Echoes in the Glass

Scott J Clauss

Published by Scott J. Clauss

Available in eBook and paperback formats.

eBook Edition ISBN: 979-8-9998212-0-1

Paperback Edition ISBN: 979-8-9998212-1-8

Cover design by Scott J Clauss

Edited by Michelle Gerbozy

Table of Contents

Acknowledgements

Though Echoes in the Glass is a work of fiction, many of the emotions, encounters, and terrors portrayed within its pages were drawn from real-life experiences—some my own, and some courageously endured by those closest to me.

First, to my wife, Chona—thank you for enduring countless hours of me being lost in thought, distracted by the world I was building on the page. Your patience, understanding, and quiet encouragement gave me the space to create, even when it meant my mind was somewhere far from home. This book would not exist without your support.

To all who lived through the moments that inspired this book: thank you for your strength, your honesty, and your willingness to remember.

My son, Charles, reminded me of events from our time in the apartment—memories I had buried but which shaped much of the atmosphere in these pages. My mother recounted the unsettling happenings that transpired in our family's home in New York, a place that still lingers in shadowed corners of memory. My ex-wife, Marta, endured the most harrowing of these experiences in our apartment in Washington. Her terror—and the trauma it left behind—left an indelible mark on us all.

To my brothers, Robert and Timothy: thank you for surviving those same long nights in that old house. Your strength and resolve in the face of the unexplained helped form the emotional core of this story.

I am deeply grateful to those who helped refine this book through their careful critiques and thoughtful suggestions. Michelle Gerbozy was a key contributor—her insightful edits and honest feedback made this a better, sharper book. My mother's unwavering belief in the story was a quiet force of encouragement. CL Stegall, friend and fellow author, offered invaluable industry advice at crucial moments. And to Shelly Vidaurri, along with her boyfriend—thank you for ensuring the storyline remained consistent, compelling, and worthy of publication.

To all of you: thank you for walking with me through the glass.
— *Scott J. Clauss*

Preface

There are some moments in life we try to forget—not because they were unimportant, but because remembering them means facing what we couldn't explain.

Echoes in the Glass is a story born from shadows. While it is, at its heart, a work of fiction, many of its darkest moments are grounded in experiences that were all too real. Places we lived. Things we saw. Nights that stretched too long, too cold, and too silent—until something moved where nothing should have been.

This story began as a way to make sense of the unspoken. It evolved into something more: a journey through grief, memory, and the thin boundary between the living and the dead. It explores what happens when trauma lingers, not just in the mind, but in the very walls around us.

The names have changed. The timelines have shifted. But the fear— the kind that lives just beyond the veil of reason—is still the same.

I invite you to step into this story not just as a reader, but as a witness. Not everything within these pages can be explained. But everything here was felt.

— *Scott J. Clauss*

Chapter 1 - Reflections

Scene 1: Shadows

Joseph awoke not to sound, but to presence.

It was the kind of waking that doesn't come from rest, but from alarm—like a thread pulled tight inside his chest had finally snapped. His body wouldn't move. His limbs, locked in place. Eyes sealed shut with the weight of sleep and something else—something heavier. A pressure filled the air, so thick it seemed to hum just above the silence.

His breath came shallow, hesitant. Something was in the room with him.

He fought against the crusted edges of sleep, his eyelids stubborn like old wood nailed shut. Slowly, painfully, he pried them open. First, only a sliver. A muted silver glow bled into the room from the window near the foot of his bed. The moon hung in the night sky, not quite full, casting its pale, indifferent light across the bedroom floor.

Joseph's bed was pressed tightly against the right wall—a deliberate choice. The solid plaster there was his fortress, his safe side. He had always believed that nothing could sneak up on him from that direction. It offered a false comfort tonight.

As his vision adjusted, familiar shapes took form. The low-set television on its rust-speckled hope chest. The knotted radiator in the far corner beside the window. Shadows wrapped themselves around these objects like thick vines, shifting subtly, impossibly.

Then—he heard it.

A breath.

Not his own.

It was long and low. Wet. Drawn through unseen lungs. It came from inside the room, not beyond the walls, not outside the window.

15

The sound sliced through him.

Joseph tightened his grip on the blanket, pulling it toward his chin. He wanted to hide behind it—bury himself—but couldn't tear his eyes away. He needed to look. To see what it was. His gaze edged to the left, inch by inch, past the bedroom door, past the quiet television, past the safe corners of the known world.

And then—the corner.

The far corner just beyond the door.

A darker shade of shadow shifted there.

Did something move? He wasn't sure. His heart clanged in his ears like a metal bell. He strained his vision, scanning for features. Was it a trick of the moonlight? A tree outside swaying in the breeze?

Another breath—closer now.

Terror crawled beneath his skin.

But then... a revelation. The wind outside was teasing the tree limbs again, their twisted silhouettes dancing across the floor. Shadows. Nothing more. With trembling hope, he let out the tiniest sigh of relief. It's just shadows.

But the relief didn't last.

The weight in the room remained. Heavy. Watchful. Wrong.

Joseph's eyes drifted toward the left side of his bed—toward the darker half of the room. That side had always felt colder somehow, as if the wall there didn't know how to hold back the night. He looked for his dresser, but saw only blackness—thicker than shadow, more absolute than night.

Even the moonlight refused to pierce it.

The breath came again.

But this time, it was right beside his face.

Joseph froze. Every muscle screamed to run, but he lay rigid. Slowly, slowly he tilted his head toward the pitch. The thick dark began to thin, just slightly, and he saw the faint outline of the left wall returning.

But something else had come into view.

It was a figure—blacker than the black it emerged from.

A shape.

Head. Shoulders.

Someone was standing over him.

Joseph's eyes went wide, and the room spun. The shape did not move, but its intent was palpable. It loomed, its face a blur of shadows that somehow stared straight into him. Then—it bent closer.

Its mouth opened.

And Joseph screamed.

A child's scream, pure and primal, tore through the room. He yanked the blanket over his head and scrambled downward, trying to disappear into the fabric, but the breath was still there—louder now, closer.

He felt something grab his foot.

He shrieked again, high and ragged, and kicked with everything he had. It was pulling him. Dragging him out from under the blankets. Joseph clawed, thrashed, tried to anchor himself in his mattress—but it was no use. He was being taken.

And then—

A voice.

Warm, familiar. Desperate with concern.

"It's ok. It's ok, dear. You were dreaming. Calm down now, honey."

Joseph gasped. His eyes flew open.

Light. Real light. His mother's face hovered over his, her arms tight around his trembling body. He was no longer under the blanket—he was in

17

her lap, held tightly, surrounded by the scent of her cotton nightgown and the soft cadence of her voice.

The Thing was gone.

But the breath lingered in his memory—cold and real.

Even as his mother gently rocked him, whispering safety into his ear, Joseph knew something else had been there.

And deep down, even at just four years old, he knew it would come again.

Scene 2: The Quiet Before

The house in Schenectady was old, older than it first seemed. When they moved in, it welcomed them with creaking floors and the scent of lavender drifting faintly from a garden out front. The elderly couple who sold it had smiled kindly, their voices as soft as the faded floral wallpaper lining the hallway. Joseph had wandered the rooms wide-eyed, already imagining where his toys would go, where he would sit and read, where he might hide when Ricky tried to scare him.

It had seemed like a dream—his own room, a staircase to slide down, doors that clicked shut like magic.

But as the weeks passed, the charm faded. What once felt warm now pressed in. The air grew heavier each night, like the house was holding its breath. Even when the sun streamed through the tall windows, Joseph sometimes caught himself watching shadows move where nothing should have cast them. At night, the house shifted. The pipes whispered. The walls groaned.

And something… waited.

But it hadn't started here. No—Joseph had known this feeling before, long before the move.

Before the city streets and honking cars, before the old stairwells and basement shadows, there had been Valatie.

The trailer park.

Nestled beside a meandering creek and surrounded by tall grass and dairy pastures, the park in Valatie was small and quiet. The dirt road twisted past scattered mobile homes, the air always thick with the smell of hay, cows, and woodsmoke in the colder months. It was a place where everyone knew each other's names, where screen doors slammed all summer and sled tracks cut clean paths in winter.

Joseph could still feel the softness of the worn carpet beneath his hands as he crawled after Ricky in their tiny trailer. Their mother laughed often back then, her voice echoing through the narrow hall like music. Their father came home each night with tired eyes and hands that smelled of oil and iron, scooping Joseph up into bear hugs that lifted him from the floor.

And then came the day Little Joshua arrived.

Joseph remembered standing barefoot at the screen door, holding Ricky's hand, watching their mother step carefully out of the car with the newborn cradled in her arms. She was glowing with joy. Ricky had been quiet, awed. Joseph only knew that everything had changed—there was someone smaller than him now. Someone to protect. Someone to share his blanket with, even if Joshua didn't yet know how to ask for it.

Their days were humble and full.

Joseph and Ricky would race sticks down the creek behind the trailer, leaping over tree roots and getting soaked to their knees. Some mornings, they walked the dusty path up to Old Man Golden's farmhouse. Mr. Golden owned the dairy farm and the trailer park, and though his voice was rough and grumbly, his wife was gentle and soft. She'd press molasses cookies into their tiny hands—so large they spilled over their fingers, still warm and sweet and spiced. Her kitchen always smelled like cinnamon, milk, and old wood.

Winters brought snow so deep it buried the mailbox. Summers, the fields swelled with green and the hum of bees. Life was simple. Whole.

19

But even then... something had stirred.

Joseph was barely more than a toddler. He couldn't speak to it then, couldn't name it. Only a memory remained, clear in ways that mattered.

He was in his crib.

The trailer's small bedroom was dim, the curtains pulled tight, sunlight leaking in around their edges like thin gold fingers. He had woken in silence. No footsteps. No voices. Just that same feeling—heavy, alert, wrong.

He turned his head toward the mirror above the dresser, the one that hung crooked with a crack in the corner.

And he saw it.

Not his own reflection.

Something else.

A face.

Pale. Watching. Waiting.

It stared at him through the glass, lips unmoving, eyes too deep to be his. And though he couldn't yet speak the words, Joseph remembered what he felt: the cold that swept through him, the breath that caught in his throat, the certainty that someone—something—was inside the room with him, and it wasn't leaving.

He never told anyone.

He barely understood it himself.

But it stayed with him. The memory. The feeling. That first glimpse through a veil he didn't know existed.

And now... the veil had returned.

Back in Schenectady, beneath layers of new paint and secondhand furniture, the old house seemed to know him. Its rooms shifted when no one watched. Its corners darkened without reason. Ricky didn't seem to notice, too busy with school and growing up. Joshua was too young.

But Joseph felt it.

And though he couldn't see it now, he knew it was near. The thing he saw in the mirror—the presence that breathed in his room—it hadn't stayed behind in the trailer.

It had followed..

Scene 3: The Years that felt like Forever

For a while, everything was just…normal.

The kind of normal that only exists when you're small and the world still fits within your block, your house, your backyard. After moving into the Schenectady house, life fell into rhythm—gentle, warm, ordinary.

Summers were made of dirt and laughter. Joseph and Ricky spent whole afternoons outside, knees stained with grass and soil, hunched over little toy trucks carving roads into the flowerbeds. Ricky would narrate the adventures: car crashes, rescue missions, monster chases—Joseph believed every word.

"He's not gonna make it!" Ricky would yell, swooping in a plastic fire truck and plowing through a wall of sticks they'd built as a fort.

"Quick, get the ambulance!" Joseph squealed, already digging a new trench beside the maple tree.

When the sun was high and the pavement too hot for bare feet, their mother would call out from the porch, "Come get some lemonade before you melt!" They'd race up the steps, dust trailing behind them, and gulp it down too fast, ice cubes clinking against their teeth.

On cooler days, they played catch in the driveway with a beat-up leather mitt that had belonged to their dad when he was a boy. Other times, all the neighborhood kids gathered for hide and seek just as the streetlights began to flicker on.

"You can't hide behind the Buick again, Joey!" Ricky would laugh, tugging him out from his not-so-secret spot.

They ran wild until someone's mom yelled that it was dinner time, and one by one, little voices vanished behind screen doors.

Sundays were slow and sweet. Their father liked to drive aimlessly after church, windows cracked, AM radio humming. Joseph sat in the backseat, watching the world blur—cornfields, corner stores, gas stations with Pepsi signs faded by the sun.

Once, when they stopped for ice cream, Joseph asked, "Daddy, where do you go every morning?"

His father glanced at him in the rearview mirror, eyes warm but tired. "To work, son. Gotta keep the lights on."

"But where?"

"Just a factory," he replied with a shrug. "Not much to see."

Joseph imagined great machines and rivers of fire, the way it looked in cartoons. He nodded solemnly. Factories sounded important.

Life was full.

At Christmas, the next-door neighbors, the Fioris, always invited them over. Their house smelled like pine and cinnamon, and Mrs. Fiori made those little chocolate crinkle cookies dusted with powdered sugar. The grown-ups talked and laughed while Joseph, Ricky, and the Fiori boys played army in the hallway, their plastic soldiers lined up on the heating vent.

"Bang! You're hit!" one would yell.

"No I'm not! You missed!" Joseph would protest.

They never stayed mad for long. Even when snow piled up taller than Joseph himself, they bundled into coats and stomped outside, carving tunnels through the drifts, building forts with milk crates and stolen shovels.

One morning, Ricky helped Joseph climb the snowbank along the sidewalk.

"From here, you can see the whole street," he said proudly, hands on his hips like a king surveying his kingdom.

The wind stung their cheeks, and Joseph felt like anything was possible up there in the white silence.

Nights were magic. In the still dark, they hunted fireflies, chasing blinking specks across the backyard with empty pickle jars. They'd punch holes in the lids with butter knives—always too big. Most nights, the bugs escaped before morning, sometimes into the living room, blinking slowly behind the curtains.

They laughed. Their mother scolded, but never too hard.

Ricky was always near. If a bigger kid tried to mess with Joseph at the park, Ricky would stand in front of him, arms crossed, unflinching.

"Pick on someone your own size," he'd say, voice calm but firm.

Joseph would stand behind him, small fists clenched, heart swelling with gratitude and pride.

Even holidays were perfect.

Trips back to Valatie brought waves of familiar faces—cousins, aunts, uncles, the old park looking just a little smaller each time. They'd drive past the creek and Joseph would press his nose to the window, looking for the spot where he and Ricky used to launch sticks like little boats.

Old Man Golden was still around, waving from his porch, and his wife still handed out molasses cookies so large Joseph had to hold them with two hands.

"Eat up, darlin'," she'd say, tousling his hair.

For two whole years, it was like life pressed pause. There were scraped knees, snowball fights, late dinners at the kitchen table. There were jokes and teasing and warm arms around his shoulders. There was love— soft, constant, unspoken.

They learned from the world itself—from falling and getting up, from chasing balls into the street and learning to look both ways, from cold hands thawing beside the radiator, from the feel of woodchips under their sneakers at the playground.

Joseph didn't know that this kind of childhood would one day seem rare. He only knew that it felt safe. Solid.

Normal.

But some nights—only some—when everyone else had gone to sleep, and the house was quiet except for the ticking clock in the hallway… Joseph would lie awake.

And he would remember the mirror in Valatie.

He never told anyone about the face he saw that day. About how it had looked straight into him.

He convinced himself it wasn't real.

Because for now, life was good.

And monsters don't belong in good places.

Scene 4: The Wall Between

Everything was normal.

Until it wasn't.

The sun had only just dipped below the trees, leaving streaks of amber across the walls of Joseph's room. The muffled sounds of the television drifted upstairs from the living room—some sitcom laugh track echoing faintly like it was coming from another world.

Joseph lay in bed, nestled beneath his flannel blanket, the cotton worn smooth from a hundred washes. He wasn't tired, not really. He just liked pretending. Liked being still and warm, liked hearing the sounds of home settle around him.

Joshua's room was on the other side of the wall.

They shared it like a secret. Joshua would sometimes babble just before sleep, his voice a soft murmur through the sheetrock. A comfort.

But that night… it wasn't Joshua's voice that broke the stillness.

It was a scream.

Not the kind toddlers give when startled. Not the cry of a child needing his blanket or a bottle.

This was shattering.

High-pitched. Desperate. Animal.

It tore through the wall with such force that Joseph jolted upright in bed, his breath caught in his throat. Before he could call out, a thud—a massive, bone-shaking slam—struck the wall between them. The whole room seemed to jump. Joseph felt it through the floorboards, through the springs in his mattress, in his bones.

Then another scream, shrill and breaking, from his brother.

Joseph couldn't move.

His body locked itself in place. Instinct took over. He slid down into the warmth of his blanket, yanking it up to his chin, eyes wide in the dark. His heart pounded so hard it drowned out the TV downstairs, drowned out even the sobbing sounds from the other side of the wall.

And then—the sound of footsteps.

Rapid, panicked.

Their mother.

He heard her sprint from the living room, her slippers slapping the hardwood stairs in a blur of motion. She didn't hesitate. The house shook as she hit the second floor and slammed open the door to Joshua's room.

A gust of wind exploded from the room.

It howled.

Not like anything from outside. It wasn't the cold wind of December. It was loud—furious—like a storm had been trapped behind that door and released all at once. The door swung back hard, hitting the wall with a crack like a gunshot. Through the chaos, Joseph could hear her:

"LEAVE MY SON ALONE!"

Her voice rang out, raw with rage and fear, shaking.

The wind roared, as if pushing against her, holding her back. Joseph could only imagine what she saw in that room—but she screamed again, louder this time, furious.

"LEAVE HIM ALONE!"

Joshua's cries pierced through the wind, frantic and broken.

Joseph's mind raced. He imagined his little brother, too young to understand, standing in his crib. Reaching out. Helpless.

And then—his mother again. Struggling. Fighting something unseen. She pushed forward, the floorboards groaning beneath her. Joseph pictured it: his mother leaning into a wind that had no source, one arm shielding her eyes, the other reaching.

Joshua was screaming, standing on the crib rail, arms stretched toward her.

But something stood in the way.

Something dark.

Tall.

Looming.

It didn't move like a person. It leaned. It bent. It watched. And it blocked the path between mother and son with an almost intentional malice. Like it wanted to be seen. Like it wanted to be feared.

Joseph trembled beneath the covers, frozen.

He didn't cry.

He couldn't.

Then—more footsteps.

Heavy. Urgent.

Their father.

He burst through the hallway, not pausing at the door. Not asking questions. Not demanding answers. He charged.

He pushed straight through the doorway—through the wind, through the Thing—and into the room.

And the Thing—whatever it was—reacted.

It leaned back, recoiling as if surprised. It hadn't expected him. Joseph could almost feel the moment shift. Just a second—long enough.

In one motion, their father swept Joshua up from the crib. The baby clung to him like a vine, face buried in his chest, still sobbing.

Behind them, the wind howled.

The Thing moved forward.

No face.

Only presence.

But their father didn't stop. He reached out, grabbed their mother's arm, and pulled her with him—ripping her away from the icy current that seemed to grip the air.

Together, they bolted for the hallway.

The Thing followed.

Joseph could hear it—no footsteps, no breath, only the feeling of motion and the roar of something wrong behind them. Then—

SLAM.

The door shut.

And the wind stopped.

The house fell silent.

Utterly.

No crying. No roaring. No movement.

Just the sound of Joseph's ragged breathing under the covers and the distant hum of the TV still playing downstairs.

A moment later, his bedroom door creaked open. His father stepped in, hair mussed, shirt soaked in sweat. He didn't say a word. He only looked at Joseph with eyes wild and wide.

"Get up, Joey," he said quietly. "We're leaving."

Down the hall, Ricky was already putting on his shoes. Their mother clutched Joshua to her chest, whispering to him, rocking him back and forth, as she tried to keep her hands from shaking.

They didn't take anything with them.

They didn't speak.

Joseph followed them barefoot through the cold hallway, his blanket still clutched in one hand.

They hurried down the porch steps into the night.

The air outside was calm—too calm. The sky stretched wide and starless overhead. Behind them, the house loomed in silence, its windows black.

They walked three doors down, to the Fioris' house. The lights were on. Warm yellow spilling onto the lawn.

Mrs. Fiori answered immediately, her mouth forming a question that never made it out.

One look at their faces told her enough.

She stepped aside without a word.

That night, they all slept in the Fioris' den—blankets piled high, floor creaking with every shift.

No one talked about what had happened.

But Joseph knew.

It had returned.

And this time, it didn't want to be forgotten.

Scene 5: Morning Doubt

The sun was just beginning to warm the rooftops of Schenectady when the scent of brewing coffee drifted through the Fioris' house. Joseph stirred on the carpeted floor, still wrapped in the blanket he'd carried from home. For a moment, he forgot where he was—the muted light, the floral curtains, the slight squeak of the radiator weren't his.

Then he remembered.

The screams.

The wind.

The Thing.

He kept his eyes shut, hoping to delay the day for just a little longer.

In the kitchen, footsteps creaked across linoleum, and the low murmur of a voice broke the morning stillness.

"Percolator's a little loud, sorry," Mr. Fiori's voice called, mostly to himself. He moved with the quiet confidence of someone who'd done this routine a thousand mornings before.

From across the room, Joseph's father, Samuel, sat up on the Fioris' sofa, rubbing his eyes and running a hand through his graying hair. He looked worn—more than just tired.

"Morning," he muttered, making his way toward the kitchen in his socks.

"Morning," Devin Fiori replied, pouring two mugs without asking. He handed one to Samuel, who took it silently, letting the steam wash over his face.

For a long moment, they just stood in the kitchen, sipping coffee.

Then Devin spoke, his voice low.

"Rough night."

Samuel didn't answer right away. He stared down at the dark swirl in his mug, the silence between them stretching.

Finally, he exhaled. "You wouldn't believe me if I told you."

Devin leaned against the counter, arms folded. "Don't be so sure about that."

Samuel glanced up. Devin wasn't smiling. He wasn't patronizing. He was just… listening.

So Samuel began.

"I heard the scream from downstairs. Thought maybe Joshua had fallen out of the crib or something. But then I heard Ellen. And when I got up there…" he paused, his voice thinning. "There was this… wind. Like a damn hurricane in his room. And something else. I don't know how to explain it. It was dark. It moved, but there wasn't anything there."

Devin nodded slowly, brows furrowed.

"I mean, it was like something was there. Standing between Ellen and the crib. But when I went through it…" Samuel shook his head, his voice trailing. "I don't know. It moved back, like it didn't expect me. I grabbed Joshua, got out of there. That's all I know."

Devin stayed quiet, letting the words hang in the space between them.

"You think it was… something supernatural?" he asked carefully.

Samuel snorted lightly. "I don't know what it was. Maybe I was seeing things. Stress. Sleep. Trick of the light. Maybe there was a draft upstairs. Who knows."

"You heard the wind too though," Devin said.

"I know what I heard. But people hear things all the time. Doesn't mean it's real." Samuel's voice grew firmer, as if reassuring himself.

Behind them, a voice cut through the conversation.

"You know what it was."

They both turned.

Ellen stood in the doorway to the kitchen, her arms crossed tight over her chest. Her hair was still messy from sleep, and her eyes were red—but there was no hesitation in her voice.

"It was evil. I saw it. It was trying to take our son."

Samuel opened his mouth to speak, but she continued.

"You felt it too. You know you did. Don't try to explain it away with pipes and shadows."

Samuel sighed and rubbed his temples. "El, we were all scared. Emotions run high—"

"No," she snapped. "No. Don't do that. Don't make this small just because it doesn't fit in your head."

Devin shifted awkwardly but said nothing.

A moment later, footsteps came from the stairs, and Teresa Fiori appeared, tying her robe as she descended. She looked over at the voices, her expression softening when she saw Ellen.

"Oh, honey," she said gently, crossing the room. She placed a hand on Ellen's back. "I didn't mean to eavesdrop, but I heard what you said. I… I've wondered about things like that before."

Ellen looked at her, still trembling. "Do you think it was demonic?"

31

Teresa's voice was quiet. "I don't know. But if it was... there are things we can do. The church. A blessing."

Samuel scoffed under his breath.

Teresa glanced at him, undeterred. "Sam, I know it might sound strange to you. But this kind of thing—it's not new. There are passages that speak of spirits and darkness. Evil walking among us."

"Oh, come on, Teresa," Samuel said, rolling his eyes. "You're talking about ghosts and demons like this is some kind of horror movie."

Teresa didn't flinch. "Ephesians six-twelve," she replied, her voice steady.

Samuel let out a dry chuckle. "Oh great, here we go with the Bible verses."

"For we wrestle not against flesh and blood," she recited, "but against principalities, against powers, against the rulers of the darkness of this world."

Samuel stared at her, the smirk fading slightly from his face.

"It's not about belief, Sam," she continued. "It's about protection. And if there's even a chance something unnatural is in that house—don't you want your family to be safe?"

The room fell still again.

Joseph peeked around the corner now, clutching his blanket, watching his parents.

Ellen looked at her husband. "We can't go back without doing something."

Samuel took a long breath, rubbing his neck.

Finally, he gave a slow nod. "Fine. We'll bring in your preacher. Say a blessing. Whatever it takes to calm things down."

"You don't believe," Ellen said flatly.

"I don't," Samuel admitted. "But if it makes you feel safer, then fine. We'll do it."

Devin placed a hand on his shoulder. "It's not about what we believe, Sam. It's about what's there."

Samuel didn't respond.

The morning light pooled on the floor beneath their feet, calm and golden. In the warmth of the Fioris' kitchen, coffee cooling in forgotten mugs, a decision had been made.

They would go back.

But they wouldn't go alone.

Scene 6: Seeking Help

Tuesday morning came heavy and gray. A mist clung to the edges of the Fioris' windows. Teresa and Devin moved quickly, ushering the Duncans—Samuel, Ellen, Ricky, Joseph, and little Joshua—toward the car. The church wasn't far, just a few blocks away. St. Helen's stood quiet, its steeple stretching into the cloudy sky.

When they arrived, Devin led the way, climbing the church steps with quiet purpose. He reached the heavy oak doors and knocked firmly.

After a few moments, the door creaked open.

Father Allen stood there, dressed in his plain clerical blacks. His silver hair was neatly combed, his expression kind but cautious.

"Devin," he said, looking surprised. "Is everything alright this early on a Tuesday?"

Devin hesitated, shifting uncomfortably. "Father... I know we didn't call. We—uh—we need your help."

The priest looked from Devin to Teresa, then over his shoulder at the Duncans standing close together at the bottom of the steps.

Teresa stepped forward. "Father, we need an emergency blessing. Something… attacked the baby last night."

Father Allen's brows lifted, but he stepped aside without another word.

"Come in."

The scent of incense lingered as they entered the sanctuary. The air was cool and still. Statues of saints towered along the walls, casting shadows that stretched across the floor. A massive crucifix loomed above the altar—Christ, sculpted in agony, staring down. The stained glass windows filtered the light into fractured blues and reds, and a brass chandelier hung silently overhead.

The group moved quietly through the sanctuary. Father Allen led them down a side corridor into his office.

It was small and cluttered with books, the smell of old parchment and wood polish filling the space. The Duncans stood close together. Joshua was asleep on Ellen's shoulder. Ricky held Joseph's hand.

Father Allen gestured for them to sit.

He looked directly at Samuel.

"Tell me what happened."

Samuel inhaled deeply. "I don't know what it was. My wife thinks it was a demon. I think…" He trailed off, unsure. "I think maybe it was a nightmare. The wind. Shadows. My kid was screaming. My wife saw something. I—I don't know."

Ellen's eyes brimmed with tears. Teresa wrapped her arm around her shoulders.

Father Allen's gaze shifted to Ellen.

"And what do you believe?"

Ellen's face changed. Her tears dried into resolve. She looked the priest square in the eye.

"It was evil. From the devil. And we need your help."

The priest nodded slowly. He opened a drawer and pulled out a Bible, placing it on the desk before him.

"There are things in this world we don't fully understand. The Scriptures speak of spirits… both holy and unholy. Cleansing a home is not a guarantee. Sometimes, it provokes more than it removes. But if you're ready—I'll help you."

Samuel scoffed, folding his arms. "Well, let's get on with it, then. Maybe this nonsense can finally stop."

Ellen turned away from him in frustration. "Thank you."

Father Allen simply nodded. "Let's begin.".

Scene 7: The Blessing

The clink of two small glasses marked the only sound in the quiet kitchen of the Fiori home. Samuel Duncan sat hunched over the table, rubbing his temples while the soft golden whiskey in his glass caught the dim light above. Devin Fiori sat across from him, silently nursing his own drink. Samuel leaned forward, his voice low.

"I don't know what's happening in that house," he said, his voice barely above a whisper, "but it's pulling my family apart."

He glanced over his shoulder, checking to be sure Ellen couldn't hear. In the adjoining living room, Ricky and Joseph were on the carpet, focused on their Lego creations. Joshua sat nearby in a bouncer, babbling softly. In the dining room, Ellen and Teresa sat in quiet conversation, Teresa's hand resting on Ellen's knee as if she'd been comforting her for a while.

"You think I'm losing it, Devin?" Samuel continued, swirling his glass. "You think this is just hysteria?"

Devin looked at him, his face unreadable. "I think something's happening, Sam. And whether it's real or not doesn't matter anymore. It's real to them."

Before Samuel could respond, a sharp knock at the front door shattered the quiet.

Everyone in the house froze.

Teresa stood, moving calmly but quickly to the door. She opened it, revealing Father Allen dressed in his full clerical attire, his long black coat billowing faintly in the warm breeze. In one hand he held a worn leather case, and in the other, a thick black Bible bound with a red ribbon.

He stepped inside without hesitation, surveying the room with solemn eyes. His gaze passed over the children, landed on Ellen, and finally rested on Samuel.

"Are you ready for this?" he asked, his voice calm but weighty.

Samuel opened his mouth to speak, but Father Allen raised a hand.

"No—don't answer that yet. You must truly be ready for this. Because what we're about to do…it won't be pretty."

Ellen stood and came to Samuel's side. "We're ready," she said firmly. "We have to be."

The priest nodded, then looked at the children.

"Should they be with us?" Samuel asked.

"If they lived in that house," Father Allen said, "they must be there. The blessing must pass through all who dwell in the home. No one can be left out."

He then bowed his head and offered a short prayer.

"Lord, grant us courage, grant us peace, and guard us from the darkness we are about to face. Amen."

And with that, they left for the Duncan house.

The walk was short, but each step felt heavy. The breeze was warm and strangely still, the kind that presses against your skin like a warning. Thunder rumbled far in the distance, low and drawn out. The house came into view, glowing with the light of the television still flickering through the window. It hadn't been touched since the night before.

Samuel approached the door, key in hand, and unlocked it. The door creaked open. He stepped aside.

Father Allen stepped into the threshold, opening his leather case and removing a bottle of holy water and a small bundle of sage. He flicked a lighter, igniting the end of the sage until it glowed and smoked. He handed it to Teresa.

"Keep it moving. Around the edges of every room."

He clutched the Bible with one hand, the holy water in the other.

"Leave the front door open," he commanded. "We begin at the back of the house and move forward. The spirit will have only one path—to leave."

Samuel led the way upstairs. The others followed, keeping a cautious distance.

They stopped outside Joshua's room.

"This is where it started," Samuel said.

Father Allen stepped inside, Teresa close behind. He began to recite scripture:

"In the name of our Lord Jesus Christ, by whose blood we are redeemed, I command every evil spirit to depart from this home. May the peace of God, which surpasses all understanding, guard the hearts and minds of all who dwell here."

He sprinkled holy water in wide arcs, and Teresa moved the sage along the walls and corners.

A sudden breeze curled into the room from the far corner, stirring the curtains.

A faint shadow rippled against the wall.

Father Allen repeated the verse, louder this time.

The wind hissed as it swept past him—cold, bitter—and rushed out the door. Ellen gasped. Samuel stared after it.

"To the next room," the priest said firmly.

Room by room, they moved methodically. Each time, the presence grew stronger, angrier. Lights flickered. Cold drafts pressed against their skin. At one point, the sage went out and had to be relit.

Finally, they reached the front entry.

Father Allen raised his Bible and began the final recitation. His voice thundered through the hall:

"I cast you out, unclean spirit. In the name of Christ, begone!"

The air changed. The shadow thickened and twisted into form.

There it was.

Dark, massive, its shape amorphous but towering. It loomed just inside the doorway, writhing with unseen energy.

The priest did not flinch.

"In the name of the Father, and the Son, and the Holy Spirit—"

The shadow lunged forward—its face inches from Joseph's. The room exploded with a deafening, otherworldly scream.

"JOSEPH!!"

Joseph stumbled backward into his brother's arms.

And then—

A great wind blew in from behind them. It tore through the house like a storm.

The spirit was ripped from the air and swept through the front door into the night.

Silence.

Father Allen stepped outside and slammed the door shut behind him. He pulled the holy water once more and blessed the doorway.

"By Christ's name, this house is sealed."

Inside, the air was lighter. The pressure had lifted.

Outside, the thunder had ceased. The clouds broke open. A silver moon bathed the house in pale light.

The house—finally—was still.

Chapter 2 - The Forgotten Door

Scene 1: The Morning After

The morning sun broke through the bedroom window in long golden beams, washing the room in light. Joseph stirred beneath his blanket, eyes fluttering open to the sound of birds chirping just outside. The air felt different now—lighter, cleaner. He sat up and inhaled deeply. No heaviness in his chest. No dread clinging to the edges of his mind.

It was quiet.

Downstairs, the unmistakable scent of frying bacon drifted up from the kitchen. His stomach rumbled in response.

Joseph climbed out of bed, stretching as he walked to the window. The backyard was soaked in sunlight, the trees swaying gently in the morning breeze. The house no longer felt like it was holding its breath. It was breathing again.

He padded down the stairs barefoot, the wooden steps warm beneath his feet. In the kitchen, Ellen stood at the stove in her bathrobe, spatula in hand, flipping bacon onto a paper towel-lined plate. The soft crackle filled the air, mingling with the smell of fresh coffee.

At the table, Samuel sat hunched behind the morning paper, sipping from a chipped mug. He didn't look up when Joseph entered.

"Morning, sweetheart," Ellen said with a small smile.

"Morning, Mom." Joseph slid into one of the chairs.

Ricky bounded down the stairs two steps at a time. "Moooom. Is it ready yet?"

"Almost. Sit down and stop whining," Ellen said, playful but firm.

Joseph looked around, soaking in the normalcy. The sunshine, the smells, the low hum of family life. It felt good—safe.

But then the question pressed in.

"Mom?" he asked, softly. "Is it... gone?"

Ellen hesitated, spatula pausing in the skillet. She turned slightly, her eyes meeting his.

"I believe it is," she said. "I do."

Behind the newspaper, Samuel grunted.

He lowered the paper just enough to glance over it. "It's gone. That's the end of it. I don't want to hear another word about this supernatural nonsense."

Ellen's jaw clenched. "You saw it, Sam. We all did. And it said Joseph's name. Why?"

Samuel slammed the paper down, folding it with exaggerated frustration. "Who the hell knows, Ellen? Who cares? It's over. To hell with it."

Ricky snorted into his juice. "Ha... literally."

Neither parent was amused.

Joseph looked down at the table, tracing the woodgrain with his finger. His mother's question echoed in his head: Why Joseph?

Why had the Thing called out to him?

Samuel drained his coffee, stood, and grabbed his keys from the counter. "I've got to get to work. Some of us don't get summer break."

He kissed Ellen on the cheek, nodded briefly at the boys, and left without another word.

The door shut behind him with finality.

Ellen sighed, turning back to the stove. "Alright, you two—plates are ready. Come eat before it gets cold."

As the boys scrambled toward the counter, the kitchen slowly came alive with normal chatter again. Ricky made faces with his bacon. Joseph poured syrup on his pancakes. Ellen hummed a tune under her breath.

The house, for all appearances, was just a home again.

But Joseph couldn't shake the chill in his bones.

It said his name.

It had screamed Joseph..

Scene 2: The Silence Between

Years passed.

The house stayed quiet.

Joseph grew, slowly shedding the fearful skin of childhood, stepping tentatively into adolescence. The memory of that terrible night— the wind, the blessing, the scream—faded like an old dream. There were no more attacks. No shadows in the corner. No looming presence watching from the dark.

But there were moments.

A whisper. A soft tug at the back of his shirt. A cold breath on the nape of his neck when no windows were open.

Nothing dark. Nothing threatening. Just... there.

He often told himself it was nothing. Maybe the wind. Maybe his imagination. Maybe... just maybe, the way life was. That we live surrounded by echoes, and every now and then, one of them brushes past.

He never thought himself special. Never claimed to be different. He figured everyone must experience something strange from time to time. It was just life.

Elementary school came and went like a breeze—carefree and filled with muddy sneakers, scraped knees, and laughter.

Middle school was harder. The sting of bullying, the slow realization that the world was more complicated than cartoons and bedtime stories. Joseph learned to be quiet. To keep his head down. He was observant, quiet, and occasionally made friends with kids who needed defending as much as he did.

By high school, the house had become strained.

Samuel's stern hand ruled with hard discipline. Ellen remained the nurturing counterbalance—too forgiving, too indulgent, in Samuel's eyes.

Joseph and Ricky grew more rebellious with age. Arguments flared often. The house, once quiet and cautious, now filled with shouting, slammed doors, and long silences that stretched like taut wires through the halls.

One afternoon, it all broke.

Ricky, now a senior, had skipped school. Again.

Samuel found out before dinner. The confrontation erupted in the living room.

"You think you're just gonna lie your way through life?!" Samuel shouted, his voice like a freight train.

Ricky stood tall, defiant. "Maybe if you trusted me once in a while, I wouldn't have to lie!"

Ellen rushed in from the kitchen, wiping her hands on a towel. "Sam, please—calm down—"

Samuel shoved past her. "This kid needs to learn what it means to be a man!"

He raised his arm.

"No!" Ellen cried, grabbing his wrist.

In a heartbeat, Ricky stepped between them. "Touch her and I swear to God—"

A scuffle. The two locked arms, wrestling in the middle of the living room.

Joshua burst into tears. Ellen was screaming, trying to pull them apart. Joseph stood frozen near the archway to the dining room, wide-eyed, fists clenched.

And then—

BONG.

A deep, resonant chime echoed through the house.

BONG.

It came from the antique clock on the mantle—Samuel's great-grandfather's clock. The one that never worked. The one with missing gears inside. For years it sat silent, a decoration. A relic.

BONG.

Three chimes in total.

Everyone stopped.

Ellen's sobs fell quiet.

Samuel released Ricky's shirt, slowly turning toward the clock.

They all looked at it. Then at one another.

And then the wind came.

It blew in hard from behind Joseph, lifting the curtains and tossing his hair forward. The air turned heavy—so dense it pressed against their chests.

Samuel's voice cracked. "I want a divorce."

Just like that.

The wind stopped.

Silence.

Not a breath. Not a word.

Joseph looked at his mother. Her eyes were hollow.

Ricky took a step back, his chest rising and falling with fury and confusion.

No one spoke.

The house had made its statement..

Scene 3: The Maze Within

The divorce was drawn-out and bitter.

Samuel fought hard to protect what he believed was his—his house, his pride, his life carved out through years of labor. Ellen, scrapping for everything she could get, had never worked outside the home. Now she had to think of the future—three boys to feed, a mortgage to face, and little certainty about anything. The world had turned upside down.

Samuel wasn't cruel, not in the traditional sense. But something unseen seemed to pull him away, and Joseph couldn't understand it. Sure, the boys had acted out, but what teenager didn't? Why was their family unraveling now? And what had happened that night with the clock? The wind? The sudden heaviness?

Was it back?

Weeks passed. Then months.

The house was different now—quieter, heavier in its silences. Joseph hadn't seen the Thing again. Not like before. But he remained cautious. Aware.

Sometimes he felt... something. A tug on his sleeve. A soft whisper in the ear that faded as soon as he turned his head. But these weren't dark or ominous. They were gentle, almost polite—as if a stranger had quietly whispered hello.

He didn't speak of them much. But one day, while sitting in the kitchen watching his mother slice apples, he asked, "Mom? Do you ever hear… voices? Or feel like someone's trying to get your attention?"

Ellen paused, knife hovering mid-air. "No, honey," she said gently. "Why do you ask?"

"No reason. Just wondering."

She turned to face him, her eyes soft. "You've been through a lot, Joseph. We all have. Everything will be alright."

But Joseph wasn't sure.

After Ricky graduated, he joined the Army and left home. The dynamic shifted again. Joseph now felt the weight of being the man of the house. Joshua was still young. Ellen did her best to hold things together, but there was an emptiness—a hollow echo of what life used to be.

Samuel visited every couple of weeks. He'd pick up Joshua, sometimes take Joseph out for ice cream or a drive. But it was awkward. Tense. Unnatural. Joseph never knew what to say, and Samuel never seemed to try.

Joseph struggled to cope. His schoolwork slipped. He rarely went out. The world outside seemed to speed forward, but inside he was stuck—buried under the weight of responsibility and confusion. He was nearing graduation but had no clear direction. What could he do to help? He didn't want to be a burden.

And that's when the dreams started.

One night, sleep came fast. The room was darker than usual, the shadows thicker, and Joseph felt himself slipping into a deep, unshakable slumber.

In his dream, he wandered through a labyrinth of darkened hallways. Endless turns. No end in sight.

Which way? Left? Right? Always uncertainty.

He walked, each corridor tighter, each corner more terrifying. The further he went, the more the fear settled deep in his chest.

And then he heard it.

A breath.

Low. Familiar.

The same breath he had heard as a child. From the crib. From the dark.

He turned a corner.

The breath was closer now. Almost at his ear. Still unseen.

He knew he couldn't turn back. The maze wouldn't allow it. Only forward.

Another turn. More shadows.

He hesitated.

Then he heard it:

"Joseph… I am here."

The voice was deep, guttural, not human. It shook the air around him.

"I seek you."

Joseph froze.

Paralyzed with terror.

His heart pounded in his chest. Sweat broke across his brow. The darkness began to churn.

Suddenly, a wind erupted around him—swirling, suffocating. It pulled at him from all directions, lifting him from the ground. He screamed, but no sound escaped.

The dark wrapped around him. And then, it appeared—formless yet solid. The Thing. Back again. Clutching him with unseen arms.

And then—

It vanished.

Joseph shot upright in bed, soaked in sweat, breath shallow.

The room was quiet.

Still.

He scanned the darkness. Nothing moved. No sound.

Was it just a dream?

Or had it returned?

Scene 4: The Weight of Inheritance

The day had finally come.

Joseph stood at the threshold of his future. High school was behind him, and the world waited with open hands—and hard choices. He'd been talking with Ricky, now stationed in another part of the country, and their long conversations had turned serious. Joseph had made up his mind: he was going to enlist in the Army.

It wasn't a decision he made lightly. Leaving his mother behind gnawed at his heart, but he needed to do this. For her. For Joshua. For himself.

That evening, sunlight filtered softly through the curtains in the living room. Ellen sat in her favorite chair, crocheting in silence, while Joseph paced, searching for the right words.

"Mom," he said finally, "I've been thinking a lot about what Dad said. About being the man of the house."

Ellen looked up, giving him her full attention.

"I want to help. I've got to help. I can't just stay here and watch you struggle. Ricky said the Army gave him a path. Maybe it can give me one too."

She placed her crocheting down and folded her hands. "Joseph, I'm proud of you. But I know this isn't just about duty. There's more, isn't there?"

Joseph hesitated. "I don't know if I can trust what Dad says. Even after what he saw... the Thing. He still denies it like it was nothing."

Ellen's expression darkened, her gaze drifting to the antique clock on the mantle.

"Do you know why your father refuses to believe?" she asked.

Joseph shook his head.

She drew in a breath. "It's time you knew the story behind that clock."

He followed her eyes to the relic on the mantle—aged wood, brass fittings, its glass face forever frozen in time.

"That clock belonged to your great-great-grandfather, Adam Duncan," she began. "He was a Union soldier in the Civil War. His unit was trapped and under siege for months. They were starving. Dying. Turning on each other. It was... hell."

She paused.

"One night, according to old family folklore, Adam fell to his knees and prayed—not just for food or rescue, but for escape from the horror they were becoming. That night, a shadow came to him. It told him to look in the mirror to find what he sought. He thought it was a dream. A hallucination from hunger."

Joseph listened intently.

"Days later, while scavenging, Adam stumbled on that very clock. He looked into the glass and saw someone staring back at him... someone who wasn't him. In that moment, a cannon blast struck nearby. The shockwave hit him so hard, it fractured his skull. He died the next day."

"What happened to the clock?" Joseph asked.

"Other soldiers thought it was his, so they sent it home with his things. Since then, strange things have followed that clock. Some believe Adam made a deal with the devil that night—and part of him never left."

Joseph's heart pounded.

"Dad knows this story?"

Ellen nodded slowly.

"Then… if he fears the clock so much, if he thinks it's cursed and brought bad things to our family, why keep it?"

Ellen looked toward the mantle, her face suddenly more solemn. "There's an inscription on the back of the clock. Carved faintly into the wood, almost worn away with time. Your father found it when he was a boy."

She paused, then continued. "It says, 'Whosoever breaks the line or casts me out shall doom their blood to live forever trapped behind the glass.'"

Joseph's skin prickled.

"He fears that inscription as much as he fears the clock. Maybe more," Ellen said softly. "I think part of him believes we're cursed either way—so the best he could do was pretend none of it was real."

"Do you think that's why he wanted a divorce? To get away from the clock? The house? Me?"

Her eyes welled with tears. "I think… something changed when the Thing came. I don't know what it is, or if the clock has anything to do with it. But something's centered around you now."

A long silence passed between them.

"I'm joining the Army," Joseph said again, firmer this time. "I'll write. I'll help how I can."

Ellen's face lit up with pride, even through the worry. "I know you will, baby."

She reached out and took his hand.

"But don't be too hard on your father. Ever since that night, he hasn't been the same. Maybe… he's just scared too.".

Chapter 3 - Haunted Service

Scene 1: Departure

The Greyhound station sat in a haze of morning mist, quiet but not silent, cloaked in the faded melancholy of a place that watched too many goodbyes. Fluorescent lights buzzed overhead, flickering now and then like they too were weary of watching people come and go. The linoleum floor was scuffed, stained with stories no one told. In the far corner, a vending machine clicked and clattered. A tired-looking woman in a frayed coat sipped coffee from a Styrofoam cup. An older man with a wrinkled hat thumbed through a newspaper that looked as worn as his eyes.

Joseph stood by the glass doors, hands in the front pocket of his grey hoodie, thumb absently running over the frayed seam. His jeans were soft from wear, and his boots—new, a gift from his mother—still felt stiff. The diesel scent of the idling bus outside drifted in, mixing with old coffee, cheap floor cleaner, and the sharp tang of nerves.

His shoulder-length hair framed his face, uncut and windblown, half hiding the uncertainty written across his features. He looked like any young man waiting for a bus—but inside, he felt like he was standing at the edge of something irreversible. Others in the depot might've been heading toward jobs, family visits, or second chances. Joseph was headed toward transformation, toward the uniform and the weight of orders, toward a life that didn't yet have shape.

Behind him stood his family. His mother Ellen clutched a balled-up tissue in one hand and gripped her youngest, Joshua, with the other. Her eyes were red-rimmed, her lips tight with the effort to keep it together. Joshua was bouncing on his heels, anxious and confused, too young to really understand the scale of the moment.

Samuel stood apart from them all, arms folded, his brow furrowed with more than disapproval—it was a storm of memory and worry, a complicated knot he couldn't untangle aloud. He had said little since arriving.

He didn't do hugs or long speeches. But his silence had a gravity to it, like something inside him was pulling tight and taut.

"You nervous?" he asked finally, voice gravelly, worn.

Joseph turned toward him, nodding faintly. "Yeah... a little."

Samuel stared at the bus through the window. "There's something about leaving a place," he said, voice quiet. "A piece of you stays behind. And not all of those pieces are good ones. Some things... they linger, waiting. Watching. Sometimes, if you're not careful, they follow you."

Joseph frowned. He didn't know what his father meant—but the weight in his tone sank beneath his skin like a cold nail. It was as if Samuel wasn't talking about nostalgia or old friends. His voice had a different edge, like a warning forged from experience.

Samuel finally looked at him—really looked at him. "Just... trust your gut. If you ever feel like something's wrong, like you're not alone when you should be—don't brush it off. Pay attention to the quiet things. The cold places. The things that don't feel quite right. I didn't, once."

Joseph blinked, trying to read behind the words.

"What happened?"

Samuel's jaw flexed. "Someone close to me... didn't make it. Not really." He looked away. "Just don't be like me and pretend it's not there. Trust what you feel, even if no one else can see it."

Ellen stepped in then, brushing Joseph's hair back gently. "You'll write us when you get there, won't you?"

Joseph nodded, grateful for the change in tone. "I will. I promise."

"Stay safe. And eat real food, not just vending machine snacks," she said, forcing a soft laugh.

Joshua tugged on Joseph's sleeve. "Can I have your comic books while you're gone?"

Joseph smiled, the tension breaking just a little. "Only if you promise to take good care of them. No folding the corners."

"I won't!"

A voice crackled over the loudspeaker, calling for final boarding. The engine of the bus outside revved softly, eager to depart.

Joseph turned to his mother first. She wrapped her arms around him and held on tight.

Then to Joshua, who grinned up at him and gave a clumsy thumbs-up.

Finally, he faced Samuel again.

The handshake between them was firm, but there was something more there—a silent transfer of things too difficult to say.

Samuel leaned in, just enough that only Joseph could hear him.

"Remember what I told you. Don't ignore the shadows. Especially the ones you carry."

Joseph's breath caught. He nodded.

Then he stepped onto the bus.

As he settled into his seat and pressed his forehead against the window, the morning light cut low and pale through the city streets. His family stood small against the depot entrance. Joshua waved, his mother wiping her eyes. Samuel stood still, arms still folded, unmoving, a statue carved from silence.

The bus groaned, lurched forward.

Schenectady began to blur.

But Samuel's words clung to him like a second skin.

Not all pieces are worth carrying.

Not all shadows are yours.

And some... follow..

Scene 2: The Weight of Marching

Fort Leonard Wood was nothing like home. Gone were the soft beds, the comforting smells of his mother's cooking, and the idle days of wandering through quiet neighborhood streets. Here, everything was hard-edged and grueling—early mornings filled with shouting, nights punctuated by exhaustion. The air smelled perpetually of metal, oil, and sweat. Joseph's civilian clothes and long, shoulder-length hair had vanished, replaced by stiff fatigues and the raw itch of a fresh buzz cut. It felt like his identity had been scraped off, layer by layer, and the remnants were buried beneath calluses and discipline.

Basic training didn't ask permission. It stripped every recruit to the bone, demanding obedience and endurance in equal measure. Reveille sounded well before dawn, dragging them from shallow sleep. Physical training came first—running in cadence, push-ups in dirt, sit-ups beneath metal pipes. Then chow. Then instruction: classes on tactics, rifle ranges, land navigation. Combat drills. Night brought either KP duty or standing guard. There was no end to the grind, only brief pauses.

But over time, something changed. Joseph adapted. His muscles hardened. His movements became sharper. And though his nights were restless, filled with strange dreams and distant whispers he never remembered upon waking, he rose each morning with increasing resolve.

He made acquaintances—Calderon, a fast-talking Puerto Rican from the Bronx who swore he'd become a chef after the Army, and Greene, a quiet, serious Southerner from Georgia with unmatched aim and steady nerves. The drill instructors were gruff, especially Drill Sergeant Miller, whose bark shook the floorboards, but whose eyes betrayed a watchful fairness. Joseph came to respect the structure, the challenge, even the pain.

One morning, a particularly brutal ruck march had them hauling 50-pound packs down a sunbaked gravel road. Dust clung to their sweat-slick skin, and their boots struck the path with the rhythm of hardship. The forest that flanked them whispered with early morning wind, the sun just cresting over the trees. After miles, Drill Sergeant Miller called for a rest.

"Ten minutes. Hydrate. Check your gear. Let's not lose anyone to heat stroke, ladies."

Joseph collapsed onto the edge of a culvert and peeled off his boots, steam practically rising from his soaked socks. He wrung them out, gulped tepid water from his canteen, and tried not to think about the aching knot between his shoulders. Around him, other soldiers lounged on rocks, swapped out socks, laughed, stretched.

Then the air changed.

It wasn't a temperature drop—not quite. It was a sudden stillness, a pressure, like the pause before a thunderclap. Joseph looked up. The sun seemed to dim behind a veil of thin clouds, casting odd shadows. The wind died. The laughter faded.

He scanned the tree line, a tickle of unease rising in his gut. Something felt... off. The others didn't seem to notice. Calderon was still cracking jokes, Greene drinking from his canteen. But the stillness clung to Joseph, burrowed into his skin.

His breath slowed. A chill ran down his spine.

He reached for his second sock, but paused mid-movement. A prickling sensation danced over his ear. Not quite touch—more like a whisper. A breath, hot and cold at the same time.

He slapped at the air beside his head.

"Damn bug," he muttered.

But it happened again.

Greene looked up. "What the hell you swattin' at?"

Joseph blinked, scanning again. "You see a bug or something? Around my head?"

Greene shrugged. "Nah, man. You're trippin'. Ain't nothin' there. Probably your imagination."

Joseph laughed nervously and shook his head, but his chest tightened. The others were right there. Why couldn't they feel it?

He laced up his boots and shouldered his pack, trying to focus. Breathe in, breathe out. Back in formation. He stood and turned toward the others—

—and was hit.

Something slammed into his ribs. Not hard enough to break bone, but with a violent, undeniable force. His body twisted sideways, and he crashed onto the gravel with a grunt, the impact knocking air from his lungs. His vision blurred from the jolt.

Gasps followed. He could hear footsteps running toward him.

"Yo, you okay?" Calderon shouted, kneeling beside him.

Greene appeared too, crouching low. "You just collapsed, man. You dizzy or something?"

Joseph stared at them, mouth opening and closing. "I—no. I think I slipped."

Calderon raised an eyebrow but didn't press. Greene didn't say anything more.

Drill Sergeant Miller's voice boomed across the clearing. "Let's move out! Back on your feet, soldiers! You're not here to sunbathe!"

The moment was gone. The men fell back into motion. Joseph joined them, brushing dust from his fatigues and refusing to look back.

But he couldn't shake it.

No rock had tripped him. No misstep caused the fall.

He'd been pushed.

His mind ran in circles the rest of the march, trying to make sense of what happened. Maybe it had been a freak muscle spasm, a sudden dizzy spell. But the sensation was too distinct. Too focused. It wasn't a fall—it was an assault.

And no one else said a word.

The rest of the ruck passed in silence. The march ended. They returned to the barracks. That night, Joseph lay in bed staring at the ceiling, his bunk creaking slightly with every breath. He could still feel that shove—the weight, the angle, the impossible presence behind it.

Something had touched him. Something he couldn't see. Something no one else could.

And for the first time since arriving, he felt something far worse than pain or exhaustion.

He felt watched.

Scene 3: Shadows at the Range

The day at the grenade range dawned under a hazy sky, the Missouri heat already thick with humidity that clung to the skin like a wet shroud. Joseph could feel sweat gathering beneath his helmet as he marched in step with the rest of the platoon, his boots crunching over gravel and dry dirt. The air buzzed faintly, a mixture of insect drone and the crackling intensity of what awaited them. Today was live grenades—no simulations, no second chances.

The range itself was carved into a hillside like some post-apocalyptic trench, its edges lined with battered concrete and rusted rebar. The approach tunnel was dim and claustrophobic, lit by long red safety bulbs that washed the narrow corridor in a hellish glow. The line of soldiers waiting their turn snaked silently forward, each of them stewing in their own nerves.

Joseph moved with them, his fingers tapping against his thigh in a nervous rhythm. His stomach churned. There was no room for error here. One mistake, one dropped grenade, and it was over.

The corridor's windows—small squares of thick glass built into the outer wall—offered a view of the range beyond. Joseph glanced at one, his eyes narrowing. The glass wasn't smooth. It was shattered, fractured in spiderweb veins of impact damage. Pockmarked and burned at the edges.

"That used to be clean," muttered a sergeant standing nearby, catching Joseph's stare. The man had a haunted look, the kind that lingered in combat vets and funeral homes.

Joseph looked back at the window.

"Couple years back," the sergeant continued, "some dumbass grabbed the grenade by the pin. Pulled it by accident. It dropped, spoon flew. Killed him and the DI. Blew part of that wall out too."

Joseph stared harder. There, embedded in the concrete on the other side, was a stain. Dark. Crimson. Permanent.

"Pit out there's got blood in its foundation."

The line fell quiet. Even the usual wisecracking private at the back said nothing. But someone broke the silence with a snicker and a cruel mutter: "Guess he pulled the wrong pin on career day."

The sergeant's glare snapped to the voice. "This isn't a goddamn game. You screw up here, you don't get recycled. You get buried."

Joseph's turn came. The DI handed him the grenade with both hands, a gravity in the gesture that made Joseph's fingers feel numb.

"This is live," the DI said, locking eyes with him. "No spoon milking. You throw when I say throw, understood?"

Joseph nodded.

He followed the DI down the narrow concrete path toward the pit. The range opened before him—an empty bowl of scorched dirt and charred debris. The air here was dry and powdery, tainted with the iron scent of spent explosives. Smoke from earlier throws still drifted low across the ground, curling around rocks and forming shapes that seemed to slither and breathe.

Joseph stepped into the pit—a waist-high bunker of thick, cracked cement. It felt like a grave.

He dropped to one knee, clutching the grenade close to his chest. The DI crouched beside him, eyes on the horizon.

The wind changed.

It rolled in like an unseen tide, cool and unnatural. Not the humid breeze of a summer afternoon. This was sharp. Dry. Hollow.

And it carried a whisper.

Joseph turned slowly toward the open range. The smoke shifted.

From within that drifting haze, a figure began to take shape.

At first it was faint—nothing more than the outline of a man. But with each breath, it gained form. A soldier, standing perhaps ten yards out. His uniform was shredded, streaked with blood and soot. One sleeve hung loose, empty. As the figure turned, Joseph's stomach dropped.

The man's left arm was missing. Torn off at the shoulder. His chest was caved in, ribs visible through blackened skin. His mouth hung open— not in pain, but as if frozen mid-scream.

Joseph's breath hitched.

He turned toward the DI, heart hammering. "There's someone—"

But when he looked back, the figure was no longer ten yards away.

He was right there.

Inches from Joseph's face.

The dead man's skin peeled and cracked, eyes like burned glass. His breath—if it could be called that—reeked of fire and blood. His voice came not from his mouth but from the air itself, vibrating deep within Joseph's bones.

"The glass does not just reflect," the apparition said. "It holds. It binds. It remembers all who pass through. Time folds inside it. The mirror sees. The mirror listens."

His face flickered, features distorting like water under heat.

"And when the line is broken… he comes."

Joseph trembled.

"We see him too, Joseph. In the In Between. We see him. And we fear him."

Then—gone.

The wind died. The smoke thinned.

"Private!" the DI shouted, his voice a thunderclap. "What the hell are you doing?"

Joseph blinked. He was still clutching the grenade.

"In the pit! Pull the pin! Don't milk the damn thing! Count to two and throw it like your damn life depends on it—because it does!"

Joseph obeyed.

His hands moved on instinct. He yanked the pin, held the spoon.

One. Two.

"Fire in the hole!"

He threw.

The DI tackled him low, forcing him down into the cement as the grenade arced, bounced—and exploded with a roar that shook the hillside.

Debris rained down. Dust filled the pit.

Joseph rose, coughing, ears ringing. But the blast wasn't what haunted him. It was the echo.

The mirror sees.

The mirror listens.

When the line is broken, it comes.

He climbed out of the pit in silence. No one said a word. The others had seen something in his face. Fear. Madness. Maybe both. But no one dared ask.

Joseph marched back to the waiting line, but his mind stayed behind—on the figure in the smoke.

And the whisper that knew his name.

Scene 4: The Ghost Whisperer

Life in the Army was beginning to settle into rhythm. With basic training behind him, Joseph now spent his days focused on AIT—Advanced Individual Training—where he learned the skills that would mold him into a reliable supply specialist. The regimented pace of study, drills, and hands-on logistics training provided structure, a kind of armor against the strange thoughts that crept in when things grew quiet.

He was good at it—efficient, methodical, calm under pressure. It came naturally. Yet, in the margins of his focus, darker thoughts drifted. Memories that refused to fade. At night, while the barracks hummed with the soft snores and restless shifting of soldiers, Joseph lay in his bunk, staring up at the stained tiles above, listening to the whispers of memory.

The figure at the grenade range had left a scar deeper than any shrapnel. The words had etched themselves into his mind like scripture carved in stone:

"The glass does not just reflect. It holds. It binds. It remembers all who pass through. Time folds inside it. The mirror sees. The mirror listens. And when the line is broken, it comes. Do not break the line, Joseph. He is waiting."

He didn't understand it. Couldn't. He ran through it again and again during quiet moments—on guard duty, while loading inventory, even during chow—trying to decipher meaning. But every time he returned to it, he came up empty. He couldn't tell anyone. Who would believe him?

Still, strange things continued to happen. Doors that closed when no one was near. Lights flickering in the supply shed. Cold drafts brushing past his neck even in the sweltering Missouri summer. He told himself it was nothing. Everyone told themselves that.

One late Friday night, the squad had gathered in the barracks common room, a rare reprieve after inspection and drill. Warm beers clinked, card games flared with laughter, and the scent of foot powder and greasy fast food filled the air. It wasn't long before the subject turned to ghost stories. Soldiers shared tales from their hometowns—haunted forests, cursed dolls, phantom hitchhikers. Laughter echoed off the cinderblock walls.

Joseph sat quietly, sipping from a lukewarm can, not offering anything.

That's when Kincaid, a lanky southerner with a buzzcut and an ever-present smirk, nudged him with his elbow.

"Yo, Duncan. You ever see ghosts? You got that 'I've-seen-some-shit' look."

Joseph laughed lightly, careful to keep it casual. "Nah, man. Just tired."

"Bull," Kincaid said. "I've seen you. Talking to yourself out on night watch like you're arguing with someone. You freeze up sometimes too, like you're hearing something the rest of us can't."

"You did freak out at the grenade range," chimed in McClure from across the room. "Looked like you'd seen a corpse crawl out of the ground."

"Probably just saw his reflection and got scared," someone else joked, and the group roared with laughter.

Joseph forced a grin. "Y'all are idiots. I'm just focused. Thinking out loud sometimes."

But they weren't buying it—not entirely.

"Uh huh," Kincaid said, narrowing his eyes. "Sure, man. Whatever keeps the ghosts away."

"Casper's Buddy," someone snorted. "I like that. That's your new call sign, Duncan."

The teasing was mostly harmless, but under the surface there was something sharper. They noticed the way he stiffened when walking past mirrors. The way he sometimes paused mid-conversation, staring at something no one else could see. A toolbox crashing off a shelf when he walked by. A whispered voice heard by only him.

But Joseph denied it every time.

"Just stress," he told them. "Lack of sleep. Everyone hallucinates once in a while."

Yet, deep down, he wondered. Not about the hallucinations—but about why it only seemed to happen to him. Why no one else heard the voices or felt the breath of something cold on the back of their neck. Why the cracked mirror in the latrine made his stomach knot every time he passed it.

He didn't think of it as a gift. Not yet. It was just… something wrong with him. Something broken.

The rest of AIT passed with mounting unease. No major events. No terrifying visions. But always that feeling of being watched. The hum at the edge of silence. The crackle of something pressing against the veil of reality.

When graduation came, Joseph stood tall, diploma in hand, commendation in his file. He'd done well. Even Drill Sergeant Miller had nodded at him with something close to approval.

Then came his orders: Panama.

A remote U.S. Army installation surrounded by dense jungle and sweltering heat. Isolated. Quiet.

It's the kind of place where time forgot to move forward.

He boarded the plane with a sense of both dread and relief. Maybe, in Panama, the silence would be clean. Maybe the whispers wouldn't follow. Maybe the mirrors wouldn't watch.

Maybe.

But even as the plane ascended into the clouds, Joseph couldn't shake the words from the grenade range. The echo of the ghost's voice still lived in the corners of his mind.

"We see him too, Joseph. In the In Between, we see him. And we fear him."

He closed his eyes.

And prayed he wouldn't see it again.

Scene 5: A Whisper Between Two Worlds

Life at the remote base in Panama settled into a rhythm, slow and oppressive like the thick, humid air that clung to everything. The tropical heat wrapped itself around Joseph's body from the moment he stepped outside his barracks each morning, seeping through his uniform and turning every movement into a sluggish chore. The weather was a far cry from Missouri's erratic seasons. Here, the sun seemed to boil the world while the jungle whispered secrets from beyond the fences.

The base was tucked deep into the hills, a speck of American routine carved into foreign wilderness. Dense foliage walled off most of the outer perimeter, green and alive and watching. At night, howler monkeys screamed from the trees like tortured souls, and thunder rolled over the mountaintops in long, groaning rumbles, like some ancient god turning in its sleep.

Despite the isolation, Joseph found it easier than he expected to fall into the daily grind. Morning formations, supply runs, endless inventory checks. His job as a supply specialist was straightforward—accounting for gear, issuing items, tracking paperwork. He did it well, fast, and without complaint. But when the tasks ended and silence returned, his thoughts always drifted to darker places.

Morales, his bunkmate, was the opposite of dark. A fast-talking New Yorker with a permanent smirk, Morales treated life like a never-ending comedy show. He tanned shirtless under the punishing sun, posed like a model in front of the mirror he'd duct-taped to their concrete wall, and could make even rations seem like a gourmet meal with his endless commentary.

One evening, while the two of them counted canteens and logged gear, the sun dipped below the canopy outside, painting the walls in bands of orange and crimson. The flickering light made shadows dance.

Joseph stood near the back shelf, handling a dusty box of spare helmet straps, when he murmured, almost to himself, "The glass does not just reflect. It holds. It binds. It remembers all who pass through. Time folds inside it. The mirror sees. The mirror listens. And when the line is broken, it comes."

Morales froze mid-count. "You quoting poetry now, bro?"

Joseph blinked, then looked over. "No. That's what a ghost said to me. At the grenade range. Back in basic."

Morales lowered the clipboard and stared. "Wait… a ghost? Like a full-on, spooky, dead-guy ghost?"

Joseph nodded slowly. "He was torn up. Like he'd been hit by something big. But he talked to me. He knew my name. He warned me."

A heavy pause filled the air. Outside, the jungle murmured with the sounds of distant insects and something else… maybe frogs. Maybe not.

"You ever tell anyone?" Morales finally asked. "Like the chaplain? Or, I don't know, medical?"

Joseph shook his head. "No. I've had stuff like this happen before. My whole life, actually. Thought maybe everyone did. Just figured it wasn't something you talked about."

Morales gave a low whistle, then exhaled through his teeth. "Man, that's some heavy stuff. You serious? Like, it happens a lot?"

"Enough," Joseph said. "More than enough."

Morales leaned back against a steel locker, arms folded. "Damn. That's not just 'weird dreams' territory, that's something else. Maybe you got a gift, man. Like a sixth sense. Or cursed blood or something."

Joseph offered a weak smile. "Back in AIT, some guys started calling me 'Casper's Buddy.' Thought it was funny."

Morales barked a laugh. "Ghost Whisperer. That's better. You ever think maybe you're supposed to see this stuff?"

Joseph hesitated, then looked away. "I don't know. Maybe I'm just broken."

Silence settled again. Outside, lightning flashed through the cloud cover, casting their shadows in stark relief. The fluorescent bulb above them buzzed faintly.

"Well, Ghost Whisperer," Morales said, grabbing his canteen and slinging it over his shoulder, "I think we need a break. Let's get off base for a bit. Find a bar, drink something cold, talk to someone who isn't dead."

Joseph glanced at him, unsure.

Morales raised an eyebrow. "C'mon. You keep staring into mirrors like they're about to speak Latin and crack. You need to breathe, man."

Joseph finally nodded. "Yeah. Let's get out of here."

Scene 6: Beneath the Surface

The pub was tucked away in a sleepy Panamanian village just beyond the base perimeter, nestled beneath sagging palms and bougainvillea spilling from cracked planters. The building looked as though it had been there forever—the wood worn smooth by decades of hands, weather, and the occasional drunken scuffle. Inside, the lighting was dim and gold-tinged, cast from stringed bulbs strung lazily across the ceiling. Ceiling fans rotated slowly, stirring the heavy air more in pretense than effect. A haze of cigar smoke curled in the rafters. Glasses clinked against wood, and low, rhythmic music floated from an old jukebox in the corner.

Joseph and Morales took a seat near the back, beneath a window layered with grime and ivy, the light outside all but swallowed by evening shadows. Their boots hit the scuffed floorboards with the tired rhythm of soldiers off-duty. They ordered two local beers, the glass sweating in the heat, and leaned back, letting the weight of the day slide from their shoulders.

That's when she walked in.

Maria.

She entered like a breath of cool air. Her long dark hair was swept over one shoulder, glinting in the low light, and her sun-kissed skin seemed to glow against the warm tones of the room. Her red dress was simple, cotton and modest, but the way she wore it made it feel like silk. Her sandals clacked softly on the wooden floor as she moved with easy grace toward the bar.

"Dios mío," Morales whispered. "Look at that."

Joseph followed his gaze, and time seemed to stall for a moment. There was something arresting about her. It wasn't just her beauty, though that was undeniable. It was something deeper—the way she carried herself, like she belonged there and nowhere at the same time.

Maria approached the bar, and both men instinctively straightened in their chairs.

Morales was first. "You from around here, or did the heavens just get tired of missing an angel?"

Maria turned her head, unimpressed. "Seriously?" she asked, a playful smirk tugging at her lips. "You've used that one before, haven't you?"

Joseph chuckled. "He has a whole book of them. I think he gets them printed on flashcards."

68

Maria turned her eyes to him. They were warm, inquisitive, almost challenging. "And what's your line?"

Joseph met her gaze, unflinching. "I don't have one," he said honestly. "I just thought you looked like someone I'd regret not talking to."

Her smirk softened into a real smile. "That's... actually sweet."

Morales feigned offense. "I bring the fire, and he gets the smile. Figures."

They all laughed, and the tension dissolved into something easy. Maria accepted their invitation to join them, sliding into the seat beside Joseph. They talked for hours—about the village, the heat, the jungle, the absurdity of military life. Maria shared that she worked as a translator occasionally, helping military families and doctors with local dialects. Her laugh was full-bodied and infectious, her intelligence clear in every sentence.

As the night deepened and the bar emptied, Maria leaned closer to Joseph. Their arms brushed now and then, and each time sent a small thrill through him. They shared drinks, smiles, and long glances that held unspoken questions. Morales eventually excused himself with a wink and a mumbled excuse about letting the lovebirds have the night.

Once they were alone, Joseph and Maria moved to a quieter corner of the patio outside. The night air was thick, perfumed with tropical blooms and the salt of the nearby sea. A single string of lights illuminated the edge of the roof, casting a gentle glow over her profile.

"I wasn't planning on coming out tonight," she said softly. "But something pulled me here."

Joseph looked at her, captivated. "I'm glad you did."

She tilted her head. "You have a sadness in your eyes. Like someone always waiting for the other shoe to drop."

He looked down. "Maybe. Just life, I guess."

Maria touched his hand, and he didn't pull away. "Maybe. Or maybe you see more than most. Feel more than you let on."

He swallowed. He wanted to tell her everything—the ghost, the whispers, the mirror. But he didn't. Not yet.

Instead, he said, "You make it quieter."

She smiled, and leaned in to kiss him. It was soft at first, then deepened, their shared breath becoming one. The jungle hummed around them, but in that moment, there was only her.

Time passed in blinks. Dinners turned to walks, nights into mornings. Each evening they met in secret corners of the village or quiet beaches under the stars. She brought warmth into his cold places. Laughter into the silence he'd carried since childhood.

One night, they stood on a stretch of beach just beyond the village. The sun was sinking behind the waves, setting the sky ablaze with streaks of crimson and gold. Joseph held her hand as they walked barefoot in the sand, the tide tracing patterns around their ankles.

She laughed at something he said and brushed a strand of hair behind her ear. Her eyes shimmered with affection, and Joseph felt the small box in his pocket weigh heavier than ever before.

He stopped walking.

Maria turned to face him. "What is it?"

He pulled the box from his pocket and dropped to one knee.

"Maria," he said, voice catching in his throat. "I don't have a perfect life. I've got my demons—real ones, maybe. But I know this. I want to spend the rest of my life protecting you. Loving you. Will you marry me?"

Tears filled her eyes. She nodded quickly. "Yes. Yes, of course I will."

They embraced, kissed, and for a moment, all was still.

But in the shadowed reflection of a tide pool nearby, a ripple stirred.

And something watched.

Chapter 4 - A Battle, A Bride

Scene 1: New Beginnings in Washington

The air in Panama clung to Joseph like a second skin—thick, humid, fragrant with the scent of mangoes and distant wood smoke, undercut by the salty tang drifting from the nearby ocean. It was a place that hummed with life at all hours, where the cries of geckos and the shrill songs of unfamiliar birds threaded through every open window. The heat seemed to settle into the walls of their modest military apartment, making everything—clothes, sheets, even Joseph's thoughts—feel a little heavier, a little slower. But inside, behind the faded curtains and the humming air conditioner, Joseph and Maria found comfort in each other and the slow, rhythmic predictability of base life.

The world outside sometimes felt far away, held at bay by the perimeter fence and Maria's laughter echoing through their tiny living room. There were mornings when Joseph would linger in bed just to listen to the sound of her voice as she sang in the kitchen, her accent lacing the air with something bright and hopeful. For a time, Joseph let himself believe he'd outrun the shadows of his past—that the lingering dread from childhood, the nightmares that sometimes woke him in a cold sweat, belonged to someone else.

It was Maria who first noticed the change, the way Joseph seemed to relax in Panama. "You smile more," she teased one evening, leaning into him as they watched a rainstorm batter the palms outside. "I like it." He didn't have the words to explain how much it meant, how the ordinary struggles of life—misplaced keys, a broken fan, the unpredictable schedule of military logistics—felt like proof that he was living in the daylight at last.

Then, just a few months into their marriage, Maria discovered she was pregnant. The news came with both joy and an undercurrent of fear—a trembling Joseph felt deep in his bones. He'd never known his own father, Samuel, to be demonstrative. Their relationship was defined by silence, by the weight of words unspoken. Samuel was a man of deep wells and locked doors, his affection revealed only in small, careful gestures: a hand on Joseph's shoulder after a baseball game, a nod of approval that felt as significant as a medal. There had always been a barrier between them, an unspoken pact to keep certain truths in the dark. Joseph sometimes wondered if it was fear or simply habit, the kind of emotional reticence handed down through generations of men who believed love was best measured in work and sacrifice, not words.

His mother, Ellen, had been different once. In Joseph's earliest memories, she'd been the heart of the home—warm, quick to laughter, her touch a salve for childhood hurts. But something changed as Joseph grew older, as the weight of family secrets grew heavier and the shadows in the house lengthened. The distance crept in quietly, widening until conversations felt forced and rare. Phone calls grew shorter. Texts went unanswered. When Joseph called home to share the news of Maria's pregnancy, Ellen's voice sounded hollow, her congratulations perfunctory, as if recited from memory rather than felt. He wondered if she resented the silence that had always hovered between father and son, or if, in her own way, she too had been consumed by it.

Within weeks of Maria's pregnancy announcement, new orders arrived. Joseph was being reassigned to Fort Lewis in Washington State—a world away from Panama's relentless sun. The transition was abrupt and disorienting. One day they were sweating over packed suitcases and trying to eat the last of the plantains, the next they were buckled into a transport plane, the sky outside shifting from blazing blue to a gray so deep it felt like the end of summer.

The Pacific Northwest was a revelation: towering evergreens, endless mist, rain-soaked roads winding past mossy forests and quiet neighborhoods. Their new home was an on-base residence tucked at the edge of a housing loop, its windows looking out onto stands of Douglas fir that seemed to swallow the light. Life slowed, then settled. The Army's daily routine became Joseph's anchor—morning formations, the hum of activity in the logistics office, the camaraderie of men and women bound by shared purpose. He wore his uniform with pride, the insignia on his chest a shield against the uncertainty he carried inside.

Maria adapted with the same quiet resilience she'd shown in Panama. She filled the house with warmth and color—handmade curtains, photos clipped to string, the gentle chaos of baby toys and blankets. Their first son, Jacob, arrived on a rainy spring night. Joseph held the boy for the first time in the pale hospital light, awed and terrified by the weight of fatherhood. He saw flashes of his own father in the boy's serious gaze, glimpses of his mother's gentleness in the curve of his mouth.

Two years later, their second son, Noah, was born. The family of four grew into a familiar sight around the base: Maria pushing a stroller down the damp sidewalks, Jacob running ahead with shrieks of laughter, Joseph following close behind, eyes alert to every passing car and dog walker. He tried to be present, to build a home free of the cold silences that had haunted his own childhood. Yet sometimes, after a long day, he'd find himself staring at his sons and wondering how much of Samuel lingered in his own bones—what quiet fears and secrets he might be passing down without even realizing it.

For five years, life at Fort Lewis was steady and predictable. Joseph found a rhythm that felt almost safe, the old anxieties fading into the background. He earned the respect of his peers, built friendships over poker games and long shifts, watched as Maria transformed every new house into a home. The future began to feel less like a shadow and more like something he could shape with his own hands.

But eight years of service passed, and Joseph faced a choice that felt both liberating and terrifying. He could reenlist, secure the routine and stability that the Army provided, or step out into the unknown for his family's sake. In the end, he declined reenlistment—not out of bitterness or regret, but because he longed for a life he could truly call his own. The Army had taught him discipline, resilience, the value of brotherhood. It had also shown him the importance of coming home.

They moved to a modest apartment in University Place, a small community not far from the base. Joseph found work at a grocery warehouse—a far cry from military life, but honest and steady. He enrolled in business classes at the local college, determined to carve a new path forward. Maria stayed home with Jacob and Noah, their days punctuated by the sound of cartoons, the clatter of dishes, the scent of homemade bread.

Evenings brought a quieter kind of noise. After the boys were asleep and Maria had slipped into bed with a book, Joseph would sit alone in the living room, listening to the wind rattle the old windows. Sometimes he caught himself staring into the shadows in the corners, feeling the hair on his arms rise for no reason he could name. Once, he thought he heard Jacob talking softly to someone in the hallway—but when he checked, the boy was fast asleep, his breathing deep and even.

There were other small oddities: cool drafts moving through closed rooms, toys found in strange places, the feeling—fleeting but persistent—that he was not alone. Joseph tried to dismiss it as the quirks of an old building, the anxieties of a man still adjusting to civilian life. But in the quiet moments, when the house held its breath and the past felt near, he wondered if the shadows he'd outrun had simply learned to wait.

He thought of Samuel, of Ellen, of all the words never spoken. Joseph wasn't sure what he was passing on to his sons, only that he wanted them to know love in ways he'd never been able to express to his own parents. And on some nights, when the silence pressed in and the air felt cold against his skin, he wondered if the distance that grew between people—between mothers and sons, fathers and children—was another kind of haunting, one that lingered long after the lights went out.

Scene 2: Ghosts of Tombstone

Joseph had always felt a strange kinship with haunted places. As a boy, he'd been drawn to stories of ghosts and old tragedies—the kinds of tales whispered at sleepovers or dramatized on late-night television. He never considered himself special. If anything, he'd always envied those who seemed oblivious to the possibility of spirits moving through the world, unseen but ever-present. His experiences never felt like a gift. They simply were—persistent, undeniable, woven through his childhood and shadowing his adult life. But for all the fleeting chills, the inexplicable shadows, the dreams that left him shaken and searching for meaning, he never thought himself truly sensitive. Not the way so many on those ghost shows claimed to be.

Joseph watched those shows religiously, fascinated by the tools—spirit boxes spitting out garbled syllables, EMF meters blinking in empty hallways, digital recorders capturing the disembodied voices of the dead. He wasn't trying to prove anything. He wasn't a skeptic, nor an eager believer. He just wanted to understand what followed him in the dark and why. For years, he had quietly accepted that his experiences were simply part of his life—unusual, but private.

So when the idea came to take the family on a vacation to Tombstone, Arizona, Joseph felt a familiar flutter of excitement. He'd read about the haunted Birdcage Theater, the gunfights and sorrow that clung to the town's battered wood and dusty streets. He'd pictured himself standing in those infamous rooms, maybe catching a glimpse of history's residue. What he didn't expect was the surprise he felt at not feeling anything at all—at least at first.

The drive in was brisk, the April air carrying the sharp tang of desert sage. The town rose from the horizon like an artifact, preserved and defiant, every plank and board heavy with stories. They checked into the Tombstone Hotel Inn History, the boys wide-eyed with excitement, Maria smiling at Joseph's boyish energy. As soon as their bags hit the bed, Joseph retrieved his EMF detector, half expecting it to start screaming the moment it crossed the threshold. But there was nothing. He swept the room—walls, corners, windowsills. The device was as silent as the grave. The same was true of the boys' room next door: no cold spots, no tingling sense of being watched. The silence was so complete, so ordinary, that Joseph found himself almost disappointed.

That night, Joseph left Maria with the boys and joined the ghost tour at the Birdcage Theater. Maria didn't mind. She had never been a skeptic, but she'd never felt the presence of spirits herself. She encouraged Joseph's curiosity with a loving patience, content to let him wander these old haunted places if it brought him peace.

Their guide, Mike, was nothing like the television hosts Joseph had watched for years. He wore a battered Tombstone cap and a scowl that suggested he'd seen his share of would-be ghost hunters. Mike's voice was even, almost bored, as he led the group through the barroom's haze of antique bulbs and whiskey-laden air. "People make things up all the time," he said, leveling a gaze at the cluster of tourists. "We've had TV crews film here—sometimes they fake it when the spirits don't show up. If you want the truth, you go to the records. You talk to the locals. You pay attention."

Joseph listened closely, Mike's words sinking into his mind. He felt a sudden self-consciousness about the EMF detector tucked into his palm, the same device that had given him nothing but silence since he arrived. He'd always thought his own experiences were small, maybe even imagined. Was he just another tourist chasing shadows?

The tour continued into the main theater, its red velvet drapes faded and heavy with dust, the ornate opera seats arrayed beneath balconies that once echoed with laughter and secret deals. Mike spun stories of the theater's wild years—gunfights, jealous lovers, the bloody echoes of lives cut short. Joseph stood at the rear of the room, near the doorway, quietly soaking in the atmosphere. He let his gaze drift over the shadowed stage, the curtains trembling slightly in the draft.

Then, something moved—a shadow, crossing from right to left behind the stage, swift and purposeful. Joseph's heart stuttered. He blinked, trying to focus, but it was gone, swallowed by the darkness. Instinctively, he checked his EMF detector. Still nothing. The lights remained dark, as though whatever passed before him wasn't made of the same energy that tripped wires or set off alarms.

He was surprised by how disappointed—and yet excited—he felt. He had always known spirits were real. His childhood was marked by whispers, half-seen figures, that feeling of being watched when no one else was home. But this was the first time he'd felt something different, something that didn't want to frighten or show itself in some obvious way. He remembered something Mike had said earlier: "Some people just have a way of drawing them out. Maybe you're sensitive—maybe you're just paying attention." The words weighed on Joseph's mind, making him reconsider his role in these encounters. Was he more than just a witness? Was he, as Mike suggested, a kind of conduit?

He stayed quiet as the group moved through the theater, letting the guide's stories wash over him. When they climbed the stairs to the faded balcony, Joseph's hand hovered over the detector. At the base of the steps, he got a single flicker—two green lights, just for an instant. It felt like a whisper, a gentle acknowledgment. He felt his skin prickle with a familiar thrill, but also something new—a sense of being noticed, chosen. The spirit's presence wasn't hostile. It was urgent. It wanted to be known, to be heard, and for some reason, it had chosen Joseph to carry its voice.

He was struck by a sense of honor—strange and unexpected—that a spirit would single him out. For so long, his experiences had made him feel isolated, different. Now, he felt a quiet relief. Maybe he was sensitive. Maybe all those years of strange dreams and inexplicable chills meant something. Maybe he was meant to give voice to the things that lingered in the shadows, desperate to be remembered.

In the dim glow of the Birdcage's old bulbs, Joseph felt the spirit's message seep into his bones. The words weren't spoken, but they rang clear in his mind: We are here. Listen. Tell them. It felt less like an intrusion and more like a calling—a responsibility, even. He looked around at the other tourists, their faces drawn with anticipation, and wondered how many of them would ever know what it felt like to be chosen.

Mike continued recounting the tale of a prostitute named Gold Dollar who, in a fit of jealousy, killed another working girl backstage with a stiletto. That room, he claimed, had the highest concentration of reports: shadows, disembodied voices, the feeling of being watched. Theaters were emotional places, he explained—echo chambers of laughter, lust, and murder.

As the group filed up the creaking staircase, Joseph felt each step beneath his boots reverberate like a quiet warning—a hollow, uncertain music played by the bones of the old theater. The balusters were slick beneath his hand, worn by decades of hands reaching upward in hope, in fear, in curiosity. Dust swirled in the narrow shaft of lamplight above, disturbed by their movement, and the air seemed to shift—thicker, heavier, like the exhalation of something long buried and half-awake. Joseph's heart tapped a quick rhythm in his chest, anticipation sharpening his senses.

He trailed at the back of the group, letting the others' murmurs and nervous laughter drift ahead of him. There was a subtle pull, almost magnetic, drawing him not to the center but toward the left side of the wide, shadowed room. He glanced around—the velvet of the balcony railings was mottled with age, the wood beneath his feet creaked in protest, and the wall sconces cast uneasy shadows that quivered across the old wallpaper. Joseph's hand tightened on his EMF detector, its weight both reassuring and oddly fragile in his grip.

Near the base of the balcony steps, he paused. His breath caught. For a heartbeat, everything seemed to hold still—the tour group, the hum of the old building, even the distant sounds of Allen Street outside. Then, suddenly, a soft glow blinked to life on his device: two green lights, faint but clear in the dimness. It wasn't much. In the world of ghost hunting, it was a whisper, a breath, a heartbeat. But to Joseph, in that moment, it felt like the answer to an unasked question. The space between his shoulder blades tingled. The air shifted, colder than before, like an invisible hand passing through the room.

He fought the urge to call out, not wanting to break the spell. Instead, he stood quietly, letting the sensation linger, studying the leftmost shadows where the stage vanished into gloom. Something had moved there earlier, a shadow that seemed to bend the darkness around it. Was it still watching? Or waiting?

Mike, oblivious to Joseph's private revelation, continued his tale, his voice echoing through the hush. "Back in the day, you didn't sit with your back to the door," he was saying, "especially not if you were holding aces." The group's attention was fixed on the guide, the tension in the room rising with every ghost story and legend.

Unable to hold his curiosity any longer, Joseph leaned toward Mike and, voice low, asked, "Have there been reports of shadows crossing from that side of the room to the other?" He gestured, hand trembling just slightly, from right to left—following the very path that had drawn his eyes and sparked the lights on his device.

Mike paused mid-sentence, his gaze narrowing as he regarded Joseph with the practiced wariness of someone who'd heard all manner of claims. For a long moment, the only sound was the soft shifting of the group and the old building's settling sigh. "Yes," Mike said finally, his tone matter-of-fact but carrying an undercurrent of respect. "We've had quite a few people report that, actually."

The answer lingered between them like a secret. Joseph felt a strange surge of validation, his nerves buzzing not with fear, but with something close to exhilaration. He'd seen something real—something acknowledged by others, something he wasn't imagining. Mike moved on, not pressing for details, and Joseph didn't elaborate. There was no need. What passed between them was an understanding—a shared recognition of the theater's restless history, alive in the shadows.

With the story finished, Mike led the group to the back of the room and pointed out the entrance to the infamous poker room below. The descent was abrupt; the stairwell was narrow, walls lined with faded photos and yellowed newspaper clippings. Joseph could almost smell the decades-old sweat and cigar smoke that had seeped into the stone.

79

The underground chamber was chilly, the stone walls sweating with old moisture. It was said that legends like Earp and Bat Masterson had played here, that the longest-running poker game in Western history had unfolded beneath this ceiling—eight years, five months, three days, cards slapped down, fortunes won and lost. As the group filtered in, a hush fell over them. Some guests, their faces drawn in the flickering light, murmured about a sudden dizziness, a nausea that curled in their stomachs. Others simply grew quiet, their curiosity giving way to something heavier.

Joseph waited for the same wave to hit him, but he felt…nothing. Not fear, not sickness. The room was just a room—old, cold, heavy with history, but empty of anything that reached for him. He felt a twinge of disappointment, then realized his mind was already drifting back upstairs. His body was here, but his thoughts circled the shadow at the base of the balcony, the faint glow of the EMF, the peculiar pressure in the air that seemed to carry meaning only he could sense.

It was as if the shadow wanted him to return, to notice, to listen.

Eventually, Mike corralled the group and announced the final stage of their tour. "Now, we head back to the main room," he said, his voice pitched low and conspiratorial. "This time, we'll do it in the dark. Get your cameras ready. You'll want to catch what you can—sometimes it's a glimmer of light, sometimes it's nothing but a shape in the corner of your eye." He warned them again, eyes scanning the group: "Cold spots. Breath on your skin. Whispers. That's normal here. Don't panic."

A subtle tremor of excitement moved through the group, and Joseph felt his own pulse quicken. They would have to retrace their steps, passing again through the haunted backstage, the very stretch of shadow that had first reached out to him. As they climbed, the anticipation coiled in his stomach—equal parts fear and longing.

He was ready, more ready than he'd ever been. The air at the top of the stairs felt charged, thick as honey. Every sense was sharpened, every heartbeat louder. He took a breath and stepped forward, certain that whatever waited in the shadows, he was prepared to meet it.

Scene 3: The Stage Remembers

Joseph was one of the last to climb the stairs, his feet dragging with a mixture of anticipation and dread. He could hear the rest of the group above—footsteps and muted voices echoing through the old wood and velvet, fading as they clustered near the center of the stage room. The air felt denser back here, humming with an unseen charge that made the fine hairs on his arms stand up. Maybe he was subconsciously stalling, savoring the moment, or maybe it was the inexorable pull—an invisible hand guiding him again to that leftmost corner of the stage room, the same shadowed space that had first seized his attention.

As Joseph reached the edge of the stage, his EMF detector sputtered to life with an urgent crackle, suddenly leaping from silence to four solid, unwavering lights. The sight startled him—his heart seized, breath stalling in his throat. For a split second, he was paralyzed. A jolt of something— electric, real, raw—coursed up his spine and flooded his chest. Every muscle clenched. Sweat prickled along his brow and temples, slicking his palms. The nausea was immediate and total—a wave that swept from his stomach to his throat, heavy as seawater, threatening to pitch him over. His skin tingled, not just along the surface but deep, pulsing with a current that seemed to short-circuit his thoughts.

His legs quivered, barely able to support his weight. His vision shimmered at the edges, tunneling slightly. The old theater spun. The sensation was unlike anything he'd ever known—alien, urgent, somehow both freezing and burning. Joseph felt as if the world had narrowed to a single, blinding point of contact. Something was here. Something wanted him.

A woman from the group, her face framed by the soft blue glow of her phone, slipped up behind him. She noticed the blazing lights on his EMF detector and the sweat beading on his skin. "Are you okay?" she asked, her voice tentative, edged with concern. "That thing's going nuts. You're sweating."

Joseph nodded, or tried to. His mouth was dry, jaw clenched. It was all he could do to whisper, "Yeah... I'm not feeling great. Please... go get Mike."

She hesitated, then raised her phone and snapped a photo, the flash bouncing off the worn walls and throwing stark shadows. When she showed him the photo a few minutes later, Joseph's knees nearly gave out. There he was, outlined against the faded wallpaper—the unmistakable shadow of his own form, the familiar bend of his shoulders, the outline of his glasses. But next to him, ghostly and pale yet undeniable, was another shadow. Shorter. Lighter. Its contours were odd, out of time: a rounded hat, bowler-shaped, hovering atop a head as if waiting for an introduction. Joseph stared, the blood draining from his face.

Before he could process it, Mike appeared, having been fetched by the woman. His eyes narrowed in concern, reading the distress on Joseph's face with practiced clarity. "You okay? Want to sit down?"

Joseph tried to find words. He shook his head, but his voice wavered. "No. I think... something was here. I felt it." It sounded simple, even childish, compared to the reality: he'd felt invaded, struck through with presence, as if someone had pressed their whole soul into his chest.

Mike seemed to understand, his expression softening. "You were the one who asked earlier about the shadows moving across the room, right?" Joseph nodded, unable to trust his voice. Mike's words were low, deliberate, carrying the weight of hard-won knowledge. "They know when someone can feel them," he said. "They reach out to people who are open, even if they don't know they are."

He pointed to a nearby glass display case, its contents shimmering faintly in the low light—ornate porcelain vessels, delicately painted bowls, and old chamber pots, each piece glazed with the soft patina of age. They looked as if they'd once lined the shelves of a long-forgotten general store, practical items now transformed into relics. "Try over there," Mike said. "That spot's been hot before."

Still trembling, Joseph forced himself upright, legs uncertain beneath him. He moved as if underwater, every step deliberate, his mind buzzing with adrenaline and wonder. He could feel eyes on him—seen and unseen—as he reached the display case. The second he stopped in front of it, his EMF detector exploded: all the lights blazed, lighting his hand and the glass in a rainbow of green and red. The energy hit him like a physical blow—a violent, roaring surge that poured through his chest and erupted along every nerve ending. It felt like being electrocuted and embraced all at once. The charge shot down his arms, curled his fingers, sent his knees buckling beneath him. For a moment, his body stopped responding. His vision fractured, sound grew distant, and the world dimmed to a smear of faces and shadows.

Joseph staggered, unable to hold himself up, and fell backward into a nearby chair. The collapse was sudden and total. He gasped, the air searing his throat, his chest fluttering with shock. "Oh my God... what the hell was that?" he managed to choke out, voice shaking with awe and disbelief. "Did you see that? That passed right through me."

Mike knelt beside him, face grave. "That's not uncommon," he said quietly, steadying Joseph's shoulder with a hand that seemed heavier than it should be. "It may have tried to manifest through you."

Joseph's mind reeled, trying to process the enormity of what he'd felt. Was it just adrenaline? Or had he truly been the bridge for something desperate and ancient? All he could focus on was the feeling that had swept through him—a feeling so not his own it left him gasping. The energy wasn't cold, wasn't painful, but it was so overwhelming and urgent that it bordered on panic. He could sense a longing behind the sensation—a wild, aching need, the kind that can't be spoken, only screamed wordlessly. The emotion washed over him, saturating his bones: desperation, a centuries-old plea sharpened by sudden hope. The spirit had recognized him, realized that, finally, someone might be able to hear it.

He couldn't let it end there. "I have to do that again," Joseph said, determination overriding fear, adrenaline burning away doubt. Mike looked at him, startled by the raw intensity in his eyes. "You sure you want to?"

Joseph nodded, steadier now, the rush of purpose lending strength to his shaking limbs. "I do."

He stepped toward the display once more, the EMF detector already flickering, the air vibrating with unseen tension. He braced himself as he neared the case—then, BAM! The same overwhelming torrent surged through him, a tidal wave of cold fire and grief. His muscles spasmed; his legs folded, and he fell again, overwhelmed by the sensation. This time, tears pricked his eyes, not from pain but from the tidal force of sorrow that tore through him. It was grief, yes, but more—it was desperation, the frantic yearning of a voice finally, mercifully heard after decades of silence.

Mike asked quietly, "How do you feel?" The question, so mundane, felt surreal. Joseph answered honestly, from somewhere deeper than words: "Desperation," he whispered. "That's what I felt. Not fear. Not pain. Just… raw desperation, like a soul trying to scream without lungs."

He sat in silence for a long moment, the shudders slowly subsiding, hands still trembling in his lap. The group had moved on, their laughter and speculation echoing down the stairs. Joseph was alone, save for the lingering sense of presence beside him. With effort, he forced himself upright and followed the others, each step down the old stairway punctuated by another flicker on his EMF detector. The tingling in his limbs had dulled, but the urgency of the spirit's need—its plea for help—remained etched in his bones.

As he reached the main room at the bottom, the REM pod Mike had placed on the table erupted into life, buzzing and glowing, pulsing in time with Joseph's racing heart. He turned to Mike, voice ragged and low. "Do you think it followed me?"

Mike met his gaze, no hesitation in his answer. "Yeah," he said. "I think it did."

Joseph sat heavily in the folding chair, eyes drawn to the darkness at the foot of the stairs. The rest of the room faded away as Mike extinguished the lights, plunging them into thick, velvet shadow. Mike called out to the spirits, his words ringing through the darkness, inviting contact. Cameras flashed, recorders rolled, the hope of some message filling every breath. Joseph waited, half hoping, half dreading what might come next.

But there was nothing more. No spikes, no voices, no spectral touch—just the echo of his own heartbeat and the knowledge that, for one brief, electrifying moment, he'd been chosen to carry a desperate message from the other side. And as the darkness pressed in, Joseph felt—beneath his exhaustion—a fragile thread of excitement. For once in his life, he wasn't running from the unknown. He was reaching out to it.

Scene 4: Whispers Through the Walls

As the group disbanded, voices and footsteps faded into the night, swallowed by the hush of old Tombstone. Joseph lingered behind, letting the others drift away in twos and threes down Allen Street, the echo of their laughter quickly dying in the distance. The town seemed to exhale, its facades settling into themselves as the excitement of the tour ebbed away. Above him, the dim amber streetlamps spilled warm, ragged pools of light onto the warped boardwalk, painting long, doubled shadows that wavered as Joseph passed. Every step on the weathered planks resonated with a soft hollow note, as if the street itself was listening.

He slipped his EMF detector into his jacket pocket, fingertips still tingling from the energy that had coursed through him in the Birdcage Theater. He walked slowly, the desert air cooling around him, carrying the faintest scent of creosote and dust. Far beyond the edge of town, the land stretched into darkness, the silence broken only by a distant coyote and the rustle of a breeze in the mesquite. Joseph shivered, uncertain if it was from the night's chill or something left behind inside him—something that still vibrated with invisible electricity.

The memories replayed themselves, relentless: the sudden EMF spikes, the shadow that wasn't his, the jolt of energy that had left him reeling. What did it mean? Why had it happened to him? Joseph's mind turned in restless circles. He'd always noticed things other people ignored—cold drafts in sealed rooms, voices on the edge of hearing, objects moving from where he'd left them. He'd written off most of it as coincidence, or tricks of the mind. But tonight felt different. This encounter had been deliberate, the energy personal. It was as though something had recognized him, reached for him, chosen him. The spirit's touch hadn't felt evil, only desperate— aching, pleading, as if he were its last hope for being remembered.

All his life, Joseph had convinced himself he was ordinary, maybe just a little unlucky, maybe just tuned into the odd static that sometimes haunted old houses and restless nights. But now he wondered—what if it wasn't luck or misfortune at all? What if he really could sense what others couldn't? Maybe, he thought, spirits had been trying to reach him for years and he'd never realized it—never let himself believe it could be real.

He found himself at the edge of the Tombstone Hotel Inn History before he'd realized he'd wandered there. Maria was sitting outside their room on a battered bench, arms drawn tight around her as if holding in warmth. She stared up at the desert sky, vast and indigo, the stars burning with a cold clarity that made Joseph's chest ache. He paused, watching her a moment, trying to steady the nervous energy that still sizzled through his veins.

Maria's lips curled into a tired smile as he approached. "Took your time. Everything okay?"

Joseph hesitated, heart fluttering with secrets he wasn't ready to share. "Yeah. I just... got a couple hits on the EMF. Weird energy in the stage room. That's all." He tried to keep his voice light, but his words sounded hollow, even to him.

She cocked her head, studying his face in the lamplight, searching for what he wasn't saying. "Weird as in... spooky weird, or just faulty equipment weird?"

He forced a shrug. "Probably just the environment. Old wood, old wiring. You know how it is." He tried for a reassuring smile, but the effort cost him.

Maria wasn't convinced. She touched his hand, her thumb brushing his knuckles. "You sure? You look pale."

"I'm just tired. That's all," he lied, feeling the weight of the unspoken pressing against his ribs. How could he explain what he'd felt? That a shadow—no, a person, a desperate soul—had reached into him, filling him with its longing? That he could still feel it, an echo in his bones? Maria was open-minded, but this would frighten her. And the last thing he wanted was to pull her into the shadow with him.

They slipped inside, leaving the quiet hush of Tombstone behind and stepping into a room that felt like another world entirely. The stark contrast to the historic streets outside was immediate—this place was modern and comfortable, every surface pristine and untouched, the faint smell of fresh paint and new woodwork lingering in the air. The carpet was soft beneath their feet, furniture sleek and inviting, the whole space gleaming with an almost unnatural cleanliness, as if the past itself had been politely banished to the other side of the door.

But what truly set the room apart was its tribute to history. Framed photographs and detailed displays were mounted throughout, each one carefully curated to tell the story of Tombstone's wild days. Every wall was a mini-museum: weathered portraits of miners and lawmen, relics encased in glass, faded newspaper clippings, and artfully arranged artifacts that mapped out gunfights, fortunes won and lost, tragedies and legends. It was impossible to miss the pride taken in weaving the story of the town into the very walls—each room in the inn a unique chapter, a museum in miniature.

Above them, the ceiling lamp was a whimsical centerpiece: crafted to look like a poker table, complete with cards laid out mid-game, poker chips splayed in a lucky scatter, and liquor glasses cleverly shaped into light sconces. Warm golden light spilled over the beds from the tableau overhead, illuminating the gleaming new linens and casting playful shadows on the walls—a perfect fusion of comfort and history, inviting guests to become part of the legend, even just for a night.

It was perfect, really. The kind of place Joseph would have taken time to admire, the sort of attention to detail that normally made him linger and study every artifact. But tonight, he was too distracted to care. The dazzling room, with all its stories and art, faded to the background beneath the weight of what he'd just experienced at the Birdcage.

He undressed in silence, movements mechanical, his mind churning as he folded his clothes with absent hands. Every time he blinked, the shadow from the photo returned—the unmistakable outline that had stood beside him, lingering just out of reach, as if still waiting for him to turn and notice. He slid beneath the crisp new sheets next to Maria, his limbs stiff and heavy, body going through the motions of rest while his mind refused to quiet.

Maria curled into him, her breath deepening as sleep claimed her quickly, but Joseph remained awake, eyes tracing the lines of the poker table lamp above. The oddity of the fixture—so carefully crafted, so charming—should have delighted him. Instead, he felt the tension coiled tight in his shoulders, his thoughts circling the shadow, the voice, and the unsettling certainty that tonight, in Tombstone, the past wasn't just a story on the wall. It was alive, and reaching for him.

The room was so quiet, it pressed on his ears. The old air conditioner rattled, floorboards creaked softly as the building cooled. Beyond the window, the night spread out, thick and absolute. Joseph's thoughts twisted, looping over the evening's events: the rush of energy, the flickering lights, Mike's calm voice explaining, They reach out to people who can hear them. Could it be true? Had he always been someone spirits tried to reach, even when he'd ignored them? Had he spent a lifetime brushing off real voices as mere static?

Sleep took him suddenly, like being pulled beneath the surface of cold water. One moment, he was counting shadows; the next, he was nowhere familiar. He stood in a space both infinite and close, the air swirling in tight spirals, full of static and the smell of desert rain. Something watched him, presence thick and sorrowful—he knew it instantly as the spirit from the Birdcage.

Wind twisted around him, whipping his hair, stinging his cheeks. The static in the air grew, a pulsing electricity, every hair on his body standing up. Then—pressure at his throat. Not hands, but something rougher, older—a rope, tightening, closing. His breath vanished. Panic clawed at his chest. Joseph struggled, vision swimming. Through the howl of the wind, a voice rose up, straining to be heard, carrying a century of grief.

It wasn't me. I didn't do it.

The words knifed through the dream. Joseph's mind flooded with sudden understanding—this soul, whoever it was, had been executed for a crime they hadn't committed. This wasn't a haunting born of hatred, but one of injustice—a desperate, endless plea to be understood, finally, truly heard.

The noose fell away. Joseph jerked upright in bed, chest heaving, heart pounding so hard he thought it might burst. Sweat cooled on his brow as he blinked into the darkness, disoriented. The voice still echoed in his ears. He reached for Maria instinctively, searching for comfort.

89

She was already stirring, her voice groggy. "What happened? You okay?"

He tried to catch his breath. "Just a nightmare, I think," he lied again, unsure if anything that happened tonight could be called a dream.

She frowned, concern wrinkling her brow as she propped herself on her elbow. Then she muttered, "The people next door need to turn their TV down. I don't care if he didn't do it and that it wasn't him—I just want to get some sleep."

Joseph froze. His scalp tingled. He turned to look at her, words catching in his throat. "What did you say?" he whispered.

She rubbed her eyes, half annoyed, half sleepy. "The TV. Next door. I thought I heard their TV."

He said nothing, his mind spinning, wondering if Maria had heard the same plea he had. Maybe she was right. Maybe it was just the thin walls, the late night, the power of suggestion. Or maybe—just maybe—he wasn't alone in his sensitivity after all.

Maria sighed and rolled over, already halfway back to sleep. "Try and get some rest, baby. We have a long day ahead tomorrow."

Joseph remained still, staring into the dark as her breathing deepened. The silence of the room settled around him, comforting and unnerving at once. He thought of Mike's words, the feeling of the spirit's desperation flooding through him, the certainty that he had been singled out for a reason.

Maybe I do have a gift, Joseph thought, his fingers flexing nervously against the blanket. Maybe he could help these lost voices find peace. If they had always been there, waiting for him to listen, what else might he discover now that he knew to pay attention?

He lay there, eyes wide open in the Tombstone darkness, heart beating fast. Outside, a breeze rattled the window. The room felt charged, alive with unseen presence. Joseph closed his eyes and waited, willing himself to listen, to hear, to finally answer the call that had always been meant for him.

Chapter 5 - The Line is Broken

Scene 1: Home Again

Returning to Washington felt different this time. The sky was gray and gentle, the fir trees on either side of the highway slicked with early evening rain, but the world outside seemed somehow quieter—stilled by whatever Joseph had brought back from Arizona. As he and Maria turned onto their quiet street in University Place, the car was heavy with road dust, crumpled receipts, and the low hum of exhausted silence. Both kids, Jacob and Noah, were slumped in their seats, their heads lolling with each slow curve. For a few moments, neither Joseph nor Maria moved to unbuckle their seat belts. The apartment complex ahead looked unchanged—identical porches, tidy shrubs, porch lights flickering on. But for Joseph, nothing felt the same.

He sat in the driver's seat, staring out at the familiar little world of home: the dull golden porch light, the towering Douglas firs swaying gently in the evening breeze, the hedge where the neighbor's cat sometimes prowled. The windshield reflected his own tired eyes. Maria leaned across the center console, her smile gentle and reassuring, and brushed his hand with hers. "We're home," she said, her voice soft, full of the quiet certainty that always calmed the children—and usually calmed him, too.

But tonight, Joseph couldn't muster the same warmth. There was a distance inside him, a kind of internal drift. It was as if Tombstone had pulled something from the depths of his childhood, some old fear or knowing that he could no longer keep contained. For so long, he had been a stranger to his own hauntings—an outsider, looking in at the oddities that seemed to follow him. Whispers in the dark. Chilly drafts in sealed rooms. Glimpses of figures caught at the edge of mirrors, just out of sight. He'd always dismissed them as the residue of an overactive imagination or the leftover static from a childhood spent on edge.

But the spirit in Tombstone hadn't left room for doubt. The moment in the Birdcage Theater—the surge of electricity, the spike of the EMF, the

92

words whispered in his mind—had felt deliberate. Directed. Chosen. The spirit had not reached for anyone else. It had reached for him. And when it spoke—"I didn't do it"—the plea was not to the room or the world, but directly to Joseph, as if recognizing something inside him that was different.

He helped Maria carry the boys to their beds, cradling Noah's sleeping form against his shoulder, and for a moment he let himself watch Maria move about the little apartment—turning on the hall light, checking that the boys had their favorite blankets, straightening the family photos on the wall. Maria had always been the steady center of their family, the gentle gravity that kept everything from flying apart. She had a way of smoothing chaos without ever seeming hurried or anxious. When the boys woke at night from nightmares, it was her voice that brought them back from the brink. When Joseph came home late from work, tired or shaken by some distant memory, it was Maria who greeted him with the same patience, the same calm acceptance. Her presence was a kind of quiet strength—unassuming but unbreakable.

In the bathroom, Maria ran water and scrubbed road dust from her hands, humming softly under her breath. Joseph stood alone in the hallway, letting the familiar sights and smells wash over him: the soft citrus of the hand soap, the faint trace of Maria's perfume, the sound of running water and the muffled giggles of the boys through a half-closed bedroom door. The apartment felt safe—small, lived-in, and peaceful—but inside him was a storm of questions he couldn't answer.

He drifted into the living room, arms crossed tightly over his chest, sinking into the old couch that Maria had picked out at a yard sale their first year in Washington. The lamp cast a pool of gold on the coffee table, the family calendar bristling with reminders—soccer practice, doctor's appointments, tuition deadlines. Normal life. Joseph stared at nothing in particular, and memory swelled within him: the voice of the spirit soldier from the grenade range so many years before.

The glass does not just reflect. It holds. It binds. It remembers all who pass through. Time folds inside it. The mirror sees. The mirror listens.

And when the line is broken, it comes. Do not break the line, Joseph. He is waiting.

Those words looped through his mind, a riddle that haunted every quiet moment. What line? What glass? Was it all connected to the clock, the same clock that had shadowed his family for generations? That damned clock—still perched on the mantle at his father's house, silent and untouchable. He remembered the story his mother told, the inscription hidden on the back, and the way his father would always change the subject or quietly leave the room when the clock was mentioned. It was just an object, and yet it had always radiated a kind of menace—an unspoken warning, a threat never voiced aloud.

Even now, hundreds of miles away, Joseph could feel the clock's weight pressing against the back of his thoughts, as if it followed him from place to place, hidden in the ticking of time and the turning of memories.

He pressed his palms to his eyes, breathing deeply, letting the night settle around him. For the first time, he wondered if he was truly different. If he was, as Mike suggested, sensitive—not just to his own fears, but to the voices of the dead. All these years, had he misunderstood what haunted him? Had spirits been trying to reach out, seeking help or absolution, and he had simply refused to listen? The possibility frightened him and, at the same time, filled him with a strange sense of purpose. If he was meant to listen, then maybe he could help. Maybe the Thing that had chosen him as a boy— the Thing that stalked his dreams and rattled the glass—had always known who he really was.

A gentle hand settled on his shoulder, pulling him back to the present. Maria stood behind him, her dark hair loose around her shoulders, eyes soft and searching in the lamplight. She sat down beside him, concern flickering across her face. "You okay?" she asked quietly, her voice a gentle tether.

He nodded too quickly, brushing off the question. "Yeah. Just... thinking."

Maria smiled, a tired but real smile, and gave his hand a reassuring squeeze. "Don't stay up too late, okay? You look like you need sleep more than any of us." She stood, pausing at the edge of the hallway, watching him for a moment longer, her presence grounding him. "Come to bed soon," she said, voice warm but edged with a gentle insistence that always made Joseph feel safe.

He watched her go, the sway of her movements, the way she paused to glance back at him before disappearing into the hallway. It struck him how much he depended on her steadiness, how easily she bore the weight of his silences and moods. Maria was not someone who let fear rule her. She faced the unknown with quiet courage, determined to hold their family together no matter what shadows pressed in. For the first time, Joseph wondered what would happen if the darkness ever turned its eyes on her— if the world he feared became hers as well.

The apartment was silent now, the night pressing gently against the windows. Joseph stared at the blank, blackened TV screen, the glass reflecting his shape. For a heartbeat, he thought he saw another figure standing behind him—a fleeting outline, gone as quickly as it came.

He swallowed, his voice barely more than a whisper in the darkness. "What do you want from me?" he asked the emptiness, seeking an answer that never came.

Only silence replied. The silence—and, somewhere in the apartment, the faint, phantom ticking of a clock he could not see but could never truly escape.

Scene 2: Mischief in the Shadows

Their new apartment was part of a modest fourplex sunken at the base of a gentle slope, nestled beneath the towering trunks of ancient Douglas firs. The exterior was wood-clad, its faded paint and moss-draped eaves blending naturally into the cool, shaded world at the edge of the complex. From their ground-floor unit, Joseph sometimes felt as if they lived in the roots of the forest, the trunks of the firs rising like the legs of giants, their bodies vanishing somewhere high above in the drifting, Pacific Northwest clouds. Out back, a sprawling common yard stretched beneath the branches—a carpet of green that felt more like a park than a backyard, perfect for neighborhood kids to run and play in the filtered sunlight. The place felt sheltered, almost hidden from the rush of the outside world—a quiet corner in the embrace of ancient trees.

But inside, the space was cozy, wrapped in a hush that Joseph had always thought came with being on the ground floor, separated from the outside world by only a thin metal door and a few inches of drywall.

The layout was simple: step inside and the galley kitchen greeted you immediately to the left, its counters always cluttered with the detritus of daily life—Maria's keys, a chipped mug full of pens, a half-read paperback, a basket with spare change and receipts threatening to overflow. The narrow strip of linoleum gave way to the living room, a small square where a thrift store couch faced a battered coffee table. The TV glowed from its place in the corner, surrounded by a fortress of VHS tapes, DVD cases, and action figures that Jacob and Noah never seemed to keep in their room. Off to the right, a short hallway branched off to two bedrooms and a single, compact bathroom that always smelled faintly of lavender and whatever bubble bath the boys were obsessed with that month.

On the surface, their apartment was the picture of normalcy. Joseph and Maria made it their haven—filling it with family photos, school crafts tacked to the fridge, and the sound of children's laughter echoing down the hallway. They settled into routines with practiced ease: Joseph leaving early for work at the warehouse, Maria getting the boys off to school, dinners together at the little drop-leaf table, nights spent curled up together on the sofa or wrestling with homework at the kitchen counter. The hum of the refrigerator, the distant drone of neighbors' TVs, the shuffle of feet as the boys chased each other from room to room—these were the sounds that defined their days.

But beneath the veneer of peace, oddities had begun to creep in. At first, they were so minor that Joseph barely noticed them. It started with the keys. No matter how carefully they placed them on the kitchen counter—a sacred little ritual for a family always misplacing things—the keys would vanish. Sometimes Maria would walk in from the store, set her keys down, and moments later, when she returned from the bathroom, find them neatly centered on the dining table. It happened with Joseph's keys, too. They both blamed each other, then the kids, then their own absent-mindedness. Joseph even set up a stakeout one Saturday, pretending to read in the living room, keeping the kitchen in his peripheral vision. Nothing happened. But the second he turned away—just a blink—the keys were gone from the counter, reappearing on the table as if carried by invisible hands.

Maria laughed it off. "Did we put the keys there? I can't remember," she'd tease, ruffling Joseph's hair or giving him a playful nudge as she swept by. She had a way of making light of small mysteries, a cheerfulness that Joseph admired, even envied. But beneath her smile, he saw something else—an edge of unease, a wariness she tried to hide. She always checked the locks twice before bed now, and Joseph sometimes caught her glancing at the darkened kitchen, as if expecting to see something move in the shadows.

The oddities escalated. One night, as Joseph and Maria sat curled together on the couch—Maria with her feet in his lap, her head resting on his shoulder, the soft glow of the TV painting their faces with shifting colors—the apartment felt especially still. The boys had fallen asleep early, a rare and precious event, and the living room was a cocoon of warmth and quiet. They were midway through a movie when it happened.

BAM. BAM. BAM.

All three bedroom and bathroom doors in the hallway slammed shut in perfect unison, a sound so sharp and sudden that Joseph nearly leapt off the couch. The air shivered with aftershock, and for a heartbeat, neither of them moved.

Joseph's eyes darted to the hallway. The doors were all closed tight, their white paint gleaming in the low light. He listened—no wind, no rattling windows, not even the steady hum of the heater. Just the echo of those impossible slams. Maria untangled herself from the blanket and stood, moving with the cautious grace she always displayed when something unsettled the children.

She stepped lightly to the edge of the hall, peered into the shadows, then looked back at Joseph. Her eyebrow arched. "Well... that's new," he muttered, trying to keep his voice casual.

Maria shrugged and rolled her eyes with a brave little smirk. "I'm not getting up to check. If it wants something, it can ask nicely," she said, her words ringing with forced bravado. She turned back to the couch, but Joseph could feel her tension, the way her fingers twisted a lock of her hair as she settled back in. They watched the rest of the movie, but neither could focus—the suspense and the flickering images blending with the uncertainty that now haunted their home.

It was never just one thing, but a series—a slow accretion of moments that pressed against their sense of safety. Another night, long after the apartment had settled into its quietest hours, Joseph woke to a dull thumping. He checked the clock: 2:46 AM. He lay still, straining to catch the sound. Thump. Thump. Then a dragging, shuffling noise, followed by a muffled clatter in the living room.

Maria murmured in her sleep, and Joseph slipped from bed, reaching for the broom propped in the closet. He gripped it with both hands, his mind racing—burglar, animal, or something else? The hallway floor felt colder than usual. He opened the bedroom door and found Jacob peeking out, his eyes big and anxious.

"You hear it too?" Joseph whispered.

Jacob nodded, his voice barely a breath. "Yeah... thought maybe someone broke in."

Joseph led the way, broom held like a katana, each footstep testing the creaky floorboards. The living room was still, bathed in the faint amber from the streetlight outside. Joseph scanned every corner, bracing for anything.

Nothing. The only movement was their own reflection in the blank TV screen.

Jacob let out a quiet laugh. "Dad thinks he's a ninja."

Joseph grinned despite himself, lowering the broom. "Hey, it's all I had."

Relief flickered between them, but it was short-lived. As they stood in the dark, Joseph couldn't shake the sense of being observed—of something playful, perhaps, but also cunning, lurking just beyond their sight. The apartment, once so safe, now felt unsettled, the air thick with possibility and secrets.

And in the silence that crept back in, Joseph realized the mischief was only the beginning. Something else was here—watching, waiting. Something darker was pressing in, ready to reveal itself.

Scene 3: Madness Between Sleep

The days were beginning to blur, melting into one another like watercolors left out in the rain. The sky over University Place was often gray, but now even time seemed clouded, the sunrises pale and indistinct, barely separating night from day. Joseph moved through it all in a trance, each dawn arriving before he felt he'd even slept. He'd lie in bed with Maria's rhythmic breathing beside him—the gentle rise and fall of her chest the only real thing left in a world that felt increasingly thin and unreal. But when his eyes closed, home slipped away. The solid warmth of her beside him faded, replaced by something colder, weightless, and without mercy.

He was somewhere else.

Night after night, he drifted into a fog-thick realm, suspended between dreaming and waking, a twilight place where the line between memory and imagination grew thinner with each passing hour. Shadows slithered along the walls of his subconscious. Sounds crept in—soft at first, then rising: distant murmurs, strangled cries, guttural whispers that echoed as if carried on a wind from the depths of a forgotten grave. Sometimes, the voices wore familiar shapes, the echoes of childhood warnings, his mother's voice calling from another room, a drill sergeant's bark, a lost friend's laughter. More often, they were alien, harsh, layered and overlapping until they became a wall of sound pressing in, suffocating him.

"Joseph… help us."

"He sees you."

"Break the line… break the line…"

The voices built until he woke with a start, heart hammering against his ribs, skin slick with sweat. The room would be silent and dark except for the faint gold glow of the streetlights leaking in around the blinds. Maria would stir, mumbling soft reassurances in her sleep, her hand instinctively reaching out until it brushed his arm. Sometimes he lay back down and closed his eyes, willing himself to believe it was only a nightmare. But the fear wouldn't leave him. It hung in the air like smoke, twisting through the corners of the bedroom, coiling around his thoughts and making every breath feel shallow and sharp.

Daylight brought no relief. The boundary between worlds was fading. Spirits seemed to pass in and out of his life with increasing boldness, like strangers slipping through a revolving door. Joseph would stand at the kitchen sink, the clatter of dishes in his hands, when suddenly the warm water would turn cold, shocking his skin and raising goosebumps along his arms. Sometimes, while sorting the mail, he'd feel a breath—cool, deliberate—brush the back of his neck. He'd glance over his shoulder and see nothing but the kitchen's gentle clutter. Shadows darted at the edge of his vision, flickering just out of sight. Whispers pressed close to his ear, only to vanish as soon as he turned. On a few occasions, a phantom touch brushed his wrist while he watched the boys play in the common yard, sunlight golden on their hair. Each time, he stiffened, mind racing, but the feeling would fade as quickly as it came.

He told no one—not even Maria. The words were like stones in his mouth. How could he speak them aloud without making them real? If he admitted what he was seeing and hearing, what he was feeling, would he tumble over the edge into madness? He feared the answer. He feared what Maria would think—what it might cost her if she started to believe, too.

So he held it all in. He stopped sleeping, afraid of what waited for him in the fog. He lost interest in food, appetite drowned beneath the weight of constant dread. Even the boys noticed. Jacob watched him with worried eyes, asking if he was sick. Noah had grown clingy, trailing Joseph from room to room, always needing to be near him as if he sensed a coming storm. Joseph forced a smile and tried to carry on, but inside, he felt himself unraveling—thread by thread, day by day.

Then the dream—no, not a dream, a descent—returned. It began as it always did, with voices. This time, hundreds of them, tangled together in a cacophony of languages and accents, their desperation growing louder, more insistent with every passing second. Joseph was adrift in a sea of blackness, spinning, tumbling through an endless void. Cold seeped into his bones, then heat, then nothing at all—a numbness as complete as death. Wind whipped around him, more fierce than ever, a cyclone of grief and agony. Faces flickered in the gale: the soldier from the grenade range, the wrongly accused man from Tombstone, strangers whose eyes were full of sorrow and accusation. Their mouths moved, pleading or warning, but their words drowned beneath the roar.

Suddenly, everything stopped. Silence crashed in, oppressive and thick. And from the center of that vast emptiness, a shape began to form—shadow given substance.

The Thing.

It had no eyes, no face, only the vague impression of limbs and billowing smoke. It loomed over him, immense and predatory, radiating an ancient intelligence and malice so deep it nearly suffocated him. This was not a simple haunting. This was something far older, far more dangerous—a being that didn't just want to frighten Joseph. It wanted to break him, to consume him entirely.

"You opened the door," it spoke, its voice like thunder rolling beneath velvet. "You let them speak. Now, I speak."

Joseph tried to scream, to force the air out, but his throat clenched in terror. The Thing glided closer, reaching into him with invisible fingers, and Joseph felt something deep within him begin to slip away—a primal fear so profound it hollowed him out.

Then, with a sudden burst, the wind returned—howling, tearing at him, scattering his soul to the far corners of the void.

He jolted awake, lungs burning, sitting straight up in bed. The room spun. Maria stirred beside him, half-awake. "Joseph?"

He couldn't answer right away. His shirt clung to his skin, soaked through. His hands trembled uncontrollably. His heart pounded a frantic rhythm against his ribs, refusing to slow.

"Another nightmare?" Maria asked softly, her eyes heavy with worry.

He looked at her, weighing all the words he could never say. The spirits. The dreams. The Thing. He wanted to tell her everything. But fear and love tangled in his throat.

102

He just nodded.

Maria reached over and rubbed his back, slow and gentle. "I'm here," she whispered, grounding him with her warmth.

He wished he could believe that was enough.

Because deep down, Joseph knew this wasn't going to stop. The darkness was only gathering strength. It was only getting started.

Scene 4: Seeking the Truth from the Past

Joseph sat at the kitchen table long after everyone had gone to bed. The apartment felt hollow and vast in the late hours, the world beyond the window reduced to distant traffic and the faint hush of rain against the Douglas firs outside. The refrigerator's low hum filled the air, punctuated by the occasional pop and sigh of settling walls, but in Joseph's mind there was only noise—an anxious tangle of restless thoughts, old wounds, and half-remembered dreams. The silence of the apartment was thin, easily broken by the smallest sound, but inside him the noise was relentless, a ghostly chorus of whispers and regrets that refused to let him rest.

He stared at his phone where it sat on the table, the black screen reflecting his face—a haunted silhouette, eyes shadowed and tired. He'd scrolled through messages earlier, hoping for distraction, but found no peace. The device seemed to vibrate with unsent questions and confessions, things he couldn't say aloud even to Maria. What was happening to him? Why did the darkness feel thicker now, closer than ever? He needed answers, but didn't know where to look.

His thoughts turned, inevitably, to his father. Their relationship was built on an uneasy civility—always respectful, always careful, as if afraid a wrong word might crack some invisible shell between them. Samuel Duncan was a man of few words, his presence quiet but heavy, and certain doors in his soul seemed forever closed. Yet lately, with the supernatural incidents multiplying and that Thing growing nearer, Joseph couldn't shake the sense that his father's silence masked not ignorance, but knowledge. Fear. And above all, regret.

Joseph picked up the phone again, fingers trembling, and hovered over Samuel's contact. He set it down. Picked it up. Set it down again. He didn't want to sound accusatory, didn't want to break their fragile peace. But the need for answers finally outweighed his discomfort. With a final breath, he tapped Samuel's name.

The next afternoon, a sullen sky pressed low over University Place, clouds bruised and heavy with the threat of rain. When Samuel arrived, Joseph met him at the door, pulling him into a quiet, somber hug that lingered just a moment longer than usual. They made coffee, but neither touched their mugs. Instead, they sat at the kitchen table, its polished surface catching the gray light. Samuel's eyes looked older, lines of exhaustion etched deep into his weathered face. He seemed weighed down by something invisible, as if he too had not slept in years.

"You look… tired, son," Samuel said at last, his voice low and hesitant.

Joseph managed a hollow laugh, the sound dry in his throat. "Yeah. I guess I am."

A tense silence stretched between them, broken only by the distant chatter of children playing in the backyard. Joseph swallowed. "I've been seeing things, Dad. Not just now—this has been going on for years. Spirits talking… shadows watching. And then there's it, the Thing. It's older, meaner." His words hovered in the air, raw and vulnerable.

Samuel's jaw tightened, lips pressed into a hard line. He looked down at his hands, weathered and trembling slightly as they wrapped around the mug. For a long moment he was silent, lost in thought. Then, voice rough, he spoke. "I meant what I said at the bus station. Parts of us stay behind somewhere. I didn't say it for effect…I said it because of your aunt Ruth."

104

Joseph blinked, startled. "Ruth?"

Samuel nodded, his shoulders sagging. He closed his eyes, the memory rising from the depths like a ghost.

FLASHBACK – LATE AUTUMN, 1982

The old barn was almost pitch-black, the air biting cold and sharp enough to see each breath. Thin shafts of moonlight stabbed through the cracks in the walls, dancing with the trembling lantern light. Sixteen-year-old Ruth Duncan paced the packed earth floor, her cloak wrapped tight, face wild and haunted by something unseen. Samuel—just thirteen—followed in her shadow, worry furrowing his brow. The scent of old hay and rust hung heavy.

"Rustle the hay, Sammy," their mother had whispered earlier. "Just until I check on supper." But Ruth had other ideas.

"No, Sam. Stay here. I need silence." Her voice was steady, but her arms were dappled with gooseflesh. From a battered toolbox, she withdrew a small, silver-framed mirror, turning it to catch the lantern's glow. The glass shimmered—rippling, something flickering behind her reflection. Ruth's eyes widened. She swallowed hard.

"Stop, Ruth," Samuel pleaded, anxiety sharpening his voice.

She shook her head and gripped the mirror tighter. "It's real. There's something inside."

Samuel, heart pounding, tried to dismiss her fears. "You're imagining things… the whispering."

Ruth's eyes burned with conviction, an edge of terror making her seem older. "Call it what you want, Sam, but it's after me."

A sudden gust rattled the barn, the lantern swaying, throwing monstrous shadows up the rafters. The barn doors creaked open as if pushed by invisible hands. Ruth flinched. The mirror slipped from her grip, shattering on the wooden floor with a sound that seemed to echo forever.

She froze, her gaze locked on the glass, listening.

"Sam…do you feel that?"

Samuel stepped closer, every muscle tense. "Let's go home."

But the air was growing thick, sour, the stench of brimstone swirling in with the cold. Shadows stretched across the floorboards, unnatural, creeping. Ruth gripped Samuel's hand tight. "I'm scared."

A guttural laugh vibrated from the walls. Something black and slow oozed from the shards—a shape half-formed, limbs too long, its outline writhing in the lantern's dim circle.

"Ruth?!" Samuel screamed, but she held him back, her face a mask of terror and strange, eerie calm.

"It fears me," she whispered. "It doesn't want to take me…it wants me gone."

A raspy, inhuman voice trailed after her: "She is special. Better destroyed than used as bait."

Ruth turned to Samuel, eyes gentle, voice steady. "Run."

He screamed her name as dry hay burst into flame. The barn erupted in searing heat and choking smoke. Samuel dove into the fire, desperate, blinded by tears. But when the flames died and the air cleared, Ruth was gone. On the blackened floor lay a single, jagged shard of mirror, still sizzling against the wood.

Samuel's voice cracked as he returned to the present, a single tear shining in the corner of his eye. "I denied it all these years. I couldn't let myself believe there was something real out there. But Ruth... she wasn't playing. The Thing was there that night. That's why I stopped—why I pretended none of it was real."

Joseph's voice trembled, pain and understanding mixing. "You believe it was the Thing?"

Samuel nodded, his voice breaking. "I was arrogant. I thought I could protect her—protect all of us. But I failed the night Ruth died. Worse, I lied to myself because it was too terrible to face." He looked up, face streaked with emotion. "I've carried this guilt... I've carried silence."

Joseph reached across the table, taking his father's hand. "You're not alone anymore."

Samuel squeezed back, eyes shining. "And you won't be. I can't let history repeat. Not with you. Not with your family."

A heavy, profound quiet settled between them—but this time, it was the silence of understanding, not dread. The inscription on the cursed clock, Ruth's sacrifice, the Thing's return—it all pointed forward now, not just back.

Joseph drew a steady breath. "If I'm the one to face it...then you'll stand with me?"

Samuel's eyes, wet but resolute, met his son's. "Yes. I'll face it with you."

As dusk deepened beyond the windows and the firs whispered in the wind, father and son forged a bond stronger than their fears, ready to confront the darkness that had haunted their blood for generations.

Scene 5: The Bedroom Incident

The silence in the apartment after Samuel left was both peaceful and unsettling—a hush that seemed to hover just above the floorboards, thickening the air, muffling the ordinary sounds of life. Joseph sat at the dining table, the fading gray daylight creeping through the window, casting long, slanting shadows across the laminate surface. The faint rings left by coffee mugs—some fresh, some faded with time—stood out like pale scars on the table's skin. Maria had taken the boys to the grocery store, and for the first time in days, Joseph was alone. Alone enough to really feel the place.

He listened to the apartment breathe: the low, steady hum of the refrigerator, the slow exhale of the heater cycling on and off, the unpredictable creak of settling wood and nails. The sounds were familiar, yet they seemed amplified now, each one carrying a nervous pulse, like a heartbeat. Outside, the towering Douglas firs pressed close to the windows, their branches scratching lightly against the siding in the wind, a whispering chorus that had always felt protective—until now. Now, even the trees seemed to be holding their breath.

Samuel's visit had stirred something in Joseph—not just old memories, but something deeper, something woven through his blood and bones. The clock. The stories. The terrible admission about Ruth. Suddenly, everything seemed connected: the hauntings, the dreams, the Thing. It wasn't just about a single cursed object anymore. There was an intelligence, a will, working behind the spirits, orchestrating them along a line Joseph could only now begin to trace. The realization gripped him with icy fingers: the spirit bound in the clock wasn't evil. It was imprisoned. Suffering. And maybe—reaching out to Joseph not in malice, but in a desperate plea for help.

The light faded into dusk. When Maria and the boys returned, Joseph did his best to smile, to help unload groceries, to act normal. But all through dinner, he was quiet, mind distant. His gaze lingered too long on the blank TV screen, the family photographs, the darkened hallway where the ticking of that old clock echoed in the silence. Maria watched him with worried eyes but said nothing, giving him the space she knew he needed.

That night, when the world had stilled and the boys were tucked into bed—Jacob tangled in superhero sheets, Noah curled up with a stuffed bear—Joseph and Maria retreated to their own room. The hallway nightlight cast a faint, amber glow across the wood floor, painting soft lines across the bed and up the walls. Maria curled close to him, her presence warm, grounding, her breath rising and falling with gentle regularity. But Joseph couldn't relax. He lay stiff, staring at the ceiling, mind racing in ever-tighter circles.

"You've been quiet tonight," Maria whispered, breaking the silence.

Joseph turned to her, her face dimly lit by the nightlight's glow. "Just thinking. About what my dad said. About the clock… about our family." He hesitated, the words heavy in his chest. "You think all of this— the lights flickering, the sounds, the dreams—has something to do with that?"

He nodded, voice barely above a whisper. "I do. I think there's something—maybe many things—trying to reach out. I feel them. They know I can hear them. And the Thing from my childhood… it's still out there. Still watching."

Maria's expression tightened with concern. For a moment, her eyes darted to the darkened corner of the room, as if expecting something to manifest. "Do you think we're in danger?"

Joseph wrapped his arm around her, the movement more for her comfort than his own. "I'm not sure. But I won't let anything happen to you or the boys. I promise."

She nodded and pressed closer, her fingers searching for his in the darkness.

They turned in for the night, doors locked, the apartment sealed as tightly as it could be. Joseph checked on the boys one last time, brushing hair from their foreheads, watching their peaceful breathing, letting the sight steady his nerves. He closed the bedroom door, flicked off the lights, and slipped back into bed beside Maria. The bedroom felt colder than before— a stillness settling over everything, pressing down on his chest like a warning. The silence wasn't peaceful now; it was oppressive, the kind that collects in old, empty places where secrets fester.

As he lay there, Joseph realized the ticking of the hallway clock sounded odd—distant, warped, as if each tick was dragging through water. The air was too thick, every breath drawn with effort. Maria shifted beside him, already drifting off, her body curled protectively toward his.

He listened to her breathing, tried to sync his own to its rhythm. But sleep, when it finally came, fell over him like a shroud. His limbs grew heavy, his chest tight, the darkness around him swelling until he felt he was sinking into it.

A whisper.

It threaded through the silence, soft and insistent, tugging at the edge of his consciousness. Joseph's eyes snapped open, but the room was gone—replaced by a void so black it seemed to swallow even his thoughts. He tried to move, to reach for Maria, but found himself paralyzed, pinned beneath invisible hands.

The air changed—grew cold, then fetid, then burning. The darkness thickened, and in it, something began to move. Joseph's heart pounded, and then, slicing through the void, Maria's scream shattered the silence. It was raw, ragged, full of terror.

He strained, fighting the weight on his chest, and saw her—Maria, beside him, upright in bed, eyes wild, hands clawing at her throat as if invisible fingers were squeezing the life from her. Her lips moved in a silent plea, eyes rolling in panic.

"Maria!" Joseph shouted, struggling to break free, but his body would not answer. A cold, crushing force pressed down on his chest, pinning him to the mattress. He felt the mattress dip, as if something massive crouched atop him. The air twisted into a vortex, swirling with the foul stench of burnt hair, old blood, and something older, more terrible—like the rot of centuries left to fester in the dark.

And then he saw it.

A shadow darker than the room itself, writhing in the air above them—a shapeless Thing, a negative space that seemed to absorb light. It hovered, growing, a billowing mass with no face, no eyes, only the suggestion of claws and a mouthless hunger. Its presence radiated ancient, intelligent malice, so powerful Joseph felt it brushing against his soul.

Maria's body convulsed, her hands flailing against the invisible grip choking her. Her feet thrashed, eyes glazed with terror. The Thing leaned closer to Joseph, so near he could feel its chill seep into his bones. A voice, impossibly deep and calm, thundered inside his head:

"I have found you, Joseph. The blood calls to me. Come to me where I dwell. Challenge me, or your soul—and theirs—will be lost. Forever."

There was no rage in the voice—only inevitability, like a sentence handed down from on high. Biblical in its weight, cold as judgment.

Just when Joseph thought Maria's struggles would cease—just as her eyes began to flutter—a blinding light burst from the doorway. It seared through the swirling shadow, casting it back, rolling it away like smoke yanked by a sudden wind. The pressure on Joseph's chest vanished. He gasped, lurching upright, and saw Jacob standing in the doorway, the hallway behind him blazing with ethereal radiance. Jacob's eyes were wide with terror, but in that moment, he was more beacon than boy.

The Thing recoiled, twisting violently as if in agony, then slipped away, retreating into the shadows at the farthest corner. The wind ceased,

111

the air grew still. Maria collapsed against Joseph, sobbing and coughing. Jacob ran to her, burying his face in her lap, his small shoulders shaking.

Joseph held them both, his hands trembling as he stared into the darkness where the Thing had disappeared. His heart hammered. The warning had been given. The line was broken.

He knew, with an icy certainty, that running was no longer an option. The Thing would not stop. It was waiting for him. Calling to him.

He would have to answer. For Maria. For Jacob and Noah. For all of them.

For the first time, Joseph realized the battle had truly begun.

Chapter 6 - The Unveiling

Scene 1: The Aftermath

Maria was still crying, curled tightly against Joseph's chest, her body wracked with silent sobs. Her skin felt clammy beneath his hand, her face drained of all color, lips trembling as she tried to catch her breath. Jacob lingered at the foot of the bed, wide-eyed and shivering, clutching the bedpost like an anchor. Little Noah had wormed his way to Maria's side, pressing his face into her hip and whimpering, his small body shaking with confusion and fear. The room was suffused with the acrid aftertaste of panic, every shadow stretching long in the pale light from the hallway, as if the house itself had not yet released its own breath.

Joseph's gaze swept the room, searching every corner, every flicker of movement, half-expecting the darkness to surge back at any moment. The air felt raw, charged, like the world after a violent thunderstorm—cooler and lighter, yet filled with the tension of something unfinished. An uneasy silence settled, not the peace of resolution but the stunned quiet that follows a scream. It was as if the walls, the furniture, the old wood of the apartment, were themselves waiting to see if the nightmare would return.

He inhaled deeply, fighting the tightness in his chest, then shifted upright, gathering Maria and the boys closer. "It's okay. It's gone," he whispered, his voice little more than a rasp, meant more to convince himself than the others. The words felt thin, insubstantial in the charged air.

Maria clung to Noah, her knuckles white where they gripped the boy's shirt. Her eyes darted around, never resting for long. "What was that, Joseph? Why did it attack me? What did it mean—what it said to us?" Her voice was rough and broken, quivering with leftover terror.

Joseph's mouth opened, but nothing came. He couldn't force the truth out, not yet—not when he hardly understood it himself. He closed his eyes, nodding as if that were an answer. "I don't know," he managed, his heart pounding a jagged rhythm in his chest.

From the foot of the bed, Jacob broke the silence with a strange calm. "That wasn't the one who talks to me sometimes." The words hung in the air, sharp and incongruous. Joseph's heart lurched. He turned to Jacob, meeting his son's haunted gaze, but Maria, still reeling, didn't seem to register the comment. Joseph filed it away, feeling the weight and meaning behind it settle cold in his bones.

He steadied his voice, forcing himself into motion. "Okay. Let's get you boys back to bed." His movements were gentle, but urgency tinged every gesture as he ushered them into the hallway, toward their shared bedroom. Each step felt fragile, as though the thin boundary between this world and something darker might tear at any moment.

In the boys' room, Joseph knelt between their small beds, brushing hair from their foreheads, whispering reassurances. The hallway light spilled in, painting a warm, golden rectangle across the clutter of toys and the crumpled superhero blankets. He wanted to freeze time right there, to hold on to the normalcy of this simple act.

"I'll leave the light on," he promised, making his voice strong and steady. "And I'll be right out here. I'm not going to sleep tonight. I'm staying up, standing guard. I promise—nothing will happen to you."

As he tucked the blankets around them, a deep tenderness rose inside him—aching, fierce. These boys, Maria... they were his entire world. In that moment, his love felt weaponized—an iron wall he

114

willed between his family and whatever horror had invaded their night. The Thing had come for him, he knew it. It wanted him. But he would be the line it could not cross.

He pressed a kiss to Jacob's forehead, then Noah's, lingering just a moment longer as if by will alone he could protect them. Only when their breathing slowed did he stand, squaring his shoulders for what was next.

Back in the master bedroom, Maria sat rigid against the headboard, her hands twisted in the blanket, face streaked with tears. Joseph moved quietly, wrapping a warm quilt around her shoulders, guiding her gently down until she lay against the pillow. Her eyes were huge, ringed with exhaustion and fear, but she didn't fight his touch.

"I'm not going anywhere," he whispered, kneeling by the bed. "Just try to rest. The light's on. The boys' door is open. I'll be right here."

She watched him for a long moment, searching his face for some unspoken reassurance. "You'll stay awake?" she asked, her voice thready.

He nodded, settling into the old chair in the corner, positioning himself between the bed and the door. "I will," he said. "I won't leave you."

The hours dragged, slow and brittle. Maria's breathing evened out, her eyes fluttering as she drifted into uneasy sleep, though her hand never relaxed its grip on the blanket. The room was still, but Joseph could feel the pulse of the night—could feel the residue of the Thing lingering just beyond the pool of light, waiting for weakness. He sat rigid, every muscle aching with exhaustion, eyes burning from the effort of vigilance. What had that Thing truly wanted? Was it a warning, a punishment, a message meant for him alone? The memory

115

of its voice—the calm, thunderous pronouncement—replayed in his head until the meaning became a drumbeat in his chest.

Should I tell Maria everything? Should I reveal the depth of the danger? Would the truth help, or only shatter her already-frayed sense of safety? He clenched his fists, the leather of the chair creaking beneath his grip. Not yet, he decided. Not until I know more. Not until I have a plan.

At some point, despite every promise, fatigue claimed him. His body slumped in the chair, posture still vigilant, spirit willing but flesh too worn to resist. He drifted in uneasy dreams, half-listening for sounds that never came.

Morning arrived as a pale wash of light, tentative and slow to claim the apartment. Maria was the first to stir, bleary and silent, her hair tangled from restless sleep. She gazed at Joseph, slumped awkwardly in the chair, his arms folded tight across his chest.

"You fell asleep," she whispered, a hint of teasing undercut by raw relief.

He blinked awake, startled. "Yeah. I'm sorry."

She smiled—just a flicker, fragile and grateful—as she tucked a stray strand of hair behind her ear. "You're not a very good guard dog," she managed, voice hoarse.

He forced a laugh, the sound shaky but real. "I tried."

Later, they sat together at the kitchen table, the morning light dappling the surface, both clutching mugs of coffee with trembling hands. The air in the apartment still felt hollow, as if the night had stolen something they'd never quite get back.

"What are we going to do, Joseph?" Maria asked, her voice still trembling with the memory. "It said something to you. Like it wants something."

Joseph nodded, staring into the depths of his coffee, searching for answers that remained out of reach.

Maria hesitated, fingers tracing the rim of her mug. "You know my friend Abigail from church?" she said softly.

He looked up, surprised by the change in subject. "Yeah?"

"There's something she told me once—something I never told anyone. Not even the other church members. She said if people found out, she could be expelled."

He frowned, curiosity piqued. "What is it?"

Maria glanced at the window, voice dropping lower. "She's... a medium. Clairvoyant. She sees and hears things. She only told me because we were new and... she wanted someone to talk to. Maybe she can help us. Maybe she can tell us what happened last night."

Joseph hesitated, his protective instincts clashing with his need for answers. He didn't want Maria drawn any deeper into the darkness, but they were out of options. "Alright," he said at last, slowly. "But let's not tell her anything. Not yet. Let's see what she says first."

Maria nodded. "I'll invite her for dinner tonight. She's alone most nights anyway. I think she'll come."

Joseph let his head fall back, exhaling as if he could empty his fear with his breath. Something had to give. If the Thing was coming for him, he needed to be ready. And if Abigail truly was a medium, maybe—just maybe—she could finally pull the truth from the shadows that haunted their lives.

Scene 2: The Summoning of Truth

The apartment was wrapped in a hush, broken only by the muffled laughter and scuffling of toys drifting from the boys' room across the hall. That cheerful noise had become their only shield—a bright, oblivious song against the shadow that lingered after the night before. The innocence of Jacob and Noah was a living, breathing barrier, their resilience restoring them to play and comfort as if nothing had ever been wrong. It was as if a gentle hand had swept clean their memories, shielding them in ways words and reason could not. For now, their world was safe.

To Joseph and Maria, however, that laughter was a thin veil—delicate as tissue, unable to truly hide the fear that still wrapped around their hearts like cold wire. They sat stiffly on the living room couch, close but isolated, the flickering light of the television washing over them both. The familiar game show blinked across the screen—one they would normally watch together, voices raised in playful arguments over the answers, cheering at a lucky spin. Now, the hosts' laughter sounded distant, distorted. Each bright jingle felt wrong, echoing in a room that was no longer home but a place of anxious waiting. The TV was just noise now, background static to their silent, shared dread. Their bodies were present, but their minds wandered—adrift in a fog of memory and fear.

Joseph sat hunched forward, elbows braced on his knees, fingers knotted tightly together. His leg bounced uncontrollably, betraying the tension he tried so hard to keep hidden. Thoughts spun through his mind like leaves caught in a gale—each one more chaotic than the last. What if the Thing came back? What did it truly want from him? Was this all some inescapable legacy, a curse written in his blood? He tried to find answers in logic, tried to construct some plan or order, but every time he closed his eyes, the memory of Maria's scream and the Thing's cold voice crashed through him and scattered all sense.

Maria sat beside him, almost as tense. She twisted her wedding ring around her finger, her eyes fixed on the screen but unfocused. She glanced at Joseph, then away, then back again—her worry and exhaustion written in every line of her face. Today was different. Today, she could feel it too: a tension in the air, the sense that nothing would ever be the same after what was about to happen.

She broke the silence, her voice thin and brittle. "What time did you tell her to come?"

Joseph dragged his gaze to the clock on the wall, watching the second hand crawl across the dial. "Any minute now," he answered, trying—and failing—to keep the tremor from his voice.

They fell silent again, the TV filling the emptiness with hollow laughter. Minutes stretched, elastic and slow, every tick of the clock a drumbeat. Joseph's thoughts looped—flashes of nightmares, memories of the spirit soldier, the Thing's biblical warning. He needed answers, not just for himself but for all of them. But confirmation meant facing a truth he had always feared.

A sharp knock split the air, echoing through the small apartment with the force of a gunshot.

Both Joseph and Maria jumped, nerves jangling. For a split second, the world felt unreal, as if the knock had come from within a dream. Joseph smoothed his shirt and shot Maria a quick, shaky look. She nodded, and he rose, walking to the door. He paused, hand on the knob, forcing himself to smile—a mask he hoped would reassure her, but he knew his eyes gave him away.

He opened the door. Abigail stood there—her smile broad and warm as the Arizona sun, her hair swept back in loose waves, a summer dress swirling around her legs, and a bottle of wine cradled casually in her arms. She looked, at first glance, like a guest arriving for a pleasant evening.

But as soon as her gaze met Joseph's, her expression changed. The brightness faded, replaced by a look of grave concern. She read the truth in his eyes—the weight, the sleepless fear. The way people who live with shadows recognize each other. She stepped back slightly, her whole bearing shifting from visitor to sentinel, her cheerful mask falling away to reveal the resolve of someone who knows she has been called not for dinner, but for something much deeper.

Her voice dropped to a gentle, serious tone. "I know why I'm here."

Maria appeared behind Joseph in the doorway, drawn by the exchange. Abigail nodded to her with a reassuring look, then stepped inside, moving quietly. She set the wine down on the kitchen counter with careful hands, then pointed to the living room. "Gather everyone and wait there," she instructed, her voice calm and unhurried.

Her eyes swept the apartment, lingering on the corners, the shadows, the small arrangements of family life. She seemed to drink in the energy of the space, her presence both comforting and unsettling.

Joseph and Maria gathered the boys, settling them on the living room couch. Jacob and Noah looked up with wide, curious eyes, their playful laughter fading into uncertain silence as they sensed the tension from the adults. Abigail gave them each a gentle, reassuring smile, then disappeared down the hallway.

First, she entered the master bedroom. Through the thin apartment walls, Joseph and Maria could just make out the sounds of her voice—soft at first, then swelling into a gentle chant. It was melodic and rhythmic, the words muffled and unintelligible, but they carried a tone of command, a resonance that made the air seem to vibrate. At one point, her tone changed—sharp and admonishing, like a mother chastising a stubborn child. The whole apartment seemed to respond: the lights flickered, a draft stirred along the floor, the air thickened, charged.

Then, abruptly, all was silent.

Her footsteps padded softly toward the boys' room. Again, she began to speak—this time, her voice lighter, soothing, almost like a lullaby. The cadence was different: warm, encouraging, as if comforting an unseen presence. The boys huddled closer to Joseph and Maria, watching the hallway with wide, uncertain eyes.

Ten minutes crawled by, slow and anxious. The laughter from the game show felt tinny and distant now. Maria squeezed Joseph's hand so hard his knuckles turned white.

Abigail reemerged at last, her face drawn and grave. She sat down in the armchair across from the family, folding her hands in her lap, her posture regal and composed. Joseph and Maria instinctively leaned forward, their entire bodies coiled with tension. Even the boys sat perfectly still, their usual restlessness subdued by the heavy air.

Abigail's eyes met Joseph's, and her words landed like stones: "There are two spirits here. One of darkness, and one of light."

Joseph and Maria felt their hearts sink. The tension ratcheted higher.

She continued, her voice even and steady. "The dark one—he's the one that attacked you in your bedroom last night."

Maria gasped, shock etched on her face. "How did you—?"

"I felt it," Abigail replied, matter-of-fact. "He found a way into this realm. For a long time, he could only reach Joseph through dreams. But last night, something changed. A door was opened. He came for you."

Joseph felt the words burn into him, like a mark.

"But he needed a weakness," Abigail said. "A reason for Joseph to act."

Joseph's voice was barely a whisper. "My family."

Maria whipped her head toward him. "Did you know? Joseph, did you know this Thing was after you?"

He couldn't meet her eyes. He tried, but the truth was too heavy. Abigail broke the tension, her tone calm. "You have to tell her."

Joseph exhaled, his voice rough. "Yes. I knew."

Maria bolted upright, fury and fear twisting her features. "You what? You knew we were in danger and said nothing?!"

Joseph raised his hand, pleading. "I thought I could handle it. I thought it only wanted me. I didn't want to scare you without answers."

Abigail's hand closed over Maria's, gentle but firm. "He was trying to protect you. But now he knows the truth. The Thing isn't just trying to scare him. It wants him afraid—paralyzed."

Maria's eyes filled with tears. "Why?! Why does it want him?"

Abigail's face darkened. "Because it's afraid."

The room stilled. Even the game show's laughter seemed to hush.

"Luke 8:31," Abigail continued. "And they begged Jesus repeatedly not to order them to go into the Abyss. The Thing fears the Abyss—a place of torment and eternal exile. In some traditions, it's called Tartarus. Your Thing is bound to this world through a soul—a distant relative of Joseph."

Joseph nodded, feeling the puzzle pieces slot into place. "Adam. The clock. The inscription. 'Do not break the line.'"

Maria's eyes widened with memory. "You told me that story… Is he still inside the clock?"

"Yes," Joseph said. "My mother told me he was bound inside the glass. If I break the line, I can set him free."

"And cast the Thing into the Abyss," Abigail finished, her voice like a bell.

A heavy silence settled, every eye turned to Joseph.

Then Jacob, his voice soft but clear, spoke up. "So… the spirit that talks to me isn't the Thing?"

Abigail smiled gently. "No. He watches over you. He's one of the good ones."

Jacob frowned, brow furrowed in concern. "He looks hurt. He's missing an arm."

Joseph's eyes widened, recognition flaring. "That's the soldier from the grenade range. Where do you see him?"

Jacob and Abigail answered together. "In the mirror."

Joseph's breath caught. "He's been watching me. Now he's watching Jacob."

"Yes," Abigail confirmed. "He entered with Jacob and forced the Thing back. He says his name is Ryan."

Maria's fear softened, awe blooming in her eyes. "He's our guardian angel."

Abigail was slow to nod. "Sometimes, light is strong. But it may not last. Spirits are like runners. Some are sprinters. Some endure. Your Ryan is a sprinter. The Thing? A marathoner."

"So he can't protect us forever," Joseph murmured.

"No," Abigail said.

Maria, exhausted and tense, pressed forward. "So what do we do?"

Abigail leaned in, her eyes blazing with conviction. "You must free Adam from the glass through a ritual. Break the line. Send the Thing to the Abyss. If you don't, it will keep attacking—and next time, it may not stop."

Joseph looked at Maria. At their sons. At Abigail. The weight of destiny pressed upon him—but beneath it, something else emerged: resolve.

"Then it's decided. I know what I must do."

And as the moment solidified, the old fear finally melted—replaced by something heavier, but somehow brighter:

Purpose.

Scene 3: The Weight of Light

The dining room was dimly lit, not out of necessity but mood. A single warm light above the table bathed everything in a soft amber glow, casting gentle halos on faces and glinting off the edges of silverware. The faint hum of the refrigerator underscored the silence, broken only now and then by the clink of silverware against ceramic plates. The aroma of roast chicken and garlic mashed potatoes hung in the air—a comforting scent that normally would have signaled celebration, but tonight, no one had much appetite.

Abigail sat across from Joseph and Maria at the modest apartment table. Her summer dress, cheerful with swirling colors, seemed almost out of place against the dimness. Her hair, now gathered in a loose, practical bun, left wisps to frame her face, and she wore little jewelry—just a silver ring and a woven bracelet, tokens from another time. Her posture was poised, hands folded lightly on the table, but a tension showed in her shoulders and in the way she watched everyone around her: measured, aware, as if reading the currents of the room. Behind her gentle smile lingered something else—a depth, an exhaustion that marked those who have lived too long with secrets and burdens. Her eyes, an unexpected green-gold, flicked between Joseph and Maria, never missing a thing. Joseph noticed it, the gravity she carried beneath her warmth, and recognized it as kin to his own.

Joseph thought reflectively. "This wasn't just about me anymore. It never was. It was about Adam. About my father. About the thing that stole Ruth. About Maria. Jacob. Noah. I had been chosen—maybe because I could hear them... maybe because I had enough fire to answer back. Or maybe, just maybe, because I was the only one left in our line strong enough to stand up to it. But there was no doubt now—this was my burden to carry."

Maria broke the hush, her voice almost apologetic. "Abigail, can you explain how it will work? The ritual? The details."

Abigail nodded slowly and gently pushed her plate aside, folding her hands in front of her. The flickering light caught on the fine lines around her eyes. "The ritual is old," she began, her voice clear, every word deliberate. "It predates Christianity, but the Church absorbed it, recontextualized it. In its most basic form, it's a binding and releasing rite. A triangle of mirrors, each representing a holy witness. A relic—in this case, the clock—at the center. Holy water, salt, and sacred scripture must encircle the mirrors. The intent must be clear: to break the chain that holds Adam's spirit hostage."

She spoke with the cadence of someone who had spent years piecing together old texts and folk stories, someone who had learned to translate the past into the present. There was a subtle intensity to her—when she described the ritual, her hands moved as if sketching symbols in the air. Joseph saw the confidence in her, but also a flicker of vulnerability, as if she knew how easily even the best-laid protections could unravel.

"Where did it come from?" Joseph asked, studying her closely.

Abigail's gaze warmed, a teacher answering a favorite question. "The earliest recorded version comes from early Jewish mysticism," she said. "The concept of souls being bound to objects appears in the Zohar, a foundational work of Kabbalah. Later, Catholic exorcists adopted some of the framework. By the time of the early American settlers, such rituals had merged with folk practices. In some parts of Appalachia, mirrors were covered during funerals because it was believed a soul could get trapped if they looked into one too soon." She paused, smiling softly. "Superstition and sacred truth, always side by side."

Joseph nodded. That felt true. It always comes back to the mirror.

Maria asked, more anxious now, "What happens if we do it wrong?"

Abigail's expression grew serious; she didn't soften the truth. "If the triangle is broken, or the incantation falters, or worse—if the

126

Thing overpowers the spiritual barrier—then Adam stays bound... and Joseph could take his place."

A chill swept through the room, as if the words themselves held power. As if on cue, the overhead light flickered violently. They all froze. A low, uneasy creak sounded from the hallway, followed by a door slamming somewhere in the apartment.

Joseph stood, scanning the shadows. Maria held her breath, gripping the edge of the table.

"That wasn't him," Abigail whispered, her eyes sharp, watching the door.

"The Thing?" Maria asked.

Abigail shook her head, a faint furrow in her brow. "No. That wasn't Ryan either. That was... something else." She said it matter-of-factly, as if she had spent her life navigating such mysteries. She always spoke the truth plainly, but with a gentleness that made even the hardest truths feel bearable.

"Something else?" Joseph asked, voice low.

Abigail nodded, leaning forward. "Other spirits have taken notice. They know what you're about to do. The Thing has ruled with terror for decades, perhaps centuries. Many are too frightened to act. They linger between realms, too afraid to cross, too afraid to challenge. They exist like mist. Quiet. Passive. But now you've stirred the water."

Joseph listened, struck by the authority in her tone—the calm of someone who had comforted the frightened, stood vigil for the dying, and negotiated with the invisible. Abigail seemed older than her years—marked by the responsibility of her gift.

He wondered, Could they help me? Could they push back? Or would they remain shadows, too afraid to cast themselves into battle? "Will they help?" he asked aloud.

Abigail's lips pressed together in a thin line. "Some might," she said, her voice quiet but firm. "But don't count on them. Most spirits are terrified of what could come next—something far worse than this place. Remember the old warnings: 'They begged Him not to order them to go into the Abyss'—Luke 8:31. That's what they fear. An emptiness so deep that even restless souls dread it."

Maria sighed, her face tight with worry. "What do we need to do? What's the next step?"

Abigail leaned in, her eyes bright with conviction. "The ritual must take place where Adam is. That means Schenectady. Moving the clock might disturb the binding and risk the Thing sensing our plan. We need to go to the source."

Joseph nodded slowly. "I need to speak to my dad. We'll need his help. The clock is still in the parlor."

Maria looked concerned. "Should Father Allen be involved?"

Abigail hesitated, considering carefully, her fingers toying absently with her bracelet—a nervous habit. "Only if he is spiritually open. Some clergy aren't. They deny what they cannot name. But if he is willing, a priest's blessing would reinforce the ritual."

Joseph met her gaze. "Would you come with us?"

Abigail nodded, her voice unwavering. "I will."

Maria glanced at Joseph, worry etched in her features. "And the kids?"

Joseph was resolute. "No. They're staying here with Mrs. Garza. I won't risk them being near this."

The lights flickered again, then steadied, the room holding its breath.

It's listening. Always listening. Watching. Waiting. But this time, it will see something new. Resistance. Righteous fury. The light.

Abigail reached into her bag and pulled out a small, battered notebook, its pages worn soft with use. "We'll need a blessed mirror, three if possible. I know someone who can provide them. Holy water can be acquired from Father Allen's church. Salt, from a kosher source. And the scripture passage must be memorized. Luke 8:30-31. The same passage the Thing fears."

Joseph recited quietly, "'Jesus asked him, "What is your name?" He replied, "Legion," because many demons had entered him. And they begged Jesus repeatedly not to order them to go into the Abyss.'"

"That's the one," Abigail confirmed, her eyes holding Joseph's a moment longer.

Maria reached for Joseph's hand across the table. Their fingers met and lingered, drawing strength from each other.

"We can do this," she said softly, voice trembling with hope and fear.

Joseph squeezed her hand. We have to.

A sudden gust of wind rattled the window, making the flame in Abigail's eyes flicker for a moment. In the distance, a whisper drifted through the apartment, slipping beneath the door and across the floorboards.

Just one word:

"Soon."

Scene 4: A Plea in Sacred Walls

The early morning light filtered softly through the stained-glass windows of the local church there in University Place, St. Matthew's Church, casting warm hues of crimson and gold across the empty pews. Joseph sat alone in the parish office, hands clenched between his knees. A nervous energy pulsed through him as he waited for the call. The church was quiet—peaceful. It was the only place he felt sure the Thing wouldn't be listening. He needed that assurance now. The church had become more than a place of worship—it was a fortress against the dark.

"If it's true what Abigail said—that it's listening, waiting—I can't risk it. Not in the apartment. Not even in the car. But here... it can't cross this threshold. Not without being invited."

Why a church? Why the need for sanctified ground?

Because he wasn't sure the Thing wouldn't hear otherwise. Joseph wasn't just protecting himself now. He was trying to shield every word, every plan. The stakes were too high.

Joseph's thoughts swirled with doubt and fear. His mind replayed the recent events like a cursed carousel: the choking shadow, Maria's screams, Jacob's terrified eyes, Abigail's revelation, and the promise of a ritual that might free Adam but place his own soul in jeopardy. And now, the call—his father, Samuel, was due to phone him from the church in Schenectady at the exact time Joseph had requested.

The church office was quiet, its windows catching the last amber hues of dusk. Candles flickered on a side table in Father Allen's office, casting soft shadows over the simple wooden cross on the wall. Samuel sat across from the priest, both men bearing a heavy stillness as the speakerphone between them buzzed with a long, expectant pause. Samuel had understood immediately. He had seen the Thing with his own eyes—years ago—and never forgot its presence.

"Joseph?" Father Allen said gently, leaning forward. "We're here."

There was a pause, then Joseph's voice came through the speaker. It was firm, but layered with strain. "Thank you both. I know this is unusual, but... I need to make sure nothing hears us. I know how that sounds."

"No," Father Allen replied. "It doesn't sound strange. Not at all."

A moment of silence followed.

Joseph's mind raced, even as he struggled to keep his voice even. *This is the right thing. It has to be. I can't ignore this calling—not after what it's done, not after what it tried to take from us.* He glanced out the stained-glass window of his own church office where he'd taken the call—where the colored rays fell across the floor like silent prayers. *But why does it feel like I'm walking into my own death?*

Joseph leaned forward in his chair. "I'm going to attempt a ritual. One that could free Adam from the clock. And break the Thing's hold."

Silence hung for a beat.

"I know how that sounds," he continued. "But Abigail confirmed it. It's not just about freeing Adam—it's about stopping this Thing. If I don't, it will keep coming. It's already crossed the veil. It's already touched my family."

Samuel spoke first. "You're serious. You're really going through with this?"

"I have to, Dad. It's the only way to end this. For all of us."

Father Allen inhaled slowly. "I've never performed anything like this… but I've read about such bindings. Rare. Dangerous. Spirit trapped in a vessel, the Thing clinging to the soul to avoid the pit."

Joseph hesitated. "That's why I need help. I want to ask—can you be there with us when we do the ritual?"

The question hung in the air like a cloud too heavy to rain.

Father Allen lowered his gaze to the oak grain of his desk, fingers tapping silently. "Joseph… I want to. I do. But this—this ritual… it wouldn't be sanctioned by the Church."

Joseph's heart sank a little. He already knew the answer, but hearing it confirmed tightened the knot in his stomach.

Father Allen continued, "The administration would say this falls under unsanctioned exorcism. No records. No authority. And I… I'm afraid of what it might invite if it goes wrong."

Samuel looked up from his seat. "But surely there's something you can do."

Father Allen's eyes flicked to him, then softened. "Yes. I can still help. I'll provide what you need: blessed salt, holy water, crucifixes, sacred oil, protective scripture. These are the tools of light, and I'll pray over each one myself."

Joseph closed his eyes, a flicker of disappointment passing through his chest. I had hoped he would stand beside me. But he understood. He's a priest. He's seen things he can't explain. He's bound by duty… and fear.

"Father," Joseph said, voice quieter now. "You were there… when I was a child. When that Thing came the first time. What did you think it was then?"

There was a pause. Then Father Allen leaned back, sighing. "I remember. I remember the air turning sour. Heavy. I remember the shadows moving when they shouldn't. It felt ancient. Patient. And hungry." He paused again, voice trembling slightly. "I thought a blessing would be enough. I hoped it would drive it away. But I see now… it didn't leave. It just waited."

The priest grew quiet, staring into a corner of the room as if he could still feel its eyes there. "And if it's stronger now… I can only imagine what you're up against."

Joseph felt a shiver run through his spine. The walls around him suddenly felt smaller, the flickering candlelight more vulnerable than protective.

"I understand," he finally said. "I just… I needed to ask."

There was another silence, but this time, it was more peaceful.

Father Allen reached for a small bottle of holy oil on his shelf. "I will prepare everything for you. You'll need strength, Joseph. Not just of body, but of spirit. Because what you're about to do—it's not just a ritual. It's a battle. A real one."

Joseph nodded slowly, alone in his parish office but feeling the weight of the entire conversation like chains on his shoulders. I have to be strong. I have to be ready. No matter what happens, I can't let this Thing win. My family, my bloodline… depends on this.

"I'll be ready," Joseph whispered.

"I'll say a prayer for you now," Father Allen said. He closed his eyes and folded his hands.

Samuel joined him, and the speakerphone crackled gently with the sound of Father Allen's voice calling upon heaven: "Lord of Hosts, grant this man Your courage, Your clarity, and Your protection. Deliver him from the snares of the enemy and fortify him with the shield of faith. For though he walks through the valley of the shadow of death, he shall fear no evil—for You are with him. Amen."

Joseph whispered, "Amen."

When the call ended, Joseph didn't move for a while. He simply sat, letting the warmth of the prayer wash over the chill left behind by Father Allen's memories. Outside, the wind rattled the stained glass gently, like a subtle warning of what was to come.

So this is it, he thought. The beginning of the end—or the end of the beginning.

Chapter 7 - The Glass Prison

Scene 1: The Ritual Plan

The apartment was quiet, but not with the hush of comfort—more the suffocating stillness that arrives before a storm. Dust motes floated lazily in the sunbeams that angled across the living room, their paths cutting through a half-light thick with anticipation. Every creak of the building's frame, every distant sound from the common yard outside seemed sharper, as if the world itself was holding its breath. Joseph stood by the window, arms folded tightly across his chest, his silhouette etched in the late-day sunlight. Shadows reached long across the carpet, spilling from the legs of the furniture like inky streams.

He watched the sway of Douglas firs in the breeze beyond the glass, but his mind wasn't on the gentle rhythm of the trees. He was somewhere else—lost in the echo of what had happened, and in the dread of what was still to come. His jaw was set, a furrow etched deep between his brows. In that moment, he looked older, harder, a man reshaped by something he could never explain to another soul.

Behind him, Maria sat on the very edge of the couch. She'd drawn her knees up, hugging them with both arms, a defensive posture that said more than words. Her hands were wrapped around a mug of coffee gone cold, its steam long vanished, the faint scent of roast now mingling with the sharper aroma of fear and dish soap from the kitchen. Her hair hung loose around her face, and her eyes were locked somewhere in the middle distance, unfocused. The golden light picked out the worry lines at her temples, the tightness in her jaw.

"It's really happening, isn't it?" she said at last, her voice so soft it barely crossed the room, as if she was confessing to the silence itself.

Joseph turned away from the window. The resolve in his face was new, raw—tempered only by exhaustion. He crossed the room and sat beside her, close but careful, as though afraid he might break something fragile. "Yeah. It is."

She looked down at the cup in her hands. Her thumb traced the chipped rim, a nervous gesture. "I'm scared, Joseph. That Thing... it came for me. It was real. It wasn't a nightmare."

He took the mug from her, feeling the cold porcelain against his skin, and set it gently on the table. Then he reached for her hands, enfolding them in his own. "I know. I'm scared too. But I have to do this. I can't keep running."

Her voice trembled. "I don't know if I can go with you. I want to, but... if it's as dangerous as Abigail says—"

Joseph squeezed her hand, gentle but insistent, anchoring her to the moment. "I don't want to do this alone. But I understand your fear, and I would never want to put you in danger. If you feel strongly that you don't want to go, I don't want you to go through with it. The Thing came after me—you were just collateral damage to get to me. You stay if you want to, but help me prepare, okay?"

Maria held his gaze for a long, silent moment, searching his eyes for any sign of doubt or bravado. Her breath shivered between love and terror. The air seemed to pulse between them, heavy with all the unspoken words, all the memories of the night the Thing had invaded their sanctuary.

Joseph placed a steadying hand on her shoulder. "You don't have to have an answer yet. Think about it and tell me later."

They sat together in that hush, the ticking of the wall clock counting down to something neither wanted but both had come to accept. The silence was so complete, even the refrigerator's hum sounded like an intrusion. The shadows grew longer. Joseph watched the light change, felt his heart stutter with each passing minute.

As if on cue, his phone rang, the sound abrupt and harsh. The screen glowed with Abigail's name. Joseph snatched it up and answered, "Hey, Abigail. We were just talking about—"

"Shh!" she hissed immediately. "Don't say anything over the phone. Just meet me at the church. Conference room. Thirty minutes."

Then she hung up.

Joseph and Maria exchanged a loaded glance—resignation, fear, determination all tangled together. Joseph stood, grabbed his keys, and nodded. "Come on. Let's see what she has."

The church was silent, not the silence of emptiness but the dense, protective quiet of a place that has seen sorrow and hope in equal measure. The side conference room felt separate from the world—its air cool, the walls thick. Candles flickered in their sconces, sending dancing halos across the spines of ancient books, loose scrolls, yellowed notepads, and the faded photographs spread across a heavy wooden table. The smell of melting wax and old parchment mingled in the air, lending the place an air of ritual and memory.

Abigail was already there, hunched over the table in her trademark whirlwind of energy. Her hair was pulled back but wild as ever, eyes bright and red-rimmed from lack of sleep. She wore an oversized cardigan over her dress, sleeves pushed up past her elbows, and ink smudges marred her fingertips. When she saw Joseph and Maria, she stood, a proud smile tugging at her lips as if daring the world to stop her.

"What is all this?" Joseph asked, eyes wide as he took in the organized chaos—textbooks on demonology, xeroxed pages in Hebrew and Latin, a battered leather-bound journal brimming with Abigail's looping handwriting, and photographs of artifacts that seemed to shimmer in the candlelight.

Abigail beamed, placing her hands on her hips, claiming the table like a general reviewing a map. "This," she said, "is your preparation and battle plan. I've been working on it all night. I think it might be enough. Please, come in. We have some work to do."

They sat, Maria beside Joseph, both feeling the gravity in the air. The light from the candles threw their shadows long across the room. Joseph's gaze darted over the piles of notes, the odd gleam of silver from a mirror half-wrapped in cloth, the shimmer of glass vials filled with holy water. His hands shook as he reached for a stack of Abigail's papers.

He felt the enormity of it all pressing in—every fear, every question. "Abigail, what if I can't do this? What if it goes wrong? What if—" He broke off, voice strained. His fists clenched, knuckles white.

"Then it goes wrong," Abigail replied, her tone flat but her eyes soft. "But if you don't try, it will keep tormenting you. Your family. It already warned you. It wants you. It won't stop until it gets what it came for."

Joseph slumped back in his chair, running a hand over his face, mind a tangle of doubt. This is insane. I'm not a priest. I'm not a warrior. I'm a father, a husband... just a man. What do I know about ancient rituals? About fighting demons? His thoughts spiraled—What if I break the mirror? What if I fail? What if it takes someone else instead?

His breath quickened, panic threatening to claw its way out.

138

But then Maria reached across the table, gripping his hand with surprising strength. "Hey. Look at me. You're not doing this alone. You're doing this for us. For Jacob. For Noah. We are your reason. You forget that, you lose. Got it?"

Joseph met her gaze, and the noise in his mind dulled, stilled. He nodded. "Yeah. Got it."

He turned back to Abigail, his voice steadier, a new resolve taking root in his chest. "Alright. Show me what I need to know. I'm ready."

Abigail smiled, her whole face lighting with a fierce, exhausted pride. She flipped open her battered notebook, the flicker of candlelight dancing across the pages. The room felt different now—not safe, not free from dread, but bracing. Joseph's spirit found its footing.

And in that wavering golden light, a new fire had started to burn.

Scene 2: Sacred Preparations

Joseph sat on the edge of his bed, the soft hum of the air conditioner buzzing in the background, a droning lull that belied the storm within him. His hands rested on the battered cover of Abigail's notebook, the skin along his knuckles pale from the grip he held it in. He let his thumb trace the indentation of the spine, feeling every groove and crease—a roadmap of sleepless nights and anxious days. Every inch of the notebook was marked by use: notes curling along the margins, symbols crosshatched in red, diagrams of mirror placements, cautionary arrows, prayers underlined in trembling gold ink. The edges of some pages were worn almost thin, translucent where Abigail's hand had pressed too hard.

Joseph turned the pages one by one, each motion deliberate, ritualistic in its own right. The pages whispered beneath his fingers. He wasn't just reading. He was reviewing, reliving: the triangle of mirrors, perfectly measured; the clock set at the center, its face staring up like a blind eye. He pictured the sweep of holy water, the glint of salt in a perfect, unbroken circle—a barrier more sacred than stone. He mouthed the steps in sequence, the choreography of faith and desperation, replaying Abigail's warnings over and over in his mind: Every detail is a lock. Every word a key.

He closed his eyes, reciting the passage again:

"Jesus asked him, 'What is your name?' He replied, 'Legion,' because many demons had entered him. And they begged Jesus repeatedly not to order them to go into the Abyss."

He whispered it, tasting the syllables, feeling the shape of the words inside his chest. This wasn't rote memorization; this was muscle memory, magic, prayer, and hope. In this battle, intention was everything. A single lapse, a single misplaced word, could shatter the chain of protection.

As dusk began to fall outside, shadows lengthened over the apartment complex. Through the window, Joseph could see the last gold rays of sun filtering through the needles of the Douglas firs in the shared yard, throwing latticework patterns across the floor. From the next room, he could hear the rhythmic thump and rustle of Maria folding laundry. Her presence was a comfort, even if they hadn't spoken much—each lost in their own silent calculations, their own tally of risks and possibilities.

She hadn't said whether she'd go with him. Joseph hadn't pressed. In some ways, it was better this way. If she stayed, he could focus—he could put every ounce of will into the ritual, knowing the people he loved most were beyond the Thing's immediate reach. He could be the wall between them and the darkness

Joseph stared at the muted reflections in the window for a long moment, then finally stood, the notebook held like a shield against his chest. He crossed the small apartment quietly, passing through the living room with its clutter of toys and the scent of old coffee still lingering from the morning. He stepped out into the night air and walked the familiar path to the nearby church, each footfall echoing with purpose.

The church was old, built decades ago and never fully modernized. He let himself in through the rear office door, the hinges sighing softly. Inside, the office was lined with heavy, dark wood—bookshelves groaning under the weight of old Bibles, works of theology, obscure tomes on saints and martyrs. Framed photographs of past priests watched him from above, their sepia faces a silent jury. On the wall above the desk hung a brass crucifix, the edges smoothed by the touch of generations.

Joseph sat in the creaky wooden chair, placing Abigail's notebook reverently in front of him. He dialed the office phone, and the waiting began—each tone a drumbeat, the steady rhythm of anticipation, fear, and something harder: resolve.

One. Two. Three. Four. Five…

Finally, a click, and Father Allen's voice, worn but warm, came through: "This is Father Allen. Joseph?"

Joseph exhaled, relieved by the familiar cadence. "Yes, Father. Are you... somewhere safe?"

"I am," Allen replied, his words careful but kind, as if he were speaking across a fragile bridge. "I take it you're calling to inquire about the items I promised you for the ritual?"

Joseph's voice was tight, almost breathless. "Yes, Father. I wanted to be sure."

"You can rest easy," Allen said, and Joseph could picture him, sleeves rolled, spectacles perched low, the soft lamplight illuminating the deep lines etched into his face. "I've prepared everything. Blessed salt, sanctified mirrors—three of them—anointing oil, holy water, crucifixes, and selected scripture. All properly consecrated and sealed. They'll be ready when you arrive."

There was a pause, and in that space, Joseph could almost hear Allen's chair creak, could picture the priest rubbing his temple, measuring his words with the patience of a man who had seen too much.

"How are you feeling, Joseph?" Allen finally asked, the concern in his voice unfeigned. "I know what you're facing. Have you made arrangements to travel?"

"Not yet," Joseph replied. "That's next. But... I wanted to ask you something else." The question caught in his throat. "I understand why you said you couldn't participate. That it wouldn't be sanctioned by the Church. But... is that the only reason?"

There was a long pause—longer than any before. Joseph felt it stretch across the miles, a silence both heavy and telling. He could almost hear the priest's slow inhale on the other end of the line.

"It's true, Joseph," Allen said finally, voice even but with a weight beneath. "The Church would never approve of this kind of ritual. Not formally. I can't officially be part of it, not in the way you might hope. And..." There was a second's hesitation, a ghost of some

142

old hurt, "there are other reasons. Some things I'd rather not discuss—not yet. Please understand. I'm not withholding out of secrecy or pride, but some burdens are best left for another day.

Joseph felt the boundaries there, the shape of secrets and scars he wasn't meant to know—at least not now. He didn't press, didn't need to. The empathy in Allen's words was enough.

He swallowed, voice thick. "I understand, Father."

"You're not the only one who's haunted, Joseph. But that's why I can't join you in the ritual. Not again. I couldn't bear another failure. I won't take that risk. But—" Allen's voice shifted, gathering strength, "—you are well prepared. You've taken this seriously. What you've described to me... it's solid. You should have full confidence."

Joseph nodded, even though the priest couldn't see him. "Thank you."

"And remember," Allen said, "you're not entering this alone. You have the strength of your faith. As it says in Ephesians 6:11—'Put on the full armor of God, so that you can take your stand against the devil's schemes.' Your righteousness, your belief, your purpose—they're stronger than any evil."

There was another long beat. Joseph could hear Allen turn pages, perhaps smoothing a palm over the old wood of his desk.

"And above all, you're doing this to protect your family. That love? It's more powerful than anything that thing can throw at you."

For a moment, Joseph's chest tightened. He felt the threat of tears, but he blinked them back, letting the old priest's faith become his own.

"I'll remember that," he said quietly.

"Good," Allen replied, his voice warm and approving, a benediction from afar. "Now go. Plan. When the time comes, walk into that place knowing that you are shielded not just by faith—but by purpose."

The call ended with a gentle click. Joseph sat for a while, the phone's quiet hum mingling with the hush of the empty church office. He watched dusk deepen through the window, felt the tension in his shoulders slowly transmute into something unbreakable.

He picked up Abigail's notebook, stood, and walked into the chapel, where candlelight flickered along polished pews and the shadows of saints stood silent watch. His spirit felt armored. His mind, focused. The battlefield was set.

He would not waver.

Scene 3: The Quiet Before

The house was quiet—almost too quiet, the kind of hush that pressed in from all sides. Outside, the long rays of late afternoon sunlight filtered in through the narrow apartment windows, slicing the living room into geometric patterns of gold and shadow. The floor, littered with the tracks of recent play—scattered Legos, a sock half-hidden under the sofa, a crayon abandoned mid-drawing—glowed and darkened in turn as clouds drifted past. The gentle hum of the refrigerator provided a low, comforting drone. Somewhere beyond the walls, the faint, rhythmic chorus of cicadas rose and fell, the soundtrack of a summer night drawing near.

Joseph sat hunched on the couch, elbows planted on his knees, fingers laced and dangling, his gaze unfocused on the hardwood at his feet. The world seemed to move around him in slow motion. He wasn't thinking about the ritual. Not the Thing. Not even the dread that had haunted every shadow of the last few weeks. He was thinking of his family—the smell of Maria's hair as she passed by, the warmth of her hand in his, the sound of Jacob's giggle, the way Noah's small arms wrapped so tightly around his neck that he sometimes forgot where he ended and his sons began.

It was as if something in the air had shifted. Lighter, yes—but also bittersweet, as if the darkness had retreated only to gather its strength elsewhere, biding its time for a final confrontation. There was a temporary reprieve, and Joseph could almost fool himself into believing that things were normal. That this was any ordinary Tuesday, any quiet evening before a family trip.

Maria padded softly into the room, a printed itinerary in her hand. The paper was slightly crumpled, as if she'd held onto it a little too tightly. She wore an old college sweatshirt, her hair pulled back in a messy knot, eyes red-rimmed from a mixture of fatigue and quiet anxiety. "I confirmed the flights," she said softly, almost apologetically. "We leave Friday morning. First to Albany, then to Schenectady. We'll stay in a motel near the church."

Joseph lifted his eyes, offering her a tired but grateful nod. "Thanks. That helps."

Maria hesitated, her thumb running along the creased edge of the paper. She lowered herself beside him on the couch, the cushions sighing beneath her weight. "I got two tickets," she said, voice tentative. "I still haven't decided if I'm going... but I wanted to be prepared. Abigail told me she has her tickets already, too."

Joseph turned, reached over, and took her hand in both of his. He squeezed, feeling the coolness of her skin, the tremor in her fingers. "Just knowing you're willing to go is enough. If you decide not to, I'll understand. You don't owe me anything—just your heart."

145

For a long while, they sat together in silence, leaning against each other, letting the room breathe around them. The afternoon sun crept higher on the wall, warming the photos above the television—the boys in rain boots, Maria grinning in the kitchen, Joseph and the boys at the zoo. The world felt almost normal again, and the quiet between them spoke volumes more than words ever could.

Later that day, Joseph devoted himself to the boys, determined to give them a memory of joy untainted by fear. They sprawled out across the living room floor, Jacob and Noah squealing with delight as they built a precarious fortress of sofa cushions and blankets. They played board games until the pieces rolled away beneath the couch, and watched cartoons with the sound turned up a little too loud. Popcorn was eaten straight from the bowl, fingers greasy and sticky, laughter erupting at every silly commercial. For a few hours, there were no spirits, no rituals, no Thing—just family, held together by love and the stubborn refusal to let go of hope.

Jacob, ever perceptive, had grown more attached to Joseph than ever. He shadowed his father from room to room, handing him socks as he packed, peppering him with questions that tumbled out faster than Joseph could answer. "Are you scared, Dad?"

Joseph paused, kneeling so he was eye-level with his son. "Not anymore. I was, but I'm not now."

"Because of Mom?" Jacob asked, his brow furrowed in genuine curiosity.

Joseph smiled, ruffling his hair. "Because of all of you."

Somewhere down the hallway, a door creaked open of its own accord, the sound sharp in the stillness. It paused, then softly closed. Neither Joseph nor Maria flinched. Maria glanced up from her packing and offered the faintest smile—a private joke, a small gesture of trust.

146

"It's Ryan again," Jacob said, matter-of-fact, his tone oddly reassuring.

The atmosphere in the apartment had changed. Ryan's presence—once a source of fear—now felt like a guardian's. Mischievous, yes, but deeply loyal, the kind of ghost who would fight for you, not against you. Joseph felt the hairs on his arms rise—not in dread, but in solemn anticipation.

Joseph looked down the hallway, spoke softly so only those who were meant to hear would hear. "Ryan, will you be there? At the ritual?"

No sound. No gust of wind. Just a hush, a moment suspended in the afterglow of the day.

"I can't make him go," Joseph said, glancing at Maria. "I hope he does... but I can't expect it. I just hope."

"I'll ask him," Jacob piped up, earnest, sitting cross-legged on the floor. "I'll talk to him tonight. Maybe he'll listen to me."

Joseph smiled, a lump tightening his throat. "Thanks, bud."

Night gathered slowly, shadows pooling in corners as Maria cooked a special dinner—chicken Alfredo, Jacob's favorite. The table was set, hands were joined, and the prayer before the meal was longer than usual, every word weighted with longing, gratitude, and unspoken pleas for safety. The meal was good, but afterward, silence returned—full, heavy, meaningful.

After the boys went to bed, Joseph lingered in the hallway, leaning against the doorframe. He watched them laugh under the covers, whispering secrets about ghosts and adventures, about things only children believe. Maria came up beside him, her voice low, "You're thinking this might be the last time."

He nodded slowly, tears threatening. "If I don't come back… I need them to remember this. Not fear. Not shadows. This."

She slid her hand into his, head on his shoulder. "Then we remember it, too."

Joseph knelt, kissed both boys goodnight, and tucked them in. Jacob hugged him fiercely, whispering, "I'll talk to him tonight. I'll make sure he goes with you."

Back in the master bedroom, Maria lay in bed, eyes closed but restless, her hand reaching out to touch his as he stood by the window, gazing at the moon.

Joseph thought of Father Allen's words, of the promise and armor of faith. But nothing fortified him more than the small, ordinary beauty of this home, this fleeting peace. He knew then—he would risk everything to keep them safe.

Even if it meant walking straight into the fire, alone.

Scene 4: The Day of Reckoning

The morning sun did little to brighten the mood. Even with the sky a pale, cloudless blue above Schenectady, the cramped motel room felt less like a safe harbor and more like a waiting room before judgment. The floral-patterned bedspread was stiff with detergent and time. Maria moved quietly around the small space, the floor creaking beneath her bare feet, each step measured, almost ritualistic. She brushed her hair slowly, running the bristles through each strand as if the act could soothe the trembling she tried to hide. Her suitcase lay open on the edge of the bed, half-packed, clothes neatly folded but pressed tight as though order alone could hold back the tide of anxiety.

Joseph stood by the window, arms crossed tight against his chest, staring out through a streaked pane. Beyond the rusting chain-link fence, a handful of cars trundled past, their tires hissing over yesterday's rain. A plastic grocery bag blew in the gutter, snagging and fluttering like a caught soul. He could smell the faint tang of old cigarette smoke—embedded in the walls from a thousand previous tenants—and the chemical sharpness of motel cleaning products.

The decision had been made. The ritual would happen today.

Maria's voice, when it finally came, was quiet but steady—an anchor in the unease. The day before, she had sat beside him on the stiff motel bed, her hands clasped in her lap, her face ashen but resolute. She'd simply taken his hand and said, "I'm coming with you." No theatrics, no trembling lip, just a truth spoken out of love and duty.

He'd looked at her, the lines of exhaustion and gratitude deepening at the corners of his eyes. "Are you sure?

She had nodded, her dark eyes shining with both fear and the stubborn courage that defined her. "If something goes wrong, I couldn't live with myself knowing I wasn't there to try. I'm scared, Joseph. But I want to be strong—for you. For all of us."

Now, as Maria zipped her bag and slipped on her jacket, that strength was being tested by the heavy, unnatural stillness in the air. It felt as though the world itself was holding its breath, waiting to see if they would succeed or be devoured.

They drove through the city in silence. The old church rose out of the neighborhood like a relic from another age—its bell tower a weathered sentinel, pale stone smudged with the grime of countless seasons. The parking lot was empty but for a scattering of leaves and a lone squirrel that darted along the fence line. Joseph parked beneath the shadow of the tower, fingers lingering on the steering wheel, eyes fixed on the iron cross that crowned the spire. Abigail sat in the back seat, leather-bound notebook clutched in her lap, her lips moving in silent rehearsal or prayer.

As they stepped out, the faint toll of a distant bell marked the hour. The sound seemed to vibrate in Joseph's bones, a summons and a warning. He felt his heart thudding in his chest, but forced his face into calm resolve.

Father Allen opened the front doors before they could knock, his white clerical collar neat, his eyes heavy with sleeplessness but still burning with a kindness that was both fierce and exhausted. His hands, rough and broad, gripped the door like a shield.

"You're right on time," he said, voice low. He ushered them in with a gentle gesture.

Inside, the church was cool and dim, the air thick with the scents of beeswax, old wood, and incense. Shafts of colored light fanned across the aisle, painting mosaics on the flagstones—crimson, sapphire, gold. Joseph tried to draw strength from the silence, from the feeling of sacred ground beneath his feet.

Father Allen led them down a side corridor and into his office, which had been transformed from a simple study into a kind of spiritual armory. The desk was cleared of paperwork, replaced by a wooden box holding vials of holy water, a pouch of blessed salt, three mirrors wrapped in white linen, a stole embroidered in gold, thick candles, and a polished wooden crucifix. The air around the table seemed denser, as though the objects themselves radiated both hope and dread.

"Is it all here?" Joseph asked, unable to keep a tremor from his voice.

Father Allen nodded. "Each piece has been prayed over. I did so this morning, before sunrise. I trust you'll know how to use them." His voice was gentle but firm, carrying the weight of past battles and remembered failures.

Abigail was already unpacking her notes, spreading diagrams and passages across a corner of the desk. Her eyes flicked to the mirrors, then to Father Allen. "I've reviewed everything again," she said, her voice quiet but sure. "I've never performed this exact ritual, but I've studied it for years. I've also had... assistance."

Father Allen's brow furrowed. "From whom?"

"From the other side," Abigail replied softly. "Those who oppose the demon's reign. I believe they've guided me to the right instructions."

He studied her face, seeking any sign of doubt. When he found none, he simply nodded. "Then may their strength be with you."

Joseph shifted, anxiety burning in his chest. "Have you... have you changed your mind about joining us?"

The priest hesitated, removing his glasses and rubbing the bridge of his nose with trembling fingers. He glanced toward the sunlight streaming through the window, then down at his folded hands.

"I prayed about that all night," he confessed. "And the truth is... I would only be a burden. My strength is not what it once was. My last encounter with a powerful force like this almost cost someone their life. If I lose focus, even for a moment, I might compromise everything." He looked at Joseph, regret and empathy mingling in his gaze.

Joseph's disappointment was sharp but silent. He nodded. "Thank you—for helping us prepare."

Father Allen stood with them in the center of the room, reaching for his battered Bible. He opened to Ephesians 6 and read in a low, trembling voice: "Lord, clothe them in the armor of God. Let them wear the belt of truth, the breastplate of righteousness, and the helmet of salvation. Let them take up the shield of faith, the sword of the Spirit, and the shoes of peace. Let them stand firm, unwavering, as they walk into the valley where evil hides. Guide their hands, steel their hearts, and protect their souls."

"Amen," Joseph whispered, his throat tight.

Their goodbyes in the shadowed foyer were quiet, but heavy with everything unspoken. Father Allen watched them go, hope and fear mingling in his eyes.

As they stepped out into the daylight, the sun seemed somehow dimmer, the wind picking up, scattering brittle leaves across the parking lot. Maria pulled her coat tighter. Abigail held her notes close. Joseph, heart pounding but spirit steady, opened the car door.

They were going home. To his childhood house. To the parlor, the clock, the Thing.

It was time.

Scene 5: The Battle for the Soul

The wind had picked up as they neared the house, howling through the towering trees and tearing at their coats with icy claws. Joseph stood in the driveway, boots rooted in cold earth, Maria pressed tightly to his side and Abigail just behind him, clutching her leather-bound notebook like a talisman. His childhood home squatted before them—familiar, yet gutted of warmth. Once, it had been a refuge; now it seemed to lean toward them, hungry, window-eyes black and unforgiving, every shadow swollen and waiting.

Above, the sky sagged, heavy and gray, a lid pressed down over the world. The sun had vanished behind thick, bruised clouds, and all color seemed to drain from the street and the house alike. The old shutters twitched in the wind, tapping out an anxious rhythm, while the porch light flickered once and died, leaving the door shrouded in gloom. The windows, smeared with grime, reflected only pale, warped shapes—a family about to enter the mouth of something ancient and ravenous.

Maria drew her coat close, fingers white around the collar, face pale as bone. Abigail's jaw was clenched, eyes narrowed in concentration. She stared at the house the way a surgeon stares at a tumor before the first incision.

Joseph's heartbeat thudded in his chest. He could feel the pulse in his throat, the slick of sweat along his spine despite the cold. This wasn't just a house—it was a battlefield. He knew something was inside, something that had been waiting a long, long time. The pressure in the air was suffocating, the silence so thick he could hear the blood in his ears.

"Let's do this before it senses our fear," Joseph said, his voice a rough whisper. Every word seemed to echo against the bones of the house.

They climbed the porch stairs, boots groaning on warped boards. Joseph paused at the top, hand hovering at the bell. When he pressed it, the chime inside sounded twisted, slow and warped—like a music box submerged in water. For a heartbeat, no one moved.

Then the door creaked open.

Samuel stood there, thin and gaunt, looking older than Joseph remembered. His face was creased and haunted, eyes rimmed red with too many sleepless nights. But when he saw Joseph, some small, fierce light flared in his gaze. He stepped forward, enfolding Joseph in a hard, silent embrace—a soldier's hug before the last stand. He squeezed Maria's hand, held Abigail's gaze a long, serious moment. "You must be Abigail. I've heard a lot about you," he said, voice gravelly but kind.

She nodded, voice steady. "It's an honor."

Samuel stood aside, hand braced on the doorframe as if to steady himself. "Come in. Welcome to my home." The word felt like a lie. The house did not welcome. It tolerated.

Inside, the air was wrong. The cold hit them first—sharp, unnatural, like stepping into a walk-in freezer. The walls seemed to breathe. Every creak and sigh in the floorboards felt amplified, as though the house itself was groaning beneath the weight of memory and malice. The smell was dense and layered: old dust, mold, something coppery and sickly sweet beneath, like spoiled meat hidden in the walls. The taste of it stuck in their throats.

Joseph strode forward, unwilling to let hesitation rot his courage. He led them to the parlor, every footstep feeling heavier, pulled downward as if by unseen hands. The old mantle clock waited above the fireplace, its face gleaming faintly in the gloom. The hands were motionless, the brass pendulum frozen. Yet, as Joseph drew near, he saw something—just for a split second—move behind the glass. A flicker, a pulse, like an eye opening and shutting.

He turned to the others, voice hoarse: "Let's begin."

They moved with rehearsed urgency. Abigail unpacked the mirrors, hands trembling but precise, arranging them in a perfect triangle around the clock—each one angled to trap and focus. Joseph and Samuel poured salt along the edges, creating a gritty, fragile barrier. Maria's lips moved in silent prayer, rosary tight in one hand, knuckles turning blue.

Abigail set three crucifixes at the points of the triangle. Then she knelt, placed a silver bowl of holy water before Joseph, and struck a match. The candles sputtered, flames crawling to life, casting warped shadows that crawled up the walls like skeletal fingers.

Light bent. The air seemed to shrink. The shadows coiled, drawn inward to the mirrors' faces.

They knelt in a ring of faith and fear. Abigail began to chant first—words old as the world, syllables sliding from her tongue like knives. Joseph followed, his voice low and strained, reciting from Ephesians: "For we wrestle not against flesh and blood, but against principalities, against powers—"

Maria's voice joined, trembling at first, but growing in resolve. Samuel's voice, rusty with disuse, rose too, a rumbling baritone that lent weight to their chorus.

Ten minutes dragged by. The room was still—a pond before the first stone. Sweat slid down Joseph's neck. His hands ached from gripping the mirror.

Twenty minutes. The air lightened. The shadows thinned. Hope flickered between them. Abigail shot Joseph a look—could this be enough?

Joseph dared to breathe. "Maybe… it's not going to fight us. Maybe it's gone."

Then—

A tick.

The clock hand jerked. Tick. Tick. Tick.

BONG.

The sound hammered through the parlor, shaking the glass in the windows.

BONG.

Again, louder, a wave of sound pressing the air flat.

BONG.

The third chime quivered through the floorboards, sending a jolt through Joseph's bones.

And then—darkness poured into the room, heavy as wet cement. The windows blackened, swallowing what little sun remained. The temperature plunged—frost forming on the glass, breath pluming in the air. The wind battered the house from within, doors slamming, pictures crashing from the walls. One candle winked out, plunging the parlor into near darkness.

Then, the voice.

It rolled from the clock, from the walls, from the very air— deep, venomous, ancient. "You came. You crossed the line that should never be broken."

The wind twisted in a savage spiral, lifting the salt and flinging it in stinging arcs. The mirrors rattled, edges screaming against the wood. Maria's hair whipped across her face as she clung to the Bible, tears streaming down her cheeks.

"Keep chanting!" Abigail shouted, her words nearly drowned by the howl.

The voice surged, louder, layered with the agony of countless souls: "Did you think you could banish me? I was forged from fear, born from blood, and I drink from despair! You are NOTHING!"

Joseph roared back, "You have no power here! I am not afraid!"

The Thing laughed—a sound like teeth scraping bone. "Lies! I feel your terror. I taste your weakness."

The shadows massed, black oil pooling, then rising—shaping itself into a thing not meant for human eyes. All jagged limbs, flickering mouths, eyes blossoming and closing, dripping with black tears. It bled smoke and cold, every breath of it tainting the air with rot and hate.

Suddenly, Abigail was yanked from her knees—lifted and flung across the room by an unseen hand. Her body hit the wall with a sickening thud. Samuel lunged, barely catching her before her head struck the hearth. "You okay?!" he yelled, voice desperate.

She coughed, nodded, blood on her lips. "Keep it going! Don't let the mirrors fall!"

The mantle clock shuddered, glass groaning, a crack crawling across its face like a vein.

Joseph locked his trembling hands on the mirrors. Maria screamed as the Thing surged, a tidal wave of shadow rolling toward her. Its fingers—long, sharp, wet—wrapped around her throat, lifting her from the floor. She kicked and clawed at nothing, lips turning blue, eyes rolling in terror.

"Let her go!" Joseph howled, every instinct tearing him in two—save Maria, or save the world?

His feet dragged forward, but the wind shoved him back, nearly toppling the mirrors.

A blinding burst of light erupted—sudden, fierce. Ryan appeared, blazing, armored in spectral fire. He slammed into the

Thing, driving it away from Maria. She fell, gasping, into Joseph's arms.

"Finish it!" Ryan roared, his body locked in combat with the Thing, their forms clashing, each blow thunder and lightning.

Joseph turned back to the ritual. The clock now ticked violently, the crack deepening. Inside, a face—a man's face—pressed against the glass, mouth working soundlessly.

Adam.

Abigail crawled back, hands raw, voice ragged. "Almost there!"

They reached the crescendo, scripture burning the air.

"They begged Him not to send them into the Abyss!"

The Thing screamed—an unholy shriek of rage and pain, the room shaking, windows shattering inward, glass raining down like sharp tears.

Ryan pushed the Thing, wielding words Joseph couldn't hear, light slicing through darkness. The mirrors blazed, refracting beams that bored holes in the shadow-flesh of the demon.

The mantle clock exploded. Glass and brass flew in every direction, shards embedding in wood, carpet, flesh. Adam's spirit burst free, radiant, golden. He looked at Joseph, tears shining in his eyes. "Thank you," his lips formed, voice a whisper in Joseph's mind.

Adam shot upward, a spear of light punching through the ceiling, the house, the sky.

The Thing shrieked in agony. The light enveloped it, folding it into itself like paper in fire.

And then—silence.

The wind died.

The candles burned calmly.

And rays of sun slipped through the broken blinds, casting golden bands of peace across the room.

The smell of smoke faded.

Abigail collapsed to her knees, breathless. Maria leaned against Joseph, tears streaming silently.

Samuel helped Abigail to sit. "You did good," he said softly.

They all stared at the shattered clock, now empty, its purpose fulfilled.

The line was broken.

The soul was freed.

And the Thing—was gone.

Chapter 8 - Deception

Scene 1: The Weight Lifted

The house felt... lighter. The air, once heavy with dread, now held a stillness Joseph hadn't felt since childhood. The lingering shadows seemed to retreat into corners, no longer menacing but simply... shadows.

Maria stood close beside him, her hand tightly clasped in his. Abigail paced slowly near the center of the room, gathering the last of the ritual tools, her hands still trembling with residual adrenaline. Across the room, Samuel knelt by the remnants of the shattered mantle clock, now cold and lifeless.

They had done it. Adam was freed. The Thing banished.

For a moment, there was no speech—just breathing. Just the soft sound of wind tapping lightly on the windows.

Abigail finally broke the silence. "It worked," she whispered, half to herself. "I think... I think it actually worked."

Maria laughed, though it caught in her throat like a sob. "Oh my God," she muttered, clinging to Joseph. "We're okay. We're okay..."

Samuel stood and wiped his hands on his pants. "I never thought I'd live to see the day," he said with a tired smile. "A weight I've carried for decades... finally lifted."

Joseph stepped aside and turned toward the wall where Ryan had vanished, his expression reflective. He stared for a long moment, almost as if expecting Ryan to return.

"Thank you," Joseph murmured under his breath. "For Maria... thank you."

But the hallway was empty. The air was calm. Ryan was gone.

Samuel stepped beside him and clapped a firm hand on his shoulder. "He was sent to help you, son. And he did. That was his mission. And now, he's gone home."

Joseph looked at his father, who gave a slow nod.

"It's over. The thing is gone, and the line's finally broken," Samuel said. "It haunted this family long enough. But no more. No more clocks, no more mirrors, no more secrets."

Abigail walked over and offered her hand to Samuel. "Thank you," she said earnestly. "For everything. I couldn't have kept going if you hadn't jumped in when you did."

He shook her hand with surprising strength. "You're braver than most priests I know. That spirit world listens when you speak. You were meant to be part of this."

They all walked to the front door together. The air outside was brisk and clear, a stark contrast to the suffocating energy they'd battled within. The sun had dipped low, casting long orange rays across the lawn.

"We should go," Maria said softly.

Samuel nodded. "I'll stay behind. There's one last thing I need to take care of."

They looked at him quizzically.

They stepped outside and hugged him one by one. Maria kissed him gently on the cheek. "Thank you, Samuel. We couldn't have done this without you."

161

Abigail offered a quick squeeze of the arm. "You're a warrior."

Joseph lingered last. "I'm proud of you, Dad. Proud of what you did for our family."

Samuel gave him a long look. "It's your family now, Joseph. You fought harder than I ever could've. You finished it."

They turned and walked to the car. As they buckled in, Joseph glanced back through the window. He saw Samuel in the backyard, standing over the remnants of the broken clock—now resting atop the rusted barbecue pit like a funeral pyre.

With a flick of his lighter, he lit the dry remnants. The fire roared to life in an instant, bright and furious. Then—an explosion. A thunderclap of flame and smoke. The clock burst in a violent flash of white fire... then shrank into nothing. The blaze vanished just as suddenly as it began, and Samuel stood quietly in the ashes, staring into the dying glow.

They drove off in silence, each lost in thought.

The church loomed ahead. St. Helen's bell tower stood against the fading sky like a sentinel of peace.

Father Allen greeted them at the side door. He looked anxious.

"Well?" he asked the moment they entered. "What happened?"

Abigail was the first to speak. "We did it. The ritual worked. The triangle held. The glass cracked. Adam... Adam was released."

Father Allen's eyes widened. "You saw him ascend?"

Joseph nodded. "He looked at me... thanked me. Then the light took him."

A deep breath escaped the priest. "Praise God."

But then he looked up, more cautious. "And... the Thing?"

Joseph hesitated. He looked at Maria, then Abigail. Their expressions grew uncertain.

Abigail answered, "We didn't see it descend."

Father Allen's brow furrowed. "What do you mean?"

Abigail continued slowly. "Ryan—our protector—he came back. He saved Maria. Then... he took it with him."

The silence was thick.

Father Allen's gaze darkened. "So you didn't see the Thing cast into the abyss?"

Joseph leaned forward. "Is that... a problem?"

The priest paused. He weighed his answer. Then gave a practiced smile. "No... no. If Ryan took it, then it must be finished. It has to be."

But Joseph noticed the flicker of concern behind his eyes.

Abigail did too. "Father...?"

But he waved it off. "It's fine. You're safe now. That's what matters."

They nodded, though Joseph's stomach still twisted with unease.

They thanked Father Allen and made their way out. The sky had deepened into twilight.

As they reached the parking lot, a sudden gust of wind hit them from the side—sharp, cool, and unnaturally cold.

They all stopped.

A low sound rose in the air... a deep, guttural growl. Distant. Faint. Almost imagined. But they all heard it.

They turned to each other.

"That..." Maria began.

Joseph shook his head. "Must be the wind."

Abigail said nothing.

They got in the car. As the engine turned over and the headlights cut through the dusk, Joseph glanced once more at the church behind them.

The wind had died down.

But something still stirred in the silence.

Scene 2: The Quiet Return

The wheels of the taxi crunched gently against the gravel as it pulled up in front of their apartment building in University Place. Rain had begun to fall in earnest, the kind that settles deep into the soil, speckling the windshield with a thousand glittering drops. Streetlamps shone halos of amber light through the mist, painting the wet pavement gold and silver. The whole world felt freshly rinsed—cool, clean, alive. Every sound—tires grinding, engine ticking, windshield wipers squeaking in their last arc—was magnified in the hush of the night

Joseph stepped out first, straightening his back with a soft groan as he stretched the aches of travel away. The night air carried the tang of rain-soaked earth and evergreen needles, a scent that always made him think of home and safety. Overhead, Douglas firs swayed and sighed in the breeze, their high crowns lost to the mist, like watchful giants hidden in the clouds. The branches dripped with rain, and droplets fell from the needles, pattering onto the hoods of parked cars. Somewhere beyond the parking lot, a distant train wailed, its lonely call threading through the soft white noise of the rain. The echo of it seemed to vibrate in Joseph's bones, a memory of movement and faraway places.

Maria followed, tugging her coat close, her hair gathering the dampness in loose curls around her cheeks and temples. For a moment, she lingered beside Joseph, both of them simply standing together under the muted porch light, watching the glow from their own apartment window—soft yellow leaking through drawn curtains, a gentle beacon against the dark. Rain gathered on Maria's lashes. Joseph brushed a strand of wet hair from her cheek, his thumb lingering, savoring the warmth of her skin in the chill.

They exchanged a look, eyes shining with a hundred unsaid things—weariness, relief, a new and unfamiliar peace. There was exhaustion in every line of their faces, but also a fierce, quiet pride. They had survived. They were home. In that small exchange, with the weight of travel and terror behind them, a tremor of laughter rippled through their tiredness. Maria squeezed Joseph's hand, grounding herself in the reality of now.

Before Joseph could reach for his keys, the apartment door flew open, scattering a wedge of warm light across the wet walkway. Jacob and Noah burst out, barefoot, arms flung wide, faces alight with pure, unfiltered joy. "Dad! Mom!" they shouted, voices echoing in the night. They barreled into their parents, arms winding tight around waists and necks, clinging as if to make up for every lost minute. Their pajamas were rumpled, feet already muddy, but they didn't care.

Joseph knelt to gather them close, squeezing their small bodies until they squealed in delight. He buried his face in their hair, breathing in the scent of bubblegum shampoo, sun-warmed skin, and the mustiness of rain. Maria laughed as she scooped Noah into her arms, her eyes brimming, tears vanishing into the rain as she pressed kisses into his damp hair. The boys' laughter rang out, unburdened and clear, louder than the train, louder than the rain.

Jacob, cheeks flushed and grinning, finally stepped back. "We missed you guys. Mrs. Garza from church took care of us. She let us stay up late and even took us to the mall. It was... actually kinda awesome." There was a note of guilt in his voice, as if joy were somehow disloyal to his parents. He shuffled his feet, almost bashful.

Joseph grinned, water beading on his brow. "That's great, buddy. You deserve a little fun. Did anything... strange happen while we were gone?"

Jacob's smile faded to a more thoughtful expression. "No. Nothing scary. It was quiet. Peaceful, actually." He hesitated, then added in a near-whisper, "I did talk to Ryan before you left. He didn't say much. But when the weird stuff stopped... I knew he'd gone with you. I knew he wasn't here anymore."

The moment hit Joseph hard—sweet, sorrowful. He nodded, his voice catching. "He was there, Jacob. He saved your mom. We wouldn't have made it without him."

Jacob looked at his shoes. "I think I'll miss him. He was like... a friend. He watched out for us."

Joseph squeezed his shoulder. "Me too, son. Me too."

They moved inside, closing the door behind them and shutting out the cold. The apartment felt almost exactly as they'd left it—shoes scattered in the entryway, the boys' toys still lined up neatly beside the TV stand, a faint scent of lavender from Maria's air freshener and a lingering trace of last week's spaghetti sauce. The air was soft and slightly humid from the rain, but there was a subtle difference—a hush, deep and gentle, as if the rooms themselves were breathing easier. Shadows curled in the corners, harmless now. The silence was not threatening, but healing. The walls, so recently tense and watchful, now seemed to relax with them.

Maria carried their small bag to the bedroom, her footsteps soft and purposeful, slippers whispering over the old linoleum. Joseph took a moment to shrug off his coat, running his hand along the smooth countertop as if reacquainting himself with an old friend. He lingered on the chipped Formica, the cracked bowl of keys beside the sink. For years, Ryan had nudged those keys to the dining table—always moving them, always reminding them of his unseen presence. Now, they sat untouched, exactly where Joseph had left them. The quiet was profound.

He picked them up, feeling their familiar weight, and set them gently in the center of the table. For a heartbeat, he waited, half hoping to see them slide back, half dreading a sign that something lingered. But the apartment held only the quiet thrum of the heater and the distant laughter of the boys. No ghostly movement. No cold wind. Just peace.

Maria returned, brushing past him in the kitchen. Her hand touched his arm, grounding him in the present. "I'll make something easy for dinner," she offered, her voice soft but resolute. "You want pasta or eggs?"

Joseph chuckled, something inside him loosening. "You've got the energy to cook?"

She shrugged, almost smiling. "I think it'll help me feel normal again."

167

He watched her move through the kitchen—methodical, gentle, every motion familiar and cherished. The sound of the wooden spoon clinking against a pot, the sizzle of butter, the laughter from the living room as the boys raced through a video game, filled the rooms with a domestic music. The lamp on the table glowed softly, illuminating Maria's face as she measured out pasta, her brow furrowed in concentration, her lips curved in the faintest smile. These were the moments he'd fought for—mundane, luminous, real.

As dinner was served and the family gathered at the small table, Joseph looked at them with new eyes. Maria, her cheeks flushed and calm; Jacob, forever curious, still glancing now and then at the key bowl; Noah, giggling, noodles hanging from his fork, splattering sauce on his shirt. The warm yellow light danced across their faces, throwing shadows on the wall, making their little home look grander than any cathedral. This was his reason. This was victory.

As the meal faded into bedtime and the apartment quieted, Joseph stood by the window. The rain had stopped, leaving the world glistening under streetlamps. No movement stirred the glass, no shadows crept beneath the door. Only the steady pulse of peace— deep, earned, and, at last, their own. The only sound was the slow, contented breathing of his family, settling into the kind of restful sleep none of them had known for weeks.

Scene 3: A Flicker in the Dark

The days since returning from Schenectady had passed like the lull after a long storm. The Duncan apartment felt quieter than ever before, cloaked in an unfamiliar peace. Gone were the creaking floorboards in the night, the cold brushes of unseen hands, the dreadful anticipation of what might be lurking just beyond the hallway.

Instead, there were soft mornings filled with warm sunlight that drifted lazily through the kitchen window, gilding the counters and dappling the linoleum. The gentle hum of cartoons floated from the living room, punctuated by the squeals and laughter of Jacob and Noah tumbling over a nest of pillows and scattered toys. Maria folded laundry with ease, humming quietly, her movements loose and unhurried as if she'd finally remembered how to relax. The rhythmic scent of coffee brewing was a comfort, filling the air with bittersweet warmth. Joseph moved through the space slowly, taking it all in as if memorizing each soundless moment—the whir of the washing machine, the clink of mugs, the soft pad of Maria's feet on the rug. Everything ordinary felt precious, as if each detail had been cleansed in the aftermath of terror.

But peace, like glass, can fracture in an instant.

That night, as the apartment settled into darkness, Joseph drifted into sleep. His breath slowed. The silence grew deep and velvety, pressing in around the edges of the apartment like a heavy blanket.

Then came the wind.

It started as a whisper—soft and distant, threading through the crack beneath the bedroom door. But soon it rose into a howl, swirling around him in the dreamworld, pressing against his skin with the bite of winter. He stood barefoot in an endless hallway, its floor gritty with dust and paint curling off the walls in yellowing strips, the air charged with static electricity that made the hair on his arms stand on end.

Something chased him. He could feel it—no footsteps, no breathing, just presence. Heavy. Malevolent. Ancient. It pressed at his back with an icy dread, a pressure that made it hard to breathe. Each

169

time he glanced over his shoulder, the hallway behind him was swallowed in writhing shadow. Two glowing red eyes glared from the void—hungry, pitiless, inhuman. It was the Thing—the family terror, the darkness they believed had been vanquished.

Joseph ran. The floor seemed to lengthen beneath him, stretching farther with every step. The walls warped and bled shadow, the plaster blistering as if something inside wanted to break free. The shadows chased, rising up like oily tendrils, reaching for his feet, tugging at his sanity.

Then—

He woke.

Gasping, drenched in sweat, he sat up in bed. His heart pounded in his chest like a warning drum, wild and insistent. The room was cool, the sheets clammy. The air, for a moment, seemed too thick to draw.

Maria stirred beside him, hair tangled over her face. "Joseph?"

He wiped a trembling hand across his face. "It's nothing. Just a dream."

But the seed had been planted.

The next morning, the air was still and warm. Breakfast was quiet. Light spilled through the blinds in stripes, pooling on the kitchen table, catching in the steam rising from mugs. The boys chatted casually about cartoons and cereal, their laughter echoing through the hallway. Maria sipped coffee while Joseph stared into his cup, lost in memory, the bitter taste grounding him.

He recounted the dream in hushed tones.

Maria's smile faded, eyes darkening with concern. "You really think it's over?"

He hesitated, then nodded, forcing conviction into his voice. "Yes. It has to be. Ryan helped us. Adam was freed. The clock is gone. It was just a dream."

The day passed without incident. Errands, chores, sunlight angling in through open windows. Light-hearted chatter drifted through the apartment as Maria sorted the last of the laundry and the boys sprawled on the living room carpet, drawing superheroes and monsters in crayon.

But as dusk descended, so did the unease.

A spoon fell in the kitchen with a clang, metal bouncing once before settling. The hallway light flickered once—then again, the bulb buzzing with static. Maria glanced up from her book, pulse quickening.

"You saw that, right?"

Joseph nodded slowly, throat dry. "Yeah... I did."

Then came the whispers. Soft and fleeting. Like a word just missed on the wind. From the corner of his eye, Joseph caught a shadow slipping along the hallway wall—too quick to be sure, too slow to forget. The air turned chill, a breeze slinking out from under the bedroom door.

They gathered on the couch, huddled together under the glow of the TV. The movie flickered on, casting dancing patterns of blue and white on the walls, but no one was watching. The sound was muted by the heaviness pressing in on all sides.

Then—

A breeze.

Gentle. Intentional. It slithered through the living room, ruffling the curtains though the windows were tightly shut.

Joseph looked up, nerves humming. "Can you close the window?"

Maria checked. "There's no window open."

They froze.

A radiant glow began to spill from the hallway, not harsh or cold—but blinding in its purity, alive with a silvery brilliance that shimmered across the ceiling and walls. It illuminated the dust in the air, making the ordinary apartment seem like some place holy, otherworldly.

Joseph rose first. Maria followed, her hands trembling as she reached for his arm. They crept forward. The light grew brighter as they neared the boys' bedroom, bathing the walls in shimmering gold.

Then the door creaked open, the hinges sighing.

And from within the light—a figure emerged.

"Ryan!" Jacob cried out, voice trembling with hope and disbelief.

The air shifted from fear to awe.

He stood tall, clothed in light like armor, his face warm with a familiar peace. Each movement seemed to ring with a clarity and strength beyond the mortal. His eyes met Joseph's, and for a heartbeat, everything else vanished—the fear, the tension, the haunted memories.

Joseph stepped forward, voice quaking with wonder. "Where did you go?"

Ryan smiled gently, every line of his face softened by the golden light. "I've been wandering... making my way back. I was told my task for redemption is complete. I can ascend now. But I came back... to say goodbye."

Jacob's eyes filled with tears, his small fists balled at his sides. "Don't go, Ryan. Stay with me."

Ryan knelt and looked him in the eye, his expression grave and gentle. "I must ascend now. The Father calls—and must be obeyed. But know this, Jacob. You and your family have been brave. You gave me purpose. And your father... is strong enough now to stand against the darkness."

Joseph stepped closer. "Darkness? I thought we defeated it. Didn't we?"

Ryan stood, his glow intensifying, light spilling across the hallway in beams. He looked directly into Joseph's eyes.

"Let not your heart be troubled, neither let it be afraid. For the Lord your God is He who goes with you, to fight for you against your enemies, to give you victory."

A radiant beam opened in the ceiling above him, an ethereal pathway to somewhere higher.

With a final nod, Ryan stepped upward into the column of light, rising slowly, hands at his side.

Jacob reached up. "Goodbye, Ryan..."

The light swallowed him whole.

Then vanished.

Silence.

No wind. No flicker.

Just darkness.

They lingered in the hallway, hearts torn between grief and hope, tears glinting in the fading light. For a moment, the world felt paused, suspended between what had been lost and what had been gained.

"I can't believe he's really gone," Maria whispered, voice ragged with emotion.

Joseph nodded solemnly, throat thick. "He was our shield."

They stood for a moment longer, letting the calmness settle in again like dust after a storm.

Then—

Boom.

A low rumble echoed from the master bedroom, the floor vibrating beneath their feet. The light fixture swayed, its glass shade rattling. At the end of the hallway, darkness seeped in like ink—thick, moving, alive. The air turned frigid, prickling the skin on Joseph's arms.

A voice—faint, guttural—muttered from the shadows, a breath not made by any living thing.

Joseph stepped back instinctively, shielding his family with his body.

Then—

The shadow moved.

And something looked back.

The darkness was not gone.

It had been waiting.

Scene 4: The Last Mirror

The apartment trembled. The walls moaned with a force that seemed to claw at the very foundation, plaster shivering, dust sifting from the ceiling in tiny avalanches. From the master bedroom came a thunderous roar, a sound so unholy it seemed to rip the breath from the air—a roar that wasn't merely loud, but alive. The floor shuddered, buckling under the pressure of something enormous, something wrong. Reality itself bent and flexed beneath the weight of the Thing's return.

Joseph was frozen at first—just a man, pulse jackhammering, lungs burning for breath. Every instinct screamed at him to run, but there was nowhere to go, nowhere safe. And so, as if a hidden hand flipped a switch, survival roared to life inside him. He hurled himself in front of Maria and the boys.

"Stay behind me!" he shouted, his voice cracked raw with terror and purpose. His arms swept wide, herding Maria and the children behind him as the hallway seemed to narrow, suffocating them with its pressing dark.

The door to the bedroom creaked open—slowly, deliberately—its hinges whining as though it protested what was about to emerge. From within spilled darkness, thick and rolling, oily and hungry. The air tasted metallic and cold, charged with a static that crawled across Joseph's skin. Shadows writhed and twined, pouring into the hallway with a will all their own.

A voice boomed out—deep, guttural, ancient. It was not a voice that belonged to the world of men.

"Did you think the chains were broken, child of dust?

That mercy rang through shattered glass?

175

No—only your faith cracked. Only your hope splintered.

You spoke the words, you lit the flame,

But I am not undone by the trembling lips of men.

It was I who whispered in Adam's ear.

I who offered him the mirror, that he might see what I needed him to see.

He made no pact... he made a path—for me.

You thought you freed a soul?

You opened a door.

And now, one must pass through.

It is in my nature to deceive.

It is in yours to believe.

So now I ask you, Joseph...

Who then is truly bound?"

A wave of cold radiated outward, brushing Maria's cheeks, making the boys whimper. Joseph's blood felt like it had frozen in his veins.

Maria clung to the children, sobbing, "You said the line was broken! You said it couldn't hurt us!"

Joseph forced the words out, desperate: "Jesus asked him, 'What is your name?' He replied, 'Legion,' because many demons had entered him. And they begged Jesus repeatedly not to order them to go into the Abyss."

The Thing's laughter ripped through the apartment—a noise like rusted chains raked across bone, unclean and triumphant. "It's too late for your verse and rituals. I shall have your soul."

And something inside Joseph—his fear—burned away, ignited by fury and defiance. He straightened, baring his teeth. "No," he growled, voice shaking, "you can't have me. You can't have any of us!"

The wind exploded, blasting through the apartment, hurling books and knickknacks from shelves. A family portrait shattered, glass raining down like icy confetti. Maria dragged the boys beneath the dining table, shielding them as the air grew thick with smoke and shadows.

Joseph's gaze shot to the master bedroom mirror—its surface twisted, crawling with inky tendrils. "The mirrors," he thought, "close the mirrors!" With a hoarse cry, he seized a heavy lamp and smashed it into the glass. Electricity burst and fizzed, showering the carpet with shards and sparks. The darkness inside the mirror seemed to recoil, hissing, curling back on itself.

"Maria!" he barked, "Take the kids—go!"

She bolted for the front door. The boys scrambled after her, but the wind shrieked, pressing the door shut. It wouldn't move, not an inch. The shadows had sealed them in.

"It won't open!" Maria screamed, panic clawing at her voice. "It's all sealed!"

The Thing roared—a noise that rattled the silverware in the kitchen drawers. Black smoke poured down the hallway. Joseph ran, forcing his way through the gale to the boys' bedroom. The mirror on the dresser pulsed, the silver glass swirling like a portal, shadows clawing at the edges.

With a wild yell, Joseph grabbed a toy firetruck and hurled it. Glass exploded, flying in all directions. For a split second, the room flashed white, then everything crashed back into dark and chaos.

The Thing howled, echoing through the walls, shaking the windows in their frames. "You think you can scatter your reflection? It is not the mirror I need—it is you. Just one glance. One gaze into the truth of your soul."

Joseph was already gone, barreling down the hallway, the Thing slithering after him—its limbs spider-like, body insubstantial and yet impossibly massive. The living room mirror loomed. Joseph ripped it from the wall, sending bits of plaster raining down, and brought it down hard onto the hardwood floor. The mirror shattered, glass crunching beneath his shoes as he stomped every last shard.

Wind screamed, howling through every crack. The Thing surged after him, its limbs writhing, its eyes burning with desperate hunger. Maria and the boys huddled under the table, hands over their ears as the air filled with the sound of breaking, smashing, shrieking.

Only one place left.

Joseph sprinted for the hallway bathroom, feet pounding the warped floor. The Thing blocked his path, shadows clawing at the walls, warping the hallway, its body undulating, boiling, enormous. At the end of the hall, the bathroom door stood open, the mirror inside reflecting a sliver of Joseph's face—his own eyes, wild with terror.

The Thing paused, just feet from Joseph, its eyes locked on the last mirror.

Joseph's voice, low and deadly: "You shall forever be damned to the abyss."

He grabbed the ceramic soap dish and hurled it with all his might. The mirror shattered, glass falling like rain—jagged pieces skittering across the tile, fragments catching the light with a thousand fractured reflections.

With a triumphant roar, Joseph slammed the bathroom door on the Thing's face, plunging the windowless room into utter blackness. The Thing's voice screamed in agony, a sound like a thousand souls being ripped apart.

For a moment, all was silent but for Joseph's ragged breathing, his body pressed against the door, knuckles white. He could feel the Thing clawing at the other side, then suddenly—the air stilled. The screaming stopped.

Heart still hammering, Joseph fumbled for the light switch, desperate to see, desperate for any sense of normalcy.

Click.

The bulb snapped to life, harsh and cold.

And there it was.

Not the Thing. His own reflection. Staring at him from the full-length   mirror hanging behind the bathroom door. He had forgotten it, in his desperation.

For one, impossibly long moment, Joseph's gaze locked with his own eyes in the glass. There was something wrong in the reflection. A flicker, a shadow curling behind the surface. And then— he understood.

He'd been tricked.

A cold, spectral laughter rose behind him, filling the room, echoing from the very walls. The Thing's laughter, triumphant, resonant, inhumanly deep.

Joseph's body froze, every muscle seized by dread. His lips barely moved as he whispered, "It tricked me.

His reflection twisted, darkening, eyes emptying into voids. The glass shimmered as if turning liquid, then everything—sound, light, his heartbeat—stopped.

The apartment fell into silence.

The wind died.

The smoke faded.

The Thing… was gone.

In the dining room, Maria slowly rose, pulling the boys with her. They crept down the hallway, the tiles cold beneath their bare feet, the air impossibly still. Maria's heart hammered, her breath shallow. She reached the bathroom and pushed open the door, hands shaking.

The room was empty. Broken glass littered the floor. The harsh bulb flickered, humming.

"Joseph?" she called, voice trembling.

No answer. No movement.

Her eyes darted around—then widened in terror.

"WHERE'S JOSEPH?" she screamed, her cry echoing through the apartment, splitting the silence like a funeral bell.

The battle was over. And the price had been paid.

Chapter 9 - The Hollow Service

Scene 1: Absence in the Morning

The air in the apartment was still. Too still—like a held breath that never quite released.

Maria stood alone in the kitchen of their University Place apartment, her fingers wrapped tightly around a warm ceramic mug. Steam curled from the black coffee within, rising in delicate, mournful ribbons that wavered and disappeared against the window. The scent was rich and bitter, familiar and grounding, yet in the hollow space of the room it felt almost intrusive, as if it had nowhere left to settle.

Rain whispered against the window just above the sink, a soft and persistent tapping that matched the ache in her chest. Each drop was a quiet drumbeat on the glass, a lullaby for a world that seemed to have lost its music. The morning light filtering through the curtains was pale and gray—thin, almost spectral, as though the sun itself was too weary to break through. Shadows gathered in the corners and stretched across the hardwood floor, mingling with the lazy dust motes that drifted in the idle air.

Somewhere in the distance, a train horn called out—a low, plaintive wail that echoed across the city. The sound shivered through the apartment, fraying the edges of silence. It was a ghostly sound, lonely, both here and far away—a reminder that life still moved on, even as Maria felt frozen in place.

She hadn't spoken aloud in over an hour. There was no one to talk to, just the rain and the muted hum of the refrigerator. Even the clock on the wall seemed reluctant to tick, as if honoring the hush that had settled over everything.

The boys were still asleep, wrapped tight in the warm cocoon of their shared room. Maria had tiptoed past earlier and paused at their door—Jacob curled up beneath his comforter, eyes squeezed shut against dreams, while Noah sprawled across the mattress in a mess of small limbs and superhero pajamas, his thumb pressed softly to his lips. The sound of their breathing—a gentle, even tide—was the only proof that time moved forward at all.

For a long moment, Maria had stood in the doorway, hand resting unconsciously on the slight swell of her abdomen. She hadn't told anyone yet. Not even Jacob, who would have understood in his strange, old-soul way. The test had confirmed it two days ago—a soft pink line, trembling in her grasp, impossibly fragile, impossibly real. Somehow, in the wake of loss and fear, new life had dared to take root. Joseph's life. A part of him still inside her, holding her to this earth like an anchor made of love and dread.

But joy felt far away—like a memory of laughter in a house that had forgotten how.

Maria let out a slow breath and turned from the window, the mug warming her palms but never quite reaching the chill that seemed to reside in her bones. She took a sip, felt the coffee burn down her throat, and shivered anyway. Even now, weeks after the ritual—the fire, the screaming, the shattered glass and the blinding light—she felt the absence in every corner. There was no sign. No voice. No message.

No Joseph.

The soundlessness was oppressive. Maria could still hear him sometimes in her dreams—calling to her, pleading, his voice warped by distance and sleep. Sometimes, waking at night, she saw his reflection flicker in the hallway mirror—just for an instant—his face pale, eyes pressed to the other side of the glass like a man trapped beneath ice. But when she blinked, it was always gone. Her therapist called it grief hallucination. Father Allen called it a test of faith. Maria wasn't sure what to call it anymore. Sometimes it felt like hope. Other times, like a cruel joke.

The apartment creaked—a single, sharp sound like a footstep on the far side of the living room. Maria jumped, coffee sloshing over the edge of her mug. Just the wood settling, she told herself, heart pounding, but the reassurance felt thin. The silence here was different now. The walls didn't breathe the way they used to. The corners felt deeper. And the mirrors—God, the mirrors—always felt like eyes.

She glanced down the hallway and called softly, "Jacob? You up?" Her voice broke the silence, fragile and uncertain, as if afraid of what might answer.

No reply. Just the steady breathing of the house, the rain against the window, the train somewhere beyond.

Maria set her mug aside and moved down the hall, her bare feet silent against the cold laminate. Each step felt tentative, as if the floor itself might fall away. Her fingertips brushed the wall—seeking comfort, or maybe connection to something unseen. At the boys' room, she paused, hearing the soft murmur of Jacob's voice.

The door was ajar, a narrow wedge of darkness between the slanting light of the hallway and the twilight gloom of the room beyond. Maria's heart skipped a beat.

"...but I don't know where he went," Jacob whispered.

A long silence. Only Jacob's voice, soft, secretive, too old for his years. Maria waited, a chill crawling up her spine. Was he talking to himself? To someone else? To Joseph?

She knocked gently, then eased the door wider. "Jacob?" she said, voice even and quiet.

The boy spun around, face guarded and careful. He was on his tiptoes in front of the tall dresser mirror, arms crossed tightly, mouth set in a stubborn line. The mirror reflected only him—small and solitary. No flickers. No shadows. But Maria felt something lurking, a heaviness in the air, like breath held too long.

"Morning, Mom," Jacob said, feigning nonchalance. "I was just getting dressed."

Maria nodded, eyes flicking to the glass. The room felt too still, the warmth from the vent doing nothing for the iciness crawling beneath her skin. "Come have breakfast," she said, forcing a brightness into her tone. "I made toast."

Jacob padded out after her, dragging his heels, yawning wide. Maria paused to glance once more at the mirror. It reflected only the room behind, but her gut twisted. Something had been there. Something was watching.

She buttered toast for Jacob, adding cinnamon sugar the way he loved, trying to settle her shaking hands. As he ate, Maria drifted to the window. She gazed through the glass, its surface beaded with rain, watching her own face return her stare. But this time, behind her reflection—over her shoulder—a shimmer, almost a ripple, moved in the silver. A distortion, quick and sinuous, like a fish darting just below the surface of water.

The In Between.

The words had come to her in a dream—a name for the space behind the glass, the place where Joseph's hands pressed desperately, where echoes lingered. The In Between. A realm of reflections and half-heard voices. A place for the lost to wander, or to be trapped.

She whipped around. Nothing. Jacob chewed toast, legs swinging under the table. But the air remained charged, uneasy. The peace was gone. In its place was an ache, a prickling watchfulness, as if something just out of sight was tracking every move.

Maria's heart thudded, slow and anxious. The silence in the apartment was no longer gentle, no longer simply empty. Now it felt alert. Waiting.

She closed her eyes, hand pressed flat to her belly, and whispered a prayer she was no longer sure how to finish.

Somewhere, something had stirred.

And Maria knew—not all endings are ever truly an end.

Scene 2: The Maze of Sleep

That night, just after midnight, the wind rose like an omen—urgent, unceasing, pressed against the glass with wet, rattling fingers. It wasn't the playful whistling of a passing front, but a constant, low moan, like the world itself had begun to grieve. The Duncan apartment, once a fortress against the unknown, felt too still. The rain's rhythm was a lullaby overlaid with something else: anticipation. The refrigerator hummed a nervous counterpoint, pipes clicked and cooled, and the walls seemed to exhale after every creak. The night was heavy with silence and threat.

But beneath that hush, something else moved. Something old. Something watching.

Jacob tossed in his bed, limbs tangled in his blanket, a small, shadowed frown creasing his forehead. In the other room, Maria flinched in her sleep, her hands clutching at nothing, chest rising and falling in stuttered rhythm. Both breathed in deep, both unknowing, both already slipping away.

The dream took them together—a sudden, plunging cold, and the world split open.

Gone was the apartment, the warmth of cotton sheets, the familiar darkness. Instead, the ground beneath Jacob's sneakers was gritty and uneven, littered with shards of glass—some the size of coins, others sharp as knives. Each step crunched, echoing in the vast, airless dark. Every piece of broken mirror caught and distorted their reflections: eyes warped, mouths twisted, shadows swallowing all color.

Gray mist choked the floor, coiling around Jacob's ankles, its coldness creeping upward, gnawing at his bones. The air smelled scorched and metallic, thick with the stench of old, burned wires and a sour tang of rot—an unyielding presence that settled on his tongue.

He looked up and froze. Endless, inhuman corridors stretched before him—impossibly tall walls of black obsidian that shimmered as if oiled, undulating in slow, unnatural pulses. These weren't mirrors. Not truly. They were alive. Watching. Breathing. Each panel reflected Jacob back at himself—thousands of Jacobs, stretching to infinity, but some did not move as he did, some stared in silent accusation, some simply stood and wept.

He tried to speak, but his words caught in the thick, icy air. Somewhere to his left, a shape moved—a familiar silhouette fighting through the fog.

"Mom?" Jacob's voice was small, trembling, barely more than a gasp.

Maria emerged, her eyes huge, skin washed ghostly in the mirrored gloom. Shadows clung to her like oil, threading through her hair and across her arms, unwilling to let her go. She was shivering— Jacob could see it in the way she hugged herself, her breath streaming white.

"Where are we?" she whispered, her voice fragile and echoing off the glass.

Jacob glanced around, his mouth dry, his own face reflected back at him in every direction, warped and multiplied until he could barely stand to look. "The In Between," he managed, voice hollow. "The mirror called it that..."

They moved, clinging to one another, each step ringing out into the void like the clang of a bell in a tomb. Every footfall was answered by a thousand ghostly echoes—some too slow, some too quick, some never stopping. Each turn of the labyrinth revealed more corridors, more walls, each one crowded with their own desperate images. Sometimes, in the reflections, Jacob thought he saw others— half-shapes, lost faces, children crying for parents, hands pressed to glass until the knuckles bled.

The silence was monstrous, an ever-tightening noose. The air grew steadily colder, the mist thickening, clinging to their clothes and hair. The further they walked, the more their hope was devoured.

Then—deep beneath their feet—there came a sound. Not above, not behind, but below: a colossal, methodical thudding, as if something impossibly large prowled the belly of the maze. The glass vibrated. The mist pulsed. The walls seemed to sweat and breathe.

Maria grabbed Jacob's hand, her fingers ice cold. "Don't let go. Whatever happens... don't let go."

Suddenly, the silence shattered.

A breath—not theirs, not human. Ragged, desperate, each inhale wet with agony. It rattled through the corridors, stirring the mist and making the reflections shudder. Something alive, but not living, was near.

At the far end of the corridor, a shape appeared. Thin. Shrouded in gray. Limping.

"Dad!" Jacob screamed, hope and terror in equal measure.

Maria surged forward. "Joseph?" Her voice broke on his name, fractured by grief and longing.

Joseph stood still, veiled by mist. His eyes were lifeless, mouth slack. The mirrors behind him flickered with grotesque parodies—Joseph screaming, Joseph falling, Joseph lost.

"Joseph, please!" Maria begged, tears streaking her face.

But then—the world twisted. The glass darkened. The temperature plunged to unbearable cold, so bitter it stole the breath from their lungs. The air filled with the reek of sulfur and decay—a burning, suffocating cloud. Shadows stretched across the mirrored floor, reaching with fingerlike tendrils that tried to drag at their feet.

The presence was here.

It fell over them like an avalanche, a tidal wave of terror and despair, pinning them in place. The mirrors hissed, mist recoiling in dread.

A voice split the darkness—a voice that crawled into the marrow of their bones, old and cruel and endlessly hungry.

"You don't belong here."

Maria spun, eyes wild, but there was nothing behind them but more labyrinth, more endless glass.

But the voice pressed closer, filling their ears, their thoughts.

"He is not yours to retrieve. Not yours to wake. He is MINE."

The walls pulsed with sickly light. Images spasmed across the glass—Joseph's life, torn and broken, scenes twisted into nightmare.

Joseph as a boy, alone and crying. Joseph drowning in a flood of shadows. Ryan burning, screaming. The mantle clock, cracking, reforming, shattering again.

Jacob whimpered, shuddering, tears freezing on his cheeks.

Maria's voice was threadbare, barely there. "Who...who are you?"

The voice was a venomous hiss. "The Echo of all things forgotten. The keeper of reflection. I was before your blood. Before the glass."

Then it howled, a sound that should have shattered them—rage, loss, hunger, despair. The mirrored walls erupted with movement: a tide of twisted reflections, each one screaming, some with mouths sewn shut, some pounding at the glass with broken hands, a chorus of agony racing toward them.

Maria turned to run—

—and slammed straight into The Thing.

It stood inches away. Its face was a mask of torment: skin stretched tight over bone, lips torn back in a smile that promised only suffering. Its eyes were black, too large, wet with ancient tears and filled with a hate that had no end. Its mouth split open—rows of teeth gleaming, cracked, stained, endless.

But it didn't roar. It didn't scream.

It laughed.

A sound cold enough to curdle hope, sharp enough to slice through memory. A sound that promised they would never, ever leave this place.

Maria's eyes snapped open, and she bolted upright, body slick with sweat, heart thrashing in her chest. The world was suddenly too quiet. Too empty.

In the distance, Jacob was crying. She ran to him, gathered him close, her own hands shaking uncontrollably.

"I saw Dad… I saw him… But it doesn't want us to find him."

Maria held him, rocking him gently, her tears mingling with his.

She didn't answer.

Because she had seen it, too—and she knew that, somewhere, in the heart of the In Between, Joseph was still lost, and the Thing was waiting.

Scene 3: The Whispering Glass

The apartment had begun to shift again.

It started with little things—the kind of details Maria would have missed, if she hadn't been trained by terror to notice them. A picture frame on the wall, always straight, now hung just crooked enough to catch the corner of her eye. The hallway lamp flickered and sputtered even after she changed the bulb. The usual creaks and groans of their old University Place apartment seemed to have found new purpose, like someone—or something—was using them as a private code.

Maria tried to ignore it. She folded laundry, she scrubbed the kitchen floor, she hummed quietly as she made dinner, anything to drown out the low thrum of unease in her chest. But the air had changed: every shadow felt a shade too deep, every mirror a little too knowing. It was the silence, she realized—the hush that settled between every noise, too heavy to be empty.

It began one evening as the sun fell behind the evergreens, leaving the apartment wrapped in a nervous blue twilight. Maria stood at the kitchen sink, rinsing out a coffee mug, when an inexplicable chill crept across her ankles. Not the gentle cool of the air conditioner, or the draft from a window left open, but something older—like a cold breath pressed against her skin from another world.

The kitchen light dimmed and brightened again, flickering as though struggling against an unseen hand. In the faint reflection of the microwave's door, Maria caught the movement—a blurry shape standing behind her. She spun with a gasp, heart pounding, but found only the empty kitchen. The only sound was the slow drip of water from the tap.

Her eyes dropped to the floor. There, in the middle of the tile, lay a spoon she was sure she hadn't used or dropped. The sense of being watched pressed closer, heavy as a blanket. Maria stepped away, the chill slithering up her back.

That night, as the apartment finally quieted and Jacob fell asleep on the couch beside her, the whispers began. At first, they sounded like the voice of the wind, or the distant hum of the building's pipes. But as the hours crept by, they grew distinct—soft, insistent, and coming from behind the bathroom door. Maria sat up, clutching a blanket, her gaze fixed on the dark crack beneath the door, where no light shone.

She rose slowly, each footstep heavy, compelled by a need to confront the unknown. The whispers stilled as her hand touched the doorknob. The bathroom's nightlight cast odd, shifting shadows along the walls. A mirror hung above the sink—old, slightly warped. Maria's reflection stared back at her, eyes wide and fearful. Then, to

191

her horror, it moved—tilting its head just a second before she did. Maria stumbled back, leaving the light on as she fled.

The next morning, Maria found Jacob standing at the end of the hallway, facing the tall mirror. His small face was pale, expression intent. He didn't seem scared. Only... expectant.

"Jacob?" Maria asked, soft and careful.

He glanced at her, then back at the glass. "He's here," he said, voice flat and strange. "But he says he's not like the others."

"Who, sweetheart?" Maria crouched beside him, tension knotting her shoulders.

A mist began to seep into the hallway, low and luminous, curling across the floor in silent tendrils. It was cold but not biting, gentle in its touch. Maria's breath caught as the mirror fogged over from within. A face took shape, slow and spectral: hollowed eyes, a weathered jaw, deep lines of sorrow.

Maria's heart hammered as she whispered, "Who are you?"

The figure's eyes, though shaded by the frost, met hers with ancient sadness. His lips moved, and his voice rolled out—not into the air, but into her mind.

"I've been searching a long time," he said, tone low and mournful. "Longer than you'd believe. I tried to reach your husband in Tombstone."

Maria's breath stilled. "Tombstone?" The memory crashed into her: the chill in the hotel, the voice she thought she'd imagined. She took a shaky step closer. "Wait. You... You're the one who said it wasn't him?" Her voice broke. "That was real? That wasn't just a dream?"

The man's form in the glass gave a slow, heavy nod. "That was me. I tried for what felt like a hundred years to get someone to pay attention. I needed the world to know—they hung the wrong man. My name is Gregory." His voice grew more desperate, more human. "All those years, I waited. Whispered. No one listened. But Joseph did. Your Joseph. He heard me. He believed me, and I finally followed him back to the hotel, hoping—praying—he'd listen to what I needed to say."

Maria pressed a hand to her mouth, memory and disbelief warring across her face. "I heard you, too. In the hotel. I thought I was losing my mind."

Gregory's smile was sad but grateful. "You both did. Joseph listened, and you… you listened as well. You have no idea what it meant, after so long. I owe him a debt I can never repay."

He looked around, as if searching for someone unseen. "I've been looking for him ever since. After Tombstone, I followed the echoes, the threads he left behind. But when I finally found my way here, he wasn't here. Not… not on this side."

Maria's hand tightened on Jacob's shoulder. "Did you see him? Did you see Joseph?"

Gregory nodded, his expression growing grimmer. "In the In Between. I crossed through places I thought were only nightmares. The In Between… it's not a place for the living. It's corridors of glass and shadow, sorrow and hunger, a place where voices wail and time gets lost." His voice trembled. "But I found Joseph. His soul… it burns bright, but it's suffering. Something ancient feeds on him. Something that's more than the Thing. Something called the Echo."

193

Maria felt her knees threaten to give. "Is he... can we save him?"

Gregory's features softened, the mist glowing around him. "I don't know. But I had to find you. I had to tell you what he did for me. And warn you. The Echo now knows your names. The In Between is watching. And the Thing... is only a servant. The real enemy is older."

The mist began to recede. "Take care, Maria. Protect your son. Listen for the small voices. I'll be searching still. For Joseph. For a way to repay what was done for me."

The mirror cleared. Maria and Jacob stood in silence, the memory of cold and sorrow lingering long after the light returned to normal.

Then, at the edge of hearing, the bathroom mirror fogged. A faint, amused laugh echoed out. Maria shuddered, gathering Jacob close. They were not alone. The shadows had returned. And the In Between was watching.

Scene 4: The Woman in Grey

Maria dreamed again that night.

She knew it before her eyes even opened—before her thoughts could form words, before the world fell away and left her in a weightless, heavy velvet silence. She felt her body drifting, as if she were sliding beneath dark water, sinking down into the depths of a place she could never touch while awake. Every sound was muffled, every heartbeat impossibly loud in her chest. The air pressed in, thick and close, smothering the space around her.

She didn't feel the comfort of her bed. There was no softness, no warmth. Only the cold, hard slickness beneath her bare feet. When she finally dared to look down, she saw what she had feared—a floor of endless, flawless glass. It stretched out in every direction, polished to a mirror's cruel sheen, reflecting the dream's pale, colorless sky above and distorting her own image into a stranger's shadow. Every step Maria took made the surface ripple, echoing outwards as if the very world was a pond disturbed by the lightest touch.

She was back in the In Between.

A labyrinth rose around her, looming through the pale haze. Twisting walls of broken, gleaming mirrors towered above, their edges jagged, their surfaces warped by age and memory. The maze was vast, and every corridor bent in directions that defied logic— sometimes looping back, sometimes spinning her around so she wasn't sure if she was walking forward or being turned around by some invisible force. Her reflection followed her at every angle: anxious, eyes wide, lips parted in silent dread.

Somewhere, faint echoes whispered through the mist. She heard footsteps that were not her own, soft and hesitant, sometimes hurried. A low, continuous hush—like thousands of voices all trying to speak at once but only managing a mournful, shivering tremor that vibrated through the glass beneath her toes. Shadows moved at the edge of her sight—shapes she almost recognized: a flash of Jacob's hair, the silhouette of Joseph's shoulders, a memory of her own childhood face—gone the moment she turned to look.

In the suffocating silence, Maria's breath grew shallow. Each inhale tasted faintly of ash and rust, old metal and burnt memories. The air was so thick with the scent of despair that she could almost feel it clinging to her skin, oily and unwelcome.

Then, through the fog, she saw movement—a flicker at the edge of vision. At first, only the hem of a dress trailing over the mirrored ground. The fabric was worn and stained, a heavy Victorian skirt that gathered dust and glided without a sound. Maria felt a primal chill crawl up her spine as she followed, drawn forward against her will.

The figure turned to face her.

She was tall and spectral, impossibly thin. Her skin was pale as bone, almost translucent, and her features were carved with sorrow, her cheekbones sharp, her lips nearly blue. Her hair was long, streaked with the grey of mourning, and tucked beneath a black lace bonnet. Her eyes, wide and haunting, seemed to swallow all the dim light of the maze, and Maria felt herself shrinking under that gaze.

The woman's dress was unmistakably mid-19th century: a mourning gown, high-collared and tightly bodiced, layers of tulle and soot-stained cotton cascading to the ground. Smoke and old perfume lingered on her, as if she'd stepped from a funeral that never ended.

Maria tried to back away, but her feet wouldn't move.

The woman floated closer—her boots never making a sound on the glass, as if she weighed nothing at all. When she spoke, her voice came as a cold whisper, layered with echoes and memories.

"You are Maria Duncan," she intoned. "The spouse of the blood-bearer."

Maria found her tongue, the words trembling in her mouth. "Who are you?"

"I am called Delilah. Delilah Mercier." The name rang with cold finality. "My mother was Eleanor Duncan. Your husband is of her line."

Maria's breath caught. "You're... you're a relative of Joseph?"

Delilah nodded. "Long dead," she said, as if it barely mattered. "But not silent. I saw the binding. I saw the glass receive the first soul."

"What glass?" Maria managed, her voice a fragile thread. "The clock?"

Delilah's eyes grew far away. "The first clock. The mirror-faced timepiece forged by Bishop Chartrand of the Concords in the Louisiana bayou. It was crafted not to destroy the Thing—but to hold it. They never intended to end the curse. Only to hide it, to pass the darkness from one generation to the next. And so the Thing fed—on the bloodline, one soul at a time."

The world around Maria grew colder. Her arms prickled with goosebumps. "Why are you here?" she asked, feeling the dread build in her throat. "Why now?"

"The veil thins," Delilah whispered. "The Thing is not the only one who stirs. The Echo wakes."

The name lingered in the glass like a poison. Maria felt her knees tremble.

Delilah lifted a hand and gestured. The mirrored corridor behind her shuddered as if struck by a deep, slow heartbeat. A pulse of blackness slid through the glass beneath their feet. For an instant, Maria glimpsed something deep in the reflection—an impossible face, all mouth, no eyes, twisting in a soundless scream.

"You are marked, Maria. The glass knows your name now," Delilah warned. "You have entered the In Between once, and it opened willingly. That will not always be so."

Maria shook her head, voice breaking. "I didn't choose this."

Delilah's face softened, and for a heartbeat, she looked almost motherly. "None of us did. But blood remembers. And the glass remembers most of all."

A terrible sound echoed through the labyrinth—a guttural groan, something vast and wrong dragging itself across the mirrored walls, its limbs making a sound like bones breaking, claws scraping over ice.

Delilah began to fade, her outline flickering like the last candle in a tomb. "I am not allowed to remain," she said urgently. "He comes. He smells fear like smoke. Tell Abigail. The symbols must be traced again. The light must be drawn before he returns."

"Who?" Maria pleaded, backing away.

Delilah's eyes widened in fear. "The Thing? No. Worse. The one who made it his jailor."

A hurricane of wind roared down the corridor, sending shards of glass spinning like knives through the air. The scent of sulfur rolled over Maria, burning her eyes and throat.

Delilah vanished, unraveling into fog and memory.

Maria turned, and her blood froze. The Thing was there—its limbs too long, its skin stretched thin, its eyes black as the void. Its mouth twisted open in a gaping smile, rows of jagged glass teeth gleaming in the shifting light. A cold mist spun around her, clutching at her limbs, squeezing the scream from her lungs.

It leaned close—so close she could taste its breath, could see the agony swirling in the black holes of its eyes.

And then—

Maria jerked awake, gasping, tangled in sweat-soaked sheets, heart pounding as if it would break through her ribs.

The bedroom was still. Jacob stirred beside her, murmuring in his sleep.

Across the room, the vanity mirror hissed—a whisper of air against glass. Maria stared, unable to look away, her pulse thundering.

But the reflection held only darkness, and Maria shivered, knowing she'd seen the true face of her family's curse—and that it was only beginning.

Chapter 10 - Maria's Calling

Scene 1: Through the Mirror

The kettle screamed, but Maria barely heard it.

She stood motionless in the kitchen, one hand gripping the counter so tightly her knuckles blanched, the other curled protectively against her stomach as if bracing for a blow. Steam billowed behind her in curling tendrils, dissipating quickly into the chill of the morning. The hiss of boiling water seemed distant, far removed from the silence pressing down on her chest—a silence so thick it was almost physical, crowding the air until every breath felt like effort.

The dawn was thin and colorless. Light filtered in weakly through the slats in the blinds, painting the floor in narrow gray stripes. The boys were still asleep, huddled together in their room, untouched by the weight crushing Maria's heart. The apartment was still. Too still. As if the walls themselves were holding their breath, afraid to make a sound.

Gregory's words haunted her thoughts like persistent smoke, impossible to wave away.

The In Between.

The woman in grey.

The maze of mirrors.

The voices—endless, mournful, echoing through the cracks in her memory.

And Joseph.

His soul dimming.

Fading.

She tried to make sense of it all, but it tangled in her mind, weaving itself through her veins until her body vibrated with worry. Her hands shook as she moved to the small table, sitting down heavily, and pulled a battered yellow legal pad in front of her. She began to write, the pen carving jagged lines across the page. Glass. Mirrors. Ritual. Something ancient. The Echo. Not dead. Trapped? Her writing became messier, more frantic. The more she tried to make sense of it, the more the answers slipped away, like dreams fading with the morning light.

Her free hand drifted to her stomach, trembling. She held herself as though something might shatter at any moment—her resolve, her hope, her life as she knew it. The secret growing inside her felt like both a promise and a threat. She hadn't told anyone. Not Jacob, not Noah. Not yet. She pressed her palm against the slight swell beneath her shirt, as if she could shield this unborn life from the horror threatening to bleed through the walls.

Suddenly, a surge of emotion overwhelmed her—grief, confusion, guilt, terror. Tears spilled hot down her cheeks. She pressed her hands over her face and let the sobs shake her, her whole body trembling. "I can't do this," she whispered into the emptiness. The words echoed back at her, thin and frail. "I can't."

And then—the air in the apartment shifted.

The lights flickered once, then twice. The temperature dropped, a crawling cold winding around her ankles and climbing her spine. It was like the apartment itself exhaled a ghost, blowing a wave of icy dread through the room.

Maria's breath caught. She wiped her eyes and looked up.

The mirror above the fireplace—an old, silver-framed glass that had hung there since they moved in—shimmered faintly in the dim light. At first, she thought it was a trick of the morning sun, but then she saw it: the glass pulsed, as if alive, as if breathing. Maria rose slowly, her chair scraping the floor, heart slamming in her chest.

And then—his face.

It formed slowly in the center of the glass, like a photograph developing under a darkroom lamp. Joseph. His features gaunt and hollow, pale as candle wax, the skin beneath his eyes shadowed and sunken. His lips moved, and when his eyes found hers, Maria felt everything inside her collapse—grief, hope, longing—twisting into one unbearable ache.

"Joseph?" she whispered, reaching out with shaking fingers. She could not touch the glass—she knew it—but still, her hand hovered, desperate to feel the warmth of his skin.

His mouth moved again, and this time she heard him—not in her ears, but somewhere deeper, in the very marrow of her bones. His voice echoed through her mind, raw and brittle, like a prayer nearly drowned by thunder.

"Maria…"

She moved closer, tears blurring her vision, her breath shaking. "I'm here," she whispered, voice trembling. "Joseph, I'm here…"

His image flickered. She saw how exhausted he was—how his eyes, once bright, were now ringed with purple shadows. His shoulders slumped, as if he carried a mountain. He looked like a man drowning, clutching for air, clinging to the last scraps of hope.

"I'm not dead," Joseph managed, his voice so thin she feared it might shatter with the next word.

Relief and terror warred inside her. "Joseph, what—where are you?"

The glass behind him blackened, and a wind—impossible, howling—whipped his hair sideways, his coat flapping violently. Shadows passed behind him, swift and predatory, circling closer with every heartbeat.

"I'm trapped," Joseph said. She heard the agony in his voice, the strain. "In the In Between. Listen—" His voice wavered, as if the effort of speaking was almost too much. "You must... collect the shards. The clock. Get Abigail. I don't... I don't know how long I have..."

"Joseph—" Maria pressed her palm to the glass, sobbing. "Don't go. Don't leave me!"

But Joseph's head jerked suddenly over his shoulder, panic in his eyes. Something huge and dark surged behind him—a tidal wave of black, swirling smoke and talons. The Thing. Its hunger radiated through the glass, a chill so deep it numbed Maria's bones.

"It's coming," Joseph breathed, voice barely more than a ghost of sound. "I have to go—before it finds you. Before it crosses."

The mirror vibrated, the image of Joseph tearing, stretching. The room around Maria dimmed to twilight. Her reflection flickered through him, as if her presence was fading too.

"Maria—go!"

The connection snapped. The mirror went black. She stared at her own reflection, trembling, tears streaking her cheeks, the echo of Joseph's agony still ringing in her ears.

A charged, suffocating silence rushed in to fill the void.

Maria stumbled away from the mirror, her legs barely holding her weight, hands pressed to her stomach as if to hold herself together. Her breath came in ragged gasps. Joseph's last words rang in her mind:

Get Abigail. Collect the shards. It's coming.

And beneath it all, so faint she nearly missed it, came another sound. A scraping. Like nails dragged over glass. Somewhere, something was coming.

Maria sank to her knees and wept, torn between terror and hope—knowing that as long as Joseph called out for her, she would never stop fighting to bring him home.

Scene 2: Desperate Measures

Maria waited until Jacob and Noah had left for school with Mrs. Garza, the trusted church friend who had become their lifeline since Joseph disappeared. The apartment felt hollow, the ticking clock on the wall too loud in the silence. She stood for a long time with her cell phone in her hand, staring at Gregory's name written in the margin of her notebook, as if the mere sight of it would conjure him from the glass.

She hesitated only a moment longer, then dialed Abigail. Each ring stretched like wire through her nerves.

Abigail picked up, her voice soft but immediately attentive. "Maria? Is everything alright?"

Maria pressed the phone tightly to her ear, fighting to steady her breath. "Abigail, I had another dream. It was different this time—worse. Jacob was with me. We were there... in the In Between."

There was a beat of silence. "You both dreamed it?"

Maria nodded, swallowing hard. "Yes. We were together. It was—" She had to pause to find her words, her free hand trembling against her thigh. "It wasn't just a nightmare, Abigail. We walked on glass. There were reflections everywhere. It was a maze of mirrors, but the reflections... they didn't just show us. They moved on their own, they remembered everything, every awful thing. It was so cold. And there were voices—so many voices, crying and moaning, like a thousand souls pressed against the glass and begging to be let out."

Abigail's breath caught, barely audible through the line. "Oh my God, Maria..."

"And then we found him," Maria whispered, tears stinging her eyes. "Joseph. Or... what's left of him. He was in the maze, but his eyes were so empty, Abigail. He looked at me, but it was like he was seeing through me, like he wasn't all there. And then something— something terrible—was there with us. The Thing. It... it laughed. I could feel it watching me. It knows my name. It knows Jacob. I felt it in my bones."

Abigail was silent for a long moment, absorbing the horror in Maria's voice. "Maria, I'm so sorry. I can't even imagine..."

"There's more," Maria pressed on, her voice trembling. "Gregory and Delilah were there. Gregory, the spirit Joseph met in Tombstone. He appeared in our mirror, told us about the In Between. He said he's been searching for Joseph ever since Joseph listened to him in the hotel. That he tried to tell him, tried to say it wasn't him, that they hung the wrong man. That Joseph actually heard him, and that set him free. But now Gregory's been trying to find him, to thank him. He finally did, in the In Between, but Joseph wasn't... he's not..." Her words crumbled under the weight of her emotion.

Abigail's voice was gentle. "You said Delilah appeared too?"

Maria nodded, remembering the haunting eyes, the ancient mourning dress. "She found me in the maze. She called herself Delilah Mercier. She told me she was Joseph's ancestor—her mother's line. She said she saw the first soul bound to the clock...a curse cast by the Concords cult. She told me the clock was never meant to end the curse—just to hide it. That the Thing has been feeding on the Duncan family, soul by soul, for generations. She warned me... warned all of us. She said the glass knows my name now. That I let something in by going there. She said the veil is thinning. That something older than the Thing is waking. The Echo, she called it. And she said the Thing isn't the real enemy—it's a parasite, and the Echo is the one who trapped it. Abigail... Delilah was terrified."

She stopped to catch her breath, a tear slipping down her cheek. "I can't just sit here anymore. I need to save him. I need to get him out. You can't imagine what that place is like, Abigail—cold, endless, a prison made of memories and regrets. And the Thing is hunting him. I saw it. I felt it. I can't lose him. I'll do anything."

Abigail's voice hardened with resolve. "You won't lose him. We're going to find a way. I already spoke with Father Allen after you called last week. We've been researching, trying to find if there's any ritual to break a curse like this, or free a soul from the glass. He thinks it's possible. But he says we need to know more—about the curse, about the clock, about your family's history with the Thing. We have to dig deeper."

Maria squeezed her eyes shut. "But how? Where do we even look?"

"He suggested the church archives," Abigail said quickly. "Did you know the Duncans have a whole collection of documents, artifacts, maps, and journals stored there? Apparently, it's the safest place to keep records like that—away from fire, flood, theft, or… whatever else. I've already started sorting through some of the files, but it's a mountain of history. I can't do it alone. Father Allen thinks the answer might be buried in your family's records. Maybe the ritual, or the true purpose of the clock, or even a way to reverse the binding."

Maria's heart leapt with desperate hope, her voice trembling. "We'll go to Schenectady. We'll go through every page, every diary, every scrap. I'll do whatever it takes. I'll stay as long as I need. I'll have Mrs. Garza watch the boys. I just—I can't stay here, waiting for the Thing to find a way through."

"I know," Abigail said softly. "We'll do this together. I want you to be prepared, Maria—it might take days, even weeks. We don't know what's hidden in the archives. But we have to try. For Joseph. For Jacob and Noah. For all of you."

Maria swallowed, blinking away more tears. "We'll go tomorrow. We can get the first flight out. Thank you, Abigail. Thank you for not thinking I'm insane."

"You're not," Abigail said fiercely. "I've seen enough to believe you, Maria. And I saw the In Between once myself, years ago. You don't belong there. No one does. But if you're marked, it means you're closer to the truth than anyone before you. And that's our weapon now. We'll use it."

Maria gripped the phone with both hands, her knuckles white. "Promise me, Abigail. Promise me you won't let me face this alone."

"I promise," Abigail said, her voice strong. "I won't let you. We go together."

As Maria ended the call, the weight pressing on her chest eased—just enough to let her breathe again. She moved quietly through the apartment, gathering her things with deliberate care. Her fingers lingered on the boys' beds, absorbing the gravity of what she needed to do, yet fully aware of the consequences if she failed to follow through.

Outside, the wind rattled the windowpanes. Maria stared at her reflection in the glass, remembering the endless maze, the echo of Joseph's voice, the terror in Delilah's eyes.

Tomorrow, she would face the darkness with Abigail at her side. Tomorrow, the search would begin.

She only prayed that they were not already too late.

Scene 3: Ashes and Answers

They arrived in Schenectady just past noon, and the day had turned colder by the time Maria and Abigail stepped onto Samuel's creaking front porch. The leaves were brittle, scattered across the yard in crisp, copper piles. Clouds moved lazily overhead, veiling the sky in a pale gray film. There was a hush to the air—like the world was listening.

Maria hugged her coat tighter around her belly and exhaled slowly. She hadn't told Abigail about the pregnancy yet. She hadn't told anyone. But she could feel the weight of it—like a quiet heartbeat just beneath the surface. And now, with Joseph's faint message echoing in her mind, it pulsed with new urgency.

They arrived at Samuel's house just as the afternoon sun dipped behind the trees. Samuel was heading inside from the porch and paused when he saw them—especially Abigail.

His eyes softened a fraction.

"Well," he muttered, offering a faint smile. "Didn't expect company today."

Abigail smiled back. "You never expect saints or storm clouds. But both show up when they need to."

Samuel raised an eyebrow, clearly amused. "Still throwing scripture at the wind, I see."

"Someone has to," she shot back gently.

There was an unspoken familiarity in their brief exchange.

With a lingering smile he gestured for them to have a seat on the porch.

"I was just about to grab some coffee and watch the sun retire for the night, would you like to join me?"

Maria was quick to decline; her nerves already primed for the exchange she knew was coming.

"I'll take some, and don't forget my cream," Abigail quipped as Samuel turned for the door.

Once they settled on the porch's worn bench,

Abigail leaned closer, her voice low but edged with curiosity.

"Tell me again what he said," she asked, eyes fixed on Maria.

Maria nodded, her voice trembling as she recounted it. "He was in the mirror. His face—God, it looked so tired. But not dead. He said he wasn't gone. Just... trapped." She hesitated. "He said to collect the shards. From the clock. And to get you."

Abigail's brows drew together, her lips pressing into a line. "Shards. Glass. The Woman in Grey said the same thing—didn't she? It will take both memory and reflection to unbind the soul?"

Maria gave a small, haunted nod. "She said the curse echoes through blood.

Through time.

That if we don't act, the glass will close forever."

Abigail stood, pacing a few slow steps. "If Joseph is still in the In Between... and if the shards from that clock are still connected to it, then maybe—just maybe—there's a path. A ritual. But time's against us."

"Then we find the pieces," Maria said, standing beside her. "And we start with Samuel."

They turned as the front door creaked open and Samuel appeared, holding two steaming mugs and sat down in a chair across from them.

His face was weathered by more than years. It was worn down by regret.

Abigail smiled softly while taking the cup he offered her and she patted his arm like she was tending gently to a wound.

Maria watched the exchange with faint surprise. There was something unspoken between them—a quiet spark, perhaps curiosity or a subtle admiration that lingered in the air.

The three chatted for a few moments as the unspoken grief about what was known and fear about that not yet known finally became too much for Maria. She stood abruptly, and blaming the coming twilight that had brought a chill to the air asked if they could go inside. Samuel led them into the small living room, where old photographs lined the mantle and the furniture smelled faintly of cedar and dust. He settled into a low chair, his movements slower than Maria remembered.

"We need to talk," she said plainly. "About the clock. About Joseph."

The mention of his son's name made Samuel's gaze drop.

"I saw him," Maria continued. "He's alive... in some way. And I think we can bring him back."

Samuel stared into his coffee. "I kept the truth from him. Thought I was protecting him. Thought I was being strong."

Abigail leaned in. "Tell us everything. Please."

Samuel nodded. His hands trembled, wrapping around the mug. He closed his eyes.

FLASHBACK – LATE AUTUMN, 1982

The barn was almost pitch-black, the air cold enough to see breath. Thin shafts of moonlight pierced through cracks in the walls. A lone lantern burned low, casting jittering shadows on the dusty rafters. Sixteen-year-old Ruth Duncan paced, cloak drawn tight around her, eyes wild and haunted. Thirteen-year-old Samuel followed quietly, worried.

"Rustle the hay, Sammy," their mother had whispered. "Just until I check on supper."

But Ruth shook her head. "No, Sam. Stay here. I need silence."

Her voice was steady, but gooseflesh flecked her arms. She removed a small silver-framed mirror from a battered tool box and held it up to the lantern's glow. Its glass shimmered—something moved behind her reflection. She swallowed hard.

"Stop, Ruth," Samuel murmured.

She shook the mirror. "It's real. There's something inside."

He dismissed her. "You're imagining...the whispering."

Ruth's eyes burned with conviction. "Call it what you want, Sam, but it's after me."

A sudden gust rattled the lantern; the barn doors creaked open. The mirror fell, shattering on the wooden floor. Ruth froze, eyes wide, listening.

"Sam...do you feel that?"

Samuel stepped closer. "Let's go home."

But the air grew thick, sour—like brimstone. Shadows crept across the floorboards. Ruth gripped his hand. "I'm scared."

A guttural laugh echoed from the walls. Something black and slow pooled from the mirror shards—limbs too long, shape twisted— in the darkness behind her.

"Ruth?!" Samuel shouted, rushing forward. But she held him back, face drained of color.

"It fears me," she whispered. "It doesn't want to take me...it wants me gone."

A raspy voice trailed: "She is special. Better destroyed than used as bait."

She looked at him, calm. "Run."

He screamed her name as dry hay ignited. The barn erupted in flame. Samuel dove into fire, choking on smoke. When he emerged, the fire had died; Ruth was gone. On the floor lay a single black shard, still sizzling on the wood.

END FLASHBACK

Samuel's voice cracked. "I denied it all these years. I couldn't believe there was something real out there. But Ruth...she wasn't playing. The Thing was there that night. It's why I stopped—why I pretended none of it was real."

Maria's voice caught. "You believe it was the Thing?"

He nodded, tears shining. "I was arrogant. I thought I could protect her—protect all of us. But I failed the night Ruth died. Worse, I lied to myself because it was too terrible to face." He shook his head. "I've carried this guilt...I've carried silence." Abigail placed a gentle hand over his. "You can't carry that forever."

He looked up, something tender sparking in his expression. "That's the first kind thing anyone has said to me about it in forty years. My parents always thought I accidentally knocked the lantern over and started the fire. I knew they wouldn't believe me if I told them what I thought I actually saw happen. So I carried the guilt and the lie all these years, and my parents—and everyone else—blamed me for Ruth's death."

Maria cleared her throat softly, pulling them back to the moment. "We need the pieces. The clock. Is anything left?"

Samuel rose without a word and crossed to the coat closet. From the back shelf, he pulled a small metal box, tarnished and cold. When he opened it, the soft clink of glass echoed through the room.

Inside—wrapped in scorched cloth—were three shards of mirrored glass. Each pulsed faintly, like they remembered what they once held.

Outside, the wind began to rise.

The sun was sliding behind the trees now, casting long shadows across the yard. The porch creaked again, this time with no footstep to cause it.

Maria felt it first—a shift in pressure. Like the breath before a storm.

Samuel looked toward the window, the light falling away from his face.

"I burned that clock," he whispered. "But something in it... it never burned."

The wind howled once, long and low, then fell silent.

In the hush that followed, the shadows seemed to breathe.

And from the distant edge of the trees, something unseen stirred.

Abigail's voice was almost a whisper.

"This time, we won't face the dark alone."

But as the sky deepened to black and the glass began to hum, Maria knew—

The darkness hadn't retreated.

It had only stepped aside… waiting.

Scene 4: Whispers Beneath the Glass

The night had fallen heavy by the time Maria and Abigail returned to their small motel room on the outskirts of Schenectady. The world outside was a cold void—the kind of cold that seeps into the bones, that finds every crack in every window and presses in with invisible, icy fingers. Overhead, the ceiling fixture buzzed faintly, its yellow light barely piercing the shadows pooling in the corners. It cast the thin curtains in a sickly hue, making their floral pattern look wilted and washed out. The threadbare blankets on the two narrow beds were pulled up tight, but they did nothing to ward off the chill that seemed to settle deeper with every passing minute.

Outside, the wind hadn't stopped—not for hours. It moaned through the eaves, made the glass rattle in its frame, and set the branches of the old maple beside the building scraping in slow, deliberate strokes against the siding. The world felt pared down to its bones. The lights of passing cars flashed only occasionally beneath the window, headlights dragging brief ghosts across the faded wallpaper before vanishing into the night.

Maria sat on the edge of the bed, her body curved inward, hunched over as if she might fold in on herself completely. Her hands were clasped tightly together, knuckles pale against the blue of her coat. Her breath fogged faintly in the cool air, disappearing almost as quickly as it appeared. She watched the floor, her gaze fixed on a thread unwinding from the rug.

Across the cramped room, Abigail sat at the small desk, elbows braced on the scarred wood, her worn leather-bound journal open in front of her. The pages were filled with prayers, notes, and hastily scribbled fragments of old rites—some written in trembling ink, others half-erased by the passage of fingers or time. Abigail's brows furrowed as she scanned her notes, lips moving silently, tracing words she'd written in the hope they might someday save someone.

A long silence weighed between them, the only sound the slow shifting of the wind and the faint creak of old pipes. Maria broke it first, her voice thin and nearly lost in the gloom.

"There's something I didn't tell Samuel," she said quietly.

Abigail's head snapped up, eyes sharp, attentive. "What is it?"

Maria raised her gaze, shadows smudging the hollows beneath her eyes. "The woman in the grey dress... the one I saw in the dream.

215

She told me the glass still echoes. That it reaches back before Adam. Before Joseph. That something older... more powerful... is behind this."

Abigail's expression darkened as she leaned forward, her figure casting a longer shadow in the light. "Not The Thing?"

Maria shook her head, hair brushing across her cheek. "No. She didn't name it, but... later, I heard a name. In the dream. In my head. The Echo."

Abigail's hands stilled over the journal. "The Echo?" Her voice barely rose above the wind.

Maria nodded slowly, each movement heavy with exhaustion. "She said The Thing wasn't the start. That it was released, not born. That it had once been... chained. And that something was waiting to take its place. Or maybe watching. Like... a judge."

Abigail set down her pen, fingers curling under her chin as her mind spun through possibilities. The lamplight caught the tired lines in her face, the trace of old scars and newer worries. "That sounds like a higher order spirit. Not demonic, not saintly. Something... in between. Ancient. Forgotten."

"The In Between," Maria whispered, the words almost too heavy to say. "That's what she called it."

Abigail pushed up from her chair, began pacing the length of the room—three steps, turn, three steps, her boots tapping softly on the warped floor. Her silhouette wavered against the peeling wallpaper, shadow stretching tall and thin. "We've been fighting shadows, Maria. Fighting symptoms. But this Echo—if it's real—it might be the source. Or the gatekeeper. Maybe even the key."

Maria turned to watch her, desperation sharpening the lines of her face. "If that's true... maybe it has the power to undo what happened to Joseph."

"Maybe," Abigail said, voice full of cautious hope, "but we can't act on a name and a dream. We need more. We need to know who the woman in grey really was. She's connected to Joseph somehow—family, that's what she said. She knew the clock. She knew Adam."

Maria's gaze flicked to the window. The streetlamp just beyond it shivered, its light sputtering in the wind, sending uncertain patterns dancing across the glass. Every shadow seemed to shift and deepen as if hiding something ancient just beneath the surface.

Abigail's pacing slowed. "And the clock—that cursed thing—it's more than just a vessel. It's a doorway. A prison. Maybe even a record. Whatever Adam did... it started there. We need to understand it before we attempt anything else."

Maria straightened, her resolve hardening despite her fatigue. "Then we find the history of it. The records. Anything that might tell us how it came into the family. How Adam was cursed."

Abigail nodded. "We start with the church. If there's anywhere old enough, sacred enough, to have kept records on something like this, it's St. Helen's."

Maria's voice came out soft, a trembling hope. "You think Father Allen will help?"

Abigail managed a half-smile, her eyes kind but tired. "He will. He's afraid, but he's faithful. And I think... he still wants to redeem himself for the role he played in what happened to Joseph."

Maria looked down at her hands. She realized she was trembling and tucked her fists beneath her thighs to hide it.

"You think there's really a way to bring him back?"

Abigail crossed the cramped space and knelt beside her, placing a steadying hand on Maria's shoulder—a grounding, living touch in the middle of so much cold and uncertainty. "I think... we don't stop until we know for sure."

The silence between them was broken only by the wind, rattling and sighing. Then, the light above them flickered, shadows crawling over the ceiling and along the far wall. For a moment, it almost seemed like the darkness pulsed, drawn to something just beneath the surface.

In the mirror above the dresser, a faint shimmer moved—like a cold breath against glass—then vanished, leaving only their twin reflections, pale and uncertain.

Maria stood slowly, rubbing her arms as if to force away the chill. "Let's go see Father Allen."

Outside, the wind rose, howling against the thin walls, setting the windowpanes quivering in their frames. As they stepped toward the door, a chill swept through the room—not sharp, but ancient and deep, the kind that reminded you how thin the world was in places. The Echo was awake. And somewhere beyond the veil of glass, it was listening.

Scene 5: The Forgotten Concord

The narrow corridor beneath St. Helen's Church smelled faintly of dust, candle wax, and old paper. Maria and Abigail descended the stone steps together, guided by a flickering lantern, thanks to the recent electrical storm. Shadows leapt from wall to wall with each sway of the flame, lending the archives a reverent, tomb-like stillness.

Maria moved ahead, still reeling from Joseph's message in the mirror—the urgency in his voice, the weight of it all. "He said to collect the shards," she whispered to Abigail. "And to find you."

Abigail touched her arm gently. "We will. And we'll do it fast. From everything the spirits have said... there may be a way to pull him back. But time's running short."

As they reached the bottom, the old lights flickered once, then hummed to life. Abigail blew out the lantern with a quick puff, and the corridor filled with dim, yellowed light. The heavy wooden door at the end opened with a groan, revealing a vaulted chamber lined with filing cabinets and sagging bookshelves. Father Allen waited inside, hunched over a desk cluttered with scrolls, parish records, and stained maps.

"You're here," he said, standing. "Good."

They didn't waste time. "Father," Maria said. "We need to know more about the Concords, the clock, and where this all started. It's Delilah. I think she was the woman in the gray dress. And I think she's trying to help."

Abigail moved swiftly to a metal cabinet, already digging. "We found a book with the Concordia Medallion—ritual instructions, their name, even Adam's listed. But the details are vague."

Father Allen nodded slowly and gestured them closer. He pulled a folded document from a drawer and smoothed it across the table. It was a parchment sketch of a relic: an ornate clock framed by twisting thorn-like vines, a reflective glass face, and the inverted triangle sigil.

"This was found among the possessions of a late bishop," Allen said. "The Concord of Reflected Grace. A cult, born in Louisiana. They believed mirrors could preserve the soul, not damn it. They said it was protection."

Maria brushed her fingers across the spine of a heavy, leather-bound ledger and placed it on the large oak table. Her eyes, sharp but weary, moved quickly over the pages—church rosters, marriage records, baptismal notes. But none of them felt right. Not yet.

Across the table, Abigail moved methodically, laying out parchment maps of St. Mary Parish and the surrounding land tracts. Some were yellowed nearly to parchment's end, corners missing, the ink faded but still whispering of something ancient.

Father Allen hovered behind them both. Though he said little, his presence was electric. Every few minutes, he would lean over a shoulder, mutter a confirmation or offer a scripture reference connected to an entry. He was deep in his own reverie, perhaps remembering sermons or whispers in this very place, many years before.

Then Maria stopped.

A narrow, cloth-bound photo album lay at the bottom of a chest labeled simply "Concordia." The stitching along its spine had nearly disintegrated, but the pages inside were pristine—preserved by the dryness of the vault. Her breath caught in her throat as she turned a page and found her.

The woman in grey.

A black-and-white photograph, stained at the edges, stared up at her. In the center stood a tall, graceful woman—slim waist, dark hair pulled into a modest bun, dressed in a pale gown of fine silk. She stood outside a sprawling plantation home with a smile that was too restrained, too polite, like something lingered behind her eyes. Shadows seemed unnaturally drawn to the edges of her dress.

Maria's fingers trembled.

"This is her," she whispered. "Abigail. Father Allen. Look."

They gathered around her. Abigail took the photo gently, peering closer. "The woman from your dreams?"

Maria nodded slowly. "She was in the house... guiding me. When I was in that In Between place. She warned me. And now here she is... alive. Real. Delilah."

Father Allen leaned over, examining the back of the photograph. Scribbled in elegant penmanship: Delilah Duncan Mercier – Spring, 1861.

Abigail set the photo beside an open manuscript written in old French and Latin. "It's her. That name—Delilah Duncan. She was a Duncan before marrying into the Mercier family. Which means..."

"She was family," Maria finished. Her voice was a mix of awe and dread.

Father Allen ran his hand over his stubbled chin. "This explains how the clock got to New York. She must've sent it north after the war. If she knew what it was..."

"And if she didn't," Abigail added, "she might have thought she was saving it. Or hiding it."

The photo, now lying flat under the flickering lantern light, seemed to darken around the edges, as though the shadows in the picture shifted just out of sight.

Maria's chest tightened. She pressed her hand over the photo, not to hide it—but to feel the chill it seemed to radiate.

"We need to know her story," she said. "The whole story. If she was trying to warn me, there must be more. She's trying to help us. I can feel it."

They looked around the vast archive—rows of shelves, heavy tomes, metal lockboxes and bins stacked to the ceiling. So much was hidden in these walls.

And they had only scratched the surface.

Scene 6: Let's Begin

The three stood in silence for a moment, the harsh fluorescent overhead lamps throwing stark shadows across the uneven stone floor. The air was dense with quiet energy, a sense that something long buried was about to be unearthed.

Maria pulled her coat tighter around her shoulders and looked out over the table now crowded with documents, journals, photos, and artifacts. There were handwritten letters from Delilah—some sealed, some partially burned, as though someone had tried to destroy them. There were brittle maps of the old Louisiana plantation, clearly marked in precise penmanship. Seals pressed in red wax bore the crest of the Concord of Reflected Grace. One scroll, when unrolled, displayed an elaborate ritual diagram, mirrored triads, and a Latin prayer invoking the binding of the soul.

Under the cold glare of the fluorescent overhead lamps, Abigail moved with the practiced confidence of someone who had done this before. She unfolded an archival folder and laid its contents out one by one: a weathered diary, its margins crowded with frantic notes; a hand-drawn schematic of an ornate grandfather clock with notations in French; and finally, a receipt from a Northern rail station noting "one crate—contents: wood & glass timepiece—origin: Franklin, LA."

Father Allen leaned against the far wall, arms folded, his eyes dark but alert. "It's all here," he murmured. "This… this is older than I thought. The cult wasn't just a whisper. They recorded everything. Like a doctrine."

Maria picked up a brittle envelope sealed with the same sigil from the clock's backside. She turned it over and back again. "They called it the Seal of Concordia. I remember now. Samuel mentioned it once, like it was a myth."

Abigail shook her head. "Not a myth. A covenant. They believed they were guarding souls—not imprisoning them, but protecting them until they could be cleansed."

"Or devoured," Father Allen muttered.

No one corrected him.

Thunder cracked above the vault. Dust spilled down from the ceiling, a soft hiss like breath exhaled from forgotten mouths. Maria stared at the ceiling as if it might break open and reveal something watching from above.

"I think we have enough here to piece it all together," Abigail said softly. "Delilah's story. Adam's fall. The origins of the clock. The cult. The rituals. All of it."

Maria stared down at the medallion now resting beside the photograph of Delilah. "It feels like she wants us to know," she said. "Like she's guiding us still."

Father Allen stepped forward and laid one hand on the table's edge. "If we're going to face this thing again… we need to know everything. We can't go in blind like last time."

A heavy silence fell.

Abigail's fingers drifted across a hand-drawn map of the Mercier plantation, then to a brittle census page listing a 'Duncan, Adam' noted as 'killed in action.' She straightened, her eyes dark with certainty.

"Well then," she said, her voice clear, "let's begin."

Suddenly, thunder clapped and the overhead lights sputtered and died, plunging the vault into darkness. Abigail fumbled for the lantern, her hands shaking as she struck a match and coaxed the flame back to life. For a breathless moment, the only light was the flicker of the lantern, shadows leaping wildly across the walls. The vault held its breath. And the past, long buried in parchment and shadow, began to stir.

Chapter 11 - Shadows over the Bayou

Scene 1: Arrival of Delilah Mercier

April   1858
St. Mary Parish, Louisiana

The sun burned low over the sweltering expanse of cane fields, its dying light bathing the Mercier Plantation in amber haze. The scent of earth, sugarcane, and the faint iron tang of the nearby bayou hung in the air. A ribbon of road unspooled toward the grand main house, flanked by gnarled mangrove trees whose arched limbs intertwined, forming a green cathedral of shadows.

The carriage rolled steadily, its lacquered wheels whispering over the crushed seashell path. Inside sat Delilah Duncan, her gloved hands folded in her lap, pale green eyes wide with wonder. Across from her, her brother Adam adjusted his waistcoat, glancing once at their mother Eleanor, who sat between them with an air of reserved dignity.

The Duncans had traveled far from New York City. Their family company, Duncan Freight & Rail, was well established along the Eastern Seaboard and across the burgeoning Midwest. But now, with the Mississippi River's commercial arteries growing more vital by the day, they had come south to open a distribution depot in Franklin—one that would link the river to their northern operations.

But they had not anticipated this.

The Mercier Plantation was a kingdom unto itself. Sprawling over 6,500 acres, it pulsed with agricultural wealth: sugarcane, cotton, corn, and vegetables stretched in regimented rows from horizon to horizon. Twin sugar mills belched smoke near the southern edge of the property, while the northern corner held a large cotton gin, both churning with labor and noise. Chickens pecked at dry earth beside sturdy hog pens, and beyond them, blacksmith and carpentry shops hammered out the lifeblood of the plantation's operations.

The carriage passed long rows of slave cabins—neat, uniform, each with a small garden plot. Smoke curled from chimneys. Children played barefoot between the dwellings, their laughter thin in the humid air. An elder sat on a worn wooden stool, gazing up at the carriage with eyes both hollow and knowing.

Delilah looked away.

Ahead, the main house loomed, pale and stately, with towering white columns and balconies trimmed in wrought iron filigree. Wide porches wrapped around the structure, shading a dozen lounging chairs and twin rocking benches that creaked with the breeze. Inside, it gleamed with imported Italian marble floors, chandeliers of cut crystal, and silk drapes framing tall windows. Servants moved like ghosts through its corridors, polishing, arranging, anticipating.

Thomas Mercier stood waiting on the broad front steps with his sons. Broad-shouldered and clean-shaven, Thomas's sharp jaw and commanding presence made him the image of a Southern patriarch. His wife Beatrice stood behind him, prim and elegant in dark plum silk. The three sons—Thomas Jr., Samuel, and Daniel— stood in a staggered line, each wearing the practiced smiles of gentry, though only the youngest, Daniel, seemed genuinely curious about the arriving guests.

"Mrs. Duncan," Thomas Mercier greeted warmly, doffing his hat. "Welcome to our home. And you must be Adam and Delilah. We are honored to host you."

"The pleasure is ours," Eleanor replied smoothly, descending with grace. "Your property is... formidable."

Delilah followed her mother, eyes taking in every detail—the soft flicker of oil lanterns beneath the porch awnings, the perfect alignment of rose bushes, the distant hum of a fiddle carried by the breeze. It was all so grand. So hauntingly beautiful.

They settled into a guest house not far from the main road. Though smaller than the mansion, it was still grand—a wide veranda, tall windows, and a library lined with leather-bound tomes. Servants saw to their every need. Despite the luxury, Adam remained guarded. Delilah, however, found herself drawn to the rhythm of the land.

One afternoon, as they strolled past the chapel near the church square, the sun casting long shadows across the brick path, Delilah heard voices just beyond the open side window. She paused. Adam walked ahead, distracted.

Inside the chapel, the Bishop conferred with two plantation priests, their voices hushed.

"The vessel must remain sealed," said one.

"Too much exposure... they'll grow curious. We can't afford curiosity," another murmured.

"Souls must be guarded," the Bishop added gravely. "The glass is not merely for reflection. It binds. It remembers."

Delilah's brow furrowed slightly. She tilted her head, trying to catch more, but the voices quieted. One of the priests moved toward the door, and she quickly resumed her pace.

That evening, at a formal dinner beneath cascading candelabras, Delilah watched the priests from across the room. Their eyes never quite settled on her, and yet she felt seen. Not entirely welcomed.

Weeks passed. Eleanor arranged the distribution depot in town, working closely with the Mercier family and local merchants. Competition among plantations was fierce, but the Duncans' northern reach and steam-powered logistics made them increasingly indispensable.

Locals began to accept their presence, if grudgingly. Even as "Yankees," the Duncans dressed the part, played the role, and brought value. Delilah found herself the subject of curiosity, especially from young Daniel Mercier, who engaged her in conversations about poetry, New York architecture, and foreign politics.

Still, there was a darkness that lingered just beneath the surface.

Delilah often passed the church, her eyes drawn to the stained-glass windows—one in particular: a faceless figure holding a golden clock, its hands spinning backwards. Sometimes she imagined the glass shimmered. Sometimes she thought she saw her reflection in its eyes.

One late evening, as lanterns were strung overhead for a midsummer celebration, casting soft golden pools along the street, Delilah stood beneath the mangroves, her gown a shade of twilight blue. Music drifted from the great house. She swayed to the distant fiddle, watching fireflies rise from the tall grass.

In that moment, with beauty surrounding her and something ancient whispering in the shadows, she knew something had begun.

Something had awakened.

And it was watching.

Scene 2: Courtship and Alliance

The summer of 1860 settled over Louisiana like a warm breath, dense with honeysuckle and the scent of river mist. The Mercier estate thrived with activity, freight wagons creaking down the main road, house servants airing linens in the morning sun, and the dull clang of the blacksmith's hammer echoing from the rear workshops. Though the war clouds had yet to darken the South, whispers of change lingered in every parlor and plantation hall.

Delilah Duncan stood at the edge of a ledger-strewn merchant's desk in downtown Franklin, her gloved hands folded demurely over her skirt. The air inside was warm, dust catching in the shafts of sunlight slanting through the window. Across from her, Daniel Mercier—youngest son of the famed Thomas Mercier—sat attentively, dark hair neatly parted, his posture straight as a bayonet but softened by the amused curve of his lips.

She liked the way he looked at her—not like a stranger, but like someone who already suspected there was more beneath her composed surface. Delilah, with her auburn curls pinned high and posture practiced from etiquette tutors, met his gaze and smiled back. There was something sincere about him, a contrast to the rigid propriety of most Southern gentlemen she'd encountered so far.

Daniel cleared his throat. "You handle logistics well, Miss Duncan. Our family has relied on northern depots before, but never with such clarity."

"My brother runs the ledgers," Delilah replied, brushing a smudge of ink from her glove. "But I do the negotiating."

That earned a laugh. "Dangerous combination."

That evening, they walked the magnolia-lined road beneath the swaying Spanish moss. The Mercier grounds shimmered in the twilight. Lanterns had begun to glow along the porch rails, and fireflies danced like spirits in the hedges. By then, Eleanor Duncan had noticed the way Daniel offered Delilah his arm so naturally, and Adam—ever watchful—had begun to keep a step closer than before.

Within weeks, the pair's courtship blossomed. Afternoon walks turned to sunset porch conversations, and Delilah soon found herself drawn to more than Daniel's charm. He asked questions no other suitor had—about her interests, her views, even her dreams. And more importantly, he listened.

One evening beneath the giant oaks behind the chapel, Daniel took her hand and dropped to one knee. A breeze stirred the Spanish moss overhead as he presented her with a modest ring set with a dark blue stone. "Delilah," he said softly, "I've known wealth and legacy, but not love—not until now. Will you be my wife?"

Her breath caught. The moment was too perfect, too sudden—and yet, she found herself saying, "Yes."

Later that night, in the flickering warmth of the family parlor, Thomas Mercier raised a crystal glass of port. "A union not only of hearts," he proclaimed, "but of commerce and legacy. The Duncans will strengthen our reach. Together, our families shall build an empire of goods and grace."

Eleanor's smile was polite but tight. Adam, beside her, sipped water and said nothing.

Only days later, Daniel gently brought up a matter that soured the afterglow.

"The Bishop wants you to join our church, Delilah. The Concord. It's… an important tradition in our family."

She hesitated. "But I don't even know what the Concord believes."

Daniel's fingers brushed hers. "It's about reflection. Spiritual unity. We hold certain rites. Some old traditions. But I won't pressure you."

Delilah, heart still fluttering with the bloom of young love, nodded. "If it's important to you, I'll join."

When she told her mother and Adam, Eleanor's brows furrowed. "You haven't even attended a service. Are you sure?"

"I trust him," Delilah said. "And this will make our marriage stronger."

Adam glanced toward the wide veranda where Thomas stood speaking to the Bishop, their heads close. "You sure this isn't more about what he wants… than what you want?"

"I'll be careful," Delilah said, brushing off their concern, but the unease remained like humidity clinging to skin.

In the weeks before the wedding, Thomas invited Delilah for a private tea. The afternoon sun slanted across the marble floors of the solarium as he spoke.

"You have a rare gift, my dear," he said, steepling his fingers. "Daniel has told me of your insights—how you sometimes speak of things before they happen. Visions. Premonitions."

Delilah's smile faded. "I don't make a show of it."

"No, but you shouldn't be ashamed. In fact, our church regards such sensitivities with great reverence."

That night, Daniel held her on the swing beneath the veranda. His arms felt safe, but his words didn't.

"I told him about your gift," he admitted. "I thought it might help. But now… I worry."

Delilah tilted her head. "Why?"

He stared at the far-off candlelight in the chapel window. "Because they'll want to use it. And I don't know what they'll ask of you."

A silence passed between them, broken only by the whispering breeze.

"I can protect you," he whispered. "But you must be careful. Don't let them know everything."

Delilah nodded, heart torn between fear and devotion.

The wedding approached with fanfare and whispers, the gown sewn in fine lace and the vows to be spoken in the echoing halls of the Concordia chapel. Yet behind every elegant curtain and fluted column, shadows gathered. Delilah Duncan, radiant and resolute, was about to step into a life more gilded—and more dangerous—than she had ever imagined.

Scene 3: Awakening and Ambition

April 1862

Mercier Plantation Chapel, Louisiana

The pews creaked with restless bodies and the heavy perfume of magnolia, sweat, and oil lamps mingled in the still air. The Bishop stood at the pulpit, bathed in the golden glow from stained glass windows depicting the saints. A man in his early sixties, Bishop Alaric Chartrand had a commanding presence, his voice rich and authoritative as it echoed through the rafters.

"There is no greater salvation," he declared, arms raised, his white robes trembling, "than the salvation of a soul caught in wicked storm. The Word tells us in Matthew 18:18—'Verily I say unto you, whatsoever ye shall bind on earth shall be bound in heaven…'"

Murmurs of amen rippled through the congregation.

He pounded the side of the pulpit. "And so, my brethren, we bind. We bind not out of cruelty, but from necessity. We bind to protect. Just as Christ bound the demons in the swine, we preserve the soul from the torments of Hell through sacred rites."

There was thunderous nodding from the elders.

"These times call for vigilance. Darkness grows long in these lands. We are the sentinels of the soul. We are the stewards of eternity."

When the service concluded, the Bishop moved through the parishioners with practiced warmth. He smiled, shook hands, and blessed foreheads. But inwardly, a gnawing tension twisted in his gut. He hurried back across the lantern-lit path that led to his modest home tucked behind the church—a white clapboard house nestled among wild roses.

He entered, hanging his cloak on the brass hook beside the door.

"Clara?" he called gently.

There was no reply.

His stomach turned. He hurried down the narrow hallway to his daughter's bedroom and pushed the door open. The air was thick with heat and the sour stench of illness. His daughter, Clara, no more than thirteen, lay limp in a tangle of sweat-soaked sheets. Her skin was flushed red in patches and ghost-pale in others. Purple shadows bruised the hollows beneath her eyes. Her breathing came in shallow rasps, and her lips were cracked, the corners crusted with darkened blood.

"Dear Lord," Bishop Chartrand whispered, falling to his knees beside her bed. He pressed a hand to her forehead. It burned.

A bowl of water sat beside the bed, steam rising from it faintly, and a cloth that had been damp now lay dry and limp. Her eyes fluttered briefly, barely able to focus on his face.

"Father," she croaked, her voice like crumpled parchment. "It hurts."

His heart shattered. Tears sprang to his eyes as he clasped her frail fingers. "I'm here, little dove. Hold on. I'll find help."

But he knew. Yellow fever. He had seen it sweep through towns before. Always quick. Always brutal.

He stumbled to the floor beside her bed, clutched his hands together, and bowed his head until it touched the floorboards.

"Oh God... take me instead! I have served You with all I have. Spare her. Please. I beg You, take my life and give her another! I would do anything, anything at all to save her. I would trade every sermon, every ounce of grace—just let her live."

After a few moments of fierce praying, the air changed. Heavy. Thick. Wrong.

A wind began to churn inside the room, passing from one side of the room to the other. A tinted black haze twirled to life and flashed in his eyes.

He lifted his head. Curtains flared out from the windows as if caught in a gale, though the glass panes were still sealed. The room dimmed. The lantern flickered violently.

Smoke poured in through the fireplace—black and twisting like ink dropped in water. The air grew thick. His breath caught in his throat.

Then, it appeared.

The Thing.

It materialized in the smoke like a beast from Revelation. Its form towered in the room—shadow and bone, limbs longer than they should be, its head brushing the ceiling, its edges blurred like a smear across reality. It radiated presence. Heavy. Crushing. Its voice, when it came, was not spoken aloud but pressed directly into the Bishop's mind:

"You called to Me, child of dust. I heard your cries from the deepest hollow. I have come."

The Bishop collapsed fully to the floor, trembling.

"You are—You are not the Lord."

"I am older than your books," the Thing thundered. Its voice was like a hundred church bells swung out of tune. "I am the answer to your prayer."

The Bishop dared look up. The Thing's hollow face stared at him from above the fireplace, its eyes two blazing orbs that pulsed in and out of the smoke.

"Your daughter will die by dawn's breath," it said. "Unless you make an exchange."

"Anything," The Bishop choked. "I would do anything."

"Then bring Me souls. A line of them. Bound in glass, in time, in silence."

"Souls?"

"You will build clocks. Ritual vessels. Each bound soul shall be a brick in the wall that keeps Me fed and away from your world. You will bring Me a line. The line must not break. If it breaks, your soul will descend to the Abyss."

"But—but it's wrong. That's… that's wickedness."

The Thing's roar shook the floorboards.

"You dare weigh sin when your child chokes on plague?"

The room exploded in pain. The Bishop's skin blistered under a sudden wave of heat, and Clara screamed from her bed.

"STOP!" he cried, sobbing. "Please. I will do it."

Silence fell. The Thing receded slightly.

"You will bring Me souls. Of all types. Sensitives give me more power, but I will accept all that are presented. I am hungry and in need of being fed."

The Bishop trembled, his eyes shut. "I… I know a man. Dying of dysentery. He is alone. I can start with him."

"Do so," the Thing said. "I shall restore her—for now. Her soul will be reserved. Fail Me… and she will be devoured first."

The Thing began to dissipate. The smoke peeled back into the walls, the fire dimmed, and the window shutters ceased rattling.

Clara's breath grew less ragged. Her fever broke. Her chest rose in slower, steadier rhythm.

Bishop Chartrand collapsed beside her bed.

He had sold his soul. And the price was only just beginning.

Scene 4: War's Shadow Falls

Summer 1863

Mercier Plantation, Louisiana

The winds of war had changed, and they howled low across the cane fields with the voice of reckoning.

News of President Lincoln's election spread like a spark across dry tinder, igniting fear and fury across the Southern states. The Mercier plantation, once a beacon of wealth and security in the bayous, now echoed with uncertainty. Confederate banners fluttered from rooftops in town, and whispers of rebellion stirred among the foremen and overseers. The port at Franklin became tense with patrols and rumors of Northern ships sailing upriver.

Inside the grand halls of the Mercier estate, the walls, once echoing with laughter and music, had grown heavy with silence. Tensions crept through even the richest curtains and across the finest china. Thomas Mercier stood on the upper veranda, arms crossed tightly over his waistcoat, his grizzled beard catching the warm wind. He watched the sun set over his vast empire—6,500 acres of sugarcane, cotton, and corn—but his thoughts were not of harvest.

He was furious. Adam Duncan, the Northerner boy he'd once shaken hands with and allowed under his roof, had joined the Union Army. Not just joined—but now, rumor claimed, was advancing southward with his regiment, marching straight toward Louisiana. Toward Franklin. The idea that Adam—who had broken bread at his table, who had walked his fields and courted his kin—would raise arms against those who had welcomed him burned hot in Thomas's blood.

"What kind of man," he muttered to himself, "makes war on his own people?"

His wealth, so meticulously cultivated through trade and toil, was now bound tightly to Confederate currency, and the looming Union blockade threatened to choke his entire operation. Steamships were fewer, rail shipments stalling. Northern clients had grown cold and evasive. Even the sugar mills, twin engines of prosperity at the back of the property, groaned with inactivity.

Thomas exhaled through his nose. A storm was coming.

Delilah Duncan sat in the rose parlor, the pale light of dusk falling across her lap. In her hands was a letter, the envelope stained with sweat and travel grime. It bore the mark of the Union Army.

She unfolded it, smoothing the creases with trembling fingers.

Dearest Sister,
I arrived yesterday with the 12th New York Infantry outside of
Brashear City. There is talk of movement toward Bayou Teche. If
this letter reaches you, know that I am well... and I miss you.
Sometimes at night, I still see the oaks of the plantation, hear the
waltz from the great house drifting on the wind. But that music feels
like it came from another world.
Stay safe. I fear what comes.
—Adam

Delilah pressed the letter to her chest. Her brother's words carved a chasm through her heart. She longed for him, for his laughter and clarity, and now more than ever, she felt the pull northward. War had fractured the nation—and now it reached into her soul.

"Is that from Adam?" came Eleanor's voice, soft behind her.

Delilah turned and nodded. "He's safe... for now."

Her mother crossed the room and laid a hand on her daughter's shoulder. "We shouldn't be here, Lila. This place—it's gilded, but it's not gold. And Thomas... I don't like how he and the Bishop whisper behind closed doors."

Delilah said nothing. She had seen the looks too. She had felt the weight in Daniel's glances—how he clutched her hand too tightly at the chapel, how his smile faltered when the subject of the Concord was raised.

She tucked the letter away and stood. "Come. I want to walk."

The workshop behind the main house rattled with the rhythm of hammer and file. A trio of men sweated over gears and polished brass faces, affixing delicate hands to curved glass. These clocks were unlike any others—intricate, oddly shaped, adorned with symbols from the Concord's seal.

Delilah peeked inside and watched from the doorway. Inside, Thomas spoke quietly with one of the carpenters, pointing to the concave curve in a mirrored surface, gesturing at where it needed reinforcement.

"These must never crack," Thomas said with weight.

In the farthest corner, a glass dome covered a clock unlike the rest—ornate, with deep etchings across the pendulum casing and six notches at its base, each containing a tiny shard of obsidian.

Delilah's skin prickled.

She stepped back, moving away from the echoing clang of metal and into the cooling twilight. A low hum met her ears—chanting. From beyond the chapel, she saw torchlight dancing across the stained-glass windows.

She followed the sound, staying hidden behind the hedge as she drew closer to the chapel's rear courtyard. There, under the yawning branches of moss-covered oaks, six figures in white robes formed a circle. The Bishop stood among them, his voice low and resonant.

They chanted not in Latin, but in a language that slid through the air like oil over water—harsh, guttural, broken by clicks and intonations that clawed at the edge of comprehension. At the center of their circle stood one of the clocks—its surface reflecting not their faces, but something darker.

Something moving.

Delilah's breath caught in her throat.

The wind turned warm and wet, the air thick with cane-sugar and rot. Shadows twitched where they shouldn't have. For a heartbeat, she thought she saw the shape of a man standing inside the clock's glass—his face long, pale, eyes empty.

A low voice, unspoken but thunderous, brushed her ear: *"The line must not break."*

She staggered backward and nearly tripped on a root, stifling a gasp.

The ceremony continued.

She fled, her heart pounding, her hands trembling as she reached the main path again, where lanterns swayed between iron posts. The breeze carried a soft music from the house, but it sounded far away now—distant, distorted, like a song played underwater.

Inside the safety of her room, Delilah shut the door and pressed her back to it. Adam's letter sat on her dresser, now seeming like a message from a dying world.

She didn't understand everything yet.

But she knew this: something was being bound inside those clocks. And it wasn't just time.

Chapter 12 - The Clock's Curse

Scene 1: The Trap is Set

April 13, 1863

Bayou Teche, Louisiana

The low-hanging moon cast silver bars across the misty wetlands of southern Louisiana, lending a ghostly sheen to the bayou's swollen banks. Beneath the swamp's humid breath, the ground was soft and treacherous, every step releasing the sickly perfume of rot and gunpowder. No-man's land stretched between two opposing lines of troops—Union on one side, Confederate on the other—positioned in tense silence beneath the still veil of night. The trees loomed like silent sentinels, their moss-draped limbs swaying gently, whispering secrets to the darkness.

Corporal Adam Duncan crouched low in the reeds, eyes darting over the dim terrain. He adjusted the strap on his rifle and patted the folded letter tucked into his breast pocket—the one that bore Delilah's shaky handwriting. The words had shaken him: "He beat me. Thomas knows everything. He's unraveling. Please, Adam, help me. Come for me."

His jaw clenched. His sister had endured enough. Thomas Mercier, their mother's political ally turned captor, had gone mad with desperation. With the war draining his wealth and influence, he had turned his fury inward—on Delilah.

Adam had made his decision the moment he read the letter. Under the cover of moonlight, while his regiment slumbered in tents and trenches, he crept toward the Mercier plantation. The distance was not far—barely a mile—but between him and his destination lay the marshy stretch of no-man's land. Every step forward was a gamble with death.

As he crept past the last line of Union pickets, one of the soldiers nodded at him silently. Private Sawyer, the same man who'd brought him the letter. There was understanding in his eyes—Adam wasn't deserting. He was going home.

Half-crouched, half-crawling, Adam worked his way through tall grass and between gnarled roots, his heart pounding with each movement. The moon lit his path, but it also made him visible. He paused now and then, scanning the tree line ahead for any sign of sentries.

Then he saw it.

A glimmer near a lone cypress tree, rising like a phantom from the earth. Something that didn't belong. Its polished brass casing gleamed in the moonlight—an ornate mantle clock, impossibly pristine amid the muck and debris. Adam froze, blinking. It was beautiful and grotesque, out of place, a jewel in the mouth of a corpse.

Curiosity wrestled with caution. Why would a clock be here? Who had placed it?

He crept closer, step by slow step, until he stood before it. The clock's face glowed faintly, its Roman numerals etched in gold. Its hands pointed nowhere, frozen in time. Reflections danced in the glass pane.

Adam leaned in.

Something moved.

His breath caught. Within the glass, something swirled—a shadow, a smear of darkness behind the face. And then, a gust of wind ripped through the trees, a howling force that came from nowhere.

Smoke. Black and thick, coiling like snakes around his legs. It poured from the clock, rising into the air, filling his lungs with the scent of burning oil and decay.

From the glass, the Thing emerged.

Towering, amorphous, shifting in and out of substance, its presence overwhelmed the clearing. It loomed taller than the tree, its form swathed in writhing tendrils of shadow and bone. Its voice struck like thunder, yet slithered like silk into Adam's mind:

"Behold, thou who art betrayed, for the hour hath come. Thy blood calleth to Me, and I have answered."

Adam stumbled back but could not look away. The air around him had thickened, and his limbs felt leaden.

"In this glass," the Thing intoned, its voice like scripture inverted, "thy soul shall rest—a beacon and a banquet. Devoured not in haste but savored in eternity."

The air shimmered. A thin, silvery mist began to bleed from Adam's chest, stretching toward the clock. He gasped, clutched his heart, but the mist continued to pull, siphoned as if by gravity.

"Thou wert chosen. Not by chance, but by cunning. For thy kin hath bartered thee in silence. The Concordia hath marked thee. And now—"

An explosion shattered the silence. Artillery.

A deafening crack split the air, followed by another and another. Dirt and debris rained down around them. The Thing hissed, its form flickering. But it did not retreat.

"Thou art Mine!"

A final boom, louder than the rest.

The blast struck near the tree, sending Adam flying. His body flailed through the air like a rag doll. He collided with the trunk headfirst—there was a sickening crack—and he crumpled to the earth in a heap. Blood soaked the grass beneath him.

The mist snapped back into his body, incomplete.

The Thing howled—a sound of rage and hunger unfulfilled. "NO!"

It surged back toward the clock, twisting and writhing, its form roiling with fury.

"He is MINE! You have defiled the vessel!"

The Thing's form collapsed into the clock in a vortex of smoke and wind. The clock tipped sideways at the base of the tree, landing near Adam's broken body, its face now dim.

A silence fell. Not the peaceful kind. The suffocating, pregnant silence of something gone horribly wrong.

The trap had been set.

But the line had begun—fractured, wounded, and cursed.

Scene 2: Aftermath of Horror

Dawn crept over the charred remains of the battlefield at Bayou Teche, its golden fingers brushing over shattered trees and blood-soaked earth. The silence was eerie, interrupted only by the rustle of boots through tall grass and the distant crackle of smoldering debris. Union soldiers, weary and hollow-eyed, moved carefully among the bodies, searching for the wounded and retrieving the dead.

Private Reynolds stumbled over a tangle of brush and froze. Just ahead, beneath the crooked branches of a scorched pecan tree, lay the broken body of a Union soldier—face bloodied, uniform torn, limbs twisted unnaturally. Beside him, gleaming like an artifact from another time, rested an ornate, brass-framed clock. Its face was cracked, but its intricate hands still pointed to a specific hour. Smoke-charred scrollwork etched with strange symbols bordered its frame.

"Got another one!" Reynolds called, waving to the medic team.

Corporal Hatch knelt beside the soldier and read the blood-smeared tags. "Corporal Adam Duncan. Damn shame. Looks like he tried to carry this back with him. Spoil of war?"

"Must be," Reynolds replied, glancing warily at the clock. "That thing gives me the chills. Look at the face... it's like something's... moving."

They packed Adam's body in canvas, gently laying the damaged clock at his side. It would be shipped north along with his effects, back to the family he left behind. No one noticed the faint warmth that still pulsed through the metal. No one heard the whispering inside the glass. Not yet.

Back at the plantation, Delilah sat alone in her room, her arms wrapped tightly around herself, bruises from the flogging still fresh. The pain in her ribs paled next to the ache in her heart. The news had come swiftly—a courier arrived, face drawn, with a simple message.

Adam Duncan was dead.

Killed in no man's land.

Her knees had buckled. The tears had come hot and fast.

Now she sat staring at the wall, the letter she'd written him clutched in her trembling hands. The very words she had poured out in secret, the warning she'd tried to send, had ended in tragedy. She never should have trusted the maid. Never should have trusted the hope.

A hard knock sounded at the door.

Thomas Mercier strode in without waiting for an answer. He moved like a man victorious, his boots echoing off the wooden floorboards.

Delilah turned slowly to face him, eyes swollen and red.

He held something between two fingers—the very note she had written Adam. His eyes gleamed with triumph.

"You fool," he said softly. "You foolish, sentimental girl."

Delilah's heart lurched. "Where... where did you get that?"

He waved the paper once, then tucked it into his vest pocket. "The maid delivered it just as we hoped. Right into his hands."

She blinked in confusion. "Hoped?"

Thomas's face lit with unholy satisfaction. "It worked, Delilah. Don't you understand? It worked perfectly. He took the bait."

Delilah's stomach churned. "What are you saying?"

"You were part of it," he said, stepping closer. "The deception. The trap. You wrote him that letter—out of love, out of desperation— and he came running. Straight into the noose."

She backed away. "No... no, I didn't know. I didn't—"

Thomas's voice sharpened. "Your brother was a traitor. He sided with the enemy. Fought against us. Against everything we built. We couldn't allow him to return, to become a symbol for rebellion. So we prepared the field. We placed the cursed clock under the old tree. We knew he would come."

Delilah's face went pale. "No..."

"Yes," he sneered. "And now, he's bound. His soul, caught in the glass. A feast for the Thing. You helped us without even knowing."

Her legs gave out and she sank to her knees. Her sobs were low and choked. "What have I done..."

The door creaked again, and Bishop Chartrand entered, his white robes stark against the shadowed doorway. He looked between Delilah's trembling form and Thomas's self-satisfied smirk.

"Is it done?" the Bishop asked.

Thomas nodded, his voice practically purring. "It is. Adam Duncan's soul is sealed."

The Bishop closed his eyes and exhaled through his nose. "How many does that make now?"

"Twenty-nine," Thomas replied.

Delilah gasped.

"The Thing hungers constantly," Thomas said. "But we feed it well."

The Bishop stepped forward, his eyes falling on Delilah. Guilt flickered across his face, but he did not speak. The silence was thick.

Delilah buried her face in her hands. "I loved him. He was all I had left."

Thomas turned toward the Bishop and chuckled. "She'll understand in time. We all serve a greater purpose."

But Delilah, shaking with horror and grief, knew there would be no forgiveness for what had been done. Not from Adam. Not from God. And maybe not even from herself.

Scene 3: Guilt and Ruins

The parlor once glowed with warm amber light and glistening chandeliers; now, it lay in a state of ruined stillness, choked with ash and memory. The walls bore the blackened scars of smoke, and the silk drapes hung in tattered strips, reeking of soot. Shattered porcelain crunched beneath Delilah's feet as she crossed what remained of the once-grand drawing room.

Outside the windows, the world was unrecognizable. The battle had swept through with the fury of a divine reckoning. The rolling fields that once shimmered gold with sugarcane and cotton were now trampled and scorched. Bodies, both Union and Confederate, had littered the land for days until the stench drove the remaining slaves to gather them into makeshift pyres. Too many to bury. Flames now consumed flesh and uniforms alike, a grotesque offering to a sky too weary to weep.

The livestock were gone—either slaughtered or stolen in the chaos. The gardens were flattened, trees uprooted, and fences splintered. Mud pooled in great swaths of earth where grass had once grown, and black water filled the ditches with rot and decay. Crows circled endlessly overhead, crying their carrion song.

Delilah stood at the broken hearth, her soot-smeared face turned toward the open doorway where wind whispered through the jagged ruin. She held the Covenant book to her chest—a leather-bound tome that smelled of old ink and dark rituals—and in her other hand, the Concordia medallion, still warm from its wooden box.

Eleanor sat quietly in a sunken armchair, one arm wrapped around her waist, the other pressing a kerchief to her swollen eyes. The fire had taken much from them, but grief had carved deeper wounds than flame.

"He's gone," Delilah whispered, her voice ragged from hours of sobbing. "My brother… he came back for me, and they fed him to that monster."

Eleanor's voice cracked like a dry branch. "I tried to warn you. I told you there was something unholy about this place. About Thomas. About the Bishop."

Delilah dropped to her knees in the soot, holding the medallion like a rosary. Her fingers trembled.

The Mercier family had fled in the night—first Beatrice, then Thomas and the sons. No farewells, no honor. Only silence, and the echo of carriage wheels vanishing into the distance. The church, too, had been abandoned. The Bishop had left without a word, leaving behind vestments, scrolls, and relics. The pews remained as if waiting for a flock that would never return.

And the slaves… Two-thirds were gone. The town, which once teemed with wealth and brutal efficiency, felt empty now. The slave quarters had been torched during the fighting. Smoldering remains stood where a village once breathed with fragile joy. The elders who remained gathered what they could, treating the wounded and burying what few they had time for.

Eleanor's gaze drifted to the broken windows. "The army's coming. They'll take what's left. They're seizing everything, including us."

Delilah closed her eyes. She saw Adam's face again—calm, determined, full of love. He had crossed no man's land for her, only to meet betrayal. Her tears felt like acid.

"This book," she murmured, "it speaks of the Line. A sacred lineage, cursed and bound to glass. The Thing—the one in the clock—feeds from the souls trapped in that line. They… they're planning more."

Eleanor turned sharply. "What do you mean more?"

Delilah held up the medallion. "Each medallion is a seal. Each seal represents a clock, and each clock—"

"A prison."

Delilah nodded.

The front door, warped and cracked, creaked open with the rising wind. Papers fluttered in the ruins of the hall, and the scent of death rose like steam from the earth. But beneath the despair, something else took root.

Resolve.

Delilah stood, her figure silhouetted against the fractured light.

"We cannot let this continue," she said. "This—this line they've created. This Concord. It is evil masked as piety."

Eleanor stood with her. "What do you plan to do?"

"Warn the future," Delilah said simply. "Write everything. Every horror. Every lie. They want to erase the past behind velvet drapes and gilded clocks—but I'll carve the truth in iron and ink."

Together they walked through the devastated hallway, past broken mirrors and blood-stained rugs, to what remained of the study. There, Delilah laid the Covenant book open on a cleared table and began to write. Her pen scratched out names, dates, rituals. Her tears fell onto the page, smearing ink. But she did not stop.

The house groaned in the wind, a skeleton of what once was. But somewhere in the ruin, a voice stirred—not the Thing's, but the spirit of a brother betrayed, a girl reborn through pain, and the courage to shatter the line.

And far in the distance, thunder rumbled over the blackened fields, but Delilah did not flinch.

She would warn them.

She would tell the truth.

Even if it damned her.

Scene 4: Vanishing Legacy

The night had fallen with the weight of sorrow upon the ruins of the Mercier estate. The parlor—once grand and brimming with laughter, polished silver, and the perfume of fine guests—was now reduced to broken timber and faded opulence. Moonlight filtered through shattered windows, casting jagged shadows across the dusty floor. The wallpaper hung in long, tattered strips. Wind moaned softly through the eaves, whispering laments through splintered shutters.

Delilah sat alone before the hearth, her shoulders hunched, a shawl drawn tightly over her trembling form. The fire had long since died, leaving only cold ashes and the faint scent of soot and decay. Her skin, pale with illness and grief, seemed to disappear into the gloom. Her once-lustrous hair had dulled, tangled from nights of restless sleep and days of silence.

Above the fireplace hung a tarnished mirror, its silver backing spotted with age. For days now, she had avoided it. The way it caught reflections felt wrong—as if it remembered too much. Tonight, though, something compelled her to look.

She lifted her gaze.

At first, she saw only herself—thin, ghost-like, hollow-eyed. But then the shadows in the glass shifted. And there he was.

Adam.

His face, bruised and gray, hovered in the silver surface. His eyes were sunken, his cheeks gaunt. His uniform was torn and bloodstained, his once-proud posture slumped with exhaustion and pain. A hollow expression lingered on his face, as though he hadn't slept for an eternity. Behind him, the shimmer of a dark corridor stretched into blackness.

Delilah clutched her chest.

"Adam…" she whispered, tears springing anew. "I'm so sorry."

Her brother's ghostly form stared back, unmoving, yet somehow aware. He didn't speak. He didn't need to. His eyes held everything—betrayal, confusion, sorrow. And worst of all, resignation. He was no longer fighting. He was enduring.

Then something else appeared.

A slithering darkness gathered in the mirror's corner, thick as tar. It loomed just beyond Adam's shoulder. The Thing.

Its form was never fully visible—just hints of shapes, jagged and wrong. A clawed hand curled along the edge of the reflection. Its

252

presence radiated cold fury. Its hunger pulsed from the glass, washing over Delilah like a tide of ice.

"No…" she murmured, backing away. "Leave him alone!"

Adam's image flickered, twisted, and was gone.

The mirror showed only the dying firelight and her pale, stricken face.

Delilah collapsed to her knees.

Her sobs echoed through the empty room, carried by the wind through the ruins of the estate. She rocked forward, her fingers clawing into the floorboards. Her breath came in gasps.

"I led him to it. I did this," she whispered to the silence. "I let them use me… and he paid the price."

She had tried to hold on—tried to make sense of what had happened—but her soul was worn to tatters. In the weeks since Adam's death, since Thomas and the Bishop had fled with their secrets and their bloodstained rituals, she had withered. Her health declined with the seasons, but the rot inside her came not from sickness—it was guilt that poisoned her.

In her final days, Delilah refused food. She spoke only in murmurs. She wandered the wreckage like a ghost, touching broken walls, running her fingers along splintered pews in the desecrated chapel. She wore Adam's old coat and sat each night before the mirror, waiting.

Waiting for the Thing.

Waiting for the chance to beg.

It never returned.

Delilah Duncan died one bitter evening, curled in a chair in the parlor beneath that mirror, her hand resting on a half-burned journal and the brass medallion bearing the Seal of Concordia. Her eyes were open, as if still watching for Adam.

Eleanor found her daughter's body and wept for the last time. Then, with no one left to protect, she went about gathering everything.

She moved through the ruins with silent resolve, wrapping the Concordia medallion in cloth and placing it into a small wooden box. The journals—Delilah's, Thomas's, even scraps from the Bishop's sermons—were bundled into crates. She scoured the chapel, stripping it of books, relics, communion sets. From the broken parlor she took the mirror, covering it with heavy canvas and securing it with twine.

In total, it filled five crates—carefully packed artifacts, ledgers, letters, and spiritual records. All of it, proof of what had transpired in that place.

The crates were labeled with care and loaded onto a Duncan Company steamboat bound for New York. Eleanor sent them to Schenectady, where the Duncan family had built its foundation decades before. There, in the quiet, dry basements beneath St. Helen's Church, the documents would be preserved.

In the years that followed, those archives would be forgotten by most. Their contents too obscure, too disturbing, too ancient. But not by everyone.

Not by those who heard the whispers in mirrors.

Not by those who felt their blood stir when the glass hummed.

In the dim light of St. Helen's underground vault, three figures stood around an old wooden table. Maria, Abigail, and Father Allen stared down at a pile of crumbling documents and tarnished artifacts. A blackened medallion glinted in the lantern glow.

"Louisiana," Abigail whispered, almost reverently.

The air was heavy with meaning.

The past had reached out through flame, through blood, through time.

And the future had just begun to listen.

Chapter 13 - Behind the Glass

Scene 1: Prison of Reflections

The silence was complete—so absolute that it pulsed like a living thing. Then came breath. Ragged, shallow. Joseph's.

He opened his eyes into darkness. Not a darkness of shadows, but one of gleaming surfaces—glass stretching in all directions, floor to ceiling, horizon to nowhere. It was a world turned inside out. A realm of mirrors, where every inch reflected back a distorted echo of reality.

The air was cold, sharp, and heavy with the reek of sulfur—bitter and metallic, like burnt matches soaked in blood. It threaded through his lungs like poison, clinging to his skin, settling into his bones. The temperature prickled against his arms as though unseen hands were brushing along his flesh.

He rose slowly. The ground beneath him was solid but strange—slick like polished obsidian, and yet soft enough that each step gave slightly, like something beneath was shifting to accommodate his weight. His own reflection stared back at him in every direction, fractured by subtle cracks in the surface. His face—exhausted, drawn, eyes hollow—multiplied across the walls in sickening symmetry.

He didn't know how long he'd been here. Time didn't flow in the In Between—it coiled, spiraled, bled. Each moment seemed endless, and yet the next came too fast. A second could stretch into hours, and a thought could last a lifetime.

At first, he was alone.

Then came the whispers.

They slithered along the edges of the glass, just out of range of understanding. Whispers of regret, of bargains struck, of pain never named. The voices carried the weight of thousands—souls bound to this place by forgotten sins and unfinished stories. Some whispered in agony. Others giggled in madness. But all of them wanted.

Joseph moved forward, compelled by something unseen. His footsteps echoed like a war drum, each one triggering faint ripples in the mirrored ground. The maze revealed itself slowly, cruelly—a winding, living thing that shifted with every turn. Some paths closed behind him, while others stretched endlessly forward, beckoning and breathing like the ribs of a beast.

He clung to memory—Maria's voice, the curve of her smile, Jacob's laughter, Noah's sleepy breathing at night. Those small sounds anchored him. Without them, the place would unravel him.

A shadow moved across a wall ahead. Then another. A flicker to the side.

Then—a voice.

"You shouldn't have come here."

Joseph stopped.

The voice wasn't human. It was layered—many mouths speaking in perfect unison, each with a different tone, a different age, a different rage. The sound hit his chest like a blow, vibrating the air around him.

He turned toward it. At first, he saw nothing. Then, slowly, one of the glass panels shifted. The reflection changed. It wasn't his own.

A face emerged. Pale. Featureless. Eyes like deep wells of starlight—cold and endless. It hovered just beyond the veil, its form difficult to focus on. A hum began—low, tremoring, just beneath hearing.

"You draw others near," it said. "They saw you in dreams. They came close."

Joseph's mouth was dry, his lips numb. "Who are you?" he managed.

The face didn't blink. It didn't move. But its presence surged like pressure behind his eyes.

"You are not theirs yet. But you are not yours either. They reach through the veil for you. And that... threatens me."

The temperature dropped. Frost crystallized in the corners of the mirror. The whispering stopped, and the silence that followed was worse. It pressed on him like water in the deep sea—crushing, suffocating.

Joseph stumbled back a step, his breath fogging before him. Behind him, the corridor began to twist. The walls pulsed with faint, terrible light.

The figure in the mirror tilted its head. "You are the tether. The balance. And if you are taken from me... I will take them."

Joseph's heart pounded. He could barely speak, but he didn't have to.

The glass behind him fractured.

Light shattered like lightning through the mirrored plane—and from the cracks rose a shape he recognized at once. Tall, grinning, coiled in darkness like a serpent in smoke.

The Thing.

It came slowly, savoring the moment. Its smile curled like a sickle, and its eyes—pits of black fire—locked onto Joseph.

Its face was nearly pressed to his. A breath like rot and sulfur spilled from its maw. Joseph's vision blurred. The mirrored corridor behind The Thing turned darker—thicker shadows rolling through the glass like a storm.

"Found you," it hissed.

Then—

Everything went white.

The sound of glass shattering, a scream (his own?), and then—silence again.

He was alone.

But the silence was different now. It watched him. Waited.

He took another step forward, his body trembling.

The whisper returned—faint, a memory on the edge of waking.

A prison with no doors.

No mercy.

And fading hope.

Scene 2: The Lost and the Listening

A dim pulse of silver-blue light glowed along the base of the mirrored walls as Joseph stumbled forward, trying to orient himself. The encounter with the Thing had left him disoriented—shaken to his core.

But something deeper had shifted too. The maze had grown quieter. Not silent, but... listening.

He stopped to breathe. The sulfur still lingered, but it was fainter now, masked beneath a different scent—old leather, gunpowder, and the faintest whisper of honeysuckle. Strange memories curled behind the smell, like smoke from a forgotten fire.

"Joseph," a voice called.

He froze.

It wasn't Maria. It wasn't the Thing. It was… familiar in a different way. Gravelly. Cautious. Touched with pain.

Joseph turned.

From a narrowing hallway of curved glass stepped a man in a weathered duster coat, a black Stetson hat hanging low over his brow. A faded red bandana clung loosely to his neck, and his boots echoed against the floor like a funeral march. His shirt was stained with time, the vest buttoned crooked as if thrown on in haste. His eyes, though dulled by death, held a righteous fire, and his ghostly skin shimmered like moonlight on gunmetal.

"Gregory," Joseph breathed.

The cowboy spirit gave a tired nod. "Took me some time to find you again. This place… it shifts. It hides what it wants."

"You're the one who helped Jacob."

Gregory gave a faint smile, one corner of his mouth twitching with restrained emotion. "Boy's got a heart like a lantern. Bright. Brave. But he don't belong here."

Joseph stepped closer, desperation swelling in his chest. "Why are you here, Gregory? Why follow me?"

The cowboy's face twisted, and he removed his hat, pressing it against his chest. "Because you listened, Joseph. Back in Tombstone. You heard me when no one else would. I screamed from the rafters, from the shadows, from every cursed plank of that place. But no one ever listened."

He looked up, emotion choking his voice. "They strung me up for something I didn't do. I begged for mercy, swore on my mother's grave—but the noose didn't care. The crowd didn't care. My name—my honor—it was all I had left. And it was taken from me."

Joseph's throat burned. "I remember. You said it wasn't you. I believed you."

Gregory's jaw trembled. "And you told others. You gave me back something I thought I lost forever—my name. My truth. That act… it's why I'm still here. Why I followed the echoes of your soul into this cursed place."

Joseph looked around at the glimmering corridors. "What is this place, really?"

Gregory exhaled. "The In Between. Neither Heaven nor Hell. Not the Other Side, not quite. A prison made of memories and reflection. Here, sorrow is stitched into the very air."

"And the Thing?"

"A scavenger," Gregory said, voice low. "Feeds on pain. But he ain't the only one. There's another—older, colder. The Echo. That one don't shout or tear. It whispers. And its whisper hollows you out."

Joseph stepped forward, nearly pleading. "Can I get out of here? Can I make it back?"

Gregory's mouth tightened. "Maybe. But this place—it don't let go easy. You're tied to it now, and it's tied to you. You stepped into its web. It knows your scent. Your memories. It'll use your guilt like a knife."

"I have to get back," Joseph said, voice cracking. "Maria— she saw me. She knows I'm alive. She's coming for me."

Gregory nodded slowly. "She's strong. Fierce. But this place... it remembers her too. If she enters, she'll be tested. Worse than you."

A silence fell between them. Then Joseph said, "Gregory… if I don't make it out, promise me you'll help her. Help Jacob. Keep them safe."

Gregory looked haunted. "If I could reach across the veil and drag them out myself, I would. But I'll do all I can. That's my bond. You gave me justice. I owe you more than I can repay."

A shiver passed through the corridor. Shadows twisted at the edge of the glass. The sulfur returned, faint but sharper this time.

Gregory turned his head, listening. "It's coming back. The Thing. It knows we're speaking."

Joseph's panic surged. "Then I need to go. I need to find a way forward."

Gregory pointed to a corridor slick with frost. "That way. Toward the oldest memories. Toward the place where the glass first broke."

Joseph hesitated. "Will I see you again?"

Gregory replaced his hat and turned. "Only if I find you before it does."

He faded into a swirl of white mist—the same spectral glow Jacob had seen before. The scent of old leather lingered.

Joseph stood alone in the shimmering hall, breath unsteady. Then, far ahead, he heard it—Maria's voice.

Calling his name.

He took a step toward it, and the mirrors began to whisper.

Scene 3: The Weight and the In Between

The corridors of the In Between twisted with unnatural angles, a fractured geometry that defied logic and reason. Joseph pressed forward through the mist, his breath visible in the air—chilled, not by cold, but by despair. Every step echoed hollowly on mirrored floors, the sound folding in on itself, as though the realm swallowed even the idea of motion.

He passed shadowy alcoves, each housing tormented figures. Faces twisted by grief, regret, and sorrow emerged from the glass walls—trapped in moments of their own unending loss. Their eyes followed him. Some reached out with spectral hands, barely visible, pressing fingers and palms against the mirror's inner surface. Not to harm, but to beg.

"Are you him?" one whispered.

"The one who freed the soldier?" another rasped, voice like cracking porcelain.

"I saw the fire... I saw the glass break..." a third murmured, drifting close.

Joseph stopped. He turned and looked around.

Souls were gathering—at first in silence, then in chorus. Some stood still, simply watching. Others moved toward him, expressions filled with desperate hope or envious pain. One clutched his face and wept openly. Another kept muttering "Not again, not again," as though he relived his death on a loop.

They pressed closer—not hostile, but overwhelming. Joseph could feel their stories bleeding into his mind. Visions of battlefield deaths, of betrayals, of abandoned children, of suicides and sins unforgiven. Their torment became a crushing weight across his chest, settling into his bones. His knees buckled.

He gritted his teeth. "Stop…" he gasped.

The In Between fed on pain. It knew how to turn love into a weapon, hope into a chain. And Joseph's soul, tethered by grief, guilt, and purpose, began to sink beneath the tide of agony pressing in on all sides.

He saw Maria's face in his mind—then Jacob's. Then Noah's tiny hand holding his. His family. The flickering warmth of life.

"I have to get back," he whispered, trembling.

The crowd of souls quieted, as if waiting. Joseph inhaled slowly, drawing from a well deep within himself. He planted his feet and straightened his spine. A shimmer of light pulsed beneath his skin. The mirror beneath his feet cracked faintly.

And then the wind came.

At first, it stirred like a sigh. Then it built—a swirling, screaming vortex that tore through the corridor. Souls scattered, weeping, vanishing into the mist.

The Thing was coming.

Joseph backed away as the wind howled louder, the mirror walls vibrating with a sickening hum. Shards of shadow peeled from the ceiling, coalescing into tendrils of night.

He turned toward the widening crack in the distance—a rent in the mirrored floor, glowing faintly with something brighter. Hope.

But behind him, the Thing surged forward.

A shape of pitch, of hunger. Its eyes glowed like coals doused in sorrow. It moved not with feet, but by unfolding itself through the mirror's surface. Its roar wasn't sound—it was the memory of every cry Joseph had ever heard in nightmares.

And just before it reached him—

Scene 4: The Echo

The Thing didn't slither toward Joseph Duncan this time—it slammed into existence like a storm, riding a wind that howled down the mirrored corridor. The gust screamed around him, bending reflections inward, shattering illusions as it carved a furious path of malice. Shadows surged in every direction, stretching and contorting like writhing bodies clawing to escape.

Joseph braced himself, arms thrown up against the wind, the air thick with sulfur and ash. The Thing's presence was unmistakable—rage without shape, hunger without voice. It had no eyes but saw everything. It didn't speak but flooded his mind with pain. It was a tempest made flesh, and it had found him again.

But this time, something was different.

A coldness, deeper and more complete than anything Joseph had ever felt, swept through the corridor like a dying breath from the earth itself. The Thing froze. The air fell still.

A new presence arrived—not with noise, but with silence so total that Joseph's heartbeat felt like an offense against it.

The Thing recoiled. Its shapeless body peeled backward like smoke retreating from flame, cringing into itself.

Then he felt it.

The floor beneath Joseph's feet cracked with pressure as a towering weight filled the mirrored realm. The reflections stopped. The air became heavier. The glass walls moaned. And then the shadows parted—not like curtains, but as if driven back by force.

The Echo entered.

It did not walk. It did not glide. It was simply there—tall and draped in rags that bled shadow, eyes like obsidian mirrors, hands skeletal and impossibly long. It radiated solemnity and fury, malevolence and restraint. A god not of light nor flame—but of memory, pain, and cold dominion.

It smelled of rot and stone and the damp air of graves long closed.

"You," it said.

The voice was not sound. It was impact. It landed in Joseph's mind like a hammer, vibrating through his bones. It came from nowhere and everywhere. It tasted of old blood and mourning. And it knew his name.

"Joseph Duncan."

The Thing shuddered.

The Echo's head tilted with reverence twisted by disgust. "You burn brighter than most. But you burn all the same. And every flame... belongs to me."

Joseph dropped to one knee, unable to breathe under its weight. The presence crushed him, not with brute force—but with truth. This was not some monster crawling through nightmares. This was the builder of nightmares. The keeper of all regret. The creator of the In Between.

"You freed one," the Echo said, its voice sharp now, slicing through thought like glass. "You disturbed the stillness. That soul was mine. A broken relic, yes—but necessary. He kept the line."

Behind Joseph, the Thing whimpered like a beast and slithered farther into the shadows.

"You dare interfere," the Echo growled. "You awaken others. Their prayers grow bold. Their hope... loud. All because of you."

It leaned close, eyes black and bottomless. "This is my domain. My expanse. Built not from stars—but sorrow. Fed not by time—but the tide of souls. The more that cross, the larger I become. I stretch beyond your comprehension. Growing. Evolving. Expanding—as your kind clings to shattered hope."

Joseph's lips trembled. His throat burned to speak, but no words formed.

"You are nothing," the Echo hissed. "A blink of resistance in an ocean of surrender. I do not fear you—I consume you. And I will break you down. Piece by piece. Regret by regret."

The Thing shrieked—a warped, bitter sound of submission.

The Echo turned toward it, disgust carved into its face. "You grow too fast, servant. You hunger too wide. Do not forget... you are bound to me."

Then it turned back to Joseph. "They will come for you. The woman. The child. The priest and the witch. They will bring light here. They will carry it through shattered glass. And when they do... I will extinguish them first."

The wind rose again, not from The Thing—but from the Echo's cloak itself, which rippled with every shattered cry ever uttered in the In Between.

Joseph screamed as the air became razors.

And then—

Darkness.

Chapter 14 - The Echo Stirs

Scene 1: Hunger in the Glass

The In Between groaned with a terrible, low vibration—an undercurrent of agony that stretched through the mirrored corridors like the hum of a distant funeral bell. The shadows that dwelled in its fractured halls had grown longer, darker, and more erratic, slithering along the broken surfaces like tendrils of oil. Something was changing. Something terrible.

The Thing prowled through its labyrinth of broken reflections, its presence dragging a foul wind in its wake. Every step it took left behind a stain of rot and despair. The enslaved spirits shrank from it, trembling in their prisons of glass and ash. Many had long since stopped speaking, their voices hoarse from unanswered cries. Others wept silently, their eyes dull and their forms dimmed to barely a shimmer.

They had been drained—not killed, but emptied.

The Thing did not merely torment—it devoured.

With each soul it ensnared, it fed. Not with teeth, but with tendrils of hunger that pierced into their memories, drawing out strength and warmth, laughter and love, until there was nothing left but fragments and fog. It consumed what made them—them, leaving husks suspended in agony.

And then it moved on.

"More," it hissed, slinking through a crumbling hall of mirrors. "More. More. I need more."

Its voice was a grating wind, gnawing at the edges of reality.

The Echo's command still lingered in the stale air, but the Thing no longer bowed as easily. It trembled at the presence of its master, yes—but a new desire had begun to burn within it. A defiant ember. The Thing wanted more than to serve.

It wanted to rule.

It had tasted what the Echo possessed—the dominion, the authority, the endless expanse. It had seen the way the In Between grew, swallowing time and space alike, its hunger matched only by its cold detachment. But the Echo did not care for the souls it kept. It wasted them. It preserved too much. The Thing saw another path.

Why preserve what could be devoured?

It knew the Echo feared Joseph Duncan's light. Feared the ripple of hope. Feared the breach of glass that had weakened its hold. But the Thing... the Thing thrived in that breach. It knew how to twist light. How to lie. How to mimic. It knew how to deceive a soul into walking willingly into its grasp.

And it would do so again.

In a forgotten chamber, four spirits knelt in anguish. The Thing stalked among them, dragging the tip of its clawed limb along the floor. Sparks danced where it touched, lighting the broken reflections with fleeting fire.

"Where is your faith now?" it whispered.

One spirit, faint and flickering like a dying candle, raised her head. Her eyes glistened with tears. "Please... I remember the sun..."

The Thing wrapped her essence in a claw of smoke and drew her in. Her scream echoed across the corridors before vanishing. The Thing pulsed with a sudden burst of energy—richer, sharper, alive. It absorbed every shred of who she was—her childhood laughter, her first kiss, the moment she held her newborn son—ripped away and consumed without mercy.

What remained was a sliver of gray mist, trembling and weak. It looked up at the Thing, empty, devoid of self.

"You are spent," it growled. "Useless."

And with a careless flick of its limb, it cast her to the floor, where her essence shattered like glass into dust.

The other spirits screamed and scattered, but there was nowhere to run.

The Thing inhaled deeply, the power still warm in its core. "I will replace her," it snarled to the walls. "With ten more. Ten who fight, ten who burn, ten who beg. Their screams will sweeten the air."

It turned to the others. "Run. Hide. It won't matter. I will have you all. And when you are spent—" it paused, relishing the words "—I will find more."

Above, the reflections trembled. The glass bent inward. The Thing turned, sensing it—its master's gaze upon it.

The Echo was watching.

The Thing lowered its frame, a twisted show of submission. But it did not stay bowed. Instead, it rose slowly, defiantly. A growl twisted up from its chest. Soon, it thought. Soon, I will no longer need to kneel.

It turned its gaze toward the next soul it would hunt, the shadows dragging behind it like a crown.

And the In Between groaned again.

Scene 2: Tremors in the Void

The In Between pulsed in silence—a vast, endless stretch of silvery glass and whispering shadows that undulated like breath. Time here had no rhythm. No forward march. Only the echo of suffering, layered one cry atop another until it became part of the air itself. And within that air, the presence of the Echo moved with the grace and terror of an ancient god.

The Echo had ruled the In Between for a time no soul could comprehend. It had watched entire civilizations rise and fall from behind the glass of every mirror. It was old—older than the first prayers whispered in firelight, older than the concept of pain itself. Its form shifted between towering shadows and fractured reflections, never fully taking shape, as if the realm itself resisted seeing its true face.

It hovered now over the obsidian pool at the center of the Hollow Bastion, its inner sanctum. The pool's mirrored surface shimmered with scenes from the Other Side—moments stolen, glimpses of lives ripe with pain and potential. But the images stuttered. Flickered. And in the deepest corner of its being, the Echo felt it: the balance tipping.

Power siphoned too quickly.

Energy collapsing inward.

A subtle drain from the edges of the In Between.

The source was not immediately visible. The Echo did not rage—rage was for lesser entities, like the Thing. No, the Echo observed. It calculated. With the patience of an immortal being, it examined the shifting tides of its domain. Concentrated flares of depletion bloomed in places that should have remained stable. The energy distribution across the mirrored corridors faltered. A tremor in the expansion. And the Echo knew—it had seen this pattern once before, long ago, when a soul with unusual resonance had disrupted the cycle.

Joseph Duncan.

The name was nothing. The soul was everything. He had cracked the line. Not by power alone—but through love, through sacrifice. The In Between had underestimated the strength of such a soul. And now, it might again.

Worse still, there was the crack in the glass—a rupture initiated by the woman, Maria. That fissure, though small, had reverberated across the foundation of the In Between like a fracture in stone. And the Thing had felt it too.

The Echo turned its attention toward its servant.

The Thing, coiled in the Chasm of Mourning, was feeding again.

It gripped a weakened soul—a flickering echo of a man who had once been a healer. The Thing drained him violently, ripping emotional energy from memory and marrow alike. The soul's screams were a melody of despair, echoing through the mirrored vaults. And when the last shred of vitality fled, the Thing discarded the hollow wisp like ash, hissing with impatience.

"More," it snarled, its voice a rasp of broken glass. "Ten more to replace the one. Twenty, if I must. I will feed, even if it cracks the sky."

The Echo said nothing. Not yet.

It moved through the halls, its presence a shiver in the very glass of the walls. It saw its jailers—hulking shades that kept the enslaved penned in place. It passed scavengers—feral, mindless remnants that roamed the outer zones, snatching at weakened souls who strayed too far. It observed the flow of energy, the ripple of torment, the cycle of agony that powered the realm.

This was its world. Built piece by piece, soul by soul. As the number of trapped echoes increased, so too did its dominion stretch outward. The In Between was not static—it was expanding, like the universe itself. But expansion came with cost. Resources were finite. Only so many viable souls walked the Other Side. And if the feeding continued at this pace, if the Thing's hunger remained unchecked, the In Between risked collapse.

The Echo would not allow that.

Still, it revealed no displeasure. Not yet. It needed the Thing. The others feared the Thing—its rage, its cunning. But the Echo... managed it.

To reprimand it now would sow discord. And the In Between needed unity.

So instead, the Echo drifted back to the heart of the Hollow Bastion and sent its thoughts across the realm, commanding the veil-watchers to keep their focus on the crack in the glass. The source of imbalance.

Joseph Duncan.

The soul with potential to fracture the very nature of the Echo's empire.

But potential was not enough.

The Echo would wait. Watch. Calculate.

And when the time came, it would ensure that every light behind every mirror... dimmed.

Scene 3: Whisper Between Worlds

Jacob lay on his bed, staring up at the ceiling as evening settled around the apartment. Noah was in the living room with Mrs. Garza, who had offered to keep an eye on them while Maria and Abigail traveled to Schenectady. The faint aroma of Mrs. Garza's cooking drifted through the doorway—spices and garlic that reminded him of simpler times, when his mother's laughter had been easy and his father had still been with them.

He sighed, turning his attention to the mirror on the dresser across the room. It was ordinary at first glance, framed in worn oak, the glass surface slightly cloudy with age. But Jacob knew better. He had learned that mirrors were not merely surfaces that reflected—they were gateways. His heart picked up speed slightly as he waited, expectant.

A gentle ripple shimmered across the glass. Jacob sat up, anticipation quickening his breath.

"Gregory?" he whispered.

The surface trembled again, and the familiar outline of Gregory appeared, solidifying as if stepping through a thin curtain of water. He wore his usual rugged attire—a weathered cowboy hat, denim jacket, and scuffed boots—as though he'd just stepped out from a cattle drive rather than from another dimension.

"Howdy, Jacob," Gregory said, his voice carrying that familiar warmth tinged with solemnity.

Jacob smiled weakly, relieved yet anxious. "Hey, Gregory. Is it about Dad?"

Gregory's expression softened into something more serious, lines deepening across his brow. He removed his hat, holding it carefully in front of him.

"Yeah, son, it sure is." Gregory hesitated, seeming to weigh his words carefully. "Joseph's havin' a mighty rough go of it. That Thing has got its hooks in deep. It's drainin' him somethin' fierce, feedin' on him constantly. If he's to be rescued, it's gotta happen soon."

Jacob's chest tightened painfully. "Is he... okay? I mean, is he still fighting?"

Gregory nodded, a sad smile tugging at his lips. "Your daddy's tougher than old boot leather. But even the strongest man can't hold out forever when somethin' like the Thing gets greedy. It's been feedin' excessively, takin' advantage of Joseph's strength. Trouble is, all that gluttony ain't gone unnoticed. The Echo has seen what's happenin', seen the imbalance Joseph's presence has caused in the In Between."

"The Echo?" Jacob asked softly, the name making him shiver. "Is it angry?"

Gregory looked grim. "Hard to say, Jacob. The Echo ain't much for showin' its cards, but it sees all. Right now, it's just watchin', measurin' things up. There ain't no tellin' how long it'll sit patient before it decides to set things right. And if it does... well, that's somethin' I ain't too keen on findin' out."

Jacob swallowed hard. "Is Dad causing the imbalance? Is it his fault?"

"Nah, son," Gregory reassured quickly. "Joseph didn't choose this. But powerful souls like your daddy's can tip scales real easy. The Echo's job is keepin' the In Between balanced, and right now, things are teeterin'."

A heavy silence settled between them, broken only by the soft clinking of pots from the kitchen and Mrs. Garza's quiet humming.

Gregory lifted his head slightly, sniffing the air. A wistful expression crossed his face. "Smells mighty fine out there. Takes me back. Reminds me of Sunday supper after a long day on the ranch. My momma used to make the best chili this side of the Pecos."

Jacob smiled faintly, momentarily comforted by Gregory's nostalgia. "Mrs. Garza cooks really well. Mom says she's like family."

Gregory nodded appreciatively. "Well, family's what matters most, Jacob. That's what your daddy's holdin' onto right now. That's what you gotta hold onto as well. You and your little brother stay close, understand?"

"I will," Jacob promised. "Gregory, can you watch over him? Can you help Dad in there?"

Gregory's eyes softened, regret clear in their depths. "I can watch over him, son, and I'll do what I can. But my reach ain't unlimited. The Thing is strong, and the Echo, well… it don't let nothin' go unnoticed. But I promise, Jacob, I'll keep an eye on your daddy best I can."

Jacob took a deep breath, nodding. "Thank you."

Gregory placed his hat back on his head, tilting it slightly in a comforting gesture. "Now, you try not to worry too much. Keep your head up, your heart strong, and let Mrs. Garza's cookin' warm your belly and soul. And I'll be back as soon as there's news."

"Okay," Jacob whispered, feeling a bit stronger. "Goodbye, Gregory."

Gregory smiled warmly, his form beginning to fade back into the mirror. "Goodbye, son. You take care now."

The mirror rippled gently one last time before settling back into an ordinary reflection. Jacob sat in silence, comforted by Gregory's presence but unsettled by his words. He could hear Mrs. Garza calling gently from the kitchen, asking if the boys were ready for dinner.

Jacob rose slowly, taking a deep, steadying breath before leaving his room. As he walked toward the inviting aromas and warmth of the kitchen, he couldn't help but glance back at the mirror one final time.

And wondered just how much longer it would hold.

Chapter 15 - Discovery and Reckoning

Scene 1: Revelation at St. Helen's

The underground archives beneath St. Helen's Church were silent, lit dimly by lanterns whose soft, flickering glow cast elongated, shifting shadows onto the old stone walls. The air was thick with the scent of ancient parchment and mildew, and the quiet rustle of pages being turned was the only sound punctuating the oppressive stillness.

Maria, Abigail, and Father Allen stood around a heavy wooden table, its surface cluttered with journals, worn documents, faded photographs, and ornate artifacts that seemed to hold whispers of the past. They had been standing there for hours, piecing together fragments of a story that had been long buried, hidden away for generations. The revelations, each more harrowing than the last, had left them shaken, their faces pale and drawn under the wavering light.

Maria's eyes rested on the old photograph of Delilah Mercier, her delicate features and distant gaze frozen in time, a haunting echo of despair. The accounts of her suffering, betrayal, and tragic role in Adam's fate were vividly detailed within the journals spread out before them. The events had unfolded in their minds like a ghostly theater—dark rituals, corrupted intentions, and the sinister trap that had ultimately consumed Adam's soul, binding him to the cursed clock.

Father Allen exhaled heavily, pressing his palms against the table as though to steady himself. "All these years… the stories were here, waiting to be uncovered. How could they have remained hidden for so long?"

Abigail's fingers traced lightly over the brittle pages of an old leather-bound ritual book. Her eyes were wide, filled with a mixture of awe and fear, as she carefully deciphered the intricate handwritten notes. "It says here that the binding ritual they used to trap Adam's soul is irreversible except by another ritual, a counter-ritual. But…" Her voice trailed off as her finger paused beneath a line written in a dark, faded script.

Maria moved closer, her breath catching slightly. "What is it, Abigail?"

"Listen to this," Abigail continued, her voice barely above a whisper. "'What is done may only be undone where it was first wrought. The soul, tethered and tormented, must be freed at the source of its binding.'" She looked up, her eyes heavy with dread. "Wherever this was done, that's where it must be undone."

A silence settled over the room, each lost in thought. Maria's mind raced, envisioning the decaying plantation house, the grandeur reduced to ruin, the fields that had once been lush now barren and haunted by the past. She felt a chill ripple through her, as if the archives had suddenly grown colder, their secrets exhaling the icy breath of old suffering.

Father Allen's voice broke the silence, somber yet firm. "This explains much. The manifestations, the disturbances—everything points to the fact that Adam's spirit, and now Joseph's, have become focal points for the Thing. It feeds from their torment, grows stronger with their pain. If Joseph is to be freed, the line must be broken. Completely."

"But at what cost?" Maria's voice trembled slightly, betraying the fear she had fought to keep hidden. "If the ritual fails, or if we misstep…"

"We won't fail," Abigail interjected, her tone quiet yet resolute. She looked at Maria with determination in her eyes, but beneath her confidence lay a flicker of uncertainty. "The instructions are clear. We know what must be done, and now we have the means."

The weight of their discovery seemed to press in on them, the dimness of the archives amplifying their apprehension. The lantern flames wavered slightly, as though disturbed by an unseen breath, sending shadows dancing wildly across the walls. Maria felt a shiver move through her, cold and deep, settling into her bones.

Father Allen picked up Delilah's photograph once more, his expression grave. "Delilah's regret was profound, her life ended in sorrow and shame because of her unwitting complicity. She left us these records hoping one day someone would come along and right the wrongs that haunted her. Perhaps her spirit still lingers, guiding us even now."

Maria considered the priest's words carefully. She had felt the pull of Delilah's anguish, had sensed her presence within the layers of text and faded ink, reaching out from the past with urgency, guiding their hand in this discovery.

Abigail's gaze shifted nervously around the dim room, her brow furrowing. "The Thing won't let us do this without a fight. It knows we're close. It can sense our intentions."

Father Allen nodded slowly, his eyes narrowing with the resolve of a man facing a storm he knew he must weather. "Then we prepare. Spiritually, mentally. This battle will be unlike anything we've faced before. The Thing will try to use our fears against us, to break our resolve. We must remain strong."

The air around them thickened further, as though the archives themselves held their breath, listening intently. A cold draft whispered through the underground chamber, ruffling pages and flickering the lantern flames, casting deeper shadows that crept along the edges of their awareness.

Maria felt a presence behind her, unseen yet unmistakably there, and turned sharply—only darkness met her gaze, a dense, impenetrable void stretching endlessly into the gloom. She steadied her breathing, steeling herself against the fear rising within her.

"It knows," she murmured softly, her voice tight. "It's watching us even now."

Father Allen placed a reassuring hand on her shoulder, his expression solemn but calm. "Let it watch. We know what must be done."

Abigail closed the ritual book gently, her hands trembling slightly. "Then we have no time to waste."

Maria straightened, drawing strength from the resolve in their eyes, knowing their fates were intertwined with those who had come before. "Then let's be ready. Because whatever happens next, we must end it."

Outside, above the ancient archives, a storm began to gather.

Scene 2: Abigail's Secret Past

The rain had softened into a faint mist outside the windows of St. Helen's Church, the stone walls humming gently as the storm that had haunted the region began to drift east. Inside the church archives, the old lantern flickered across weathered shelves and stacks of parchment, and the air smelled of dust, candle wax, and something ancient—something waiting.

The trio had spent hours uncovering the horrors left behind in the fragile pages of the Concordia texts. The ritual, the names, the clock—it was all beginning to make an unbearable kind of sense.

Maria, Abigail, and Father Allen now sat in a heavy, exhausted silence, each of them staring at the cracked leather tome lying open on the table.

Father Allen rose with a groan and stepped away to examine a document they had found in the archive vault, leaving Abigail and Maria in the warmth of the dim light. Abigail sat in a chair, her hands folded in her lap, her eyes distant and unreadable.

Maria glanced at her friend, noticing the unusual stillness. "You've gone quiet," she said softly.

Abigail blinked and offered a tired smile, but there was something deeper behind her eyes—something old and buried, finally pushing its way free.

"There's something I've never told anyone," Abigail said after a moment. "Not even Father Allen."

Maria leaned in. "You don't have to—"

"No," Abigail interrupted gently. "I think I do. After what we've seen, what we've read, I know why I've been drawn to this. Why I've always known I'd be part of something like this. I think you need to understand... who I really am."

She looked down, then folded her arms tightly across her chest as though bracing herself.

"I died once."

Maria sat up straighter.

"I was thirteen," Abigail continued, her voice low and trembling. "There was a car accident. I don't remember the crash—not the metal, or the sound, or even the pain. I just remember the quiet afterward. Like being underwater, but weightless. Everything was... still. And then I saw it. A place between. It was full of light and shadow, mirrors, shards of memory and possibility. I saw things there. People I hadn't met. Places I hadn't been. And I saw things I wish I could forget."

She looked up, her eyes glistening. "They said I was dead for three minutes. Clinically. No heartbeat. But I remember so much from those three minutes that I couldn't even explain. When I came back, it didn't stop. The visions. The feelings. The knowing."

Abigail's hands trembled slightly. "At first I thought it was just trauma. Or dreams. My parents sent me to doctors. Therapists. But nothing could stop it. I'd walk into a room and feel someone's sorrow like it was mine. I'd see glimpses—echoes of things that hadn't happened yet, or had happened long ago. The mirror became something I couldn't look into for long. It would show me too much."

Maria reached out and gently placed her hand over Abigail's. "You've been carrying this alone?"

"I had to." Abigail's voice cracked. "You tell people something like that, they don't think you're blessed. They think you're broken. Or dangerous. So I hid it. I trained myself to be quiet, to act normal. Church became my sanctuary, ironically. People don't ask too many questions when you serve quietly."

Maria gave a sad smile. "But it's not a curse."

"For years I thought it was." Abigail's tone turned bitter for a moment. "There were nights I prayed to be rid of it. Cried until I fell asleep asking God why He chose me to carry this. But over time... I saw things I could stop. I warned people—subtly. Sometimes I made a difference. And now—now I know. It wasn't a curse. It was preparation."

Abigail looked into Maria's eyes, and for a moment there was no fear, only certainty.

284

"This—what we're doing—it's why I was given the gift. To help stop this cycle of pain and possession. To stand between the innocent and what waits beyond the glass."

Maria nodded slowly, overcome by emotion. "You're the only one who could've done this with me. You were meant to be part of it."

Abigail hesitated, then gave a shy smile. Her cheeks flushed a gentle pink. "There's something else."

Maria raised a brow.

"I think I've... fallen for someone."

Maria grinned. "Oh?"

Abigail laughed nervously. "Samuel. It's strange, isn't it? With everything going on. But I feel like I've known him forever. Like we're... tied together somehow."

Maria's eyes softened, and she reached across the table to squeeze Abigail's hand. "He's had such a hard life. And he needs someone who understands. Who sees him."

Abigail nodded. "I do see him. The pain. The walls. The guilt. But I also see his heart. He's a good man. And I'd never take a step forward if I thought it would hurt you."

Maria laughed gently through her emotion. "Abigail, you have my blessing. Truly. If there's anyone I trust with his heart, it's you."

The moment hung in warm silence. Outside, the rain had stopped, and a pale moon began to rise through a veil of broken clouds. Within the church walls, the past, the present, and the future were winding themselves into a single thread.

Abigail leaned back and closed her eyes for a breath. "Then let's finish this. For Adam. For Joseph. For everyone who never had a voice."

Maria nodded. "And for you. The girl who came back from the In Between with fire in her soul."

Scene 3: Urgent Call to Action

The weight of the room felt tangible, pressing down heavily upon Maria, Abigail, and Father Allen as they reviewed the final pages of the ancient, fragile documents strewn across the expansive archive table. The air had grown stale and oppressive, a reflection of the somber history they had just unraveled. Maria's heart was heavy with the truths they'd uncovered—secrets long hidden, souls bound and suffering. She ran her fingers gently along the edges of the brittle parchment, careful not to tear the delicate material, but feeling the raw emotional weight as keenly as if it were a physical presence.

Abigail stood beside her, eyes scanning pages filled with hastily scrawled notes and diagrams, her expression a mixture of sorrow and determination. Her clairvoyance had always been a burden, but in moments like these, Maria saw clearly how it weighed upon her, the visions and whispers from unseen sources etched in the quiet lines of Abigail's thoughtful face.

Father Allen paced slowly, occasionally stopping to peer closer at a passage, his brow furrowed deeply beneath his graying hair. His own history of confronting the supernatural had left him with scars visible and hidden, but Maria saw in his quiet strength a reassuring resolve. He had faced demons before, both literal and figurative, and he carried an aura of quiet courage that steadied Maria's anxious thoughts.

The silence in the archives felt almost reverent, each of them caught up in their own reflections on the revelations they had pieced together. The dim glow of the emergency lantern cast elongated shadows across the stone walls, the occasional flicker making the room feel even more isolated from the outside world.

Then, as abruptly as it had vanished earlier, the overhead lights surged back to life, flooding the archives with stark brightness. Maria flinched at the sudden illumination, blinking rapidly as her eyes adjusted. Abigail released a breath she'd been unknowingly holding, visibly relaxing her shoulders. Father Allen paused mid-stride, his eyes momentarily lifted toward the ceiling as if in silent thanks for the return of normalcy, however fleeting.

In that brief moment of relief, Maria's phone suddenly blared loudly, startling them all from the fragile comfort of restored light. Heart racing, Maria quickly reached into her pocket, pulling out her phone with trembling fingers. Jacob's name illuminated the screen, and Maria felt her breath catch.

"Jacob?" she answered urgently, pressing the phone firmly to her ear.

"Mom?" Jacob's voice was tight, filled with a quiet anxiety that Maria knew all too well. "Gregory was here. He said things are bad, Mom. He said Dad's in trouble."

Maria felt her stomach twist painfully. "Slow down, honey. What exactly did Gregory say?"

Jacob's voice quivered slightly as he continued, "He said Dad is being drained. The Thing is feeding off him more than it should. Gregory said if Dad is going to be rescued, it has to be soon, because the Echo is noticing what's happening. He said the Echo sees the imbalance Dad created in the In Between. Gregory said it won't wait forever to fix things. He didn't say what that meant, but… it sounded bad, Mom."

287

Maria's gaze locked onto Abigail and Father Allen, both of whom watched her intently, reading the urgency in her eyes. "We understand, Jacob. We're going to take care of this. Stay with Noah and Mrs. Garza. Keep an eye out for anything strange, and call immediately if anything happens."

"Okay, Mom," Jacob said, a slight steadiness returning to his voice. "I will."

Maria hung up and stood quietly for a moment, the weight of her son's words hanging heavily in the restored brightness of the archives.

"What did Jacob say?" Abigail asked gently, stepping closer.

"It's Joseph," Maria said quietly, her voice tight with controlled fear. "Gregory warned Jacob that Joseph's soul is being drained by the Thing. Time is running out. The Echo is becoming impatient. If we don't move now, we may lose Joseph forever."

Father Allen exhaled sharply, his gaze filled with determination. "Then we have no choice. We must perform the ritual as soon as possible. And it must be done where the binding began. Franklin, Louisiana."

Maria's heart sank further, an additional worry clouding her mind. "I can't leave the boys alone, not now. I need someone I trust watching them in case something happens."

Abigail touched Maria's arm reassuringly. "Then call Samuel. He'll protect them. He owes that to Joseph."

Without hesitation, Maria dialed Samuel's number. His gruff voice answered quickly, almost as if he'd been expecting her call. "Maria?"

"Samuel," Maria's voice shook slightly, betraying the strain she tried to hide. "I need you to go to Washington and stay with the boys. I can't leave them unprotected, and there's no one else I trust right now."

A heavy silence lingered for only a heartbeat before Samuel responded with unwavering certainty, "I'll be there. Nothing will happen to those boys. I promise you. I owe Joseph that much."

Relief flooded through Maria, briefly easing the ache in her chest. "Thank you, Samuel."

She hung up, turning again to Abigail and Father Allen, her voice now firm with purpose. "It's settled. We're going to Louisiana. Joseph needs us, and we're going to bring him home."

They exchanged quiet nods, the weight of their shared mission evident. They had no choice now but to face what awaited them, trusting that their bond—and their courage—would be enough.

Scene 4: Whispers in the Mirror

Samuel had taken the red-eye flight, landing in Seattle just after sunrise. By midmorning, he arrived at the quiet apartment in University Place, rubbing the sleep from his eyes and carrying only a worn duffel bag and the weight of his own guilt. Maria had greeted him at the door with a tired hug, and Abigail had already laid out coffee. The boys were still asleep, and Mrs. Garza, after a few gentle reassurances, had returned home.

Now, Samuel stood in the hallway, unpacking in the master bedroom that Maria had offered him. The apartment was hushed, with only the occasional creak of floorboards and the low hum of appliances to break the silence. But even those familiar domestic sounds seemed dimmer than they should have been—muted by something unseen.

Too quiet.

The hallway light flickered.

A chill slithered through the apartment, as if some unseen wind had crept in through the cracks in the world. It was a suffocating cold—not the gentle bite of winter air, but a deep, marrow-chilling presence that pushed against the skin and crawled down the spine.

Jacob sat up straighter on the couch, eyes locked on the mirror at the end of the hallway. "He's coming," he said.

Samuel turned. "Who?"

Before Jacob could answer, the mirror convulsed.

It rippled like a black pond struck by a sudden wind. The surface shimmered—not just in reflection, but in texture, warping and twisting like a liquid membrane torn open by something clawing through. The hallway lights sputtered violently and then dimmed to a dull glow.

From the mirror poured a darkness so absolute it seemed to devour the hallway itself. The Thing emerged.

It came like a shadow bleeding into the world, stretching, slithering, forming grotesque limbs that twisted like smoke and bone. Its body pulsed with hunger, eyes burning with desperate fire. It moved with a feral urgency, dragging its formless mass into the space with wet, slick sounds that made the skin crawl. Its mouth—if it could be called that—unfurled in a soundless wail.

Jacob froze.

Samuel leapt into the hallway to shield the boy, but the Thing's appendage lashed out, striking with brutal force. Samuel flew backward, crashing into the wall and collapsing to the floor in a stunned heap.

The Thing lunged again, reaching for Jacob with a clawed tendril of blackness.

But then—the mirror trembled.

The lights exploded with a burst of static. Glass cracked in the bathroom down the hall. Every shadow deepened.

A new chill descended, different from the Thing's. This one was colder still—but not ravenous. It was sovereign.

A pulse rippled through the air. The mirror churned again, swirling like a vortex of memory and storm. And from that maelstrom came a presence even darker than the Thing, but quieter. More commanding. The air bent to it. Time seemed to pause.

The Echo stepped forward.

Where the Thing twisted and shrieked with hunger, the Echo moved with stillness that drowned out breath. It stood tall, its body half-seen and cloaked in shadow, its face unreadable. Eyes like dull stars burned behind a veil of black mist. Around it, the world dulled. The wind stilled. Even the ticking of the clock stopped.

The Thing recoiled.

It screeched—a noise that clawed at the ears and rattled the bones—as if defying an ancient master it wished it could destroy. It thrashed against the pull of the Echo's presence, its form unraveling in tendrils of oily smoke.

"You've taken too much," the Echo said. Its voice was not loud, but it echoed in the walls, in the floorboards, in the hearts of those who heard it.

The Thing hissed, its mouth folding open like a wound. It didn't speak, but its defiance was clear.

"You upset the balance," the Echo continued. "This soul is not yours to drain."

The Thing lashed forward again—but not toward Jacob. It clawed at the edges of the mirror, resisting the pull, shrieking with frustration. Its body spasmed, claws scraping across the hardwood floor and walls as if it were being forced back.

"I will come again!" the Thing screeched, its final wail like a dying storm. "He is mine! He is strong—too strong to be wasted in the light!"

The Echo stepped closer. "He is not yours. Not yet."

With a final, furious shriek, the Thing was yanked back into the mirror. It dissolved into mist, claws raking across the surface as it disappeared. The hallway lights snapped back on with a pop.

Jacob stood frozen. His breath came in ragged gulps, his eyes locked on the now-still mirror.

The Echo turned its face to him.

And then it was gone.

The mirror cleared. Only the faintest crack marred the glass.

Samuel groaned from where he had fallen, pushing himself upright.

"Did… did that just happen?" he croaked.

Jacob nodded slowly. "Yeah."

And from the master bedroom, Gregory stepped into the hall, jaw tight, his eyes unreadable beneath the brim of his hat.

"I reckon we best talk," he said.

Both Jacob and Samuel turned to find Gregory standing there, his hat in one hand, the other casually tucked into the pocket of his worn duster.

"Gregory?" Samuel asked, narrowing his eyes. "You... you're the cowboy Jacob talked about."

Gregory tipped his hat. "The one and only." He turned to Jacob. "Didn't mean to spook ya, partner. Just wanted to make sure you were all right. That Thing's gettin' bolder. And hungrier."

Jacob frowned. "It's after my dad, isn't it?"

Gregory nodded slowly. "He's bein' drained. Fed on. That foul thing's gluttin' itself on your daddy's soul like a pig at a trough. And now the Echo's noticed. Balance in the In Between's startin' to tip, and that ain't good. Not good at all."

Samuel rubbed the back of his neck. "What happens if the Echo decides to act?"

Gregory's eyes darkened. "Ain't no tellin'. He restores balance by any means necessary. Sometimes that means takin' more than he gives."

He moved toward the kitchen, inhaling deeply. "Well I'll be... y'all got roast and potatoes goin' in that crock pot?"

Samuel blinked. "Yeah. Left it on low all morning."

Gregory smiled. "Smells like my mama's Sunday dinner. Lord, it's been a long time since I could taste a thing."

He looked back to Jacob. "I'll stay close, partner. Keep watch. I need to show your mom something. She needs to know this to be prepared for what she has to do. But I ain't as strong in this world as I am in the In Between. My time here's short. You got a job to do. And I reckon it's comin' sooner than any of us want."

Jacob nodded solemnly. "I know."

Gregory touched his hat once more, then turned and walked toward the back of the apartment, fading as he went, his boots silent against the floor.

Samuel looked down at Jacob. "You sure you're up for this?"

"I have to be," Jacob said.

Outside, thunder rolled again.

Inside, the mirror remained still.

—for now.

Scene 5: Maria's Vision

Maria lay in bed at the hotel in Schenectady, her window slightly ajar to let in the thick summer air. A storm had passed only hours before, leaving behind the scent of damp earth and the rhythmic drip of water from the rooftop above. The hum of cicadas filled the spaces between the raindrops still pattering against the window ledge. In the distance, a low rumble of retreating thunder rolled like the echo of something ancient.

Sleep had come fitfully, uneasy with the knowledge they were leaving for Louisiana in the morning. But eventually, the weight of exhaustion and prophecy overtook her, pulling her under into the black.

In the dream, she stood barefoot on glass.

Around her, the world shimmered like heat rising from asphalt. Jagged shards stretched endlessly in all directions, forming twisting corridors and crumbling hallways. A single flickering lantern floated at her side—no flame, no wick, just a pulsing orb of pale blue light. Gregory's silhouette appeared from the shifting shadows ahead. His features were indistinct at first, as if the In Between had trouble remembering who he once was, but his presence was familiar. Calming.

"Come," he said softly, voice like water over stones. "We don't have long."

Maria followed him through the fractured maze. Each mirror they passed showed something different—memories, regrets, moments lost to time. One reflected her sons' faces, both bathed in golden light, calling her name. Another showed Joseph, pacing a dark corridor, a mirror fragment clutched in his bleeding hand.

But most showed suffering. Screaming souls clawing at unseen walls. Eyes wide with terror, mouths agape in endless wails, their voices swallowed by the silence of the glass.

They reached a precipice—an open platform surrounded by broken columns, suspended above a pit of swirling black. In the center stood the Thing.

It was feeding.

Maria froze, heart hammering in her chest. Gregory placed a gentle hand on her shoulder. "Watch."

The Thing loomed tall, its body shifting constantly—a silhouette stitched from shadows, smoke, and glistening sinew. Its arms reached out, talon-fingered, dragging soul after soul from nearby shards. Each victim was suspended in midair, writhing and crying out as tendrils of darkness coiled around them. The Thing inhaled deeply, and with each breath, the soul dimmed, until it flickered like a dying ember.

But there was something else. Despite the horror, Maria noticed the Thing falter.

It trembled.

It leaned against a pillar, momentarily drained. As it fed, its form pulsed, but between those pulses, it withered. Weakness. Hunger unfulfilled. Like a beast too long denied.

Maria turned to Gregory. "It's starving."

He nodded grimly. "Yes. Its power grows with each soul, but hunger is its weakness. The more it feeds, the more the veil between worlds tears—but it also drains itself. That is when it is most vulnerable."

Then the ground shook.

A thunderclap—so loud it shattered several nearby mirror walls—rippled through the air. From the far edge of the platform, something vast emerged from the gloom.

Maria fell to her knees as the Echo arrived.

It did not move. It did not speak. It simply was—colossal, ancient, still. Its form, half-seen, half-felt, pulsed with power that made even the Thing shrink back. Where the Thing was chaos and hunger, the Echo was order and judgment. It towered over the Thing like a warden over a wayward prisoner.

The Thing hissed, bowing its head. But the Echo did not acknowledge it.

Instead, the Echo turned its unseen gaze toward Maria.

A pulse tore through the realm. The mirrors around her vibrated, their surfaces boiling with light.

Maria gasped and fell backward—

—and awoke with a start.

The hotel room was bathed in early morning gray. Rain still whispered against the windows, and summer humidity clung to her skin. Her nightgown was damp with sweat, her breath ragged.

She sat up, pressing a hand to her heart.

"I saw it," she whispered. "I saw everything."

Later that morning, the rain had lightened to a mist as Maria, Abigail, and Father Allen loaded their bags into the rental car. The sky was still overcast, casting the city streets in soft blue and silver. As the car pulled away from the hotel, Maria sat in the passenger seat, eyes on the passing trees and quiet buildings.

"Maria?" Abigail asked gently. "Did something happen last night?"

Maria turned slowly. "Yes. I had a dream… a vision. Gregory led me into the In Between. We saw the Thing, feeding. But it's hungry—desperately so. And that's its weakness. It consumes, but it can't sustain itself. It's losing control."

Abigail's brow furrowed. "And the Echo?"

Maria nodded. "It's real. It's ancient. Towering. It stands over the Thing like a warden over a chained beast. It has power over it. Gregory said the Thing is vulnerable when it feeds."

Father Allen, in the driver's seat, gripped the wheel tighter. "Then perhaps we can strike when it's weak."

Maria exhaled, then looked between them. "I know what we have to do now. The ritual book—the phrase: 'What is done may only be undone where it was first wrought.' We have to go to Franklin. That's where it began. That's where it ends."

They drove on in silence for a few moments, the rhythmic swish of the wipers the only sound.

Maria stared out the window, watching the storm remnants drift behind them.

"We know what to do," she whispered.

And ahead of them, somewhere beyond the clouds and timeworn memories, Louisiana waited.

Chapter 16 - The House Remembers

Scene 1: The Parlor Waits

The road stretched before them in a serpentine line, winding through moss-laden oaks and muddy culverts, the afternoon sky still slick with the remnants of a summer storm. Louisiana's humidity clung to their skin, thick and suffocating, a vaporous presence that made each breath feel just a little too heavy. Maria wiped her brow with the back of her hand as she stared out the SUV window, her eyes tracing the narrowing trail of dirt and broken asphalt that wound toward the place none of them had dared speak aloud for miles.

They had driven this road before, not in body, but in memory. Delilah's memory. The journals, the letters, the echoing words in parchment and dream. They knew this was the path she had taken with Adam and Eleanor, full of hope, ambition, and innocence. But now, the road was no more than a haunted artery leading into the carcass of the Mercier estate.

"God," Father Allen whispered under his breath as the main gates creaked open. He gripped the steering wheel tighter, knuckles white against the leather. "It's like time gave up on this place."

The estate rose out of the fog like a dying giant. The once-pristine fencing lay shattered in the underbrush, tangled with creeping vines and broken stone. The main house loomed in the distance, its white-washed facade now weather-stained and peeling like shedding skin. Gables sagged. Windows stared out like blind, hollow eyes. The grand oaks that had once flanked the entry drive now stood crooked and gnarled, their branches like arthritic fingers stretching into the mist.

As they rolled toward the front steps, Maria leaned forward and stared in silence at the shell of what had once been Southern grandeur. Even in its decay, the architecture clung to remnants of pride—the ornate iron railings, the rotting wooden columns still wrapped with faded carvings of laurels and angels. But the angels were chipped. Their wings broken.

Abigail opened her door and stepped into the wet grass. Her boots sank slightly into the soggy ground, but she didn't flinch. The house called to her.

Maria followed close behind, her eyes narrowing as she approached the broad staircase. Mold mottled the stone steps. The door, heavy oak with rusted iron fixtures, hung half off its hinges.

"It's waiting," Maria said, almost too softly to hear.

Abigail turned. "What?"

"The house. This place. It's been holding its breath."

Inside, the air was still. Not quiet—there was a difference. It was heavy with the kind of silence that presses against your eardrums, makes your pulse louder. Dust coated everything, filtering the sunlight into pale shafts of haze. The wallpaper peeled in long, curling strips. Water stains stretched across the ceiling like the veins of something long-dead.

Father Allen ran his hand along the banister as they climbed the stairs to the main corridor. "How many walked these halls thinking they were safe?" he muttered.

"Too many," Abigail replied.

They explored in silence, splitting apart to examine each room. Most were caved in or gutted, mold consuming the edges of faded rugs and crumbling wainscoting. The once-glorious ballroom was littered with broken glass and the skeletal remains of a chandelier.

Eventually, they reconvened in the parlor. The room was oddly intact. A cold hearth gaped like an open mouth beneath the cracked marble mantle. On top sat a mantle clock—familiar in shape, yet foreign in its presence. Brass hands frozen at 11:03. The glass face smeared with time.

Abigail walked slowly to it, her fingers hovering just inches away. "This is it," she whispered.

Maria and Father Allen looked at one another. She nodded.

"This is where it begins. Or ends."

Abigail turned. "We need to make this our base. There's something about this room... it holds echoes."

Father Allen sighed deeply, wiping his glasses on a kerchief. "Let's start setting up."

They unpacked in a quiet flurry. Salt. Shards of mirror glass. Silver bowls of anointing oil. The Concordia medallion, wrapped tightly in cloth, gleamed faintly as Abigail unwrapped it and set it on the mantle beside the clock.

Maria knelt in a corner, drawing the first of many salt lines with trembling fingers. The parlor felt smaller now, as if the walls had drawn inward, inching closer with every passing minute. She looked up and out the cracked window toward the barn in the distance. Once a hive of labor and life. Now silent. Rotting.

As she rose, she pulled out her phone and dialed.

"Samuel?"

His voice came through static-laced but strong. "I'm here. We're watching the mirror. Jacob's asleep. I've got it covered."

"Keep the mirror veiled unless we call you. If something happens... we may need to use it. As an exit."

A long pause. Then, "Understood. Be careful."

She hung up, her fingers lingering on the screen. Her eyes scanned the room. There were shadows dancing now. Not visibly—not yet. But something had shifted.

Abigail returned from the hallway carrying a bundle of black candles. She knelt near the hearth and began placing them in a circle.

Maria turned to Father Allen. He sat stiffly on a faded armchair, his Bible resting closed on his lap. His eyes were distant, not tracking anything in the room.

"You alright, Father?"

He looked up slowly. "I've been here before," he said quietly.

Abigail looked over, pausing her candle work. Her eyes lingered on him, searching.

He said nothing more. Just stared into the hearth.

Abigail exchanged a glance with Maria, then stood. "We prepare tonight. No more delay."

Maria nodded and crossed to the mirror above the mantle. She wiped a streak through the fogged glass, her reflection pale and fractured.

"We finish this," she said. "And we don't look back."

Outside, thunder rumbled far in the distance. The storm hadn't truly passed. It had simply made way for something worse.

Scene 2: Ritual Rehearsal

The late afternoon sun struggled to pierce the storm-washed clouds that lingered above the decaying Mercier plantation. Inside the parlor of the old manor, the air was thick with the scent of mildew, smoke, and something far older—a spiritual rot that clung to the wallpaper and cracked woodwork like mold on dying fruit.

Candles flickered along the mantle and window sills, their flames casting long shadows across the warped floorboards. Salt lines had been poured with trembling hands, forming broken circles and sacred triangles, reinforced by jagged shards of mirror glass and iron nails driven deep into the threshold. At the center of the room sat the Concordia medallion, now polished and gleaming despite the dust-choked gloom.

Abigail stood at the heart of the configuration, holding the ritual book close to her chest. Her eyes had not left its pages for over an hour, but her voice remained steady as she read aloud the incantations in Latin, repeating them over and over so Maria and Father Allen could commit each word to memory.

"We must speak as one," she reminded them, her voice calm but strained. "The rhythm matters more than the force. The thing we're confronting listens for doubt. It will seize on it."

Maria wiped her palms on her jeans, nerves fraying like the threads of her resolve. "And if we misstep?"

Abigail hesitated.

Father Allen finally spoke, his voice low, gravelly. "Then we risk loosing something into this world that was never meant to be free."

That hung in the air like smoke. Even the flickering candlelight seemed to falter.

Abigail drew a breath, searching their faces. "We won't fail."

She didn't say it with force. She didn't shout. It was a whisper—a desperate attempt to offer hope, but one she didn't fully believe. This time, her visions hadn't come. No flashes of the future. No guiding presence. Only silence. That terrified her more than the Thing itself.

Father Allen paced along the mirror shards embedded in the floor, his fingers pressed tightly together, murmuring prayers under his breath. His lips moved steadily, but his eyes told another story. Each time Abigail glanced at him, she saw that same haunted stare. Something inside him was unraveling, and she knew he would speak of it soon. But not now.

Far away, back in Washington, night had fallen across the small home where Samuel and Jacob stood vigil. The mirror in Jacob's room had been covered in thick black cloth, but the air around it pulsed with unnatural cold. Samuel had barely slept in days.

"They'll be starting soon," he said, standing at the doorway of Jacob's room.

Jacob sat cross-legged on the bed, a small wooden cross in his hands. "I can feel it. Like... thunder in the distance. It's not here yet, but it's coming."

Samuel nodded. "You did good telling us about the mirror. I know it's scary. But we'll keep it under control."

A faint tapping sounded from behind the cloth. Then another. Jacob went stiff. Samuel turned slowly toward the mirror.

Then came the warping. The cloth swelled and twisted, rising outward as if something inside was pushing against it.

A sickly, rasping voice seeped through the veil.

"Innocent child. Flesh veiled in light. I see your soul, unbroken, untainted. It shall be mine."

The mirror strained. The cloth shook violently.

"Samuel..." Jacob whispered.

Samuel reached for the cloth. But before he could touch it, a blast of cold surged from behind the mirror, sweeping the room.

A second voice joined the first.

"He is not yours to take."

Gregory.

Within the mirror, unseen but clearly audible, a struggle erupted. Blades of sound clashed. Screeches, growls, and guttural cries slammed against the glass.

The Thing snarled, voice like fire and brimstone. "I am famine unending! I drink the marrow of time! I shall feast on him, and the children of his line!"

Then came the shudder—a low rumble from inside the mirror that made the dresser tremble and Samuel's bones ache. The air distorted. Time stilled.

Another voice, deeper and more terrifying than even the Thing's, echoed from within:

"GLUTTON."

It wasn't shouted. It didn't need to be. It rang like the sound of the world breaking.

A screech followed, loud and agonized.

Then silence. Dead and total.

The mirror went still.

Samuel covered it again, stepping back as if burned. His breath hitched in his chest.

Jacob looked up at him, pale but calm. "That was the Echo. Gregory said it wouldn't let the Thing take me."

Samuel could barely nod.

Back at the plantation, Abigail finished another round of rehearsal. She lowered the book, her fingers trembling now.

Maria approached, placing a hand on her arm. "You okay?"

Abigail looked at her, eyes shimmering with emotion. "No. But I will be."

Father Allen finally broke from his trance. "This must be perfect. No missteps. No faltering. If any part of the mirror triangle cracks, we seal ourselves in forever. If the salt line is broken, the Thing comes through without resistance."

Abigail nodded. "We know."

But she looked back toward the cracked mirror leaning near the hearth—and for just a second, she thought she saw Joseph's face.

The ritual was coming. And none of them would be the same afterward.

Scene 3: Father Allen's Reckoning

The candlelight in the decaying Louisiana manor wavered across Father Allen's face, revealing the tension etched into the deep lines of his brow. Abigail watched him closely as he sat on a cracked velvet armchair in the corner of the parlor, shoulders hunched forward, fingers absently twisting his rosary. Maria stood at the table, arranging the remaining ritual components in silence. Outside, the storm that had rolled in earlier now lingered as a mist, a breath held in anticipation.

"You've been quiet," Abigail finally said.

Father Allen didn't look at her. "I've seen what happens when you reach too far into the dark. When you believe so strongly you're doing good that you don't realize you're crossing a line."

Maria looked over. "What do you mean?"

He exhaled slowly, the weight of memory pressing on him. Then, his eyes drifted into shadow.

FLASHBACK – UPSTATE NEW YORK, 1995

The Mallory house stood like a crooked tooth against a backdrop of deep woods and withering dusk. Father Patrick Allen had arrived just before nightfall, clutching a leather satchel of relics and rites. The storm in the distance mirrored the anxiety in his chest. The Mallorys had begged him to come. Their daughter—Elise—was no longer herself.

307

The front door creaked open, and Mrs. Mallory stood pale and desperate, hands clasped at her chest.

"Father, please. She's been speaking to... things. In the mirror. She hasn't slept in days."

He followed her into a dim parlor. Every curtain was drawn. The air was stale, damp with the scent of mildew and lavender. In the center of the room, Elise stood before an ornate mirror. Her reflection didn't quite match her posture.

"They whisper," she said, voice cracked and far too calm. "They tell me secrets. About the others who got lost. They want me to go with them."

Father Allen approached slowly, laying down his kit. Basil bundles. Holy water. Vials of blessed oil. Salt.

"This isn't you," he whispered. "This is not what God wants for you."

She blinked, eyes glazed. "God doesn't come here anymore."

He drew a circle of salt around her, lit incense, began reciting verses. Psalm after Psalm. Latin phrases he wasn't authorized to use. Prayers meant only for trained exorcists.

The mirror began to cloud.

The air turned sharp. The salt hissed. Thunder shattered the silence. The faces in the mirror moved. Not Elise's—other faces. Hollow-eyed. Grinning.

Elise screamed. A sound so raw it flayed the soul. Her back arched as her limbs convulsed, lifting from the floor, body snapping like a marionette with tangled strings.

Father Allen flung holy water at the mirror and it shattered in a shriek of glass. A storm wind burst through the room from nowhere. The crucifix in his hand burned against his skin.

"Elise!" he yelled. "You are not theirs! In Christ's name, I command it!"

She collapsed, twitching. Blood leaked from her nose. Her mouth opened, no sound. Mrs. Mallory screamed, dropping to her knees beside her.

For a moment—Elise didn't breathe.

Patrick fell beside her, hands shaking. He had gone too far. Used forbidden rites. Broken the order.

Then—a gasp.

Elise's eyes fluttered open. She blinked, the girl returned. Her voice quaked: "Thank you..."

He couldn't speak. Only weep.

Back in the present, his voice cracked. "She survived. Barely. But I don't know if what I brought back was completely her. I never did."

Abigail knelt beside him and placed her hand gently on his.

"You meant to save her," she said.

"And I almost lost her to something worse," he whispered. "After that, I swore I'd never perform another ritual. Not one. Not unless the Lord Himself called me to it. I've lived with the guilt of that night ever since."

He looked at Abigail and Maria. "But now... This family. Joseph. Your son." He turned to Maria. "They deserve to be saved. And I will face my past, even if it means giving everything."

Silence filled the room. But something had shifted. The resolve was deeper. The weight shared.

Abigail's voice broke gently. "Then let us stand together in the fire. This time... no one faces it alone."

Scene 4: The Shimmering Veil

Twilight draped itself in shades of bruised purple and deepening gold over the ruins of the Mercier plantation. The once-magnificent estate now hunched in silence beneath the heavy Louisiana sky, its broken rafters and collapsed outbuildings casting crooked shadows across the trampled grass. The chirping of insects had stilled. Even the cicadas, tireless heralds of Southern dusk, had gone mute.

Inside the parlor, the air hung like wet wool. Each breath was a labor. The dust stirred not from movement, but from the mounting tension that now gripped every wooden beam, every cracked windowpane. The hearth was cold. The walls felt closer than they had hours ago, as if the very house leaned in to listen.

Maria stood at the center of the parlor. Around her, mirrors lined the walls, angled precisely, reflecting each other endlessly in a corridor of repeating reflections. Salt lines, thick and white, were meticulously drawn at the base of the walls. Shards of broken glass had been arranged in ritual sigils around the perimeter, glinting like teeth. The Concordia medallion, darkened with age and wear, rested at the heart of it all on a folded linen cloth.

Outside, the wind began to gather.

Maria hugged her arms around herself, the cool damp of the air seeping through her skin and into her bones. Her thoughts spiraled. She had gone over every step of the ritual twice, then again. Yet the question clawed at her: What if they failed?

In her mind, she saw Joseph as he once was—smiling, laughing, with Jacob perched on his shoulders, and little Noah running circles around them in the golden grass of their old backyard. That memory shimmered and slipped like water through her fingers, replaced by the haunting stillness of their home after Joseph vanished. She had fought so hard not to believe he was gone, but the emptiness had crept in, steady and suffocating.

What if this brought him back—only broken?

What if it made things worse?

She turned and looked toward Abigail.

The clairvoyant moved slowly, pacing the parlor with beads of sweat glistening on her brow. Her voice, low and rhythmic, wove Latin and old Creole into a humming chant, calling out to the unseen—guides, ancestors, protectors. She cast glances toward the mirrors, sometimes speaking as if to someone who stood there but could not be seen.

Father Allen sat against the far wall, just outside the circle of ritual elements. The rosary clenched in his hands had long since left impressions in his fingers. His lips moved in prayer, silent, steady, like the ticking of a watch whose time had nearly run out. His eyes were distant, staring toward the hearth—toward the clock above it.

The mantle clock.

Its once-polished cherry wood casing had dulled with time and dust. The glass over its face was cracked, hairline fractures splitting outward like veins from the center. Its hands—bent and rusted—had frozen at 11:03.

No one had touched it.

They hadn't dared.

The wind outside howled, rattling the shutters like bones. A deep pressure sank over the plantation, a shifting of the world's weight. The animals in the surrounding woods had long since gone silent, but now the very air seemed to brace against itself.

Maria paced to the window and looked out.

The surrounding land, once a thriving kingdom of cotton, sugarcane, and sweat, now resembled the burial ground of forgotten gods. The trees leaned, bare and diseased, as if watching the house. The fields were blackened husks, long untended. The silence was not peace. It was waiting.

A presence was drawing near.

She turned back, catching the glance between Abigail and Father Allen. Neither spoke, but all three shared the same understanding: something was coming. Something had been stirred. This land remembered. And now, it breathed again.

The air thickened further.

Maria's hands trembled slightly as she returned to her place at the center of the ritual. She bent to touch the medallion, her fingertips brushing the cold, metal surface. It pulsed faintly with energy—not warmth, not life, but something.

A hush fell over the room.

The wind outside ceased.

The very world paused.

And then—

BONG.

One sharp, resounding chime split the silence.

It came from the mantle clock.

No one had touched it. The clock hadn't worked in decades.

BONG.

It echoed once and faded like a stone sinking beneath still water.

Maria's breath caught in her throat. Abigail stopped chanting. Father Allen opened his eyes and stared directly at the clock.

None of them moved.

The sound had not been a mechanical anomaly. It had been a message. A warning. A presence.

The Thing knew they were here.

It was waiting.

In the mirrors, reflections deepened. Shadows within shadows layered over each other like sediment. A flicker passed through the glass—quick, like a blink in reverse—but it left the room colder.

Maria took a long, steady breath.

"It knows," she whispered. "It's watching."

Abigail slowly nodded. "Then we begin at dawn. No more rehearsals."

Father Allen gripped his rosary tighter. "And we end it."

But as the candlelight dimmed—just slightly, just enough—they knew something else was listening, waiting in the wings of glass and dark.

The veil had begun to shimmer.

And there was no going back.

Chapter 17 - The Soul Crossing

Scene 1: Passage into the In Between

The first hint of dawn crept through the shattered remains of the plantation's stained glass windows, casting fractured beams of amber and rose across the ritual chamber. The parlor smelled of candle wax, scorched herbs, and salt-soaked earth. The air was heavy, not just with the thickness of the Southern humidity but with something unseen—a weight of presence that pressed on the skin, crawled along the spine, and whispered in the bones.

They hadn't slept. Not one of them.

Maria sat cross-legged within the chalked boundary of the ritual circle, her palms resting atop her knees, eyes bloodshot and hollow. Her hair clung to her face with sweat, though she had not moved in an hour. Every breath she took felt thin, like sipping air through a broken straw. Each heartbeat ached. Every nerve in her body was pulled taut.

Beside her, Abigail stood over the Concordia medallion. The relic glowed faintly in the early light, pulsing like a living thing. Her voice had long since fallen silent, replaced by the sound of her breath, deep and slow, fighting to remain steady. Her hands shook from exhaustion. Her mouth was dry from hours of incantation, her soul worn raw from the pressure of what loomed just beyond the veil.

Father Allen knelt on the floor, clutching his worn Bible so tightly the leather binding creaked. His face, usually composed with stoic resolve, was etched with fear. Not fear of death—he had long

315

made peace with that—but fear of damnation. Fear of unleashing something worse than the devil he hoped to defeat.

They had completed every preparation, followed every instruction written in the tattered ritual book. Mirrors, placed in a triangle around the room, reflected infinity upon themselves. Shards of blackened glass, taken from the original clock, lined the inner circle. Salt formed protective barriers between each mirror and the next, and candles burned at the cardinal points—each flame casting shadows that danced in unnatural ways.

They were ready.

And had been ready.

But the ritual required daylight. Dawn had to kiss the ground for the portal to the In Between to open.

That was the rule.

And so they waited. The last two hours had passed like centuries. The Thing had made its impatience known, rattling the mirrors violently just before twilight, sending tremors through the floorboards and raising a distant howl from the far ends of the house. A warning. Or a greeting. Or both.

Maria thought the waiting would kill her. The silence screamed in her ears louder than the Thing ever could. She thought of Joseph, of his face before he vanished, his touch, his warmth. She thought of Jacob, and how his eyes had changed since his father's disappearance. There was a weight in their son's gaze now—a weight too old for a child.

She would not let that darkness take him too.

"It's time," Abigail whispered.

Maria opened her eyes.

The sun had risen. Its rays now pooled like liquid fire against the floor of the parlor.

Father Allen stood. "Let us begin."

Abigail lifted the medallion and placed it at the circle's center. The moment it touched the salt, the air inside the room contracted—a sudden stillness, as though all breath had been drawn inward and held.

Abigail began the chant.

Low, guttural words in an old tongue no longer spoken by the living. Latin laced with the guttural intonations of ancient Creole. Her voice echoed through the chamber in unnatural ways, bouncing against mirrors and circling back upon itself.

Maria added her voice. Father Allen followed.

The flames of the candles began to dance wildly.

Then the mirrors began to pulse.

At first it was subtle, a shimmer like heat waves. But then the glass quivered as though submerged underwater. The reflections within them began to distort—faces blurred, rooms stretched, shadows rippled.

A wind began to howl. Not outside—within the chamber.

The medallion lifted off the floor and hovered. The salt lines ignited in blue flame. The room spun, not in motion, but in sensation, as if the very fabric of the air twisted around them.

Then—the crack.

A jagged split tore through the space between the mirrors, as though reality itself had been sliced open.

And there it was.

The threshold.

The passage to the In Between.

Maria was the first to step forward.

It felt like passing through water boiling on the surface but frozen at the core. Her vision stretched and warped. Her skin prickled with pins and needles. Her soul screamed in protest as her body was drawn through the slit in the world.

Then everything shattered.

The In Between.

The world beyond.

It wasn't black. It was absence. The color of void. A realm not of shadows, but of emptiness where light came from nowhere and fell on nothing. Jagged glass jutted from every angle, floating in the air like the shards of broken eternity. The ground beneath their feet was not earth, but a twisted reflection of it—grey and featureless, like stepping upon memory.

Wind tore through the realm with the fury of a thousand screams. The sound was unbearable. Not loud—but wrong. A frequency of despair that churned in the gut and turned the brain against itself.

Maria dropped to her knees. Her ears bled.

Abigail staggered beside her, her hand clutched tightly around the medallion. Her eyes darted from one floating mirror to another, searching for a path.

Father Allen bent low, shielding them both. "Stay together! Do not break the line!"

All around them, glass spun in slow spirals, catching glimpses of other worlds. In one, Joseph stood at a mirror, whispering. In another, a woman with no eyes wept against the glass. In another, a child floated motionless.

The deeper they walked, the more distorted the realm became. The ground tilted. The light dimmed. The wind screamed.

Far in the distance, a sound like dragging chains echoed through the vastness.

The Thing had noticed.

They had entered its domain.

Maria clutched her chest, her heart pounding not from fear—but from hope.

Joseph was in here.

And they were going to bring him home.

Scene 2: The Wandering of Joseph

The In Between had no sky. No floor. No horizon. It stretched in all directions like a broken reflection of the world, where light could not fully form and sound hung suspended like breath never exhaled. It was a place made of glass and smoke, each step echoing forever across a surface that shattered and reformed beneath Joseph's boots.

He wandered.

His breath, once steady and warm, now rasped like paper against flame. The air offered no comfort, only the dull sting of despair. Cold pressed in from all sides, not the kind of cold that froze skin, but the kind that seeped into the marrow and whispered, You are forgotten.

Joseph had stopped counting the days. If time even passed here. Hunger didn't gnaw at him anymore. Thirst was meaningless. Pain had dulled into something worse: acceptance. The realization that perhaps he had always been meant for this place, that maybe this void was where the thread of his life had always led.

Around him, mirrors floated in pieces, drifting like dying stars in black space. Some were whole, suspended midair, showing twisted versions of places he once knew—the kitchen in Washington, the broken staircase of his childhood home, the church with shattered pews. In each reflection, something was always off: too many shadows, faces that turned before they should, eyes that followed.

And then there were the souls.

They came without sound. Pale figures made of smoke and memory. They shimmered into existence, drawn by his presence. Their mouths moved silently at first, eyes wide with longing, hands stretched toward him like branches reaching for sun.

"Please..." a voice finally formed.

Joseph turned. A woman—or what was left of one—floated before him, skin like cracked porcelain, eyes sunk into pits of lightless grief. "You freed one before. You can do it again."

Another joined her. Then another. Soon a dozen.

"I saw what you did," whispered a man with no face. "You broke the line. You opened a path."

Joseph stumbled back, pressing a hand to his temple. Their voices were not shouts but waves, crashing over him, wearing him down. Every plea burrowed into his soul, their suffering thick as mud in his lungs.

"I can't..." he gasped. "I don't know how anymore."

His legs buckled, and he fell to his knees on nothing. A mirror shattered beneath him and reformed around his body, trapping him momentarily in a cage of his own reflection. He saw himself from every angle—older, drained, his eyes bloodshot and rimmed with shadows. His skin had grown ashen. His lips cracked.

Then, a pressure. A suffocating presence, like gravity had found him.

From the periphery, a tide of blackness began to form. The souls sensed it and recoiled, vanishing into the dark like dust blown away.

The Thing.

It did not walk. It did not fly. It unfolded. Vast and formless, a skeletal mouth etched in flame and shadow. Its voice came before its shape—

"Fallen son of the blood-stained line... you tremble with power yet unused. The In Between remembers your defiance. It will not forget."

Joseph cried out as tendrils of smoke wrapped around him, brushing his arms, his throat. The Thing did not touch to bind. It touched to drain. To taste.

"You burn with the memory of light. Your hope is a wine, and I drink it slowly."

A searing pain wracked his chest. His vision dimmed at the edges. The energy in him—the strength he clung to in desperation—

began to leak from his pores, not as blood, but as shimmer. The Thing feasted on it with quiet ecstasy.

"So many come for you. So many believe. You are the flare in the dark, the candle the flies would die chasing. I let them come... for each adds to the meal. Their desperation feeds the storm."

Joseph struggled to stand, legs trembling beneath him. He staggered away, dragging his feet, leaving faint trails of light that evaporated into mist.

He couldn't let it end here. Not yet.

But the void offered no direction. No escape. Only reflection after reflection, each showing twisted possibilities. He saw Maria— screaming in the church. Jacob—reaching for his father across a sea of glass. Abigail—eyes wide with knowing grief.

"Why are you showing me this?!" Joseph roared.

The Thing laughed.

"Because the soul breaks faster when it forgets why it began to fight."

A new mirror flashed before him. He saw the parlor in Louisiana. Abigail. Maria. Father Allen. All there. Preparing something. A flicker of hope jolted his chest.

But the image rippled. Darkened. Their eyes turned black. Their mouths stretched too wide. The Thing laughed again.

"Even your dreams betray you here."

Joseph collapsed again, curled against the void. The mirrors pressed closer now, like teeth around prey. The souls murmured in the dark, no longer pleading, just watching. Waiting to see if he would fall like them.

And he was falling.

He felt himself fading from within. Pieces of him cracking away like chips from an old statue. He didn't even know what was left. Was there anything left?

He closed his eyes.

"Maria..."

Her name was a whisper from his soul, a thread cast into the black.

The Thing paused. Its presence loomed, but it did not speak.

For now, it fed slowly.

Because Joseph was still alive.

And as long as he lived, the Thing could savor every last drop of light.

Scene 3: The Thing Stirs, The Echo Watches

The In Between grew colder.

Not in degrees measurable by flesh, but by something deeper—something ancient and merciless that tugged at the soul. The air shimmered around Maria, Abigail, and Father Allen, not with warmth, but with pressure, thick as oil and twice as suffocating. They pressed onward through a corridor of shadow and shattered light, each mirror-framed path warping reality into impossible angles. The glass underfoot cracked but didn't break, flexing like cartilage beneath their steps.

Abigail stopped mid-step.

"It knows," she whispered.

Maria halted behind her, breath caught in her throat. "The Thing?"

Abigail didn't answer immediately. Her eyes scanned the mirrors around them. Every reflective surface trembled—not from impact, not from wind, but from an unseen ripple of intention. The In Between wasn't reacting.

It was awakening.

From far ahead in the mirrored maze, a screech rang out—glass on glass, a sound like knives dragged across porcelain. The path flickered violently, a strobe of shadow and light, and then from the walls came a rising sound, subtle at first.

Wind.

It began as a low whisper, brushing past their ears like unseen hands. Then it grew stronger, swirling around them with rising shrieks, until it howled like a hurricane ripping through a cathedral of mirrors. Every shard vibrated in its frame. Some fractured with sharp, shrill cries.

And beneath the wind—a rhythm.

Not natural.

A pulsing thrum like a heartbeat from something vast and malignant.

Father Allen fell to his knees. His hands trembled as he clutched his rosary. Blood wept from his nostrils, and he grit his teeth to keep from crying out. Maria grabbed his arm, her own legs weak. The ground beneath them felt unstable, rippling like a living thing.

Abigail turned slowly. Her face was pale, eyes wide but focused. "We need to move. It senses us now. Not fully—not yet. But it knows we're here."

As if on cue, the mirror behind them exploded inward with a blast of wind and shards. None of the glass touched them. The fragments stopped midair—hovering, trembling, then reversed direction and reassembled themselves. Maria gasped.

"What the hell was that?"

"Warning shot," Abigail murmured. "A game. It's playing with us."

Shadows stretched from the broken mirror seams, rising like tendrils. They didn't slither—they prowled. Darting just beyond the periphery of light, they circled, growing more daring by the second. Figures made of smoke and memory, hunting with breathless anticipation.

Maria shivered. "Is that the Thing?"

Abigail shook her head. "The Thing doesn't hunt like this. These are its servants. Fragments."

Above them, the ceiling warped. The void pulled back like peeling bark to reveal a swirling funnel of darkness, framed in jagged glass and echoing wind. Through it, something stirred. Not the Thing—not fully—but its essence, like a scent preceding a predator.

And then—a pause.

The wind died. The shards stilled. The darkness held its breath.

All three of them froze.

The silence was worse.

It was expectation.

And then, at the farthest point of their sight, beyond the maze of shifting glass and darkness, something vast loomed.

Not moving. Not threatening. Just watching.

It didn't resemble the Thing. Where the Thing was chaos wrapped in hunger and blasphemy, this presence was order forged in incomprehensibility. It had no eyes, no mouth, no form—just mass. Scale. Gravity that bent the very reflection of the world around it. The mirrors bowed inward, light dimmed in its presence. A sound like a deep organ note hung in the air.

Maria grabbed Abigail's arm. "That... Is that it?"

Abigail nodded slowly. "The Echo."

Maria's throat tightened. "Should we be afraid of it?"

Abigail hesitated. "Only if we do something it doesn't want us to do."

Maria stared at her. "Are we?"

Abigail closed her eyes, focused. The swirling energy around them responded to her presence, brushing past her skin like reverent air.

"No," she said after a beat. "Not yet. We're out of place, not out of line."

A crack ran through one of the mirrors. The path ahead warped.

From somewhere unseen, a distant voice screamed. Not in pain, but in recognition. A soul pulled toward the Thing, or away from it, they couldn't tell. All they could do was move.

"We don't have long," Father Allen murmured, rising shakily. "We find Joseph. Now."

As they began to move again, the air thickened. The shadows gathered behind them like wolves.

But the Echo watched.

And for now, it did not stop them.

Scene 4: Reunion and Rupture

Their breath steamed in the gloom, even though there was no cold. The In Between twisted around them, not like a place, but a pressure. Walls of mirror fragments rose and shattered again with each uncertain step. The floor beneath them cracked like frostbitten glass, though it never broke. Maria led the way, her body trembling with both fear and urgency, the Concordia medallion clutched in her fist like a dying ember of light.

"There!" Abigail whispered. Her voice echoed back as if spoken in a cathedral of bones.

In the distance—no, not distance, for space bent in the In Between—a flicker of movement, a silhouette hunched beneath the jagged arch of a fractured mirror. Joseph.

He sat slumped on a shard-throne, his head bowed low. The shadows around him pulsed with faint cries. Ghosts, dozens of them, clawed and whispered, their translucent faces strained with longing. They swirled near Joseph but did not touch him. Not yet.

Gregory stood watchfully beside him, his expression weary but unyielding. He looked up as the trio approached, his eyes luminous even in this realm of bent light and dead echoes.

"He's holding on," Gregory said. "Barely."

Maria didn't wait. She sprinted forward, stumbling across the broken terrain. "Joseph! Joseph, it's me!"

He didn't lift his head at first. Then, slowly, as if waking from beneath a crushing weight, Joseph looked up. His eyes were dulled, surrounded by bruised sockets and cracked veins, but as they met hers, light flared in them.

"Maria?" His voice was sand, brittle and dry. "Is it really…?"

She dropped to her knees before him and reached for his face. "Yes. I came. We came."

Behind her, Abigail and Father Allen reached the shard-throne. Gregory stepped aside, nodding with approval.

"I can't…" Joseph whispered. "It's too much. They're everywhere. Hungry."

"They're not for you to carry," Maria said, tears streaking her cheeks. "You've done enough. And there's something you need to know."

She took his hand and placed it on her abdomen. "You're going to be a father again."

For a breathless moment, Joseph stared. Then the flicker of a smile cracked through the exhaustion on his face. A light—not from the realm, but from within—bloomed behind his eyes. His body straightened. He stood. With renewed energy, the paleness of his skin turned rosy pink. The sparkle in his eye returned.

"I have a reason," he said. "I can go back. I have to."

Abigail blinked. "Pregnant?" she whispered.

Father Allen's brows rose, stunned. "Blessed Mother…"

But then—

A low tremor rumbled beneath them.

All heads turned.

From the broken sky of glass and shadow, something stirred. A wind began to howl—not the natural sort, but a cacophony of voices twisted into gale. The shards that made up the In Between shook and buzzed with energy. Gregory's eyes widened.

"It knows," he muttered. "The Thing has felt him."

From the east—a direction that meant nothing here—came a vast, coiling cloud of black smoke, slashed through with thin, wormlike streaks of pale light. In its center: glowing eyes, far too large, far too many. A crown of jagged horns shimmered through the mist.

The Thing.

"Run!" Gregory barked. "It's not ready. The bridge isn't sealed."

He turned from them and sprinted toward a narrow fracture in the mirrorworld's ground—a jagged line of silver and black that pulsed with the scent of Jacob's world.

"Where's he going?" Maria cried.

"To the crack," Abigail said, realization dawning. "The mirror. He's going to stop it from escaping."

Joseph staggered but found his footing. "No—he'll get trapped out there!"

"We'll get out," Gregory called over his shoulder. "If I don't seal the gate, that thing follows you. Follows your child."

Behind them, the Thing let out a bellowing groan—like the tolling of a funeral bell—but layered with language, guttural and biblical:

"I smell purpose. I smell promise. The seed of man's line swells within her. Ripened fruit upon cursed vine. Give it to me. Feed me, and I will leave you whole."

"Don't listen to it," Father Allen growled, pulling Joseph close. "It lies in scripture and sings in sin."

Abigail dropped into stance, holding the Concordia medallion up high. "Stay behind me! We have to prepare to shift!"

The world fractured around them. Shards of mirror lifted like daggers from the floor. Winds howled in all directions. Joseph held Maria's hand as if she were his anchor.

At the crack in the veil, Gregory stood before the jagged mirror. In the Other Side, Jacob and Samuel would see his silhouette beginning to form within the bedroom mirror. He raised his hand.

"You'll not have him. Nor his son."

The Thing screamed. An orb of black lightning erupted, slamming into Gregory's back—but he held.

Inside Jacob's room, the mirror quaked.

Jacob clutched Samuel's hand. "Is that… Gregory?"

The reflection shimmered.

"Yes," Samuel whispered. "He's sealing it."

A sudden screech cut the air. A second entity—massive and formless—loomed behind the Thing. Glowing white eyes. A soundless mouth. Towering.

The Echo.

330

In the mirror, it whispered: "Glutton."

The Thing snarled and recoiled.

And in that pause, Gregory sealed the gate. The crack shimmered, closed.

Back in the In Between, Gregory stumbled and fell to one knee. "Go," he gasped. "Now. While it's distracted."

Abigail opened the way. "Joseph, take Maria. Step into the mirror. Hurry."

Joseph turned to Gregory. "Come with us!"

"I can't. I belong here now."

Father Allen ushered them in, one by one. As Joseph and Maria stepped through, the Thing howled—starved, thwarted.

Gregory watched from behind as the mirror closed. Standing as a sentry at the gate. The darkness closed in. The Echo hovered nearby—not helping, not hindering. Just watching.

He bowed his head.

"Let them be free."

The storm of glass and shadow howled around him. But the bridge was sealed.

For now.

And somewhere on the Other Side, in a quiet room, the clock ticked once.

Chapter 18 - Sacrifice and Banishment

Scene 1: Delilah's Guidance

The air in the In Between was cracking.

It wasn't sound, exactly. It was the sense of something breaking inside reality—a spiderweb fracture of truth and time splintering beneath every step. The wind had turned shrill, keening through the mirror-laced shadows like a choir of the dead. Maria, Abigail, Joseph, and Father Allen ran through this madness, glass terrain shifting with every heartbeat, their limbs heavy with dread.

The Thing followed.

Its form roared behind them, a monstrous storm of black sinew and lightless void, its eyes multiplying in the dark. Each step it took left scorched pits in the mirrored landscape. Shards twisted and rose like thorns from the ground, bleeding silvery mist as it pursued the living.

Maria stumbled. Joseph caught her, pulling her upright. But even in this haunted place, something else shifted.

A light.

Warm, pale, and steady. Not the biting glow of spirit-torches or the sick shine of the Thing's malice—but something human. Hopeful.

Delilah.

She emerged from behind a tall fracture of broken mirror, her white dress torn and faded with age, her hair floating as if suspended in water. Her eyes shimmered, deep wells of sadness and strength. She looked not at Joseph or Abigail, but straight at Maria.

"You carry life," Delilah whispered.

Maria froze, her arms around her stomach. "How did you know?"

Delilah smiled faintly. "Because the Thing knows. And now the Echo does, too."

Above them, the shadows groaned. The In Between shifted. The air became syrup, impossible to breathe. A low thunder rolled through the cracked horizon. Something stirred above the cloud veil—massive, slow, watching. The Echo.

"You must listen to me," Delilah said, approaching. She reached out, not quite touching Maria's cheek. "I was part of the sin that cursed this line. My brother... Adam... I failed him. I helped doom him. But I have a chance now, a moment to undo it."

Abigail stepped forward, breathless. "You know the ritual? The shattering one?"

Delilah nodded. "It must be performed by bloodline and bond. A soul born of love, guided by sacrifice. The Concordia seal must not just be undone. It must be reborn. Reforged in light."

Joseph looked at Delilah, dazed. "Why now?"

"Because the child changes everything," she said. "The Thing craves innocence—unmarked, powerful. He's not just trying to keep you here, Joseph. He wants to replace you. Your child's soul would feed him for centuries."

A sound like a grinding tomb split the air.

From beyond the rift, the Thing howled in jubilation.

"Ripened fruit! Seed of light! Born of shadow—mine! I claim what grows inside!"

A circle of shattered glass exploded around them, sending everyone to the floor. Maria clutched her stomach. Joseph shielded her.

Delilah remained standing.

"We don't have long," she said. She turned to Abigail. "Draw the seal. Use the medallion. And Maria, you must speak the binding prayer. Joseph—you must offer your soul freely for her protection. Only then will it shatter."

Father Allen rose shakily. "And me?"

Delilah looked at him for a long moment. "You already know your part. You always have."

They moved quickly. Abigail traced the ritual circle with shimmering shards and lines of salt etched in the glass. The medallion hummed in her hand, the Concordia seal glowing gold and blue. Maria stood at the center, hands trembling, eyes closed.

Joseph stepped forward, bruised but steady. He took her hand. "If this is the price—I give it. All of it."

"I don't want to lose you again," Maria whispered.

"You won't," he said. "Not forever."

Delilah stood beside them and began to chant.

Abigail joined, holding the medallion aloft. The words burned in her throat. The mirrored ground began to crack and rise. The seal glowed. The wind howled.

Above, the Thing loomed.

"A soul for a soul!" it bellowed.

"Give me the child—I will give you back the broken man. Trade the unborn for the damned. A soul for a soul!"

The Echo stirred.

Its eyes opened. Its attention fell.

Delilah turned toward it, her voice full of fury.

"You see! You see what has been done in your silence! This cannot be allowed to continue!"

The Echo did not respond. But its shape loomed closer.

Maria took a breath. She began to speak the ritual words. Her voice wavered at first, then grew louder. Stronger.

The seal beneath her feet flared with burning white light.

The Thing screamed.

Delilah reached out, her form beginning to unravel, her sacrifice fueling the ritual. Tears ran down her face.

"Tell Adam... I tried to make it right."

Her body fractured into light.

The seal cracked.

The ritual surged.

And somewhere beyond the veil, the first link in the chain of souls... began to shatter.

Scene 2: The Final Stand of Father Allen

The glass underfoot shattered like brittle bone with every desperate step. Maria gripped Joseph's hand as they fled through the In Between—an endless void of reflective blackness, broken only by the ghostly shimmer of fractured mirrors that hung like dying stars in a collapsing sky. The Thing pursued, its howls a chorus of starving madness. But louder than the Thing's roar was the storm building in the unseen firmament above them.

The Echo.

They could feel it watching. No longer distant. No longer indifferent.

Abigail, her cloak torn and hair wild from the wind that blew without direction, hurled a vial of sacred oil against a wall of glass. It hissed, flared briefly, and lit a path. "This way!" she shouted, her voice ragged with fear.

Father Allen ran at Maria's side, his hand clutched around the Concordia medallion. Blood leaked from his palm, but he didn't stop. He couldn't.

Behind them, the Thing howled again.

"Do not run, carriers of light," it bellowed, its voice cracking the mirrored walls like lightning strikes. "You bear the seed of power. The infant soul—pure, unmarked. I smell its spark! I will drink of it, and never hunger again!'"

Maria gasped, nearly stumbling. Joseph steadied her, but her face was white. "It knows."

"Then we finish this now," Father Allen said, teeth clenched.

They reached an open space where the In Between seemed to inhale. Shards circled overhead in slow orbit, catching flickers of memory—faces, screams, flickering flames—a surreal sky of grief. In the center stood a broken altar of black stone, its surface pulsing with ancient runes.

Delilah had vanished into the shadows. Her part was done.

"Here!" Father Allen said. He dropped to his knees before the altar and flung the Concordia medallion into its center. It cracked the stone and released a pulse of golden light that threw the Thing back into the gloom.

Abigail stepped beside him, eyes wide, hands trembling. "This is where it ends."

Joseph shielded Maria as the light began to grow. But the Thing didn't flee.

It advanced.

With each step, the void cracked and peeled away, revealing screaming souls fused into the walls of the In Between. Their voices formed a chant of despair. The Thing moved through it, mouth unhinged in a grotesque grin.

"You dare unbind what was sworn?" it roared. "You would undo my feast with petty light and old prayers?"

Father Allen began the ritual. Words in Latin. Words never meant for mortal lips. Each one tore at his throat like glass.

"Et lux in tenebris lucetet tenebrae eam non comprehenderunt!"

Light surged from the medallion. It cracked the altar wider. Maria cried out as a wind stronger than any storm surged through the void. The Thing howled, not in pain—but in defiance.

"I will not be cast out! I am the hunger beneath creation! I am the womb of oblivion!"

The Thing struck. A wall of mirrored spikes burst from the ground and impaled the altar, shattering it. The light flickered.

Father Allen fell back, coughing blood. Abigail screamed.

"No! We were so close!"

Joseph moved to help the priest, but Allen shoved him away. "No… this is mine to finish."

Then he stood. Broken, bleeding. The rosary clutched tight.

"God," he whispered, eyes raised. "Forgive me again."

He turned back to the remnants of the altar and threw his body upon it. The medallion flared once more. The light pulsed outwards— a heartbeat of golden flame.

The Thing screamed. Shadows twisted like writhing serpents, trying to smother the light. But Allen began to glow. His soul— burning from within—became the final offering.

"A soul for a soul!" the Thing shrieked.

But the light was too much. The broken altar began to rise. The medallion lifted into the air.

Above them, the Echo descended.

It came not like a beast, but like a rift in sanity. A hole in existence. Its shape was unshapeable, vast, silent. Eyes—if they were eyes—blazed with ancient knowing.

Maria clutched her stomach.

"Is it coming for me?"

Abigail stared upward, pale as bone. "I… I don't know. It's watching everything. I think it's watching him."

Joseph pulled Maria close. "We have to trust Father Allen. We have to."

The Thing turned toward the Echo. "He is mine! The child is mine! I claimed them before the light broke the sky!""

338

The Echo said nothing. But its silence thundered. The air grew denser, impossible to breathe. Maria fell to her knees.

Father Allen, glowing now, reached upward. His final breath left his lungs in a whisper: "Protect them."

And then he exploded in light.

The medallion surged. A radiant wave spread through the void. The Thing was thrown backward, screaming. Its body fractured. Mirrors shattered across the realm. The Echo began to descend further.

But the light was fading.

Only Abigail remained standing between the Thing and Joseph, Maria.

Her eyes met the shadow.

And she whispered, "Then come through me."

Scene 3: The Severing

The air of the In Between had grown viscous, like walking through water churned with ash and oil. Mirrors groaned overhead like a living ceiling, flexing in the airless vacuum, trembling with the weight of aeons. The Thing hovered in the maelstrom, swirling and stretching, trailing streams of corruption like smoke dragged through broken glass. Its eyes—if one could call them that—blazed with hunger and rage. It sought the soul it had tasted: Joseph's. But more than that, it desired the unborn.

Abigail stood at the center of a scorched clearing in the mirror field, the Concordia medallion glowing faintly in her hand, its heat blistering her palm. Maria knelt with Joseph behind her, cradling his head, whispering prayers as his strength faded again. Father Allen's sacrifice had brought a moment of reprieve, but it was already vanishing.

"We don't have long," Abigail said, voice shaking. Her skin was pale with sweat, her eyes red with unshed tears and exhaustion. "I have to finish this. I have to seal the line."

She held up the medallion and began to chant. The words came in Latin and something older, darker. The symbols etched into the medallion shimmered, casting warped shadows on the shifting ground.

The Thing coiled above, retreating momentarily, recoiling from the light.

"Yes," Abigail growled through gritted teeth. "Run, you bastard. This is your end."

But it wasn't over. In a swift, violent motion, the Thing turned and plummeted downward. Not toward her—not yet. Instead, it dove into a cluster of wandering souls, tearing through them like a shark in a school of fish. One cry rose louder than the others: the cry of a soul too close to the edge, too weak to resist. A fractured spirit, broken and drifting.

The Thing devoured it whole.

The shift in power was instant. The wind screamed. The darkness deepened. The Thing grew.

Abigail stepped back in horror. Her voice caught in her throat. The ritual faltered.

It lunged.

She gasped, instinctively thrusting the Concordia medallion out before her like a shield. It flashed, silver in the sickly light, but it was a frail, desperate thing—hopeless against what loomed above her. The Thing bore down with claws of vapor and glass, its rage erupting in shrieks that seemed to fracture the very stone. Its voice twisted through the vault, spitting curses in tongues older than language itself, the sound an agony that scraped at Abigail's bones.

And then—

A silence more suffocating than any scream. Not stillness, but an abrupt void. The hurricane wind fell dead; candles snuffed out, shadows froze. The Thing, caught mid-lunge, hung in the air as if a fist had closed around its throat. Time itself seemed to draw breath and hold it.

Another shape now stood between Abigail and the Thing. Towering. Luminous. Its presence bent the air, distorted the world— a colossus of shifting light and darkness. The Echo.

It was not beautiful. It was not human. Its edges flickered, halos of pale fire and geometric shadow, its face a mask of mirrored facets that revealed nothing and everything at once. Where it looked, the world seemed to tremble. An ancient gravity radiated from it—a force of will, purpose, and inexorable judgment.

The Thing shrank back, glass splintering from its limbs, its many eyes seething with terror and hate. It tried to twist away, but the Echo turned its focus upon the Thing, and its voice—if it could be called that—boomed without sound, reverberating in every nerve, every inch of stone and spirit.

"I have watched your feast long enough," the Echo intoned, its speech a grinding of centuries, the tolling of clocks, the slow breaking of worlds. "You devour beyond your measure. You gnaw at the root of all that divides the living and the lost. You were set here to contain—now you consume. You have made a prison of my balance. Traitor."

341

The Thing howled, twisting its form into impossible shapes, eyes flickering red and gold. "The In Between is dying! You grow fat on power and leave me scraps. I am owed! I am HUNGRY!"

The Echo's radiance flared, harsh and cold. "You envy the seat you were given. You envy my will. Your hunger distorts the In Between. I have judged you. And I have judged enough."

It shifted, its gaze—if it had eyes—falling on Abigail. She felt its judgment like an avalanche, crushing, immense. The unfinished ritual hung in the air, the words trapped in her throat. The lines of salt and light she had begun to draw lay broken at her feet, the spell unspoken. She hadn't finished—.

"Witch," the Echo pronounced, its voice cutting through her mind like a blade. "Your meddling is a trespass. The In Between is not your domain. Your sorcery fractures the veil."

Abigail's hands trembled, the medallion suddenly unbearably heavy. "Wait—please! Maria—Joseph—they're still—"

"Enough," the Echo boomed, and the world twisted. Space folded, the air howled—a primal wind, older than breath, older than blood. Light exploded beneath Abigail's feet, consuming her. She screamed, the sound torn away, lost in the roaring white. She was wrenched upward, helpless, rocketing toward a fissure in the veil—the thin, sealed crack Gregory had left behind.

The last thing she saw as she vanished was the Thing, shrieking, writhing in the Echo's grip—a wraith dragged before judgment, a parasite called to account by its master.

And then Abigail was gone, scattered in light, hurled back toward the world of the living. The ritual was unfinished. The line was not broken.

And in the silence left behind, the In Between shuddered, waiting for what would come next.

Back in Washington, Samuel and Jacob sat silent on the boy's bed, staring at the covered mirror. They had waited for hours, braced for the unknown.

Suddenly, the air changed. A hum began, low and vibrating the floor.

"What's that?" Jacob asked, scooting closer.

Samuel stood. "I don't know. Stay behind me."

The mirror pulsed.

Thunder rolled—not from outside, but from within the glass. A cyclone of shadow bloomed behind the cover.

Samuel reached for Jacob, clutching him to his side. "Hang on, boy. I don't know what's coming for us."

The dresser began to rattle. The lights flickered.

Then the cover on the mirror burst outward. Black smoke coiled and billowed from the mirror, obscuring a view of the mirror itself. A scream exploded through the room, followed by a body, flung violently from the veil.

Samuel grunted as he caught it in his arms, stumbling back into the wall. They both crashed to the floor.

He panicked not knowing what came through, friend or foe? He looked down.

"Abigail?"

Her eyes fluttered open. Her clothes were torn, face scraped, eyes wild.

"I—I'm lucky to be alive," she gasped.

Samuel cradled her upright. "What happened? How did you get here?"

Abigail coughed and tried to sit up. "The Echo. It cast me out. I tried to seal the Concordia line, but the Thing stopped me. It was going to kill me. But the Echo... it intervened. Threw me out before it got worse."

Jacob stood at their side, eyes wide. "Is Mom okay? And Dad?"

Abigail turned to him and brushed his cheek. "They're still in there. Father Allen—he... he gave his life. Maria and Joseph are holding on. But I don't know for how long."

She looked up at Samuel. "Do you have a phone?"

Samuel nodded and handed her his. "Call them. See if they're through."

She dialed Maria's number.

It rang once.

Twice.

No answer.

They looked at one another.

The mirror pulsed again behind them.

Scene 4: The Judgment of the Echo

Only Maria and Joseph remained.

The vast, shuddering expanse of the In Between stretched around them—a liminal realm of fractured time and haunted memory, endless and lightless except for the chill gleam that spilled from splintered glass. The very air shimmered with threat and possibility; with every breath, Maria tasted the bitterness of centuries. Broken mirrors spun above a ground that was not stone or soil, but a foggy reflection of suffering—rippling and scarred, pocked with the echoes of all who had ever been trapped here. Here, every secret was an open wound.

They held hands as if they might drown without each other. The emptiness pressed closer, so heavy it became its own gravity, dragging at their limbs. Maria felt her pulse in her wrists, in her throat, in the secret, hidden place beneath her ribs. Her other hand instinctively shielded her belly. She could feel the life there—a flutter, fragile and luminous, an ember she refused to let go out.

Behind them, the detritus of battle littered the void: Abigail, wrenched from their side; Father Allen, gone in a flash of martyr's fire. The Concordia Seal—wrought with sacrifice—still sparked faintly in the ruins, but the shadows only shifted, growing denser, gathering for what came next.

Then—like a storm at the horizon—the Thing returned.

It reared up in a cyclone of hunger, a devouring spiral of smoke and teeth, the nightmares of a hundred generations twisted into its monstrous form. Tendrils snaked and split, eyes boiled and multiplied. Its mass writhed, swollen with stolen power, every soul it

345

had ever claimed now pulsing and gnashing in its depths. It had grown monstrous, transcendent, drunk on imbalance.

Maria flinched, putting herself between Joseph and the oncoming horror, even as she felt him press her back. The Thing's focus fell on her, on the tremor of new life inside her, and its eyes— if they could be called that—lit with an ancient, bestial glee.

"You carry life," it hissed, the words burning, twisting the space around them. "Unspoiled. Unseen. Unclaimed. An innocent soul… boundless. Untouched. I have waited for an eternity to taste such power, and now—here you are. I could reign forever."

It drifted closer, its mouth parting in a leer, talons stretching wide. Joseph, battered but unyielding, stood between them. "You won't touch her," he growled.

The Thing laughed, a sound like tombstones cracking. "Choice? Soldier, you forfeited choice when you meddled in realms beyond your reach. You broke the chain, but left the lock. That," it gestured at Maria's stomach, "is mine by right of conquest. The In Between hungers. I hunger."

The mirrors overhead began to shriek, shattering one by one. The ground beneath their feet buckled. All around, the suffering of the trapped pressed forward—wailing, reaching, desperate for escape or vengeance. Maria's heart hammered in her chest, the terror and the hope mingling until she thought she would burst from both.

And then—a crack. The world split, the wind dying as if God had held His breath.

A presence descended: not as an angel, nor as any ghost, but as Judgment itself. The Echo.

It arrived not with a step, but a command. Reality parted for it, its form coalescing out of light and shadow, towering, terrible, and beautiful in the way of storms or the edge of a blade. Its features could not be seen—its face a shifting constellation of mirrors and cold stars, its outline radiating force. The universe recoiled.

The Thing recoiled too, momentarily shriveled by the presence. But something in it—years of gnawing, of envy, of rage—made it bold. It rose, coiling itself even larger, baring all its stolen souls.

The Echo's voice rolled out, deep as ancient bells and sharp as breaking glass: "Your gluttony has ruptured balance, Parasite."

The Thing did not cower. Instead, it surged forward, voice raw with spite. "Balance?" it spat. "Your balance was always a prison! You feasted on worship while I starved. You sealed me here to do your bidding, to collect your debts. I am the shadow that gives you meaning. I am the hunger your rules create!"

The Echo's light grew harder, colder—a noose of gravity forming around the Thing. "You were set as warden—not king. You guide the lost, not devour them. You overreach. You covet dominion that is not yours. You envy what you cannot be. You have become the cancer in the marrow of the In Between. For this—betrayal—you shall be cast out."

The Thing bared its teeth, shrieking. "You have no right! This place belongs to those who bleed for it—who die and are forgotten. You are nothing but a judge, sitting in silence while I did your work. If you send me away, who will protect your precious walls? Who will gather the dead? You are afraid. You need me!"

The Echo's form blazed, a radiance that erased shadow and color alike. Its voice thundered, a thousand years of wrath compressed to a single syllable: "Be silent!"

The Thing fell, writhing, its tendrils shattering glass, its souls howling in a deafening cacophony.

The Echo raised its hand and spoke, the words ringing with the force of the Gospels:

"And they besought Him that He would not command them to go out into the Abyss." (Luke 8:31)

The Thing shrieked, writhing in agony, every lie and cruelty it ever spawned rising up in judgment. Mirrors shattered, souls burst free like flecks of starlight. Space folded upon itself. The Abyss yawned, black and bottomless.

"Traitor," the Echo intoned. "You have eaten the world's sorrow for the last time."

With a final, sweeping gesture, the Echo flung the Thing into the darkness. It fell, dissolving into howls, snatched and devoured by a darkness deeper than the In Between itself—gone, at last, without hope of return.

Silence.

The world felt newly raw, as if every wound and scar lay open to the air. Maria and Joseph collapsed to their knees, crushed beneath the aftermath. The Echo turned, its gaze implacable, its light unsoftened.

"You do not belong here," it decreed. "You are of the Other Side. You have trespassed upon a realm forbidden, led by love but driven by fear. You know the way between worlds now. That knowledge is a threat. You cannot remain."

Maria gripped Joseph's hand. "Please—he only wanted to be free. We never meant—"

The Echo cut her off. "No bargains. No pleas. I am not your judge—but your guardian. You will return to your world and never seek the In Between again. Should you trespass once more, the Abyss will open for you as it did for the Thing. This is mercy. Take it."

Joseph, tears streaking the dust on his cheeks, nodded. Maria sobbed, clutching his hand, whispering gratitude, apology, promise— all the things left unsaid.

The Echo's arm swept downward.

Mirrors cracked, spilling golden light in rivers, swallowing the darkness and every last echo of despair. Maria and Joseph were lifted, torn upward in a cyclone of brightness, the agony replaced by the fierce, burning ache of hope.

Memories and prayers spun around them—Father Allen's last blessing, Abigail's faith, Jacob's longing—and the In Between receded, folding away behind the curtain of fate.

They landed hard, together, in the silent parlor of the old house. Night pressed against the windows. The clock was silent. The glass was empty.

Joseph wept in Maria's arms, both of them clinging to the reality they had fought to reclaim. There, at last, they found the breath to laugh and weep and whisper all the promises they had carried through hell and back.

The war behind the glass was over. But in the hush of that ancient house, the ripples of judgment and mercy moved still— unseen, but eternal.

Chapter 19 - Homeward Light

Scene 1: The Ruined Parlor

The world swam back into being with a gasp of stillness.

Maria sat upright first, hands pressed into the cold, cracked wooden floor of the old parlor. The taste of ash clung to her lips, and her skin stung with the memory of fire and fear. The In Between was gone. The weight of it had lifted, like an invisible yoke she hadn't realized she'd been carrying until it was suddenly gone.

Beside her, Joseph stirred. He groaned faintly, coughing as dust from the floor rose around him. His face was smeared with soot, and a thin line of dried blood traced the corner of his mouth. But he was alive. Flesh and bone. Eyes that opened and locked onto hers.

"Maria," he whispered.

She leaned forward and wrapped her arms around him, holding him as tightly as her trembling strength allowed. Her breath hitched in her chest as his arms came around her. The embrace was not one of celebration but of anchoring—proof that they were back. That they were whole.

The parlor was nearly unrecognizable now. The once-faded wallpaper had peeled back entirely, curling like burnt parchment. Dust choked the air, thick and unmoving. The shards of the mirror triangle they had assembled earlier were strewn across the floor, fractured and useless. And yet, despite the ruin, there was something new in the air: a breath, a hint, a whisper of peace.

Then it happened.

One by one, the mirrors lining the parlor walls began to crack. Faint lines appeared first—thin spiderwebs stretching from corner to corner—before a sound like ice fracturing echoed through the room. It wasn't violent. It was final.

Crack.

Snap.

Fracture.

Every pane of mirrored glass exploded inward, not with fury but with relief, as though releasing the last gasps of haunted breath. Glittering shards rained across the floor, some bouncing, others settling silently into the dust. The echo of the shattering seemed to cleanse the air.

Then, light.

A golden beam pierced through the grime-caked windows, illuminating the ruined parlor with a warmth that none of them had felt in what seemed like ages. The rising sun had broken through the storm clouds outside. Its rays bent through the gaps in the boards and glass, finding the two souls who had returned.

Maria turned her face into the warmth and let the light wash over her. It painted Joseph's skin with amber and gold, softening the bruises and dirt. Tears slipped from her eyes before she could stop them.

They had made it.

She looked down at her stomach and placed her hand gently against it. For the first time since learning the truth, she felt the presence of her unborn child not as a burden or danger, but as life—precious, sacred life. A flicker of hope where darkness had once laid claim.

Joseph, still leaning against her shoulder, let out a ragged sigh. "It's over," he said, almost disbelieving.

Maria nodded. "For now."

A moment passed, thick with unspoken words. Then she pulled away gently and stood. Her legs were weak, but she held fast. Joseph followed, slower, each movement a struggle, but he refused to fall.

The room bore scars of what had occurred, and yet in the hush of dawn, it felt sacred. A temple of ruin. A battlefield turned sanctuary. It was then that Maria noticed something glinting where the center mirror had once stood—in the very place where the ritual had begun, where it had nearly ended them.

She stepped carefully across the glass-littered floor.

There, resting amid the rubble, was the Concordia medallion.

It gleamed in the light, clean and whole, untouched by soot or flame. As if preserved. As if waiting.

She knelt and lifted it in her hand. It was warm. Steady. Vibrating softly with something deeper than sound. She held it to her chest and closed her eyes.

Delilah's final act. Helped by Abigail.

The seal had been remade.

"It's still here," Joseph said quietly.

Maria turned. "What is?"

He looked around the room, his eyes scanning the broken mirrors, the empty shadows. "The silence."

Maria nodded. "We took something from this place. But we left something behind too."

They stood together then, surrounded by broken glass, bathed in the light of a new morning.

Outside, the wind stirred. Leaves rustled through cracked shutters. The sound of birds, tentative and distant, filtered in through the broken windows. Nature, timidly, was returning to the forgotten estate.

Maria stepped toward the door, placing her hand on the worn, weathered knob. Behind her, Joseph followed without question. As they stepped into the sun-drenched corridor of the old Mercier house, they knew nothing would ever be the same.

But they were free.

And morning had come.

Scene 2: Jacob's Whisper

The morning crept into the house in Washington like a guest too polite to knock. Sunlight filtered thinly through the curtains in Jacob's room, tracing warm lines across the floor and over the scattered toys that had gone untouched for days. Dust motes floated, suspended in the stillness. It was a peace too fragile to trust.

Jacob sat on the edge of his bed, legs dangling over the side, clutching the blanket in his small fists. His eyes were locked on the mirror across from him—the one atop the tall dresser, the one that had shimmered, bent, and whispered to him more times than he could count. It was just a mirror now. Just glass. Just reflection. But he didn't blink.

Beside him, Samuel stood with arms crossed, watching the boy with a protectiveness that masked his own gnawing unease. And in the corner, seated in the old rocking chair that had once belonged to Samuel's wife, Abigail sat silently, hands folded in her lap. She had said little since being cast out of the In Between. Her face was pale, drawn tight with exhaustion, her eyes fixed on the same mirror that had flung her back into the world of the living.

The room was thick with tension. The kind that only comes when everyone is pretending they're not waiting for something.

Jacob finally spoke, his voice thin. "It's quiet."

Abigail nodded slowly. "Too quiet can be a blessing or a warning."

"I don't think it's coming back," Jacob said, not taking his eyes off the mirror.

Samuel exhaled, a sound of both relief and doubt. "Let's pray it's the first one."

A breeze stirred outside, and a soft groan rolled through the old house's wooden frame. The mirror remained still. No shimmer. No distortion. Just the boy's reflection, and Samuel's, and Abigail's—three survivors holding onto hope with knuckles white.

Then, Jacob blinked. He leaned forward, his breath catching.

The mirror trembled.

Abigail stood. Her breath hitched. "Did you see that?"

Samuel's hand instinctively went to Jacob's shoulder.

A single ripple moved across the glass, like water disturbed. And then—nothing. The glass returned to stillness. Flat. Normal.

Just a mirror.

Jacob stared hard. "It's… gone."

The words were a whisper, but in them was the weight of finality.

Abigail stepped closer, her hand brushing the edge of the dresser. She leaned down, peering into the reflection, searching for anything—any sign of the Thing. But there was only her face, drawn and weathered, and behind it the faint shape of Jacob's room.

She backed away. "It's really gone."

Jacob nodded slowly. "Gregory said it couldn't get me. He said the Echo wouldn't let it."

Samuel knelt down beside the bed, placing one hand on Jacob's knee. "Gregory was right, then. He kept his promise."

Abigail crossed her arms and looked out the window. Her voice was soft, almost distant. "The Echo saw what the Thing had become. It let me go. Not because I earned it… but because it was watching him."

Jacob looked up. "You think they're safe? Mom and Dad?"

Samuel looked at Abigail. She met his gaze and nodded faintly.

"They're strong," she said. "And they're not alone."

Just then, the sharp ring of the phone shattered the quiet.

All three of them jumped. Samuel shot to his feet, racing from the room. Jacob scrambled after him, heart pounding.

Abigail remained frozen in the doorway.

Samuel grabbed the phone from its cradle in the kitchen, nearly dropping it. "Hello?"

A pause.

Then Maria's voice: "We're back."

His knees buckled slightly, hand gripping the counter for support. "Thank God…"

He looked over his shoulder at Abigail and Jacob. "It's them. They made it."

Jacob's face lit up, a smile breaking across his tired face. "Mom!"

Samuel held the phone tightly. "Maria, Abigail's here too. She made it out. The Echo sent her through the mirror."

From the other end, Maria's voice choked with emotion. "She's safe?"

He turned to Abigail, who stepped closer. He held out the phone to her. "Tell her yourself."

Abigail took the phone, hesitated, then raised it to her ear. "Maria… I'm okay. I'm here. I'm so glad you're safe."

Tears filled her eyes, and she turned away slightly as they fell. She handed the phone back to Samuel.

He spoke again, voice thick. "We'll see you soon."

Then he hung up the phone.

Jacob threw his arms around Abigail. "I knew you'd be okay."

She knelt down, embracing him tightly. "Thank you for believing in me."

He didn't say goodbye. He didn't need to.

He turned, eyes glistening, and met Abigail's gaze. She already knew. Relief cracked the dam of her composure. She stood shakily as Samuel crossed the room, and they collapsed into each other's arms.

No more secrets.

No more holding back.

Their kiss was not rushed or passionate—it was slow, reverent. A recognition of survival. Of what they almost lost. Of what still remained.

"Grandpa!" Jacob burst out, running toward them and throwing his arms around their legs. "Is Mom okay?"

Samuel smiled through tears and hugged him tight. "She's home, son. She's home."

Samuel stepped closer, arms wide, and they all folded into a three-way embrace. For the first time in what felt like years, the house no longer felt haunted.

The mirror in Jacob's room remained still. But in its silence, there was no threat.

Only peace.

Scene 3: It Watches Still

The rhythm of life had returned, or at least some version of it. Days passed like ripples on a quiet lake, each one carrying Maria and Joseph further from the horrors of the In Between. The apartment in Washington had regained its familiar sounds: the hum of the refrigerator, the whisper of the heater kicking on, the occasional muffled voices from neighbors next door. Outside, early autumn rain tapped the windows, a gentle percussion that reminded them of time moving forward.

Maria had resumed her prenatal checkups. Joseph, though still healing, had begun working remotely, his eyes often drifting toward the framed photo of their family on the desk. They no longer spoke much about what had happened. There weren't words for it—not yet.

But they smiled more, laughed when they could, and held each other often.

Abigail had returned to her small cottage across the city, though she checked in frequently. Samuel had gone back to Schenectady, where he busied himself restoring the old study room at St. Helen's. He had become more active in the church again, and Jacob would call him almost every night, just to hear his voice.

The days blurred into one another in a way that felt comforting—normal. Jacob was back in school, Maria was showing more with each week, and Joseph had resumed teaching Jacob how to build model airplanes in the evenings.

But sometimes, when the lights flickered or a door creaked without cause, they paused. Just for a moment. Just long enough to wonder.

Tonight was one of those nights.

The apartment was hushed, wrapped in the quiet lullaby of the city after dark. The wind brushed against the windows, and a streetlight outside flickered sporadically, casting uncertain shadows through the blinds.

Jacob was asleep in his bed, his small body curled beneath his worn cartoon blanket. His favorite stuffed animal—a faded lion—was clutched in one arm. Joseph sat nearby, dozing in the rocking chair, a book half open in his lap. Maria had fallen asleep on the couch, the TV casting a soft blue glow as the credits of some forgotten movie rolled.

In the corner of Jacob's room, the mirror atop the dresser stood silent and reflective. It showed only what was there: the room, the boy, the shadows, and the slow, rhythmic rise and fall of his breathing.

For a while, nothing changed.

Then the air grew colder.

Not suddenly, not dramatically—but enough that Joseph stirred. He rubbed his arms, blinked at the thermostat, and shrugged it off. The wind had likely shifted. The old building always responded with uneven heat.

Down the hallway, a door creaked softly. Then another.

Maria turned in her sleep, her brows knitting faintly. Her hand slipped protectively over her belly. Her dreams were restless—images of Joseph drifting from her mind into smoke.

In Jacob's room, a faint hum began. So low it could've been the refrigerator, the wind, or a neighbor's TV through the wall. But it pulsed, like something alive.

Then the lights flickered.

Twice.

Joseph snapped awake. He looked around the room, then to Jacob and Noah. Still sleeping.

But the mirror—

A ripple.

Tiny. Barely visible. Like a single drop had fallen into the surface of the glass.

Then another.

Joseph stood. He stepped closer, eyes narrowing. "No," he whispered. "Not again."

The ripples faded. The mirror stilled. His own reflection met him, tired but alive. Real.

Then, behind his reflection—a flicker of darkness. A shape.

It moved.

For the briefest second, a shadow slithered along the edge of the glass. Thin, long, unnatural. It curled behind Jacob's sleeping form in the reflection, then vanished.

Joseph spun around. Nothing.

Just Jacob and Noah.

Peaceful.

Still.

He looked back at the mirror.

Only his face.

Only his eyes.

But then, something whispered.

Not a voice from outside. Not in the air.

From within.

A single phrase. So soft he wasn't sure he heard it at all.

"It watches still."

His breath caught.

The mirror held his gaze.

And then—nothing.

The hum stopped. The lights stilled. The air returned to warmth.

Joseph stood there for several more seconds. Minutes, maybe.

Then he turned, walked back to the chair, and sat.

He watched Jacob sleep. He listened to the silence.

Somewhere out there, behind glass and time and balance, something had seen them. Had spared them. Had warned them.

And though the apartment was whole, and the family was reunited, Joseph understood what that whisper meant.

The story wasn't over.

Not yet.

The End

Epilogue - The Glass Watcher

The room was quiet, bathed in the soft blue glow of a moonlit sky filtering through thick nursery curtains. Stuffed animals lined the edge of the toddler's crib, their stitched eyes standing sentinel in the shadows. The baby—no longer quite a baby, now standing with chubby legs and curious eyes—clutched the edge of the crib rail, blinking slowly in the calm hush of the night.

All was still. A gentle hum came from the baby monitor. In another room, the muted voices of late-night television murmured through the drywall, unintelligible and far away. A lullaby projector flicked soft starlight shapes onto the ceiling, casting slow-moving constellations that traced lazy circles above.

A mobile above the crib spun lazily, its tiny plush moons and clouds swaying, nudged not by machinery but by the faintest breath of air. The curtain beside the window pressed inward just slightly, the sash loose and giving way to the smallest breeze. The mobile turned with a faint creak.

The child stirred, not alarmed, just curious. He looked up.

The mobile turned again—once, then twice, rhythmically, then slowed.

The rocking chair in the corner shifted.

It was subtle at first. A single creak. Then, another—slightly louder. The chair moved back, then forward, as if someone had just stood from it. But no one had been sitting there.

The child blinked. His attention drawn now, alert and wide-eyed, he tilted his head slightly. A soft sound—the hint of a whisper, not threatening, just... present—floated through the room, the syllables too faint to decipher.

The child turned toward the source of the sound. Toward the dresser.

And the mirror above it.

The moonlight caught the edge of the mirror's frame. A few inches more, and a shaft of pale light spilled across the glass, breaking the surface into planes of silver and shadow. The whispering stopped.

The child cooed softly.

Then—

Movement.

Inside the glass.

A mist, faint as breath on winter glass, began to swirl on the surface. The child stared, transfixed, his fingers now gripping the rail tighter. He didn't cry. His breath caught. His eyes grew wide with something between wonder and hesitation.

The swirling thickened. The mist congealed, and a shape began to form.

First a shoulder, faintly defined—like light behind water. A fold in fabric, the faint suggestion of a shirt seam. The shoulder rose, angling naturally into the neck. Then the arc of an ear began to take form, real enough that if one pressed close, it might seem tangible.

Still, the face remained hidden.

The child leaned forward.

Outside, the wind gathered strength. It pushed against the loose sash, pressing the curtain into the room with a soft hiss. The fabric flared, shifting the light just a few degrees. And with that, the last veil lifted.

The figure inside the mirror faced the child.

It was a man—his face calm but sad, eyes heavy with purpose and burden. His features etched with time, with sacrifice. With finality.

He did not blink.

He did not move.

But he watched.

The child tilted his head again, not in fear—but recognition. Some instinctual tether tugged gently between their gazes, like the echo of a lullaby heard long ago.

The man's hand—faint and silvered—rose and pressed slowly against the inside of the glass.

His palm met the surface in silence.

And it was Father Allen.

Trapped in the glass.

Forever watching.

About the Author

Scott J Clauss

Raised amidst the rolling farmland of Valatie, NY, Scott J. Clauss learned early on to listen—to both the earth beneath his feet and the echoes of old stories carried on the wind. A childhood spent exploring fields and creaking farmhouse hallways later led him to a quieter upbringing in suburban Schenectady, NY, where he discovered a deep fascination with history and the unseen.

Scott's journey eventually took him overseas in the Army, where he met his wife, and later to the Pacific Northwest to build a life rooted in family and community. Along the way, pockets of uncanny experiences—fleeting shadows, whispers of distant voices—would intersect with his day-to-day, never overtaking his sense of reason yet lingering long afterward.

These moments found their way into his writing—not as claims of mystical power, but as threads woven into a larger tapestry. Wanting to explore them creatively, Scott crafted this novel as both storytelling and catharsis—a way to share the emotional truth of unseen encounters without preaching or self-proclamation. At its heart is a simple offering: an invitation to feel the quiet tension between history, family, and the shadows that sometimes lie just beyond sight.